Erotic Tales
of the Victorian Age

Erotic Tales
of the Victorian Age

Bram Stoker, Richard Burton,
Frank Harris, "Walter,"
Charles Devereaux, Emile Zola

Prometheus Books
59 John Glenn Drive
Amherst, New York 14228-2197

Published 1998 by Prometheus Books

Erotic Tales of the Victorian Age. Original hardback edition copyright © 1995 by Michael O'Mara Books Limited. Paperback edition copyright © 1998 by Michael O'Mara Books Limited. All rights reserved. No part of this publication may be reproduced, stored in a retrieval system, or transmitted in any form or by any means, digital, electronic, mechanical, photocopying, recording, or otherwise, or conveyed via the Internet or a Web site without prior written permission of the publisher, except in the case of brief quotations embodied in critical articles and reviews.

Inquiries should be addressed to
Prometheus Books, 59 John Glenn Drive, Amherst, New York 14228-2197
VOICE: 716-691-0133, ext. 207; FAX: 716-564-2711
WWW.PROMETHEUSBOOKS.COM

07 06 05 04 03   6 5 4 3 2

Library of Congress Cataloging-in-Publication Data

Erotic tales of the Victorian age / Bram Stoker . . . [et al.].
    p. cm.
    Originally published: Victorian erotic tales. London : M. O'Mara Books, 1995.
    ISBN 1-57392-205-6 (alk. paper)
    1. Erotic literature. 2. English fiction—19th century. I. Stoker, Bram, 1847-1912. II. Title.
PN6071.E7V53 1995
823'.80803538—dc21
                                                                      98-13806
                                                                         CIP

Printed in Canada on acid-free paper

CONTENTS

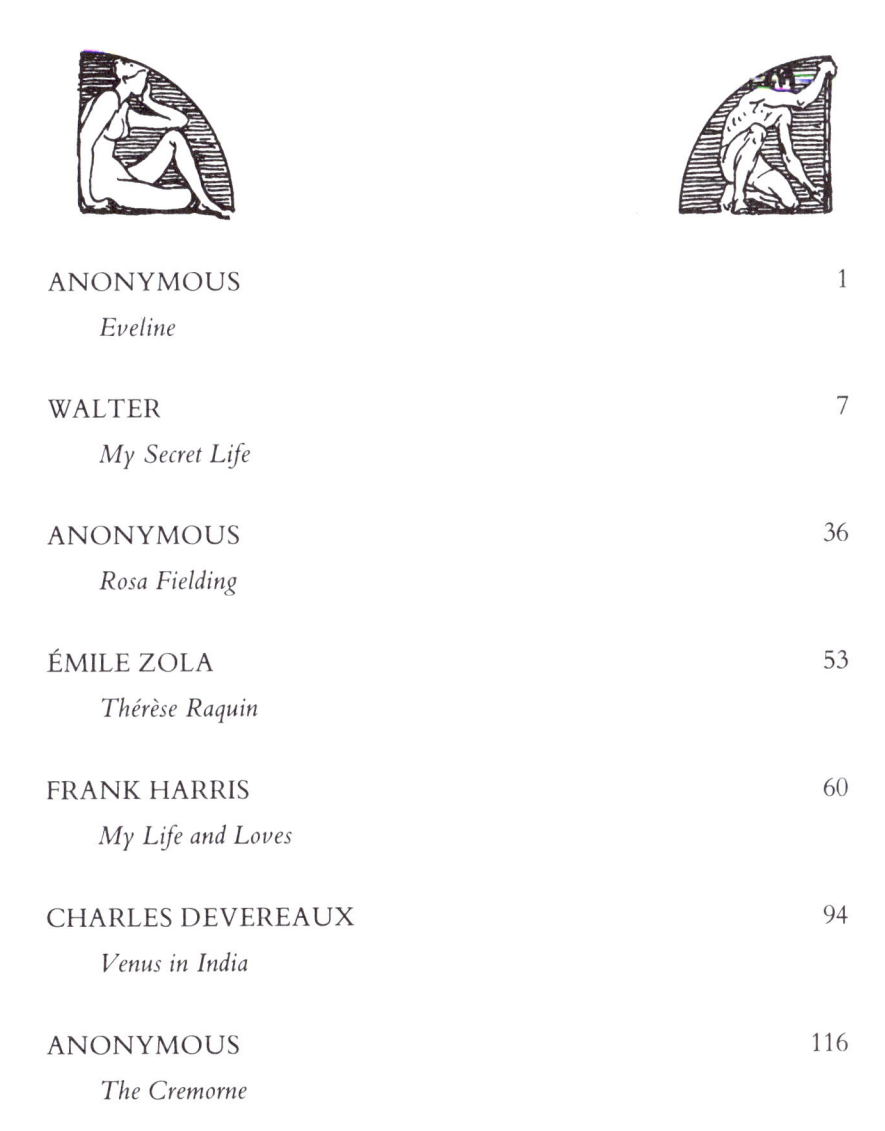

ANONYMOUS   1
Eveline

WALTER   7
My Secret Life

ANONYMOUS   36
Rosa Fielding

ÉMILE ZOLA   53
Thérèse Raquin

FRANK HARRIS   60
My Life and Loves

CHARLES DEVEREAUX   94
Venus in India

ANONYMOUS   116
The Cremorne

ANONYMOUS   138
    The Voluptuous Night

ANONYMOUS   150
    Flossie

SIR RICHARD BURTON   198
    The Perfumed Garden

BRAM STOKER   229
    Dracula

ANONYMOUS   232
    The Lustful Memoirs of a Young and Passionate Girl

ANONYMOUS

from
Eveline

Eveline is one of the best-known Victorian erotic novels. Nothing is known about the author but it was probably first published in an 'underground' edition in 1843.

Its enduring success is a tribute to the author's ability to tease and tantalize. Eveline, in her search for sexual gratification, undermines everything Victorian society expected a woman to be.

ONCE more the train to Calais, once more the dreadful sea sickness. I am free. No more school; no more *pensionnat* for Eveline! My father had returned from India. His term of service had expired. He had received his C.B. He was now retiring as a Major General. His breast was covered with the medals he had won, yet except some mere scratches, he had never received a wound. He was still a young and vigorous man in the prime of life. He was also a lineal descendant of an ancient family, and a Baronet.

I was seventeen. I was considered to have arrived at an age when I might bid *adieu* to educational routine. I was to spend a few months at home in Mayfair, to improve the occasion in the reception of music and singing lessons from the first professors. Not that my mother desired my return; she had her own reasons for her unwilling assent. Lady L—— had never overcome her antipathy for her only daughter. Sir Edward, however, had a distinct desire to have me at home. It was to him I owed my emancipation. We had not met since I was a child of eight. My sympathy was all for him. I shared his desire to meet again after so long an absence.

Sir Edward was absent shooting in the North when I arrived. My mother was suffering, so she informed me, from rheumatism. She kept to her room. My time did not hang too heavily on my hands for all that.

I had plenty of liberty. The carriage was at my disposal. We were rich. The house was commodious. The servants were numerous and well paid. They were evidently overjoyed to welcome me to my home, and have someone to break the monotony of their existence.

I very soon began to discriminate among them. There was the senior footman, John Parker, who was particularly polite and attentive to me. My mother preferred to take her meals in her own room upstairs. I dined all alone, save when I invited a young friend of my own age to share my meal. On the occasions when I was quite by myself, John would venture to suggest various choice portions from the dishes set before me. He cut and arranged them on my plate. He interested me. He was a man of some eight and thirty, not very tall for a footman, but stout and broad. I thought in my ignorance he was magnificent in his handsome livery, with his gold garters, black silk stockings, and his crimson plush breeches. He made a great impression on me. I suppose I showed my interest in him too plainly. He soon became more attentive, more subservient – more familiar.

'How long have you been here, John?'

From the first I could never bring myself to call him Parker.

'Three years, miss, come Christmas.'

'You must find it very dull now Sir Edward is away and Mr Percy in Canada. I expect you have gay times downstairs, when your work is over in here.'

'Well, miss, not so much. The others are not a very gay lot and the cook goes out when the work is done. The girls both sit upstairs with my lady's own maid. Now you're here, miss, if I may be allowed to say so, the house is not at all the same. It seems quite lively – at least to me, miss.'

'Where is my maid, John? She has not brought my shoes. I cannot bear these boots any longer, I am tired.'

'Mary is upstairs, miss, shall I call her?'

'No, John, if you will be so good as to undo these laces, I can sit more comfortably at the table.'

I pushed out my foot. I placed it on a stool. John stooped over it. He began to fumble at the knot. His hand trembled.

'I am afraid, John, you are not quite a lady's maid, but I think you are very nice all the same.'

John chuckled. I gave a little kick out with my foot. It touched his plush breeches.

'Oh, you hurt me, John – no – not your knuckles – it's the lace at the back of the instep – see here – '

He took my foot in his hand. He touched my ankle.

'It's just there, John, please rub it a little.'

John set to work to rub the ankle. As he rubbed, so I swayed my foot backwards and forwards upon his plush breeches. Something hard seemed to grow up under my foot.

'What have you got in your pocket, John? Is it a flute?'

'No, miss, I am not musical. I don't play any instrument.'

The man blushed scarlet as his breeches, and seemed quite confused.

'It feels exactly like one, John, and it gets bigger and bigger.'

I pushed my little kid boot into closer contact with the thing, John's hand was now on my calf, and my black silk stocking evidently delighted him, for he made pretence to linger where he was.

I put on my most innocent and childish air.

'Do all the men have those things there, John? The girls at school told me lots about them.'

'I don't know, miss, I suppose so. I – really! Miss! I'm afraid someone may come.'

'Don't be alarmed, John, no one will come. I want to feel it.'

'Good Lord! Miss – if they should know – if I am found out I shall lose my place.'

'But you won't tell, John, will you?'

'Oh dear, no, miss! But you might let it out unawares-like.'

I sprang forward. I seized the object in his red plush breeches with my hand. John stood quite still and breathed hard.

'Good Lord, miss! If they come, if we're found out!'

'They are all upstairs – we are alone. I must feel it. I know what it is, John. My goodness! How it throbs – how big it is getting now – let me feel it.'

The footman submitted with a good grace. It was clear he was by no means unwilling. He evidently enjoyed my fingering. I slyly undid the corner button of his flap. I audaciously slipped my hand in. I ran it quickly down his belly. I encountered his nice clean shirt all warm. Then my hand fastened on his limb. I pulled away his shirt. I grasped his naked member. It felt very fat and thick. It was still stiffening. I gave it a sudden twist. It stood up now against his belly.

'Is that nice, John?'

'Good Lord! Yes, miss, it's heavenly, but I'm afraid we may be caught at it.'

He appeared to have an enormous limb, not so long as the horrid *concierge*, but very thick and strong. I managed to pull back the skin. I felt a big, soft, beautiful knob on the end. He turned towards me. He favoured my toying, but the space was too confined to enable me to finger it as I liked.

Just then the front door bell rang.

I withdrew my hand. John buttoned up. The next minute he was opening the door with the grand air of a butler who could crush the comer with a glance.

I set to work to scheme a way to arrive at the sum of my desires. There are some things one must do for oneself. I nerved myself for the occasion. I went to a quiet street in Soho. I had noted a second-rate shop which was fitted up as an apothecary's – as we say in London, chemist and druggist. I entered. I had chosen the quiet time in the early afternoon. No one was in the shop. A good-looking fair-haired young man advanced from the back room.

'Good morning. I want a syringe – a female syringe; show me some of your best.'

'Certainly, miss, please to step this way.'

He led me to the further end of the counter. He produced from a drawer a number of the articles in question.

'These are all good, but this pattern is the one we specially recommend. It is of vulcanite. It cannot break, or do any mischief.'

I looked them over with a professional air.

'Yes, you are right. I will take the one you recommend.'

Probably he saw I was a little awkward in handling the thing. I looked him in the face with a smile. His eyes sparkled.

'Do you understand how it should be applied, miss?'

'Well, not properly, perhaps.'

He smiled this time. I laughed softly.

'How do you fill it, and with what?'

'We have a detergent always made up, miss. If you will wait a moment, I will get some water and explain the action.'

I nodded gently. He went into the back room. In a few moments he returned.

'Please come in here, I can show you how it works.'

I followed the good-looking, fair young man. He filled the syringe with water, and squirted it out again into a basin.

'You should always wipe it after use and return it nicely to its case – thus.'

I laughed again softly.

The young man laughed also. I was wicked enough to encourage his hilarity. He evidently took me for a representative member of a class to which I had not the honour to belong. I determined to humour him. He grew more familiar.

'After all, it is not at all equal to the real thing. Would you like me to try it for you? I shall be delighted to serve you, miss.'

'Thank you, but I should prefer *the real thing*, if it acts at all like the imitation. Probably you have none in stock?'

He laughed outright this time. He glanced around. We understood one another in a moment. He caught me round the waist.

'You beautiful little devil! Where do you come from?'

'Are we quite sure to be alone? Suppose someone enters the shop?'

'They must wait. I can shut the door. See, there is a muslin curtain. We can see out. They cannot see in.'

'Then try the real thing – if you have one!'

He had roused my lust. He was very good-looking. He locked the door. He pushed me towards a leather sofa.

'You really mean you will let me do the job for you, eh? You are awfully pretty, you know. I never saw such a beautiful girl. You are so beautifully dressed. I am not rich, you know, you will not want to bother me afterwards?'

'I ask nothing. I should not like to disappoint you.'

'Oh, my God! What fun! I never had such a chance. How sweet your kisses are! Let me feel.'

'Where is your syringe? Oh my goodness! What a beauty! It is much larger, though, than the imitation. Kiss me!'

'Yes, much larger and almost as stiff. It holds nearly as much also, as you will soon find. Oh, your kisses are sweet.'

I held his limb in my gloved hand. His fingers were in the moisture of my slit. He was beautifully made – not nearly so large as the *concierge*. I was dreadfully excited. I longed for him to 'do the job', as he called it. He was stiffly erect.

I had not long to wait. I was utterly devoid of modesty. I fancied I knew how best to please him. I played my part.

'Be quick – I want it! Come!'

I pulled up all my clothes. He saw all my nudity.

'My God, what lovely legs! What fine stockings! What exquisite little boots. My God! Oh – what a chance!'

The young man mounted quickly upon me. In an instant I felt him penetrating my orbit. My slit was all on fire with longing.

'My God, how tight you are – keep still – it's going in now. Oh, my God, how nice! I'm right into you now!'

It was true. I tasted the pleasure of coition for the first time with a full-grown man. I could not speak – I could only sob and moan in the ecstasy of that encounter. I clutched him by the shoulders. I felt the light hair of his belly rub on my flesh. He thrust vigorously. His limb grew stiffer and harder. It seemed to push to the extremity of my capacity. The pleasure was divine.

'Oh, Christ! I'm coming! I'm – coming! Ugh! Ugh! Ugh!'

'The syringe! The syringe! Give it me all!'

The young man discharged – gush after gush. He had spoken the truth. His syringe was ample. His sperm squirted into me in a flood.

'You beautiful little devil! How deliciously nice you are. Now you must make use of the imitation. I will get you some water.'

'Thanks. Remember to wipe your syringe and return it carefully to its box.'

I walked home. I was no longer afraid of John now.

WALTER

from

My Secret Life

My Secret Life is thought to have first been published in the 1880s in France and became one of the most famous underground classics of its kind. The identity of 'Walter' has never been discovered.

At Aldershot. – The postage stamp. – The Major's mistress. – The Railway carriage. – Carnal hints. – Carnal practice. – A pretty foot. – At the garters. – Head near tail. – A seductive priapus. – Upon the floor. – Upon the seat. – After dinner. – The Major's tool. – The lady's vulva. – A screaming gamahuche. – Good bye. – Madeline the milliner. – My amatory career. – The sexual law. – The Crystal Palace. – After the dinner. – A brooch and garters. – A thigh recipient. – Overflowing testicles.

In the month of **** I had been at Aldershot to visit a friend. He came back with me to the railway station and left me there, the train to London had not arrived. – When it did, and just as I was about to enter a carriage, a tall, dark-eyed, handsome, and elegantly dressed young woman came up in haste and asked for a postage stamp of the guard. He said he could not get one, there was no time to go to the station master. The train was a quarter of an hour behind time. 'Oh! do, pray, it's most important,' said she. – 'I'll put it in the box Ma'am without a stamp.' – 'Oh-no.' – At the instant I pulled out my pocket book and took out a stamp. 'Here's one, give me the letter.' She handed it to me, and I put on the stamp. 'Wait, guard, a second only,' – and I rushed to the station master who just then appeared, and gave it him, turned back, saw the lady looking anxiously out of a first class carriage, jumped into it with her, winking at the guard, who locked the door, and almost before I was seated, the train went off. It was an express to Waterloo.

The lady said she was deeply indebted to me and explained, as if in apology, why it was so important the letter should go off that night. Of course we got into conversation, and confidence begat confidence. – She had been to see Major **** of the ***** regiment by arrangement, and on arriving there found he had gone away. A telegram had sent him off to his mother who was dangerously ill – 'Here is his letter,' said she, and I read it. It was in very affectionate terms, and signed – 'John.'

Then I found out, tho she did not admit it in those words, that the Major kept her – I am too old a bird to believe all a woman tells me, but her tale seemed probable. Not that she volunteered much, but in talking it all came out; and I in return let her know something about myself, and the reason for my being at the camp.

Gradually I ascertained that she had not seen the Major for a fortnight. His regiment had moved from ***** to Aldershot recently, and while arranging for moving, it was useless for her to have visited him. He liked all to be quiet when she went there, he objected to his brother officers knowing too much about her, and he did not know where his quarters for a night would be, and so it was impossible for him to get to town to her. – All was I knew quite in the order of things, when a regiment was changing quarters. It taught me at the same time that this fine young creature, who didn't look more than three and twenty, must have been without a prick for a fortnight, unless she had had one that did not belong to the Major; and therefore must want that article badly, unless she had frigged herself vigorously or been licked by her maid, if she had a faithful fanatic at such amusements. – But I did not reason with myself much on the detail. – A fortnight without a lover, was enough to make me know she then must want a poke. I came to that conclusion before I had been in the carriage ten minutes.

The sensual fire which always seems smouldering in my balls then began to burn brightly. I had sat opposite to her, looking at her; now I moved to her side, saying that I didn't like the wind in my face. Leaning on the arm which divided the seats, our faces were now closer together, and our breaths mingled. She had turned towards me, as I had towards her. But there was no desire in her eyes. – They were a dark pair, bright but quiet-looking. – I noticed that she was thin, had but slight signs of breasts and not much of backside. – Those two exquisite parts of a woman that I love to see full and round, and feel solid and smooth. She didn't seem my sort at all in form, but her face was lovely. Then I noticed that her foot looked thin and narrow, tho not very small, and was in a natty boot, and she had a little hand. Altogether she seemed a sweet and pleasing variety of the sex, and as I thought of her part by part, my cock swelled slightly.

'You miss the Major – you expected a husband and must remain a widow,' – said I, delicately feeling my way – 'I wanted to see him of course.' – 'Of course, and it's hard to be disappointed as you meant to stop all night.' – 'Yes, and had brought my things, but only to stop two days,' – and she pointed to a small valise, which had been put on the netting above us. – 'It's only a change, for he expected to come back to London with me.' – 'To where?' said I. – Smiling, she replied, 'To our house.' – 'Let me go to the house with you, he won't be there.' – 'Oh, I dare not, what a proposal.' – But I saw a voluptuous smile in her face. 'Let's make this a house' – I was getting warmer and warmer. – 'What a house,' said she, turning her eyes away, and I saw she understood me. – 'A railway carriage isn't much like a house.' – 'Or a bed, but I've used one as both before now.' She laughed heartily. – (Neither sleeping cars, nor any convenience for night travelling then existed on any railway in England.)

She turned the conversation to theatres, but soon I got it to the amatory tone again – asked what she'd do sleeping alone, and got the usual evasive replies which a woman knows how to give when she doesn't want you to see that she understands you. But all my questions and suggestions were to the bed and male society, for I know the subject heats a cunt that has been once fucked. – I played with her hand and buttoned her glove. – She let me do all that. – Then risking it, as lewed intentions made me bolder, 'You must give me a kiss for my postage stamp.' – 'No thank you, not for a penny.' – 'You'd have given me fifty sooner than have lost the post.' – 'That I would,' and she laughed. – 'Then I'll have them now,' and putting my hand round her, I pulled her to me and kissed her half a dozen times; there was but little difficulty in doing it. – 'Now you kiss one of the fifty.' – 'No thank you.' – Then I asked her to dine with me. As she wasn't expected home, there would be no dinner there. – No, but she should get some tea and make it do.

I got as close to her as the arm between the seats (a fixture) allowed. – My leg met hers, and she didn't move it away. Carelessly I laid my hand on her knee, and, pinching up a bit of the silk dress, admired it. – A minute after. – 'You garter below knee,' I said, determined to see how far I could go, for three quarters of an hour would take us to London, and there was no time to lose. – 'That I don't, I garter above knee, how rude you are.' – 'My God! I feel rude, and can scarcely sit still,' – and, again taking the seat opposite to her, praised her foot and boot, and asked who her bootmaker was. – 'I shan't tell you.' – 'Well, let me look at your foot, it's a slim and pretty one.' – Up she put it on the seat by the side of me. – I felt it, pinched the ankle, and as she didn't flinch, rapidly ran my hand up to her knee, felt the garter, and just the flesh beyond, before she put her foot down.

She was angry, I was taking a mean advantage – I apologized, I could not help it. – 'Your beauty has put me in such a state of desire that I'm in actual pain for want of you – how smooth your flesh is – and you do, I find, garter above knee' – and much more. To all she made no reply, but kept first looking out of the window, then at me, and so on.

Again I asked her to dine with me – would she give me her address. – 'I won't, I dare not. – It would do you no good, and it might do me harm.'

There was something in her manner which for the moment kept me at a distance from her. – But soon I went on quietly again, talking of the officers in camp who had their mistresses there, and told of one who made such a noise when with his lady, – 'Embracing her in bed, you know,' – (I perceived that she knew well what I meant) that several heard him outside the hut, and chaffed him about it at mess. – Something of that sort had been told me, and I exaggerated it, and at intervals I felt my ballocks outside my trowsers, looking her in the face, till she turned her head to the window and smiled at my remarks. I knew that she guessed the condition of my pego, that some of her smile was at that, and felt sure that lust was stirred in her. Now every second she looked at me, and then out of the window, then at me again, and I saw in her eyes voluptuous wants.

Then I seated myself again by her side. I soon clutched her to me and kissed her and said I was madly in love with her. – 'It's your fault – my God, what a state you've put me in! – Show me your lovely foot again.' – Coquettishly she put one foot on the opposite seat, I stooped, and had my hands on her thighs in a second. She crossed them catching my hand between them, but it was embedded in the hair. – I had not only broken ice but gone clean thro it, and went on trying to force my hand further. 'My darling, let me feel your cunt, only for a minute, let me feel it, just feel it, and I'll take away my hand.'

'You shan't, I'll get out at the next station – Oho – ho – you – shan't' – she cried as I threw myself on my knees, lifted her petticoats, and got my face on her thighs. Tho she resisted, my lust now unbridled made me strong. – Violently I got her thighs apart, my head between them, my nose on her motte, my lips near her clitoris. I could not get my mouth lower, but smelt the stimulating smell of a nice cunt that was yearning for a fuck – I am sure that the cuntal aroma in the sweetest women, intensifies, gets ranker even, when want of the male is on her. I cried, 'I can smell your cunt, it's delicious, open your thighs, let me kiss it, do, love.' I tried to pull her forward, but did not succeed, but I kept my head on her thighs and motte for some minutes, feeling round her buttocks, talking lewedness under her petticoats, till she ceased striving against me.

My head still where it was, I pulled out my prick, and rubbed it hard against her calf. 'What am I rubbing against your leg? – Oh, let me have you.' – 'Get up, get up now – don't be foolish – Oh! if the guard should come. – I'll call out for the guard.'

Up I got recklessly lewd, and sat down; my prick standing up stiff in front of her. Her eyes were humid and she stared hard at me. – 'Oh, take care, here we are at the station.' The train just then slackened pace, and seemed as if going to stop. 'Oh! how you frightened me, suppose it had stopped. – What should I have done? – how foolish you are.' – 'I'll put it by if you'll feel it, – feel it,' said I. – Taking her gloved hand, I put it round it. How smooth the kid felt to my sensitive rammer.

Soon her glove was off and she was feeling it with her naked hand; whilst my fingers were rubbing between the lips of her cunt, and how moist it was – I pulled her to me and kissed her. 'Let me have you, let us fuck, love.' – 'I won't, how can you talk so, we can't here. – Now leave me alone. – Oho – don't – do leave off. – We shall be seen.' – We whisked past a station. 'Oh, if my husband knew, I should be ruined for life. – Oh – I *will* dine with you then, and you *shall* after dinner. – I can't take you home, I daren't tell you where I live. – Oh! – I *will* after dinner – oh – now,' – and her backside and thighs moved with that uneasy yet voluptuous movement, that restless, wriggling of belly, buttocks, and cunt that a woman can't help giving when a man is frigging her and the luscious sensation of complete lewedness, and the want of fucking, are coursing through her body.

I thought she might give me the slip at the station, and my chance would be lost. – I saw victory before me now and frigged on. – 'We'll fuck now, love, all's safe here.' I rose up standing before her, my prick almost touching her face, as she sat with her eyes fixed on it, whilst I begged her. – 'I won't, – I can't lie down on the floor.' – 'Take off your bonnet then and sit where you are.' She did – I put cushion after cushion on the floor, to bring myself to a convenient height, then, kneeling down, I opened her thighs, threw up her petticoats, and, gently pulling her forward till her cunt was well away from the edge of the seat, and she was leaning back, I inserted my prick. Altho the angle at which it stood, and that of her cunt was not quite favorable, it glided up deliciously and plugged her to my balls. – Then, putting my arms under her thighs, I fucked her. – We looked in each other's faces till our eyes closed in the swooning pleasure of the crisis, my prick gushed out its sperm, her cunt tightened, gripped, and liquefied, in the blissful spasms of spending, and mingling our sexual juices.

Recovering ourselves, she gave no signs of desire to uncouple. Looking speechless in each other's face (How I longed to know what she was thinking of), we held together. She was thin, but neither skinny nor bony; her backside not being great nor her cunt fat-lipped; it was well on to me and kept my prick wonderfully up her, spite of the movement of the train. (Some thin women, I have since noticed, can.) In the lovely warmth and embrocating moisture of her cunt, I lingered long; but at last withdrew my softened priapus from the Paphian temple. Putting my hand under it as I did so to receive it, a little flood of spendings rolled out after my prick left her. Telling her to be quiet, I got out my pocket handkerchief and put it to her cunt, which she wiped with it. Then I wiped my hand. 'Ah, it's nasty,' – said she. – 'Nonsense my love, neither prick nor cunt nor spunk are nasty at any time.' – Then we sat and talked. – 'It was awfully quickly over.' – 'It was – where is my bonnet?'

'That's the consequences of asking for a postage stamp,' said she. – 'Lucky for me,' I replied – We then talked about the Major ★★★★. 'Oh don't mention him, poor fellow, he'd shoot me and himself, too, if he knew what we have done. – I've never before been unfaithful.' – 'But he won't, my dear. – Let me feel it.' – 'No, don't, it's so wet still,' – but I did, and was feeling it, and she my prick, and just then the train went slower and then stopped. – We thought we were at a station, but something had gone wrong with one of the carriages. Then a carriage was detached, the passengers distributed in other carriages, and the train moved off again. The guard had locked our door.

Whilst waiting, she stood looking out of the window, I sitting felt her bum, and by the time the train moved off, was game for another fuck. – She refused. – I insisted, pulled her up from her seat, and getting her to kneel upon the seat diagonally, with her backside towards me, I fucked her standing, and never enjoyed a cunt more. – 'Oh! if Major ★★★★ knew,' said she again. – 'But he never will, my love, for you've no tongue in your cunt, and it can't speak.' – 'Well, I never did hear such a beast.' – 'You compliment me,' – I went on talking baudy, and she burst out laughing.

When we arrived at Waterloo, she wanted to leave me. There was no dinner for her, for she was not expected home, so I drove to K★★★s, got a private room, and ordered dinner. – We washed hands and face, and prick and cunt got their share of soap and water. – Then: 'Now I will, it's of no use your struggling, you shan't leave this room till I've seen it' – and I did.

I saw her slim but well-shaped thighs, and a small looking, rather pouting, but thin-lipped cunt between them. It had not much hair of a nut brown color. – Clitoris and nymphæ were scarcely visible. – It was not a lovely cunt, tho no fault could be found with it, but it was a novelty, and again I stiffened, put my prick up, gave a dozen or two shoves, but not feeling impetuous desire, withdrew it. – The bedroom was only given us to wash in, and we could not have it afterwards, so we got thro dinner as quickly as we could and drove off to a house. When we got there she was a little groggy.

At dinner she refused wine, saying that a little got into her head. – I thought it sham, pressed her, and filled her glass. – The champagne was good, and this was the result. – 'Oh I've drank too much, how shall I get home?' – 'No you mustn't – I won't tell you where, – I dare not.' She scarcely seemed to lose her wits, tho staggering, and I couldn't get out of her either where she lived or her name. She laid on the bed at once, let me undress her, and said she was sleepy. 'I'll fuck you first.' – 'Yes, fuck me.' – It was the first lewed word she'd uttered. – But a whim seized me. 'No, I'll gamahuche you.' – 'What's that.' – 'Lick your cunt, may I.' 'The Major does it more than anything' (laughing.) 'Doesn't he fuck you?' – 'Sometimes' – I pushed my enquiries about his sexual tastes.

I am always curious about other men now – 'Has he a big prick?' – 'I don't know, I think it's little,' and she laughed. 'Where do you live?' – 'Shan't tell you, ain't you going to do it?' – 'I'll gamahuche you.' – 'No, don't, it makes me scream.' – 'Scream?' – 'Yes,' she said thickly – 'it hurts me as well.' – Nonsense I thought. – Bringing her to the side of the bed, I wiped her cunt with a towel and began the libidinous exercise. It must have been because there was scarcely a vestige of clitoris or nymphae which made me, for never have I yet seen a vulva so devoid of those appendages. When the lips were opened, nothing was to be seen but the red lining and the vagina.

I found the excitable spot just above the little bone, and licked away gently. She soon felt my tongue, tho I thought she was nearly asleep. 'Oh don't! – oh put it in me.' – I went on furiously, – 'Oh! – I'm coming – leave off – he – ha – hi' she yelled. 'It hurts – hi – I'm spending' and she clutched my hair till I thought she'd scalp me. Ceasing, all was quiet for a minute. – I recommenced. She was a shorter time in spending, and I never heard such screeches given by a woman in her pleasure. – 'Oh – hi – her – hi – hi – ha – oh, I can't bear it!' – She half raised herself, and then fell back, spending and exhausted. – 'If you do it any more, I shall have a fit. I'm obliged to stop *him* sometimes, I've had fits through his doing it.'

I was still between her legs, squatting on my heels, when she said she should have a fit. But that, and her screeching, tho it irritated me, seemed at the same time to stimulate me to continue. – I felt as if I must have been giving her intense pleasure, and that delighted me. I threw her legs over my shoulders again, grasping them tightly, buried my mouth in her cunt and recommenced gamahuching. – 'Oh don't – I'll have a fit' – grasping my head, she tried to raise herself up, but fell back again as I tilted her thighs with my shoulders, spluttering out, my mouth half buried in her cunt. – 'Spend, spend, love, – spend.' – On my tongue went, as rapidly as tongue could move. – Her bum shook, her belly heaved and jerked. – 'Oh – leave – off – oh – my God – I am coming. – Oh – Ahrr – oho' – she screamed till the room rang, and just as her pleasure spasm ceased and her backside lay tranquil – a servant knocked at the door and wanted to know what was the matter.

The sexual excitement then seemed to have sobered her, and a strong cup of tea I had brought revived her. I laid her on the bed again by my side, and heard all about the strangely exciting effect of gamahuching on her. I came to the conclusion that tickling her clitoris with his tongue, was the Major's principal amusement and that he preferred it to fucking. – No doubt also from her description, his cock was a very small one. But as she sobered, she got less free in her revelations. – She had, however, declared that the Major two or three times had gamahuched her, till she had had some sort of fit – I never heard anything of the sort before, in any woman.

I stroked her twice more before leaving and really enjoyed her very much. Her cunt was deep and elastic, and such is the effect of novelty on me that I thought its thin externals gave it a great charm and added to my pleasure. – Certainly I laid unusually long up her after spending. Her cunt seemed to fit round my prick afterwards like a glove, and I put it in her and the sperm as well, till I withdrew. But her thighs and belly made it not such a luxurious bed to lie on after fucking as a stout, large-thighed woman with a soft belly does.

(Tho I never heard a woman screech so loudly and painfully when being gamahuched, I have known more than one scream in a subdued but half maddened tone, but a tone of delight, when she spent, and several ejaculate the baudiest words and thoughts as erotic images rose up in their brain. – I myself cry out now in similar manner, when a charming creature draws the sperm out of me into her mouth. It is pleasure, to utter lewed words as my sperm issues.)

After the second fuck she was anxious to go, she had no latch key and began to wonder if *they* would be out, and up to tricks in her absence, as they didn't expect her home; but I couldn't learn who *they* were. –

'No.' She became as close as wax. 'Give me some silver, I'm unnerved – now don't you follow me.' – I gave it to her and nothing more, and off she went. She made me no promise of seeing me again. – No. If even she might like it, she wouldn't, it would ruin her prospects. – If ever I saw her in camp. 'If you're a gentleman you won't notice me. – I'm sure you wouldn't like to ruin a poor woman.' – I was in camp several times afterwards, but forgot both the name of the Major, his regiment, and branch of service, so made no enquiries. – She named a place for me to write to, and gave me a name. I did write but never had a reply. She gave me a day's delicious amusement. – I have had many such, but without such curious incidents.

Some weeks before this affair with the postage stamp lady, I began a flirtation with a pretty creature named Madeline S***h, without meaning anything but to have the pleasure of talking to and being with her. – It ended in a liaison, very short and very sweet, and there was a voluptuous incident in it occurring to myself, and not of an everyday kind – I have in the after talk of dinners, and in the salacious disclosures of men in club smoking rooms, heard of similar physical crises occurring to men, and once, if not twice, recollect similar things having occurred to me. – Perhaps under sexual excitement they have occurred to many men in strong health. But I approach middle age, so the incident rather surprised me, tho it was gratifying as evidence of my sexual vigor and strength.

Sometimes I wonder at the amatory course I have run – and whether these temporary connections with women, these liaisons of lust, are forced upon me by circumstances, or whether I am instinctively seeking them? Whether it is the women who bring them about – or myself? – Which is it? – I cannot answer. – I know certainly *when* I seek them, *when* I am cunt hunting, as I term it. – But so many women (not courtesans) have fallen to my embraces (and in this narrative I have only told of my amours of a special character), as it seems to me by pure force of opportunity and circumstances, pure chance as it were; unless those seeking to form them were the women. Does a thirsty cunt and a hard scrotum set men and women together, without either of them intending or thinking about coition, until lust steals on, and strengthens, and modesty gradually vanishes, till the barriers of conventionality are broken by one or both, and they bend under the spell of concupiscence till they fuck? – Is it not the law of animal life that the male and female shall blindly and instinctively seek each other for copulation? Is it not in the great scheme of creation that they should? If so, why should they be blamed for satisfying this imperious want, this universal law, this blind necessity of fucking? Why should man frame laws, legal and social, for hindering man and woman from coupling, blending, and satisfying their love or lust whenever they like? – Love and lust are terms identical in meaning, synonymous; tho often the former is called pure, the latter foul. It is the priest who determines that. But again I ask myself, was it mine, or the women's *fault*, or rather by whose *virtue*, that we fell into each other's arms and copulated? – and whose fault or virtue was it, that Madeline and I came sexually together for a brief while?

A few days after I had had the postage stamp lady, I went to the Crystal Palace (then a fashionable lounge on certain days, it not having been opened many years), expecting to meet a nice creature, a dressmaker, who was about twenty years old. – She had worked at my house for years previously when quite a girl, but was now well grown and womanly for her years. – I had often noticed her years before, and one day gave her a sly kiss, and half a crown on some pretext. – I lost sight of her when I gave up that home as a freed man, and then met her by chance one evening a year or so after. I found she was still a milliner, and seemed as modest as one might desire, took her, spite of her reluctance, to have a glass of wine, and, giving her my arm, walked some part of her way home with her. It was in the suburbs, and in the dark I gave her a kiss, which she liked, then tried to feel her unsuccessfully; tho I got a touch on her thigh and made her cry, gave her a sovereign, and a kiss which I made her return, and never saw her again till recently, two years *after* my unsuccessful attempt at groping her. Now she seemed to me quite gay and frolicsome, she was an under forewoman at Mrs ***** a dressmaker, and had she said, a sweetheart. She was a very handsome creature, with soft grey eyes and lovely auburn hair. – I got it into my head that she, like most milliners, fucked on the sly, a little for love and a little for silk dresses. She told me when I met her, which I did three days after my visit to Aldershot, she was going on Saturday to the Crystal Palace. I said I should do the same. She remarked that she knew that I could do as I liked now. – Her name as already said was Madeline S***h.

To my annoyance, I found she was with a friend, a milliner, who looked to me as frisky, as if two pricks would suit her better than one. Getting hold of Miss S***h, I told her I was so vexed, for I wanted her to dine with. She was sorry, but her friend's young man would meet them at four o'clock. – Then said I, 'Well miss them, and you come out and dine with me.' That she agreed to, I went off, found a quiet sort of half restaurant, half tavern (houses of that class were just then springing up there), ordered dinner in a private room, paid half down at once, and went back to the Palace.

It all came off as arranged, and at about five o'clock, when some music was over, which she wanted to stay for – we left quietly and had dinner. She eat and drank well, and seemed as frisky as a grasshopper. – I'd not hinted at anything. Beyond the convenience of the sofa in the room, and my hoping it would bear the weight of two restless people, I had said nothing concupiscent in its tone, tho I was longing for her during dinner. For since the unknown postage stamp lady, I had kept myself from women. – The cloth removed, the waiter gone, I brought her to the window to look out, put my arm round her waist, kissed her, and said I thought she ought to kiss me for the dinner. – After a very little sham she did, and we kissed each other quite amorously. Then I sat her down on the sofa where I meant now to experiment on her virtue, and pulling the table a little nearer, and pouring out wine, began.

As I usually do, I first told suggestive stories, then smutty ones, but without baudy words. She laughed at them all. – 'Oh, my! – He *was* up to his tricks.' – 'Oh what a shameful story!' and so on. – She didn't blush, but got excited, and I thought all was right. Ever and anon I kissed her. She wouldn't tell her sweetheart, she said, for she had one who was going to marry her. Then I began about her garters, asked if her lover had ever put them on for her. What next should I imagine. 'Of course not.' – Why should she refuse him? I asked. – 'It wouldn't be proper.' – 'That's not the reason.' 'What is it then?' – 'You fear he'd put his hand higher up between your thighs?' – 'Oh, you blackguard, to talk like that.' – She tossed her head. – 'And feel your cunt, Madeline?' I continued – she gave me a smack on my head. – 'If you talk like that I'll go.' What a lot of women have said they would smack my head, and some have, but not very hard.

'What's the harm, my darling, even if your lover did, and what's the harm of calling it *that* if I say your *thing*, you know it means the same.' – 'Oh, you blackguard!' – I went on in the same strain and pinched and tickled her till she screeched. 'Oh, you blackguard, leave off.' – 'The waiter will be coming in if you make such a noise,' said I, getting up and bolting the door. – 'Well, don't you do that to me.' 'I can't help it, I'm madly in love with you.' – For a time we were quieter, then I pulled her back on the sofa and began spooning. 'You know your lover's been in bed with you.' – That he hadn't, she shouldn't be such a fool. – 'Let me.' – 'What?' – My arm was round her waist, my lips close to hers, my hand on her lap. I grabbed at her clothes just above her notch. She must have felt the clutch on her motte, and I said, 'Fuck you,' and kissed her with mad lust on me.

She slapped my head hard now and threatened to go, but didn't rise. – 'Did I hurt you?' – 'Don't do it again, or talk like that, or I'll never speak to you again.' – Again we kissed, I gave her more wine, and spilt some over her dress. – 'You've ruined my dress,' said she anxiously. – 'Never mind love, tell me what it cost, I'll pay for another,' – and I took out my purse. – 'You were always kind, but perhaps I'll get it out.' – 'Well here's a sovereign to clean it' – she wouldn't take the money.

Some years before I had bought a lot of pretty, small priced brooches. – Most had been given away to servants and other women, and even to favourite doxies. I had put one in my pocket now, and also had brought two pairs of beautiful garters with me.

Ah, what a repetition – how many times has nearly the same occurred – I seem to have been rehearsing it half my life, but thus it occurred now. 'Now isn't that a pretty brooch?' – 'Oh, it is.' – 'I'm going to give that to a lady friend.' – 'Oh!' said she in such a tone that I saw at once it had crossed her mind that I was going to give it to *her*. – 'And a pair of these garters as well, on one condition.' – I produced them. – 'What's that.' – 'That she'll let me put them on.' – 'Will she?' – 'I think so, I did so once before, and she's a nice little lady.' – 'Not much of a lady.' – 'She is tho, and married.' – 'She ought to be ashamed of herself then.' – 'Pough! my dear, who'll know but she and I? The last pair I put on her legs as she laid on the bed, and then I got on to the bed with her, and then.' – There I stopped. – '*You – are – a – regular scamp*, I've been told so,' said Madeline, blushing. – 'Why my dear?' – 'For tempting a poor woman so.' – 'Nonsense, my love, *she* tempted *me*, but which pair would you like?' – 'This pair.' – Then I said I'd give them her if she'd let me put them on. – She refused.

I chaffed her. 'You tie yours up with string don't you?' – 'Wouldn't you like to know.' – 'Yes, and to feel.' Saying which, I made the attempt, didn't succeed, and got another slap on my head. – She rose up, saying she wouldn't stop any longer, but after a little consideration sat down again.

On I talked in the same strain – all she replied from time to time was, 'Oh, you scamp.' But I thought she looked as if the talk was affecting her sensually, and she let me kiss her easily, after every time that she called me that name. – At length, by constantly asking her, the bait took. She selected a pair, and, with just the same precautions that other women have taken, one after another the garters were put on. – As I fastened the last, I put my mouth down, and kissed the little bit of thigh which was just clear above the stocking. – The sniff of the warm flesh exalted my randiness, lust then overpowered me, and pulling her back on the sofa, kissing her rapturously all the time, I got one hand up her clothes, and just felt the thighs and the hair of her mount. – She repulsed me instantly with a loud cry. – 'Let me fuck you, my love. I'm dying for you.' – 'Oh, you blackguard, get away.' – 'Look what a state you've put me in,' and out I pulled my glowing rod, which pulsated as if going at once to discharge the semen which lay in my balls.

Up she got, leaving me sitting on the sofa, with my pulsating, crimson tipped, cunt-rammer out. 'You mistake me altogether if you asked me here to behave like that. – I'll go at once.' – She meant it. – No. She'd go back to the Palace by herself. It had been arranged that we were to find her friend there, and all go to town together. She said a lot more, all the time standing close by me, and looking every instant at my nodding engine – looking spite of herself I expect. I got her round the waist, and swearing I would go no further, got her sitting again on the sofa, and hid my prick in my trowsers. – She was upset. The sight of a good sized, stiff prick always upsets a young woman whether she has been fucked or not, and stirs up lewed sensations in her.

She didn't know exactly where to go to find her friend, or I believe she would have gone off without me – I now saw I shouldn't succeed in having her, and that she was wide awake. She had a sweetheart who was going to marry her, and wouldn't run the risk of getting with kid, I thought. I also felt sure she'd been poked. I've had a dozen young milliners, and only one was a virgin, and altho this woman lived with her parents and seemed respectable, I know that the more women living as she was are fucked out of doors, the more careful for a time they are to hide their games from their parents and employers. – Disappointed for the minute, I ceased.

It was getting dusk, she was anxious to go, I more and more anxious to have her. My prick would not subside, but threatened to spend in my trowsers. – It was on the Monday that I had had the postage stamp lady, and since then had been keeping myself chaste, with the pleasurable hope of deluging Madeline's cunt with rich spermatic juices. – Again I grasped and kissed her. 'There is the brooch, I'll give it you, but am awfully disappointed, for I do so long for you, and no one would know but you and I.' – 'Don't be foolish, don't be a beast.' – 'Oh, let me then just feel your flesh, by the eternal God, if you'll let me feel your thigh, only half way above your knee – I'll be content, I'll go no further.' – 'You beast, let me get up,' and she made a half attempt to rise. – Was lewedness subduing her? – It was a miserable small sofa, with scarcely room for one person to lie down, she was reclining sideways, I holding her so that one of her feet was on the ground, the other nearly so, and she contemplating the brooch most of the time, was seemingly delighted with it.

I have often wondered since if it was the brooch which absorbed her thoughts and made her careless, or gratitude for it, which made her half indulge me for the moment. Or did she feel a sensuous pleasure in my attempt, secure in the knowledge that she could repel my hand when she listed? Was she lewd at that moment and therefore yielding? – What a pity that some visible sign of lewedness is not in a woman; that she hasn't something which will rise up and stiffen as a prick does. – A man has always that sign of his lustful state, and a woman need be in no doubt about it.

She went on looking at the brooch, pinning it on her breast, then taking it out to look at it, whilst I went on kissing, coaxing, pinching her thighs outside, and attempting slight liberties. 'No, I won't.' – 'Only one thigh – a little bit of the flesh only this side. Now do.' – Holding her round the waist, I hitched up that side of her clothes, and got my hand on to her thigh just above the garter. – With both hands she stopped me. – 'There now – you've done it, now leave me alone. – I'm foolish to let you. – Now don't. – Oh, what are you about?' and she dropped the brooch.

Rapidly I pulled away the only button which kept my prick within my trowsers, and out it stood rampant; raised her clothes on that side, put one hand under the thigh, with force hoisted it a little up, and turned more towards her, with the intention of letting my prick touch her flesh. I had neither hope nor idea of getting into her. – The thought alone of my prick touching her flesh filled me with voluptuous delight. – I pushed my prick wildly, now holding the thigh still more exposed with both hands, and pressing my body to it. – My prick spite of her struggles touched her. – She cried out loudly. 'Leave off – oh you scamp, don't.' – I heeded not, heated by the contact, I went on. – A spasm of delight shot through my prick, and an ungovernable movement of my buttocks shoved it to and fro. – Its tip rubbed against the tiny bit of naked thigh, pulsated violently, and before I knew if I could control it, or she free herself from me, shot out a torrent of hot, thick sperm on to her thigh. It ran down to one of my hands, whilst I sighed out. – 'My God – I'm spending – it's on your – thigh.' – Then I sank, half fainting with pleasure, upon her shoulder.

'Don't – what are you doing – let me get up' – was all I heard, and by that time she had pulled down her clothes, covering up sperm and all, and I had fallen back on the sofa holding my prick. – The whole affair, from the time I got hold of her thigh, had not occupied the time it takes me to write a dozen of these lines.

★   ★   ★

Madeline's lover Richard. – Mrs B**t*n's mischief. – Complaisance in cab and house. – Bertha the fruitress. – Male chaffing. – An erotic vision in the shop. – Is she virtuous? – Madeline again. – A ruptured membrane. – Mutual fucking sensations. – Inheritance of a marbly rump. – A woman's virgin spend. – Absent at Paris. – Madeline's lover is reconciled. – Onanistic emissions. – French letters and cunt sponges. – The influences leading women to copulate. – Madeline's intentions and admissions.

She rose, picked up the brooch, put it on the table, and put on her bonnet silently and hastily. I arose feeling ashamed, enclosed my still swollen machine, and said I was so sorry for what I had done, I couldn't help it, that it was her fault. – She made no reply beyond, – I'll never dine or speak with you again, you're a blackguard.' – 'If you'd only let me.' – 'You're a scamp.' – I chattered on, she begged me to be quick, 'I'd go without you but I can't find the place, what will Mrs B**t*n (her milliner friend) think about my being late?' – I didn't want to injure her, so rapidly paid my bill, and we got to the rendezvous late, but not too late. – There was Mrs B**t*n alone, her male friend had gone. – She approached Madeline and said, 'Richard's been here and has gone off nearly mad. – I couldn't say you were not here, so told him you'd gone with a lady friend, etc. etc.' – Madeline began to cry, saying to me, – 'You've made plenty of mischief for me,' – and turned sulky. The two held a long conversation apart, Mrs B**t*n seemed excited. – Madeline cried, till, with a rush for the train, we got seats.

It was then a long way across London, from the station to the neighbourhood where Madeline lived – I got into the cab with them – Madeline sulked all the way – I knew where she lived, and she insisted on being set down at the end of the street. Only her companion alighted with her – I bid them goodbye, hoping her young man wouldn't be angry long. – Madeline said it was a misfortune for her my meeting her at the Palace – and we parted. I had heard from Madeline that her friend the milliner lived in the heart of London, not far from another workshop, and knowing she would have to get there, put my cab away from the end of the street, and on foot waited myself in sight of Madeline's house – I had noticed in the cab Mrs B**t*n's glances, which were curious, and as much as to say, 'I know what you've been up to together.' She seemed also I think a little lewed – I had heard she was a widow. She was about thirty, and a smallish, thinnish, matured, well-shaped-looking little woman. – Really feeling anxious about Madeline, and hoping not to have done her any injury, I waited to catch Mrs B**t*n to make enquiries.

It had taken a long time to get from the Palace to **** (done in exactly half the time now, owing to railways.) It was about half past nine when Mrs B**t*n appeared, and was astonished to see me. Would she take a seat in my cab, and I would drive her home. – She accepted at once. – In a minute afterwards. 'What have you two been up to together?' said she inquisitively, and laughing suggestively.

'Nothing.' I had known Madeline a girl and liked her looks, met her by accident at the Palace, and, going myself to have some food, offered her some. Nothing more. – 'Was that all?' We had been a long time. – 'I wish it hadn't been all, for I'd give twenty pounds to have her.'

'Hush,' said Mrs B**t*n putting her hand right over my mouth. – 'I don't believe you' – but I repeated it, said she was a lovely creature, but I wouldn't on any account harm her, and directly I got to **** St and sat Mrs B**t*n down, I'd go to the Argyle and get a woman for the night.

'You're a nice boy. – I've heard of you before, you'd better go home *now*.' 'No,' said I, 'I'll have a woman first.' In five minutes after I was kissing Mrs B**t*n, in another five minutes was feeling her cunt, ten minutes afterwards was in a baudy house, and five minutes after that, a dose of sperm had been administered to the red-lipped, hair-encircled, moist, warm, aromatic organ, which she, like other women, had lying between her thighs, bum hole, and navel. – As quickly as possible afterwards, she had another dose. – Neither of us undressed, for Mrs B**t*n, tho evidently liking prick exercise in her, and altho a widow, also lived with a friend and got home at early hours.

In the interval between the fucks she told me all about Madeline. – She believed her virtuous, and didn't believe she'd been fucked. I made her say those words. It is a great pleasure to me to make a woman who is not gay speak baudily. – A young man, of her own condition in life, meant to marry her. He had come to the Crystal Palace to meet her, having heard by chance that she was going there. – Mrs B**t*n's male friend incautiously said she had gone to dine with a gentleman, and the sweetheart in a rage went off, swearing he'd have nothing to do with her any more, and would blow his own brains out. Mrs B. had told Madeline that she had told Richard it was with a lady she had left. That was to calm her – I have since fancied Mrs B. was not a true friend.

I met Mrs B. two days afterwards and fucked her. She took a little present this time. Madeline had heard nothing of her sweetheart, and thought she had lost him, so did Mrs B. – I fancy from her silence that Madeline had said nothing about garters and brooch, or my spending over her thigh, she had said that I behaved as a perfect gentleman. 'Well, I shan't meet her again at the Crystal Palace or elsewhere,' I observed, but I tried to catch Madeline on her road to and from her work, and failed. I expected that she and her swain had made it up, and that she avoided me. I didn't go near Mrs B★★t★n, and almost forgot all about the affair, for I was, and had for a month or two previously, been on the cunt-hunt, and now was on the trail rather smartly, which put Madeline out of my mind, and I had given up all hopes of getting her. – Dinner wine, baudy talk, and trying to grope her, the sight of my prick, my spending on her thigh had all failed. – No, most likely she's been fucked, but sees the chance of marriage, and will run no further risks; so ran my thoughts, and in my heart I did not blame her.

[The narrative now goes back a little. – The liaison with Madeline has been told hitherto consecutively – (a custom usually observed in this history of my secret life). But one with a girl named Bertha, commenced whilst I was courting Madeline, – the amusement with the postage stamp lady already told of – and a Paphian ball yet to be told of, also took place whilst my amours with Bertha and Madeline were going on, and I find it difficult to arrange the narrative in my usual manner, so much were all these amours intermixed and also mixed in the manuscript.]

A few months before I met Madeline, I had been a good deal into the city speculating. – Buying something one day at a very little fruiterer's shop – I noticed a pretty girl who served there. – She was shortish, sturdy, dark-haired, and dark-eyed, and had a look and manner superior to shop women generally. I thought her twenty but she was not eighteen. I shall call her Bertha.

The mistress had two shops and was usually at the other and Bertha alone at this one. The customers seemed almost exclusively well-to-do city men, and usually bought their goods after midday. They chaffed her at times broadly, which she didn't seem to mind, and at times returned. – A look in her eye made me think she was amorous, women can't help feeling lewed, and how they manage to look perfectly modest with clipping, perspiring cunts, puzzles me. – At length I found myself going often to the shop, and then chaffing her like the others. – Then I noticed some of the men say 'Keep the change, I can't bear coppers' – so to ingratiate myself I did the same. One day I snatched a kiss which she didn't seem to mind at all, and giving her a sovereign for some goods, and a half sovereign being among the change, I pushed it to her and told her to keep it. – She eyed me fixedly and curiously for a few seconds, and then refused it. 'Oh, dear no, that's too much,' said she, pushing it away. – On saying that I should take it out in kisses, – 'That you won't.' She would not take it, and a few days after being in the shop, which happened to have a quick succession of customers, the following occurred to me. – One of the strangest, and most complete, yet almost unconscious efforts of erotic fancy I ever had. It more resembled an erotic dream.

Without any sexual desires as far as I know, and certainly without any sexual intentions, I sat looking at her pretty face, and particularly at her mouth, which was unusually small, and with little handsome fat lips; lips which make me want to kiss them whenever I see them. – After a while looking – I wondered if her cunt had thick lips. – I know the idea of their being fat on account of those of her mouth being so was absurd; and that a small mouth does not imply a small cunt, nor thick lips above, mean thick lips below; but there is no accounting for the association of ideas, however absurd they may be. Then I felt suddenly a desire to see her cunt and to fuck it, and sat thinking about its size, its hair, and its looks, whilst I talked to her and looked in her eyes, and at her mouth. Then my cock tingled with lust, then swelled, then stood erect and hard for an instant, and just then she turned to someone who came in, to serve him.

Whilst she did so I shut my eyes, violent lewdness seized me, and I fancied my sperm was spurting into her – I had all the pleasure of imagination, without the physical reality. – I saw a lovely little fat-lipped cunt, with a little bush around it, and fancied I saw the voluptuous pleasure in her eyes as my prick gradually entered. – Ah! what exquisite joint sensation of mind and body, experienced as the glans is first pressed by the cunt and feels its road. – No doubt the female experiences similar thoughts as her cunt feels the distention by the smooth prick tip, and she knows it will search to its innermost depths.

Said I to her, 'I've been dreaming awake about you, whilst you were serving those people.' – 'What was your dream?' – 'It would make you blush if I told you.' – 'Then don't tell it.' – Then I began wondering if she were virgin or not, and half thought not, for I saw a young man attempting to kiss her as I entered the shop soon after, and thought it improbable that a mere shop girl, serving well-dressed men and gentlemen both young and old, could have so long kept her cunt to herself, under the temptations which I fancied she must be subject to there. I began to long for her, tho I was fucking ****** about that time, and varying her pleasures with Paphians both English and French, and a big German woman as well, tho I had soon done with *her*.

I came to the conclusion at last that she was no more virtuous than she should be, and that I might as well be one of the happy ones. Yet I didn't approach the subject till one day, seeing another fellow kiss her, I said, 'Hulloh, Miss Bertha, I'll tell Mrs C★h★n.' – The same young man I had talked with one or two days before was eating strawberries and laughed with me. 'We all kiss you, don't we Bertha?' said he. – 'No, don't you tell stories about me to that gentleman, I let some of you, and Mrs C*h*n knows it, I shouldn't be here long if I made a fuss about every thing that's said to me. Miss *** was turned off because she did, and *you* lost her her place.' Then she turned to a customer who entered. – I remarked to the man that I supposed she was pretty intimate with some fellow. 'I expect so, and plenty have tried.' Then, nodding to me, he left.

Directly afterwards she told me not to believe what that man said, he was a nuisance and was always annoying her, but was such a good customer that she didn't like to offend him. – 'He wants to get to bed with you, Bertha.' – 'He's like a good many more then, but they'll be disappointed,' – said she, looking me in the face and not all abashed. – 'Don't disappoint *me* or I'll hang myself.' – 'The sooner you do it the better.' – This coolness astonished me. I didn't think about what a hardening moral process incessant amatory chaff is; how soon a young maiden learns to return it, and how pleasant veiled allusions to marriage, to the pleasure in having company in bed, and other indirect allusions to fucking, are, – how they keep the mind and body in a slight state of voluptuousness, particularly pleasing to a woman, who feels, among other things, complimented by the allusions being made to her; for a woman always feels pleased at a man's desiring to possess her.

Then I was sitting on a little stool in the shop one day, and she told me a lot about the business and herself. – She lived with an aunt, and nightly went home by herself. Their business was generally over by eight o'clock, sometimes they kept open till ten, if the weather was bad for keeping fruit. – 'Come and sup with me, and say you've been late at shop.' – 'No thank you, I know what you mean by that.'

Another day I took her the last of my Neapolitan brooches. – She was delighted. Soon after she had to stand upon a stool to reach something down, and I risked putting my hand up her petticoats. 'That's not fair,' said she angrily, getting down. – 'I didn't expect that of *you*.' – 'I'm mad for you, dying for you, I'll not leave you alone till I've had you.' – 'I've heard that said many times.' – 'Goodbye, I shan't come again.' – 'Why.' – 'Because you won't let me.' – 'Goodbye, don't be foolish, I should be sorry if you don't come, you talk nicer than most of those who come here, but I know all your little games. – There's a middle-aged man comes here, who's had the impudence to offer to keep me, and give me five hundred a year; and I've seen his wife and his children here with him – a blackguard.'

Thought I, she's a little out of the common, but if she's not been already fucked, she will be soon. I went there less often, then was away from town. – When I returned she wondered why I hadn't been. –

'Because you won't come and dine with me.' – 'It will be no good to you if I do' – again I put my hands on to her ankles, and she seemed less angry – I did it another day, but couldn't get to her garters, she was too quick for me.

'If anyone comes in and catches you trying that on, you'll lose me my place; kissing doesn't matter, but improper things do.' – 'Come to dinner with me then.' – 'Oh! you do so plague me. I will some day, but it will be no use to you, mind.' – There the matter rested, for, having lost money, I ceased speculating, and did not go to my stockbrokers, and amused myself by tailing my doxies.

Again I went, and, chatting with a man in the shop whom I knew a little of, he said that he thought Bertha up to snuff, and that Mr ***** had had her. She seemed very pleased to see me, and I, being very bold and hot that day, got my hand up her clothes on to her thighs, at which she was excessively angry and declared that if I ever made such an attempt again, she would neither speak to me, nor serve me, and would tell the shop owner – 'and I will never dine with you.' – Off I went and didn't see her for some time.

A few days afterwards, I met in the street Madeline (I cannot make up my mind whether she threw herself in my way or not). We talked, and she began to cry. She had never seen her young man since. – He had written to say he had done with her, and it was all my fault, she said. I couldn't admit that. It was an unfortunate accident, nothing more. – She never would meet me or anyone else again, but it ended that day in her agreeing to dine with me the day following, to talk over what was to be done.

At the ***** hotel, I took a bedroom and sitting-room, leading out of each other, and took a small trunk there; feeling sure that she had been poked, and was coming to poke, and that the hotel would be more comfortable than a baudy house.

She was punctual, had a good appetite, and, tho crying at intervals when I mentioned her Richard, was in good spirits. – She was still dressmaking at Mrs ****'s, but being out of sorts through the loss of her young man, had been fit for nothing; and her mistress had told her she must improve or go. Madeline seemed to me in a reckless frame of mind about that, said she must do what she could. If she must leave, she must; she couldn't help what her parents said, and so on. Hers was the sort of Devil-may-care manner which I have seen in women of her class who are tired of their work and position, and who want pleasure. – In fact as a main cause of that, and perhaps unconscious of it, want fucking; and are half disposed to get a prick up them at any risk. – Her coming to meet me again after what had taken place between us led me to think she might be in that state, and from her answers to, and sometimes evasions of, my questions, I came to the conclusion that Richard had been up the red inlet to her body, which she had between her thighs like other women.

Dinner over, we sat on the sofa and I began kissing her. – She was so far complaisant. Talking about Richard, she had heard he was now, 'Sweet upon another young woman,' and, altho she then whimpered, said she didn't care much. I found that it was the loss of a husband, and one who was so respectable, that she fretted about, more than the individual. I began to doubt then if she'd had Richard up her, and joked her about her not getting a bedfellow so soon as she'd expected, offered myself instead, talked about matrimony, on the absurdity of a man and woman who liked each other not doing before marriage all that nature prompted them to do, and how they lost pleasure, which they couldn't take too young. She sipped wine and got amative in manner, I held her to me, and our kisses were many. – 'That's enough,' said she, as if it had just occurred to her that she was giving way too much.

My prick now got on the ramp, and I resolved either to get her or let her go. Tho I'd promised her never to refer to what had taken place at the previous dinner, I asked her if she'd washed her thigh since, and if she looked at her chemise after it. – She coloured up and rose to go, I pulled her down, said I'd forgotten my promise and couldn't help it. – I'd like to do it again to her, or if she'd let me, do something better. – Women are so cunning, you never can make them, until they have long had a man, confess, their lust; but I've no doubt that, with this talk, Madeline's cunt was beginning to sweat inside. The half bashful way she looked at me, and the ridiculous resistance to my kissing which she now offered for a second or two, made me feel sure that she wanted fucking at that minute, and was struggling against it. – Women can control their passions to a certain point, and then they droop, and yield helplessly all at once, I have found.

She really was angry once, yet returned each of my kisses. 'Have you the garters on?' – 'Yes.' – 'Let me see them' – and I made the attempt. – 'No, no, you shan't,' and she struggled, but I got my hand on her thigh.

She got it away, but in another minute her head was over my shoulder, I was kissing now her ear, now her cheek, and whispering baudiness. – I had reduced her to silence, whilst speaking of my sperm on her thigh when it ought to have been in her cunt, and she have had pleasure as well as me, whilst my prick discharged it. 'Let me feel your thighs. – Do – if you don't I'll do that again.' – 'Oh don't,' said she in a half whisper. – 'Well, let me see your garters, I will,' and, letting go her waist, I pulled up her clothes, saw garters and thigh, and, stooping, kissed the flesh before she could prevent me. She gave a slight cry, but next moment I was clasping her round her waist, again her head was on my shoulder, my fingers on her cunt, and I was whispering about carnal love into her ear, and titillating her clitoris.

[How commonplace it all seems as I write this afresh now. – To how many women have I done as nearly as possible the same, and how many under similar circumstances have behaved like Madeline? It can't be varied. – A woman's a woman, a cunt's a cunt, everywhere. Voluptuous sensations are common to all, lewedness makes the man attack, and the woman yield. All the world over it's the same, and ever will be. – Yet each woman who is fresh to me in copulating preliminaries gives as much pleasure to me as if she was the first I had. I feel as if I never had such sensual felicity before as at that moment, and was still to have with her.

Does the woman mean to let the man have her when she meets him, or from the moment he touches her cunt, or when, or at all, or does she unconsciously acquiesce, and gradually yield, as sensations overcome all sense but that of carnal voluptuousness? – Do visions of his prick entering the hitherto sacred precincts of her cunt pass through her brain as he gently masturbates her? Few women can answer this themselves, I find.]

Absorbed in feeling her cunt, and the delight of giving the sweet creature pleasure, wondering if I dare put my finger lower down and try the passage, I titillated her in silence. All was silent now, excepting the gentle smacking of my kisses on her upturned cheek and lips. – I frigged gently between tightly-closed thighs, till in that charming way a woman has, when she feels the premonitory thrills of the coming spend, and doesn't like to show her pleasure; she moved her face up from my shoulder with a start. – 'Oho! aha! leave off now. – You shan't'; and, with a jut back of her haunches, she removed my finger for a second. I instantly recommenced, frigged quicker, still quicker, harder. Now I ceased kissing her. 'Spend darling, spend, love,' I said, looking into her face, which was again on my shoulder. – Her eyes were closed, her mouth slightly open, rapid breathing and quick sighs of pleasure came from her. – Ah, that quiver of the thighs and belly, that tremulous shiver in her bosom, I knew it well, and the squeeze of the thighs on my hand, – tight for a second – then the convulsive opening of them, again the tight closing, and then the languid opening of the fleshy columns. – I knew it well, for I have frigged scores of the angels, and knew that Madeline had spent.

Whilst her thighs in voluptuous languor lay loosely, I slipped my hand between them and grasped her whole cunt, and my fingers lay between the lips. She started up and pushed my hand away. On it as I withdrew it, were the copious evidences of her pleasure. – 'You've spent, love. – I've frigged you. – Ah! if my prick had been in you, how much more pleasure you'd have had. Come to the other room, let us – come.' She sat looking at me full. What was she thinking of? Again I cuddled, kissed and fondled her, again my hand touched her clitoris. She was passive, my fingers moved over all the moistened surface, and then her thighs closed again. – 'Come with me, come.' – Gently and uninterruptedly I frigged on, murmuring 'Come, love,' till with a sudden rousing, she pushed away my hand, gasping out slowly and hesitatingly, 'No – I – can't.'

'Feel my prick then,' and I put her hand round it. She was now sighing, her head again fell on my shoulder with eyes closed, my prick in her hand, when I recommenced frigging. – 'Oh leave off. I can't.' – 'Come to the bed, or my spunk will go all over you again. – Oh, how wet your cunt is. – My love, let's go, or I shall spend.' – She was almost insensible to everything but lust and didn't reply. I rose, seized her hands, and gently pulled her up. – 'Come.' 'No.' – But gradually and easily I led her into the bedchamber – She wouldn't get on the bed. – 'I won't let you now.' – 'What nonsense, then I'll leave you – get on love, and I'll only frig you.' – On she got.

I got on the bed unbuttoning as I did so. There was no light excepting what came through the sitting-room door. For a moment I frigged her, gradually pressing her on to her back, then slowly mounted her. – 'I'll do it so. – I'll spend over your thigh so, and frig you after, be quiet dear.' – She knew what I was going to do, tho she feared it. – My legs pressed her thighs apart, I lodged my prick and gave a gentle push, to my astonishment, it did not enter. With a little wriggle she murmured 'Oh, don't!' – Then she is virgin! – Oh, the delight as I grasped her buttocks for a forcible thrust, had her firmly in hand, guided my prick low down (I know the point of entry well) and lunged, – 'Oho – oha' – lunge – 'oho' – lunge. 'Oh, don't' – I felt that never-to-be forgotton sensation which a hymen when splitting up gives a prick, the tightening round it, then the loosening, and the next instant the shaft was up to its roots in her cunt.

That was a short business, but not a quick fuck, for I had fucked the night before. – I enjoyed both the sensation and the idea of the virgin cunt which I had ruptured, but fucked slowly till nature urged me on faster, and spent as her cunt tightened and her murmurs of pleasure reached my ear, as I lay with my head over her shoulder. Coming to myself I felt the stem of my prick yet up her, and sanguinary proof I found. 'You've never been fucked before,' said I. – 'What?' – said she astonished.

[Some men, and some women say that females don't spend at the fuck which destroys their virginity; generally they do not, but I have had several who did, and can swear to it.]

I locked the bedroom door, which I had not done before, lighted candles, wiped her cunt myself with a towel, and inspected her jagged slit. – She objected, and I almost used force. – 'What nonsense, to the man who's just fucked you.' – Then she seemed faint. – We came into the sitting-room, I gave her wine, and she sat with my handkerchief against her quim, for she bled unusually. – In an hour we fucked again, and soon after she went away still bleeding. She wanted to get home early; I stopped all night at the hotel.

Next night she could not meet me, the next she did. I could not get to the same hotel again, but knew of three where they shut their eyes. – At one I hired a sitting and bedroom. The dinner was not so good, but was wholesome, the wine excellent. – A charming tête-à-tête meal we had, and a comfortable bed there was to go to afterwards. 'We are going to get into bed presently Madeline.' – 'Oh, no.' – 'Oh, yes you are,' – and so it was. What a fuss she made, but at length, in chemise only and I in shirt, I forced her up on the bed, and, throwing up her chemise as fast as she pushed it down, and insisting on my right, I had her thighs wide apart, and gloated on her private charms, and kissed and smelt them (for I liked the smell of her cunt) till my impatient prick would let me look no longer. Then into bed I got, and pushing up chemise and shirt to our necks, covered her sweet fair body with mine.

I recollect nothing in my life more exquisite, than the minute when my prick glided up Madeline's cunt the second time that night, with a slow movement which it pleased me to make. Going up it inch by inch, resting between each stroke, watching her face, hearing the slight cry of pain which her lacerated and still sore cunt forced from her, whilst voluptuous sensations higher up in her cunt coming at the same time, issued in a lovely murmur. A murmur expressing mainly the pleasure that fucking was giving her. Her irritated, heated, spunk-filled vagina was longing to relieve itself by a discharge of its lubricating mucus to meet my spermatic injection, and thrilled her with burning lust. I lay a minute, letting her enjoy the complete distension of her cunt, that pretty little cunt, tight, stretched and gorged with my prick, which never was larger or stiffer. Then I thrust hard, banging its red tip against the portals of her womb, which made her jerk her bum back but stimulated her to a crisis of pleasure. – All this time I was wondering at my luck at having her a virgin and my stupidity at having thought she was not. Thus I lay in her arms, clasping and kissing, and thinking with that rapid evolution of lascivious thoughts which go thro my brain as my prick is in a cunt.

After our second fuck, as recovering from our elysium of lasciviousness I lay tranquilly between her smooth legs, and restlessly began feeling her satiny flesh from hips to thighs, and lower, I became conscious of much hardness of the lower part of haunch and backside; and still later on when we had exhausted ourselves in each other's arms, and she had washed and was preparing to put on her clothes, I felt her all about those fleshy parts, and looked at and kissed the fair globes, and found that her bum had an unusual hardness, a hardness far beyond what would be called solid, but was even marbly in its solidity; such as I have felt perhaps in half a dozen women, but not more.

She was conscious of it. It was solid when a girl, and in rising womanhood, sleeping with other young women, her hard bum had been noticed. – I suppose they felt each other, and why not? – I have always hitherto found that substantial flesh, in the arses of stronger, coarser-built women. In this slighter and more delicate town-built woman it was an agreeable novelty. She had told that in a moment of jocosity, her mother had once told her that she also had one of the hardest bums, and that if she put a walnut on a wooden chair and sat with naked bum upon it, she could crack it. – This I suppose was figurative, but possibly may be true. So Madeline inherited her mother's solid buttocks. I am not sure that such hard flesh there is beautiful. A slighter solidity, and more elasticity, is preferable to the feel, I think. It is pleasanter to clutch an elastic rather than an inelastic arse, when fucking.

She was a beautifully made creature; slim, with fine bones delicately covered, and had a most exquisite foot in size and shape. Her cunt was small both in look and feel and had but little hair on it. – In her armpits there was scarcely a hair visible. I don't recollect before seeing a woman of her age without hair there, tho I have seen some with very little. I never saw a more ragged jagged edged split than my prick had made in her hymen. She told me that, before fucking, she couldn't quite insert the tip of her little finger, in the orifice thro which her courses drained off. She had a fair sized clitoris and trifling inner lips, and that is all about her cunt.

She could not get out next night, but on that following she met me again. – We dined as before and took our pleasures directly afterwards. – What a difference in her manner! In the cab I felt her cunt and did what I liked, there was no fuss about the groping, and by the time I reached the hotel, we had felt each other till I was stiff, and she was moist and lewed. – How charming at dinner to sit opposite to the pretty creature, knowing what was to follow, that there was no part of her fair body which I had not seen, that she knew the size of my prick, from its normal state of quiescence to its utmost and active rigidity. Such thoughts passed through *my* mind, and similar ones no doubt passed through *hers*, tho, with the hypocrisy so common among women, she denied it when I asked her.

She could not stop out till eleven o'clock anymore, for her parents became inquisitive. But a woman who wants fucking will risk anything to get it. So she afterwards left her business early on some excuse, and we went to a brothel, and I had her almost nightly for a week or two. Often it was only one fuck she could wait for. I waited impatiently for her every night, so fresh and nice was she, so intensely did she enjoy me, and I her, in teaching her postures and the art of love in all its ways and shapes. Then I again got her to dinner at a hotel, and in bed began talking about her future, and Richard's name came up.

Said she: 'It's of no use now if Richard came after me again, for he'd find out that I've done it, and I couldn't marry him.' I told her that half the men had never had a virgin, or had had only one in a state of tremendous excitement, and with a little skill that she could deceive him. – He'd gone off and had left his place, and she had quarrelled with her milliner friend, Mrs B★★t★n whom she heard had told Richard that she (Madeline) had gone to dine with a regular swell (myself) who had met her by appointment at the Palace. Richard had written her that. – Mrs B★★t★n was jealous of her, for Richard was a fine man. Then Madeline got spooney on me and hinted at my keeping her. I was going over to Paris (which I did, to see for the last time the French lady whose ravishment I have told of). She burst into tears and hoped she wasn't in the family way. – I told her that in such an event, and she couldn't get her courses on, that I would provide for her (and would have done). But she now had taken to fucking, so that I feared in my heart that, when away, she would get another prick in lieu of mine. Cautioning her against that, I went to Paris.

I was gone nearly three weeks, on my return wrote her to meet me, and she did. – At first she would not go to a house with me. – When in one, I sat down on a chair, and, clasping her naked backside with both hands, pulling her towards me, and asking her if she wasn't longing for a fuck, and how many times she'd frigged herself in my absence, she, standing up, still with bonnet on, said she couldn't let me do it any more. – No, it was not her poorliness and she was not, thank God! in the family way, and didn't want to be, for Richard had come back to her, and would marry her in a year.

I was pleased, but it made me want to fuck her more than ever. –

'Well take your bonnet off.' – 'For a little time, but I won't let you.' – A kiss and cuddle on the ample sofa followed. – 'Let's feel each other a bit, and stop, I *will* look at it first. – Oh! what a lovely little cunt!' – and I kissed it again and again. – Then I felt her, and she felt me, our tongues met, distilling their liquids, and we were both sighing with the languid pleasure our hands gave us. 'I shall spend in your hand.' – 'No, don't.' – 'In your cunt then.' – 'Oh, no. – I'm coming Walter,' – for she knew my name – I left off, not meaning her to come. The gentle wriggling of her backside and belly ceased, her thighs were quiet, we relinquished each other's genitals and looked lewedly at each other, she with petticoats half up her thighs, I with prick vertical. – 'Let's do it, and I'll pull it out when my spunk's coming.' – 'Be sure you do, if I get in the family way you know I'm done for.' – She got on the bed as nimbly as she could, for her cunt was craving for a stretch, was hot and moist with desire for the male.

The pause let our juices subside, but soon the pleasurable friction of prick and cunt roused them again. – 'I'm coming love, are you?' 'Aha – yes – aha – don't do it in me. – Aha.' – 'No – aha.' – 'I'm spend – ing!' – At the crisis we both forgot. She clasped me to her, her cunt constricted and held my prick with that peculiar, grinding grip which a cunt gives when spending, whilst my prick, with short wriggling thrusts, shot out my spunk into its proper place.

'Get out and wash quickly,' said I, ere pleasure was well over or my prick done spending. Getting off with her, I put down the basin, poured out the water, and soon saw the pearly lumpy, stringy sperm, which ought to have been still comforting her cunt, at the bottom of the basin. She looking as I did, rubbing her cunt with a towel, and hoping it was all out. – 'That's the stuff which comes out of a man's thing?' – 'You've seen it before?' – 'Never.' – 'More was on your thigh five weeks ago.' – 'But it was all on my chemise when I looked.' She took up the basin, and looked curiously at my semen. – 'I hope it's all out, you didn't keep your promise.' – 'I couldn't, your cunt gripped my prick into you so. – You should have jerked my prick out when you found I was spending.' – Madeline had certainly not had then enough experience to know to a second when a man is going to spend; I dare say she does by this time.

We talked, with passions appeased. 'No, not again' – but frigging recommenced and altered her mind. – I called out for the servant and told her to bring a French letter, a bit of sponge, and a piece of thread. – All were brought, and the maid laughed. I gave Madeline the experience of a prick covered with sheep's gut, but neither of us liked it. So I pulled it off, and we fucked till consummation approached, and then put it on. We did the same with the sponge. I tied it by the thread, and pushed it up her cunt a little way, she further, and my prick pushed it right up – and so we fucked on to the pleasurable discharge. When I drew out the sponge holding my sperm, and she had washed her cunt out again, we agreed that our pleasure was much destroyed, both by the gut and the absorbent zoophyte – Madeline learnt something that night. I wonder if she has applied that knowledge since.

Fucking creates such a tie between man and woman, that, altho she said she wouldn't ever meet me again, added, 'I'd better not, had I?' and altho I agreed not to ask her, yet I did a few days after by letter. – She came and was on heat – I knew it by her looks and manner, and told her she was lewed. She laughed and, colouring up, said she did feel as if she'd like me. – This time, not wishing to injure her, I took a nice little round sponge, and my sperm spat into that absorbent, but we half fucked before I put it up. I got her to dine that night, and we were both in fine condition. Her parents were told there was late work (the usual milliner's excuse) and I gave her a sound ballocking. Her poorliness she expected on every hour, and such was the state of lewedness which our heated genitals got into that, at the last fuck, we did without sponge, for I couldn't that time spend with the sponge in her. – When my pleasure was coming on, and my glans touched the sponge, so intensely sensitive was I that it stopped me spending. – When I did, I pulled my prick out nearly to the top and spent thus, she washed directly and took no harm.

That night we parted for good, and I made her take ten pounds – I was to see her again some time afterwards as it happened.

I incline to think, now that a few years have passed since this intrigue, that Madeline came to the second dinner with me, intending to let me have her. – Her little struggles and resistance may either have been shams or timidity at the last moment, when I was getting to victory. Was it annoyance at the loss of her lover, a desire for a change of life, a speculation of becoming my mistress, or even my wife – or lust? – Lust does not influence women usually so much before they lose their virginity as it does men (unless so hot cunted as but few are). It influences women more afterwards, when they know the delights of a cunt plugged by a prick. Curiosity is powerful with them, and numbers fall under a mistaken notion of their own powers of resistance. 'I did not mean to let him do it, tho I didn't mind his larking or feeling me,' said Maria ***** once to me. Many have said the same when I have closely questioned them. – That's it. – The idea of feeling and being felt by the man, the sensuous delight increased because forbidden, – of having a little baudy chaff about sleeping together, and so on, is permissible. – Even the hurried feel, the glance askant at the stiff prick, is charming, and all very well. But they don't reckon the consequence of the chance of his getting his fingers on to their clitorises and their not being able to get them away. – A five minutes' good frig, whilst a woman is kissed, and lewed suggestions whispered by the man, settle most women. That is my experience. Half ready to spend, lewed images in their mind, curiosity at work, they almost helplessly let the man do his will. – 'Open thighs – enter prick – exit hymen. – All is over, my love. Swab up the bloodstained sperm from your cunt, and prepare for the next ramming. You are a woman now, in for a penny in for a pound. The gates of pleasure are opened, let the promenaders walk in.'

Indeed that was the sum of Madeline's confession to me when we talked about the affair. She didn't think I'd dare to try to do what I did. 'Why did you come again?' – 'I don't know really, I wanted to come and didn't want, I like dining with you. I wondered what you'd do.' – 'You didn't think I'd be quiet and respectful.' – 'No – I don't know really, but thought you might put your hands up my clothes, that I really did.' – 'And show you my prick?' 'Well, I did.' – 'Now you were lewed and came to be fucked.' – 'That I declare before Heaven I didn't, for I'd made up my mind if you did what you did before that I'd run out of the house.' She didn't know her own strength of resistance, and they are nearly all alike. Nature has made them so. – Prick is potential. – Altho a woman cares less about seeing or feeling a prick than a man does a cunt, (for females have seen pricks all their lives, it's incidental to their sex as nurse, and they see them from their infancy), yet a stiff stander shown at the moment when the fingers have raised lust thro the clitoris, is an invincible persuader. 'Open sesame,' and the female opens. – It is her destiny.

ANONYMOUS

from
Rosa Fielding

Rosa Fielding *was first published in 1867 under the title* Victim of Lust! or Scenes in the Life of Rosa Fielding. Depicting the Crimes and Follies of High Life and the Dissipation and Debauchery of the Day. *It is a remarkable example of late Victorian Erotica and was designed to outrage Victorian morality.*

IT was a fine morning in May, and the dull, little frequented High Street of the small country town called Rutshole seemed absolutely cheerful, as if inspired by the exhilarating atmosphere.

So at least thought Mr Bonham, a portly widower of fifty or thereabouts, as having left his carriage at the inn, he proceeded down High Street leisurely, but with the usual solemnity on his countenance (which he considered dignified and respectable), much lightened by the cheering weather. He stopped at the door of a small shop, on which was inscribed, 'Trabb, Hosier and Glover'. Here he entered.

Now that capital woman of business, the widow Trabb, was engaged in suiting a stiff-necked old maid with a pair of mittens; but even if she had not been so occupied, we very much doubt if she would herself have attended to a gentleman customer. The worthy woman knew that there are other means of making a shop attractive besides the excellence and cheapness of the wares therein sold: and she had enlisted in her services a pretty girl of sixteen, whose remarkable grace and modesty had already attracted numerous young squires, young farmers, and officers from the neighbouring garrison town, as real or pretended customers, to the manifest advantage of Mrs Trabb's till.

When therefore, she saw the rich and respectable Mr Bonham enter her shop, she summoned her aide-de-camp with 'Rosa, attend to the gentleman!' and continued her attention to her customer. Now Mr

Bonham, though nearly fifty as we have said, and of a very staid and even strict outward demeanour, was by no means so elderly in his feelings and capabilities as would have been judged from outward appearances. He had been early left a widower, and the very fact of his having to keep up the said outward appearances and his ambition to have a saintly character among his neighbours and friends, had forced him to restrain his indulgences within very narrow bounds, and to be circumspect and moderate in the enjoyment thereof. So that this self denial was of a double benefit to him; among the saints of his acquaintance he was esteemed as 'one of the elect and a babe of grace', while he himself was pleasingly conscious that, thanks to his regular but very generous diet, and his habit of self control (not abstinence) as to the softer sex, he was enjoying what is called a green old age; and was when on the verge of fifty, pretty confident that his latent powers when called into action would be found quite equal to those of many a worn out young roué of five and twenty.

He was remarkably struck with Rosa's beauty, and well he might be. Long, flowing, golden hair; deep blue eyes, a sweet but by no means insipid expression of face, combined with a graceful figure, and manners very attractive even in her humble occupation; all detained Mr Bonham in purchasing a pair of gloves, longer than he had ever been in his life before. Certainly he was very difficult to suit; and Rosa had to take the measurements of his hand more than once. At last he was suited – as far as gloves were concerned – and was about to leave the shop when a bright idea struck him. He turned back to where Mrs Trabb was standing, that estimable woman had just got rid of her Low Church looking customer triumphantly, she had clapped two pence extra onto the price of the mits, and then after some bargaining submitted to rebate a penny. So both parties were satisfied, and Mrs T felt not only 'at peace with all men' (that she generally was) but with all women too (which was not so frequently the case).

'Mrs Trabb,' began the respectable gentleman, 'I would like to consult you about a little matter of business that may be a source of gain to a trades woman in your line; besides being conducive to the moral benefit of a tribe of benighted heathens.'

'Dear me, Mr Bonham,' exclaimed the gratified hosier, 'step this way – very kind of you I'm sure – a glass of cherry brandy? – do now – and sit down and rest yourself.'

So saying, she ushered the artful old gentleman into her snug back parlour; and producing the refreshment alluded to, awaited further disclosures.

We will not weary the reader with a full account of the proposed mercantile transaction. Suffice it to say that Mr Bonham disclosed a case of soulharrowing destitution among the Fukkumite Islanders recently converted to Christianity.

The interesting females had not the wherewithal to cover their bare bottoms, but used to display those well rounded features to the unhallowed gaze of the unregenerate sailors of whale ships calling at the islands. Now the missionaries considered that if any bottoms were to be displayed by their precious converts, the exhibition should be made in private to their spiritual advisers. And to end the story, the benevolent gentleman, by way of advancing the moral and physical comforts of the Fukkumite ladies (to say nothing of the missionaries) asked Mrs Trabb if she would like to contract for the supply of say to begin with, one thousand pairs of frilled pantalettes.

'Really very kind of you, Mr Bonham, to give me such a chance,' said the gratified shopkeeper, 'but may I ask you, sir, if the creatures, or converts, or whatever is most proper to call them, are to wear nothing else but those trousers?'

'No, I believe not,' was the answer. 'Why?'

'Because sir,' replied the experienced widow, 'a woman's pants are made, to speak plainly, with openings at the front and rear corresponding to her natural openings; so really, though I shall be very glad to undertake the contract, I must tell you before hand, for fear of having my goods thrown back on my hands, that the garments proposed are no obstruction whatever to a man who is determined to violate a woman.'

'Very proper of you to make the remark, Mrs Trabb, very businesslike and fair; but then of course the women should have opportunities for performing their natural functions conveniently; and then our self-sacrificing brethren, the missionaries, they must have facilities for their comforts.'

'Oh, of course, sir,' was the response.

'Then send in your estimate, Mrs Trabb, I'll see that you have a good chance. By the bye, Mrs Trabb, who is that modest looking and rather attractive young person who attended to my requirements in your shop just now?'

Aha! thought the sharp widow, that's it, eh? (Rather caught I should think.)

'That young woman, sir, is a daughter of the Fieldings. You know, sir, farmers about three miles from here. Rosa her name is – a very nice girl and as good as she looks. Take another glass, sir!'

'No, thank you, Mrs Trabb, send in those estimates as soon as you can and good luck to you.'

Exit Bonham.

The very next morning he mounted his fine weight-carrying cob and riding out leisurely, as if for exercise, had no sooner got out of sight and hearing of Rutsden Lodge, as his residence was termed, and out of the ken of his sharp daughter Eliza, than he spurred his good hackney into a smart trot, which pace being occasionally varied by a canter, very soon brought him to Elm-Tree Farm.

Farmer Fielding was out, which his visitor was not altogether very sorry for, as he thought it would be better in every way to begin his tactics by talking the old lady over. She received him very kindly and hospitably, though evidently puzzled to know the object of his visit. Mr Bonham was not long in breaking ground, for he knew the farmer might return in five minutes. He recounted to the gratified mother how he had been struck by the elegant yet modest and quiet appearance of Rosa, and how he was pleased to learn from Mrs Trabb, that she was as good as she looked; that notwithstanding the great respectability of Mrs T and her establishment, and the high opinion he had of her moral worth, still he could not but be aware that a position behind her counter was pernicious, if not absolutely dangerous, to a girl of Rosa's attractive personal qualities.

'Why my dear madam,' urged the moralist, 'I am informed that the young squires and farmers will ride a couple miles out of their way to deal in Mrs Trabb's shop; and then those dragoon officers come all the way from Baboonfield Barracks. I know that man of Moab, their Colonel, Earl Phuckum the first, gets all his clothes from London, and I'd like to know what he wants in Mrs Trabb's in High Street.'

'Perhaps dear Rosy will make a good marriage,' simpered the fond and foolish mother.

'Perhaps, madam,' interposed Mr Bonham sternly, 'she may learn something what ought to come after marriage but never before. How would you like to hear of her bolting off to London with one of those swells who perhaps is married already, and her returning to you in about twelve months, neglected, sick and heartbroken, with a baby in her arms? Now listen to me, Mrs Fielding,' continued Mr Bonham, gazing attentively into the good dame's horror-stricken face, 'I am not too old to have my fancies. Moreover, my daughter will soon be married and off my hands, and I have no one else to interfere with me.'

With this introduction, the model gentleman proposed a scheme of his own, namely that Rosa should be placed in a first-rate school in the neighbourhood of London; that all the expenses, including her equipment, should be borne by him; and that in twelve or eighteen months, if Rosa had been well behaved and steady, and had improved in body and mind, as there was every reason to suppose she would, he, the speaker, would make her Mrs Bonham, and mistress of Rutsden Lodge.

This grand proposition fairly took away the good old lady's breath, and there is no doubt her reply would have been a ready acceptance of Mr Bonham's proposition but then there appeared old Fielding and the whole story had to be commenced over again.

He did not receive Mr Bonham's offer as enthusiastically as his wife had done; but he owned at the same time the risk that Rosa ran in her present situation; and in plain blunt speech detailed how Susan Shufflebum had been seen behind a hayrick with her legs over young Squire Rootlepole's back.

'And I suppose, missus,' continued the worthy man. 'I needn't tell ye what he was a-doing to her; and Harriette Heavely went a-walking in Snugcroft woods with one of the danged soger officers, and when she got home her white petticoats was all green with damp grass, and she was so sore between her thighs that she has not been able to walk rightly since. But still, Master Bonham, although your proposal would take our Rosa out of the way of danger; leastways out of a good deal, for a young good-looking lass is never to say quite out of danger; yet I don't quite like the girl brought up above her station. She'll maybe look down on her old father and mother, and maybe she'll be looked down upon and made to feel the difference by them that's born of better families.'

This sensible speech of Farmer Fielding's was combated pretty sharply by the other two parties to the conversation; the old woman being anxious to see her daughter made a rich lady, and loth to miss the present chance; and Mr Bonham continuing to urge that his being almost entirely without relations and that his daughter being about to be married, would place Rosa in a far different and much more pleasant situation than is usually the case under such circumstances. He even went on to say that although Fielding had a right to deal as he liked with regards to his own daughter, yet he considered it would be almost sinful for him to throw away such a good chance to have her well educated and married, and that too in the fear of the Lord. Half badgered to death between the pair of them – the old farmer yielded a reluctant consent, upon which Mr Bonham and Mrs Fielding went at once into matters of detail with regard to preparation of outfit and so on.

One thing was determined upon, that the matter might not be talked about more than was absolutely necessary; Mr Bonham in particular to conceal his philanthropic schemes from his daughter Eliza, lest peradventure she had been addicted to wrath. And Farmer Fielding thought that the less said about Rosa until she appeared as Mrs Bonham the better.

We do not intend to weary our readers as to matters of outfit, suffice it to say that Mrs Trabb was in high glee and began to think that Mr Bonham, what with his missionary zeal on behalf of the sweet Fukkumite savages, and his philanthropic intentions regarding Rosa's welfare was going to make her fortune. Certainly she never had had two such orders in one twelvemonth, much less in one week. One remark of hers to Mr Bonham is worthy of notice.

With the natural sharpness of a woman and a widow to boot, she took it for granted that Mr B would like to know some particulars about the under-garments she had been furnishing for his pretty protegee, and after expatiating for about an hour or so about silk stockings, cotton stockings, chemises, night-dresses, petticoats, and the Lord only knows what besides, she concluded with:

'And I quite remember your sensible remarks Mr Bonham, about those trousers made for those converted cannibals. Miss Rosa's are much finer of course, and prettier altogether, but they are equally convenient, they are quite open back and front.'

This remark was made with a good deal of emphasis and meaning; but the venerable Philanthropist merely replied, without moving a muscle of his face:

'You are quite right, Mrs Trabb, and have acted very judiciously; one never knows what may be required in case of emergency!'

It was reported to a few friends and neighbours that Rosa was offered a situation in London as a nursery governess and that as Mr Bonham was going to town on business he had kindly offered to convey the young lady thither in his own carriage; being, as he said, altogether safer and pleasanter for a young unprotected girl than the public conveyance. This excuse passed currently enough, and if some of the envious or captious neighbours shook their heads and said Old Bonham was a sly fox, what business was it of theirs, after all?

Rosa enjoyed the ride immensely. Her guardian, as she took to calling him, was so kind and so affectionate (the fact was that he kept kissing her a great many times, and much more warmly than there was any occasion for) that she considered herself a very fortunate girl. And then he took such an interest in minor matters, he wanted to know how Mrs Trabb had executed his orders – with regard to her wardrobe – and in his anxiety to know if everything was nice and proper, actually commenced to investigate Rosa's underclothing. He expressed his opinion that the petticoats would do; but that the outer one was hardly fine enough, but that defect would be repaired in London; his researches became more interesting when the chemise was put upon its trial.

'And now, Rosa darling,' said the ancient voluptuary, 'let me see if

Mrs Trabb has obeyed my orders about your trousers. I told her to have them made a certain way or you were to wear none at all.'

'Oh, dear me, Mr Bonham,' exclaimed Rosa, who all this time had been dutifully holding up her clothes to facilitate her guardian's exploration, 'you will make me ashamed of myself!'

'Not at all, my dear girl,' was the reassuring reply, 'it is my duty to see that you have everything nice and proper, and your duty to submit to the enquiry; so put your graceful right leg over my left shoulder.'

Trembling and blushing, the innocent girl, fancying that it was not quite right and yet not knowing very well how to refuse, did as she was requested and made a splendid exposure of her secret parts immediately.

'Ha!' exclaimed Bonham, 'I see that Mrs Trabb has not neglected her duty; your trousers are well open in front certainly, though for the sake of seeing your thighs I would have preferred no trousers at all. But your cunt shows very nicely – golden hair, I see – not quite as much as you will have in twelve months, but a very fair show for a young girl of sixteen – and very nice lips.'

Here the moral gentleman inserted the first two fingers of his right hand in Rosa's tender orifice, at which the poor girl could not help an exclamation and making some slight appearance of resistance. On this her companion remarked:

'As you are going to be married to me in twelve or eighteen months, my lovely Rosa, I regard you already as my wife, morally speaking, and if the jolting of this carriage will allow, I will give you a practical proof of it.'

'A practical proof sir?' stammered Rosa.

'Yes, my beloved child, look here!' So saying, he unfastened his trousers and brought to view his cock, and a very good, useful, stiff-standing, domestic piece of machinery it was.

'Take hold of it, my little pet, do not be afraid, it won't hurt you.'

'What is it?' asked Rosa, who had never seen anything like it before, but who was clasping it as she was told, in a way that was increasing the weapon materially in size and stiffness.

'How hot it is,' she remarked.

'Yes love,' said her guardian, 'he is rather feverish, and there is considerable irritation, but you have a little warm bath between those lovely thighs of yours; and he will be quite cured after I have plunged him in and let him soak a couple of minutes.'

'I shall be very glad, my dear guardian, to do anything to contribute to your comfort or to show my gratitude for the kindness you have done me; but I do, I certainly do think that this thing, this part of your person (I hardly know what to call it), is far too large to go into the slit between my thighs – which just now you called my cunt. Of course, you have a right to do as you please with me, and are perfectly welcome; but I fear you will hurt me dreadfully, even if you do not actually split my belly open, or extend my little orifice as far back as my bottom hole.'

'No fear, my sweet charmer,' replied her guide, philosopher and friend, 'your sweet orifice is destined by Providence for these assaults, and is wonderfully elastic; there is no risk therefore of my splitting your belly up or knocking your two holes into one – I should be very sorry to destroy such an elegant specimen of nature's handiwork, especially as I hope to live and to enjoy you for fifteen years to come – so open your thighs as wide as you can possibly stretch them, with your feet placed upon the opposite seat.'

Trembling, but obedient, the girl did as she was required, producing, as any of our readers will find, if they choose to try the experiment, a very favourable position.

(N.B. Should the seat on which the lady's bottom is situated be too high, a small carpet bag, a folded cloak, or an extra cushion under the gentleman's knees will raise him to the desired height.)

After this slight digression, let us proceed. However confidently Mr Bonham might have expressed himself as to his facilities of entrance into Rosa's virgin sanctuary he still did not neglect the only precautions which were at hand. It had never been his intention, until stimulated by the girl's outward graces and secret charms, to violate Rosa in his carriage, and therefore he had not provided himself with any cold cream or pomade, so the only lubricant he possessed was his mouth, and of that he proceeded to make such good use, that his pretty friend, who at first shrank nervously from the operation, as he proceeded, found it endurable, and at last actually began to like it, at least if her leaning complacently back with a half-smile upon her face, and endeavouring to stretch her thighs beyond their present extension could be interpreted as signs of such a feeling. We think so, and it is quite evident that her guardian thought so too, for murmuring to himself: 'Now's the time!' shifted his posture so as to bring his priapus and appendages into the situation just previously occupied by his mouth. The lips of Rosa's cunt were still open, and Mr Bonham had a fair chance and greatly to his credit he availed himself of it manfully. In he went about an inch and a half, and – there he stuck. Now had he attempted Rosa's maidenhood when first his prick came to full stand, we do not know what he might not have effected; but he had retained his member's tension too long, and had excited himself too much; consequently after getting in a short way as we have described, and making Rosa cry with his efforts against her barrier, his eager pushes were brought to a close in the most natural manner possible; viz. – by the arrival of the moment of delight, which certainly in this instance was a one-sided pleasure, and indeed hardly that, for we hold that even to give the man his proper share of transport, the injection must be performed when he is fairly within his companion, for spunking about the lips and mossy hair, or even an inch or so into the passage, as Mr Bonham did on this occasion, can hardly be called a satisfactory termination to a fuck. On this occasion it was not quite as bad as it might have been; for Rosa, who had gathered from some expressions of disappointment on the part of her friend, and a sort of intuitive feeling that all girls possess, that all was not right, was spared for the moment the pain of a burst maidenhood, and if her guardian were not quite satisfied, he was at least quieted, and that did quite as well, particularly as by this time the carriage was entering the suburbs of London – to say nothing of the risk of Thomas the coachman, or John the footman, becoming accidental spectators of his little game, and reporting him at home accordingly. So by his advice, Rosa wiped herself dry, and he looked as fatherly and demure as he could; and from his long practice in what we hardly choose to call hypocrisy but something very like it, succeeded very well. And by the time the carriage arrived at the gate of Mrs Moreen's Seminary for young ladies in Clapham nobody could have guessed from his manner that anything had transpired during the short journey irreconcilable with the fatherly manner he exhibited towards Rosa.

Mrs Moreen was most favourably impressed with his manner, and indeed was prepared to welcome him cordially, in consequence of the liberal arrangements entered into in the correspondence that had already passed between them.

She was also much interested in Rosa, being quite judge enough to see that, country bred and uneducated though she might be, she had all the capabilities of making a very elegant and showy young lady.

Leaving Rosa then thus happily situated; and her protector sitting down to a late dinner at a hotel in Covent Garden, for the old sinner made an excuse to himself for passing the night in London, being that his carriage horses would be knocked up by the return journey on the same day – besides, had he not business of some kind next morning? – leaving then these friends of ours so comfortable, we will return to Rutsden Lodge, and entering a small room where a tall, dashing-looking young lady with dark eyes and raven hair is writing a letter, we will take the privilege of narrators who are ex-officio invisible and ubiquitous, and peep over a round white shoulder.

The letter began: 'My dearest Alfred,' and after a few ordinary remarks, got business-like and even warm.

'I am afraid,' the letter ran, 'that my father is going to make a fearful fool of himself. There was a baby-faced girl in a shop here and the old idiot, I fear, has seen her and fancied her. If he would only give her a fucking and a five pound note,' (this was the style the young lady wrote in) 'there would be no harm done, but I believe, though don't know anything for certain – that she has got a governess's place in London, and he has conveyed her there in his carriage. He had to go up to town on business.

'Now I no more believe in his business than in her governess's situation – for she is not fit for one; and I believe the whole thing is a blind. And what's more, her stupid old mother has been talking nonsense about her Rosa being a lady, all which, without being absolute proofs, make up a strong case against the old gentleman. Just fancy me with a mother-in-law! – a vulgar, uneducated country girl, about sixteen or seventeen years old. Of course, my dear Alfred, I know that you will marry me as soon as you can; indeed I think that in gratitude for the numerous privileges I have granted you, you should make a point of doing so – not that I regret that I allowed you to fuck me for I have enjoyed it very much, and trust entirely to your honour. But, then you see my dearest cousin, that somebody else can fuck besides you, and as sure as that stupid old party, my respected father, marries a young fresh country girl, he'll get her with child – just you see if he doesn't! And then my inheritance will be lessened at his death, or perhaps cut away altogether. And as for you, my dear cousin, you will come in simply for nothing at all. But you had better get a few days' leave and come here on some pretext or other and we will have a consultation on the subject. You see if you or some of your brother officers could get access to this girl, give her a good rogering and get her with child, or turn her upon the town, it would settle the question at once. And I think it might be done. I will try to find out her address from that foolish old mother of hers. But do you come here at any rate, my dearest Alfred; for I rather think that I want something else besides a consultation; indeed the night before last I had a dream about you, awoke with a wet night-gown; so if you do come you had better take the precaution of bringing a dozen preventatives in the shape of French letters in your pocket. For I suppose you will be wanting as usual to make the best use of your privileges both as a cousin and an engaged lover; and I know how those affectionate liberties usually terminate.'

This was in effect the termination of the young lady's letter, with the exception of a few strong and passionate expressions of enduring attachment.

It was addressed to Captain Alfred Torrant, 51st Dragoons, Baboonfield Barracks, where it was duly received by that meritorious officer. He read it over twice, so as to read, mark, learn and digest the contents; then prudently and properly burnt it.

Then he relieved his feelings by swearing a good deal; having by this precaution blown off any surplus steam, he at once applied to his commanding officer for a few days leave of absence, which was forthwith granted; then he took his departure for Rutsden Lodge, travelling in a dashing tandem, as a gentleman holding a commission in HM's Dragoons ought to travel.

* * *

As the gallant Captain Torrant alighted from his dashing equipage, he was met at the hall door by Miss Bonham's attendant, a pretty, impudent girl, always ready to be kissed or pulled about by any handsome young gentleman, though habitually reserved and discreet with young men of her own station in life. She received the commander smiling, as he, as a matter of course gave her a kiss and a squeeze, together with his 'Good morning Lucy, how blooming you look today!'

'You had better keep all that sort of nonsense for my young lady, Captain Torrant!' was the reply, 'for I know she is expecting you!'

'How do you know that my dear?' enquired the dragoon.

'Easy enough,' replied the lady's maid, 'as I helped her to dress she made me take out her prettiest morning frock, and moreover put on white stockings and her nice little bronze slippers. And I pretty well know what that means,' added the soubrette, archly nodding her head, as she tripped upstairs, leading the way to her young mistress's sitting room.

There the young captain was neither unexpected nor unwelcome. We need not retire, as did the discreet Lucy after ushering in the guest, but remain witnesses to the affection, not to say transport, with which he was received by Miss Eliza Bonham.

'My own darling Alfred,' she exclaimed as she flung herself into his arms, kissing him most rapturously, 'how good of you to answer my note so quickly!'

Nor was the young gentleman one whit behind hand in reciprocating her profession of love. He glued his mouth to hers, pressed her to his breast, and even began with his right hand, which he purposely disengaged, to make a demonstration towards the lower part of her person. But this performance Eliza eluded, not from any dislike to the proceeding – oh, no! but from prudential motives.

'Stop, stop sir!' she laughingly exclaimed, 'not so fast, if you please – I understand you came here to talk over a disagreeable business matter;

and besides, Alfred dear, you really must cover your beautiful instrument with that sheath, or condom, or whatever you call it. I have no notion of having a pretty white belly, bow-windowed before marriage! – indeed I shan't particularly care about it after marriage!'

But the gallant young officer had not driven over from the barracks for nothing, and begged to assure his beautiful cousin that in his present state of mind and body, it would be quite impossible for him to give proper attention to any serious business, until his burning love for her received some temporary gratification (the plain English of this being that he had a tremendous cock-stand, and felt that if it was not allayed pretty quickly that he must burst), and that as for the sheath, she might set her mind quite at rest, for he had brought a dozen with him.

'A dozen!' exclaimed Eliza, lifting up her eyes and hands in pretended astonishment, 'what on earth does the man mean by bringing a dozen? You are not going to fuck me a dozen times, I can tell you that, sir! And I don't want my waiting maid spoilt, mind that, and who else you intend to favour, of course I don't know – '

Here her speech was brought to an abrupt termination by her cousin covering her mouth with kisses and begging her to seat herself in a low easy chair, while he prepared himself for the promised treat. Fastening the door was a precaution taken as a matter of course, for Lucy knew that it was as much as her place was worth, to permit any intrusion in the neighbourhood, and Mr Bonham was not to arrive until the following day.

Coat off and trousers down, Alfred produced a bundle of safe-guards, and selecting one of the filmy looking coverings, besought his lovely cousin to put it on for him. Of course he could have put it on himself perfectly well, but he was too great an epicure to miss any piquant delicacy in the approaching banquet. Accordingly, Eliza's delicate fingers as she performed the required office, added new fire to his already terribly inflamed prick, so that the scarlet knob absolutely turned purple and the whole nine inches, from the hardened balls to the orifice at the end, throbbed with excited lust. This was heightened by Eliza's appearance for (being almost as eager as her gallant cousin, and that's saying a great deal), as she seated herself she drew up her clothes, and put one of her splendid legs over the chair on which she sat. Consequently, her rump being advanced quite to the extreme edge of the cushions, she made a most admirable display; her excitement and her lover's embraces had produced the usual result, and the lips of her cunt were slightly opened, temptingly inviting an entrance; while her bushy black hair showed off to advantage the creamy whiteness of her belly and thighs.

No wonder that as soon as the condom was securely put on, Captain

Torrant fell down on his knees, and expressed his adoration of the shrine he was going to enter by covering it with amorous kisses. Under this treatment, the pink lined portals expanded more and more and as Eliza flung back her head with a smile and a sigh, the young officer saw that the auspicious moment had arrived – not that he was an unwelcome visitor at any time in the mossy retreat, so getting his charger well in hand, he put his head straight for the gap and rushed in. It was indeed a short lived pleasure as may be conceived: the fact being that the gentleman was in that state of lust that two or three judicious rubs from the hand of his fair cousin would have released his evacuation; and as for the lady, if her hot lover had continued on his knees before her, kissing her cunt one half minute longer, he would have had some warm cream over his moustache, of a kind not generally sold by Rose or Gillingwater. So three good shoves, actually only three, did the business most effectually, and, no doubt to their great mutual satisfaction. But there was no mistake as to Miss Bonham's prudent regard to the sheath, or the Captain's good sense in acceding to her wishes.

For his beautiful antagonist met his attack so grandly and discharged her battery so promptly in reply to his, that if the latter had not been retained by the discreet covering, very serious consequences to the lady would have almost inevitably made themselves apparent in nine months' time or thereabouts.

And in our humble opinion gratification is not increased by running any risk. On the present occasion both Miss Bonham and her lover congratulated themselves on having enjoyed each other thoroughly, and without any fear of the result.

Their extreme transports being over for the present, the young gentleman applied himself to putting his dress in order, while Eliza rang the bell and desired Lucy to send up the lunch.

While this acceptable refreshment was being done justice to, the loving pair proceeded to consider what was to be done in regard to Mr Bonham's infatuation. Captain Torrant's first step was prompt and business like. He told his man Robert, a smart soldier, to take a walk through the fields in the neighbourhood of the Fieldings' Farm, and, by getting into conversation with some of the farm lasses, he would most likely find out something as to Miss Rosa, the great probability being that the old dame would not be able to keep her mouth shut, but would have been dropping boastful hints as to her daughter's great prospects, being made a grand lady of, and so on.

'Find out this for me if you can Bob,' said his generous master, 'and I will give you free liberty to do what you like by way of amusing yourself with any of the girls.'

'Cert'nly sir, thank you sir,' replied that valuable domestic, saluting as he marched away on his errand.

Leaving him for a while to enjoy his country walk, we will attend at the consultation between the lovers.

'You see, my darling Alfred,' began Eliza, 'I fear there is considerable truth in these reports that are going about. I don't believe all I hear about the girl's beauty '

'Oh, of course not,' said the Captain, inwardly chuckling.

'I dare say she is a pretty, dowdy doll; but when a man of my father's age makes a fool of himself, he does it with a vengeance. And if you were to speak to him seriously on the subject, he would ask you what business it was of yours, quarrel with you, and perhaps cut you out of his will, or turn you out of the house and forbid our marriage.'

'That would never do,' interposed the young gentleman warmly.

'No indeed, dearest Alfred,' replied the lady looking at him warmly and lovingly.

'What plan would you propose then my pet?' asked he, 'supposing that your governor does contemplate making a jolly jackass out of himself in his old age?'

'Well, Alfred, if he could be put out of conceit with the girl in some way – if he found anything against her character – something to disgust him in short – '

'I perceive,' replied Captain Torrant reflectively, 'but there is some danger. In the first place, proof may be difficult to get to support the accusations; and in the second place any one setting such reports on foot would be liable to heavy damages.'

'Pooh, pooh,' replied Eliza, 'you have plenty of young scamps among your brother officers who would be delighted with the chance of taking a pretty girl's maidenhood. Only let me find out her address, and then you can give one of your friends the information, and let him make her acquaintance and seduce her; fuck her well, get her with child – anything – so that she is quite ruined and spoilt as to any purpose of becoming a step-mother to me.'

To this hopeful scheme, the gentleman assented, merely remarking that it would never do 'to trust any of our fellows with such a delicate business'.

'I see how it is sir,' exclaimed Eliza, 'you think that if there is any maidenhood taking to be done, you can do it pretty well yourself. And so you can, I can testify; only I think that your regard for me, that you profess so largely about, might keep you from straying after such a nonsensical baby-faced doll.'

'My darling Eliza, I did not propose to do anything of the kind,' replied the aggrieved dragoon, 'I merely said that I would not venture to entrust such a piece of business to any of our youngsters.'

'Ah well,' said the lady, 'I would rather have avoided this part of the business; but I suppose what must be, must; and if the girl is to be seduced and rogered, you will have to do it. Of course, it is all fun for you, but I can't help but feel a little bit jealous. You don't care for her I know, as you care for me, but still all you young reprobates like a little change, and I am told that she is fresh and rosy-looking, with golden brown hair; while as for poor me, I am sallow and colourless, and my black hair looks dismal – I know it does.'

We must presume that Miss Bonham made these remarks in full consciousness of her charms; for she really was a splendid woman. And of course her lover judiciously lost no time in informing her of the fact, accompanying his protestations with the warmest caresses. So that at last the young lady, fairly vanquished, promised to be no more jealous – than she could help; that she supposed Alfred would have to like Rosa a little – just a little bit – or he would not be able to seduce her; and that when that nice little bit of business was done, he must leave her in some gay house, or in keeping with one of his friends, or somewhere or other; Miss Bonham was not particular, only that Alfred must never see the girl again; and must marry her – Eliza – as soon as it could be managed, and then they would live happy forever afterwards, as the story book says. On this there followed more kisses and caresses, and the lovers went out for a walk in the garden.

Leaving them in their happiness we will follow Master Robert on his excursion to the Fieldings' farm; an excursion taken on his master's account as far as business was concerned, but not without an eye to his own amusement should opportunity occur. The day was fine, and he walked leisurely along, thoroughly enjoying the feeling of having got away from the barracks, and of having nothing to do; not that Master Robert was particularly over-burdened in that respect at any time. He had asked directions as to his road from one or two country louts, and was following a side path which bordered a wood when he caught sight of some chimneys in the distance; this he thought might be the farm he sought; and while he was considering the matter he perceived in the adjoining wood a girl and a boy gathering fallen sticks. He spoke to the couple, desiring to know whereabouts Farmer Fielding's might happen to be. On this, the girl said her brother should show him the way, while she went home with the sticks.

But Master Robert, who had his eyes about him, and perceived that the girl, though coarsely dressed was a stout, buxom, fresh-looking lass of about seventeen, proposed that she should show him the way, and that her little brother should take the sticks home. The girl seemed to hesitate; but the boy being presented with a penny, cut the matter short by running off to spend it, and thus left Robert, as he wished, alone with the nice looking girl guide.

She was for going to the farm by the path, from which indeed, as she said, the house was easily to be seen; but Robert knew better than that, and said he was sure the wood must be a shorter way, and putting his arm around the girl's waist, led her along to where the bushes appeared to grow tolerably close. She laughingly declared that the way he was taking did not lead to anywhere; but did not seem to object nevertheless, even when Robert, spying a mossy bank, pretty well sheltered from observation, proposed that they should sit down there and rest awhile.

Finding that the girl was not at all ill-disposed for a little love-making, though she might be a little shy, the jolly dragoon proceeded to seat her on his knee, taking the precaution in the first instance of raising her petticoats, so that he might have facilities for exploring her bare rump. And of course, when he had got her great fat arse thus comfortably established, he lost no time in shoving a couple of fingers up her cunt. As he found no maidenhead, he asked his rustic friend if she had any sweethearts among the country lads, to which she replied, smiling and shaking her head:

'No, no, Susan Flipper she had a sweetheart and she let him shove his cock into her, and she had a child and it gave her a great deal of trouble – no, no sweethearts for me, thank you!'

'But what do you do, my precious, for something instead of a cock, and how do you happen to have lost your maidenhead?'

'Well, I don't know much about a maidenhead,' was the reply, 'but when I feel queer like, I get a carrot and ram it into me, into the slit between my thighs, that you've got your fingers in; and it makes me feel so nice – only one day I did it rather too hard, and burst through something and hurt myself.'

'Let's see,' said the astute Robert, as he turned the damsel over on her hands and knees, and pulling open the lips of her cunt, took a deliberate inspection, 'I can manage to give you a deal more pleasure than you can get from a carrot, Nelly (if that's your name) and without any risk of getting you with child.'

'Could you really now,' said the simple country girl. 'Is your cock quite harmless, then?' she asked.

'Certainly,' replied Robert, uncovering about nine inches of a wholesome looking and decidedly thickish prick, 'you perceive my dear, that if you go down on your hands and knees and I just shove in the red end of this machine, no harm can possibly happen to you; it is only when a girl is laid down on her back – with her thighs open, and her sweetheart gets atop of her and shoves the whole length of his tool up her that she gets big with child.'

'Ah, I know that's true enough,' replied Nelly, 'for Susan Flipper told me, that was the way her John got her down in the cow house, one day when she was milking.'

'If you'll just go down on your hands and knees – on the soft mossy bank, I'll fuck you very gently.'

'Well, you are a nice looking young gentleman,' replied the rustic lass, 'and your cock is certainly an uncommon nice one, and a big one – I only hope it is not too big, and so – '

'And so, I may! Isn't that what you mean to say, my pet?' interrupted Robert.

Then, taking consent for granted, he placed the strong well-shaped girl on all fours, with her jolly rump prominently stuck out, and the whole of her regalia completely displayed. As she was pretty tight, he at first kept tolerably well to his promise about not going further into her than the knob, but every shove made a difference, and by the time he had got to the fifth push, he was in up to the hilt, simply as far as his weapon would go.

Nelly did not reproach him greatly for his perfidy, on the contrary, she wriggled her bottom about, and even shoved it out to meet his furious lunges so that Master Robert enjoyed himself even more than he expected to do. That Nelly did the same may be pretty well inferred from the fact that when he was spunking into her, she was actually sinking under him with pleasurable emotion.

ÉMILE ZOLA

from
Thérèse Raquin

Émile Zola's highly charged account of an illicit love affair created an outcry when it was published in 1867. It was considered to be obscene and Zola was reviled as a pornographer. We can now see it as the masterpiece it is – a truly honest portrayal of sexual desire. His description of unrestricted passion is as powerful to read today as it was a century ago.

FROM the beginning, the lovers felt their affair to be something necessary, inevitable, and utterly natural. At their first meeting they spoke familiarly and kissed without any blushing or embarrassment, as if their intimacy had already been going on for a number of years. They were quite calm and at ease in their new situation, and they lived completely without shame.

They worked out how they would meet. As Thérèse could not go out, it was decided that Laurent would come round to her. In a clear and confident voice she explained to him the arrangement she had thought up. They would see each other in the bedroom. Her lover would come up the side passage which led off the arcade, and she would let him in through the door at the top of the stairs. Meanwhile, Camille would be at his office and Madame Raquin downstairs in the shop. Such a bold plan could scarcely fail.

Laurent agreed. For all his prudence, he had a kind of animal daring, the daring of a man with huge fists. His mistress's calm, serious air was strong encouragement to come and taste of a passion so daringly offered. He picked an excuse, his boss gave him two hours off, and he hastened round to the Passage du Pont-Neuf.

As soon as he set foot in the arcade, he felt a strong tingle of anticipation. The woman who sold costume jewellery was sitting right opposite the door to the side passage. He had to wait until she was busy, selling a brass ring or some earrings to a young working woman. Then he slipped quickly into the passage and climbed the dark, narrow staircase, pressing against the damp, sticky walls. Every time he stumbled on one of the stone steps, the noise gave him a burning sensation in the chest. A door opened, and there on the threshold, dazzling in the white glow of the lamp, he saw Thérèse in her camisole and petticoat, her hair tied up tight in a bun. She shut the door and flung her arms round his neck; she had a warm scent of white linen and newly scrubbed flesh.

Laurent was astonished at how beautiful he found his mistress. He had never before seen this woman as she really was. Thérèse, lithe and strong, hugged him and threw back her head, her face lit up by smiles in which passion burned. It was as if her features had been transfigured by love; her expression was wild but caressing, her lips moist and her eyes shining; she was radiant with joy. With her body wound sinuously around his, she was beautiful with the strange beauty of complete abandon. It was as if her face had been illuminated from within and flames were leaping from her flesh; and the fire in her blood and the tension in her muscles filled the air around her with warm exhalations, bitter and penetrating.

From the first kiss, she showed an instinctive skill in the arts of love. Her hungry body threw itself into the experience of pleasure with total abandon. She was emerging from a dream and awakening to passion, and passing from the feeble arms of Camille into the muscular embrace of Laurent; this approach of a powerful man was like a sudden jolt which had shocked her body out of its slumber. All the instincts of a highly strung woman now burst to the fore with incomparable violence, as her mother's blood, that African blood which burned in her veins, began to pulse furiously through her slight, still almost virginal body. She offered herself to him with a total absence of shame, and she was racked from head to toe by long drawn-out spasms.

Laurent had never known a woman like this, and it disconcerted him, made him ill at ease. He did not normally receive such a passionate welcome from his mistresses; he was used to cold, indifferent kisses and tired, satiated love-making. Thérèse's moans and fits almost frightened him, while at the same time stimulating his sensual curiosity. When he left her he was tottering like a drunkard. The next day, once he had regained his caution and his rather forced composure, he asked himself whether or not to go back to this lover whose kisses so inflamed his passions. At first he firmly resolved to stay at home. Then he began to weaken. He wanted to forget Thérèse, the sight of her naked body and her sweet but brutal caresses, yet there she still was, implacable, holding her arms out to him. The physical pain which this vision caused him soon became unbearable.

He gave in, arranged another meeting, and returned to the Passage du Pont-Neuf.

From that day on Thérèse became a part of his life. He did not yet accept her, but bowed to her will. There were hours when he was filled with horror, and moments when all his cautiousness came back, and all in all the affair was an unpleasant disruption; but his fears and misgivings always gave way before his desire. One assignation was followed by another, then many more.

Thérèse had no such doubts. She gave herself to him unsparingly, going straight where her passion led. This woman, who had been bowed down by circumstances and was finally standing up for herself, laid bare her whole being, and explained to him her past life.

Sometimes she would put her arms around Laurent's neck, pull herself up along his chest, and say to him in a voice still breathless with passion:

'Oh, if only you knew how much I have suffered! I was brought up in the clammy heat of a sick-room. I had to sleep next to Camille; at night I tried to move away from him to escape the disgusting stale smell of his body. He was tetchy and stubborn; he refused to take his medicines unless I shared them with him, so to please my aunt I had to drink all sorts of potions. I don't know why it didn't kill me . . . They have made me ugly, my poor darling, they've stolen everything I had, so you can never love me as much as I love you.'

She wept and she kissed Laurent, then went on with hatred smouldering in her voice:

'I don't wish them any harm. They brought me up, took me in and protected me from destitution . . . But I would have preferred abandonment to their hospitality. I had a desperate need for wide-open spaces; as a little girl, I dreamt of roaming barefoot along dusty roads, begging alms and living the life of a gypsy. I was told that my mother was the daughter of a tribal chief in Africa; I often thought of her, and how close I am to her in my blood and my instincts; I wished I had never had to leave her, and that she might still have been carrying me across the desert on her back . . . Ah! What a way to grow up! Thinking about the long days which I spent in that bedroom with Camille coughing and groaning still fills me with disgust and anger. I used to squat in front of the fire, mindlessly watching his infusions boil and feeling my limbs grow stiff. I couldn't even move around; my aunt used to scold me whenever I made a noise . . . Later on I did have a taste of real joy, in the little house by the river, but by then I had already been too much repressed; I could hardly walk and I fell over whenever I tried to run. Then they buried me alive in this awful shop.'

Thérèse breathed heavily as she squeezed her lover in her arms; she was taking her revenge, and her delicate, supple nostrils quivered nervously.

'You wouldn't believe how vicious they've made me,' she went on. 'They've made me into a hypocrite and a liar – They so smothered me in their bourgeois comforts that I can't understand how there can still be blood in my veins . . . I looked down at the ground and put on the same dismal, stupid expression, and lived the same dead life, as them. When you first saw me, I looked just like some dumb animal, didn't I? Gloomy, cast down, no initiative? I had no hope left, I was thinking of throwing myself in the Seine one day . . . But before I reached that state of dejection, how many nights of rage I spent! Back in my cold room in Vernon, I used to bite my pillow to stifle my shouts, and hit myself and call myself a coward; my blood was on fire and I could almost have torn my body to pieces in my rage. Twice I wanted to run away and just keep going, out into the sunshine, but my courage failed me; they had turned me into a docile pet with their flabby benevolence and revolting affection. So I lied and kept on lying; I stayed put, all sweetness and silence, when I really wanted to hit out and bite back.'

The young woman stopped, wiping her moist lips on Laurent's neck. After a moment's silence, she added:

'I don't know any more why I agreed to marry Camille. I didn't protest, out of a sort of disdainful indifference. I took pity on the poor child. When I used to play with him, I felt my fingers sinking into his limbs as if they were made of clay. I took him because my aunt offered him to me, and because I had no intention of putting myself out for him. And in my husband I found that same poorly little boy next to whom I'd already had to sleep from the age of six. He was just as frail and complaining, and he had the same stale, sickly smell which had so nauseated me all those years ago . . . I'm telling you all this so that you won't be jealous . . . I felt a kind of disgust rising in my throat; I remembered all the potions I had drunk, and I moved away from him; I had some dreadful nights. But you, you . . .'

And Thérèse lifted her upper body, arching her back, with her fingers caught in Laurent's strong hands, looking down at his broad shoulders and enormous neck.

'I love *you*, I have done since the day Camille first pushed you into the shop. You may not respect me, because I gave myself to you all at once, everything . . . Truly, I don't know how it happened. I am proud, I'm impetuous too, and I felt like hitting you that first day, when you kissed me and threw me to the floor here in this bedroom . . . I don't know how I can have loved you; actually, it was more like hate. The sight of you annoyed me, I couldn't stand it; when you were there, my nerves were stretched to breaking-point, my mind went blank, and I saw red. Oh, how I suffered! Yet I wanted my suffering and longed for you to come; as I moved round and round your chair I sensed your breath on my body and felt my clothes brush against yours. It was as if your blood were radiating warmth as I passed, and it was this burning aura surrounding you that attracted me and held me close to you, despite my inner urge to rebel . . . You remember when you were doing the painting here? An irresistible force attracted me to your side, made me breathe in your atmosphere with painful delight. I realized that I seemed to be begging for kisses and I was ashamed to be so enslaved; I knew I should fall if you only touched me. But I gave in to my weakness, shivering with cold while I waited for you to deign to take me in your arms.'

Then Thérèse fell silent, still quivering, proud and avenged. She held Laurent, drunk with passion, to her breast, and in that bare and freezing bedroom there were enacted scenes of fiery passion, sinister and brutal. Each new meeting brought still more violent ecstasies.

The young woman seemed to thrive on her daring and impudent behaviour. She never hesitated or showed any fear. She threw herself into adultery with a sort of frantic energy, facing danger with alacrity and taking pride in doing so. Whenever her lover was due to come round, her only precaution was to warn her aunt that she was going upstairs for a rest; while he was there, she would walk about, talk, and do everything with no attempt at concealment, without every worrying about making a noise. Sometimes, in the early days, this scared Laurent.

'For heaven's sake,' he would whisper to Thérèse, 'don't make such a racket; Madame Raquin will be coming up.'

'It's all right!' she laughed. 'You are a real worrier. She's stuck behind her counter; what do you think she'd come up here for? She'd be too afraid of being robbed . . . Anyway, let her come up if she wants to. You can always hide. I don't give a damn about her. I love you.'

Laurent was scarcely reassured by her words. His sneaking peasant's caution had not been entirely stifled by passion. Soon, however, by force of habit, he came to accept without undue terror the difficulties of these assignations in broad daylight, in Camille's own bedroom, only feet from the old haberdasher. His mistress kept explaining to him that danger spares the bold, and she was right. The lovers could not have found a safer place than this room where nobody would ever come looking for them. Incredibly, they were able to satisfy their desires there quite undisturbed.

One day, however, Madame Raquin did come up, fearing that her niece might be ill. The young woman had been upstairs for nearly three hours, and she had now taken her daring to the point of not even bolting the door between the bedroom and the dining-room.

When Laurent heard the old woman's heavy tread coming up the wooden stairs, he snatched up his waistcoat and hat in a panic. Thérèse began to laugh at his peculiar expression. She grabbed him forcefully by the arm, made him bend down at the head of the bed, in a corner, and said to him in a quiet, self-possessed voice:

'Stay there . . . don't move.'

She threw on top of him all the men's clothes that were lying about, and over the whole pile she spread a white petticoat which she had taken off. She did all this with swift, accurate movements, without becoming at all flustered. Then she lay down, her hair in disorder, half naked, still flushed and quivering from their embrace.

Madame Raquin opened the door quietly and crept on tiptoe towards the bed. Thérèse pretended to be asleep. Laurent was sweating beneath the petticoat.

'Thérèse, my dear,' asked the haberdasher with concern, 'aren't you feeling well?'

Thérèse opened her eyes, yawned, turned over, and replied in plaintive tones that she had a terrible headache. She begged her aunt to let her go back to sleep. The old woman went away just as she had come, without making any noise.

Silently laughing, the two lovers kissed each other with violence and passion.

'You see,' said Thérèse triumphantly; 'we have nothing to fear here. All these people are blind, they aren't in love.'

Another day, the young woman had an odd idea. She could behave at times as if she were quite crazy, her mind wandering.

François the tabby cat was sitting upright in the middle of the room. Solemn and motionless, he stared at the two lovers with his big round eyes. He seemed to be scrutinizing them unblinkingly, lost in some devilish reverie.

'Just look at François,' said Thérèse to Laurent. 'He looks as if he understands what's going on, and he's going to tell Camille all about it this evening . . . Wouldn't it be funny if he suddenly started to talk in the shop one of these days? He'd have some fine stories to tell about us.'

Thérèse found the idea of François starting to speak extremely amusing. Laurent looked at the cat's big green eyes and felt a shiver run down his spine.

'Here's what he'd do,' Thérèse went on. 'He'd stand up, point at you with one paw and me with the other, and shout out: "Monsieur and Madame get up to all sorts of naughty things together in the bedroom; they take no notice of me, but since their illicit affair makes me sick, please would you put them both in prison so they won't disturb my nap in future."'

Thérèse joked about like a child, imitating the cat by stretching out her fingers into claws and rolling her shoulders in feline undulations. François, still sitting perfectly still, watched her all the time; only his eyes seemed to be alive, while two deep wrinkles at the corners of his mouth put a laughing expression on his stuffed-animal face.

Laurent felt a chill in his bones. He thought Thérèse's fooling around was ridiculous. He stood up and put the cat out of the door. The truth was that he was afraid. His mistress had not yet taken him over altogether; deep down there still lingered a little of the unease he had felt when Thérèse had first kissed him.

FRANK HARRIS

from
My Life and Loves

Frank Harris was a friend of Oscar Wilde and knew everyone who was anyone in the literary society of the late Victorian and Edwardian period – he died in 1931. His autobiography – My Life and Loves *– written in old age – was published in 1922 – and was designed to be the most honest autobiography ever written. It duly offended almost everyone. The most shocking sections of the book deal with his sexual exploits. Colourful, candid and highly explicit* My Life and Loves *is a key work in Victorian erotica.*

I AM again, however, running ahead of my story. The second evening of the voyage, the sea got up a little and there was a great deal of sickness. Doctor Keogh was called out of his cabin and while he was away, someone knocked at the door. I opened it and found a pretty girl.

'Where's the doctor?' she asked. I told her he had been called to a cabin passenger.

'Please tell him,' she said, 'when he returns, that Jessie Kerr, the chief engineer's daughter, would like to see him.'

'I'll go after him now if you wish, Miss Jessie,' I said. 'I know where he is.'

'It isn't important,' she rejoined, 'but I feel giddy, and he told me he could cure it.'

'Coming up on the deck is the best cure,' I declared. 'The fresh air will soon blow the sick feeling away. You'll sleep like a top and tomorrow morning you'll be all right. Will you come?' She consented readily and in ten minutes admitted that the slight nausea had disappeared in the sharp breeze. As we walked up and down the dimly lighted deck I had now and then to support her, for the ship was rolling a little under a sou-wester. Jessie told me something about herself, how she was going to New York to spend some months with an elder married sister and how strict her father was. In return she had my whole story and could hardly believe I was only sixteen. Why, she was over sixteen and she could never have stood up and recited piece after piece as I did in the cabin; she thought it 'wonderful.'

Before she went down, I told her she was the prettiest girl on board, and she kissed me and promised to come up the next evening and have another walk. 'If you've nothing better to do,' she said at parting, 'you might come forward to the little promenade deck of the second cabin and I'll get one of the men to arrange a seat in one of the boats for us.' 'Of course,' I promised gladly, and spent the next afternoon with Jessie in the stern sheets of the great launch where we were out of sight of everyone, and out of hearing as well.

There we were, tucked in with two rugs and cradled, so to speak, between sea and sky, while the keen air whistling past increased our sense of solitude. Jessie, though rather short, was a very pretty girl with large hazel eyes and fair complexion.

I soon got my arm around her and kept kissing her till she told me she had never known a man so greedy of kisses as I was. It was delicious flattery to me to speak of me as a man, and in return I raved about her eyes and mouth and form; caressing her left breast, I told her I could divine the rest and knew she had a lovely body. But when I put my hand up her clothes, she stopped me when I got just above her knee and said:

'We'd have to be engaged before I could let you do that. Do you really love me?'

Of course I swore I did, but when she said she'd have to tell her father we were engaged to be married, cold shivers went down my back.

'I can't marry for a long time yet,' I said. 'I'll have to make a living first and I'm not very sure where I'll begin.' But she had heard that an old man wished to adopt me and everyone said that he was very rich and even her father admitted that I'd be 'well-fixed.'

Meanwhile my right hand was busy. I had got my fingers to her warm flesh between the stockings and the drawers and was wild with desire; soon, mouth on mouth, I touched her sex.

What a gorgeous afternoon we had! I had learned enough now to go slow and obey what seemed to be her moods. Gently, gently, I caressed her sex with my fingers till it opened and she leaned against me and kissed me of her own will, while her eyes turned up and her whole being was lost in thrills of ecstasy. When she asked me to stop and take my hand away, I did her bidding at once and was rewarded by being told that I was a 'dear boy' and 'a sweet,' and soon the embracing and caressing began again. She moved now in response to my lascivious touchings, and when the ecstasy came on her, she clasped me close and kissed me passionately with hot lips and afterwards in my arms wept a little, and then pouted that she was cross with me for being so naughty. But her eyes gave themselves to me even while she tried to scold.

The dinner bell rang and she said she'd have to go, and we made a meeting for afterwards on the top deck; but as she was getting up she yielded again to my hand with a little sigh and I found her sex all wet, wet!

She got down out of the boat by the main rigging and I waited for a few moments before following her. At first our caution seemed likely to be rewarded, chiefly, I have thought since, because everyone believed me to be too young and too small to be taken seriously. But everything is quickly known on seaboard, at least by the sailors.

I went down to Dr Keogh's cabin, once more joyful and grateful, as I had been with E. . . . My fingers were like eyes gratifying my curiosity, and the curiosity was insatiable. Jessie's thighs were smooth and firm and round: I took delight in recalling the touch of them, and her bottom was firm like warm marble. I wanted to see her naked and study her beauties one after the other. Her sex, too, was wonderful, fuller even than Lucille's, and her eyes were finer. Oh, life was a thousand times better than school. I thrilled with joy and passionate wild hopes – perhaps Jessie would let me, perhaps – I was breathless.

Our walk on deck that evening was not so satisfactory: the wind had gone down and there were many other couples and the men all seemed to know Jessie, and it was Miss Kerr here, and Miss Kerr there, till I was cross and disappointed. I couldn't get her to myself save at moments, but then I had to admit she was as sweet as ever and her Aberdeen accent even was quaint and charming to me.

I got some long kisses at odd moments and just before we went down I drew her behind a boat in the davits and was able to caress her little breasts; and when she turned her back to me to go, I threw my arms round her hips and drew them against me, and she leant her head back over her shoulder and gave me her mouth with dying eyes. The darling! Jessie was apt at all love's lessons.

The next day was cloudy and rain threatened, but we were safely ensconced in the boat by two o'clock, as soon as lunch was over, and we hoped no one had seen us. An hour passed in caressings and fondlings, in love's words and love's promises; I had won Jessie to touch my sex and her eyes seemed to deepen as she caressed it.

'I love you, Jessie. Won't you let it touch yours?'

She shook her head. 'Not here, not in the open,' she whispered and then, 'Wait a little till we get to New York, dear,' and our mouths sealed the compact.

Then I asked her about New York and her sister's house, and we were discussing where we should meet, when a big head and beard showed above the gunwale of the boat and a deep Scotch voice said: 'I want ye, Jessie, I've been luiking everywhere for ye.'

'Awright, father,' she said. 'I'll be down in a minute.'

'Come quick,' said the voice as the head disappeared.

'I'll tell him we love each other and he won't be angry for long,' whispered Jessie; but I was doubtful. As she got up to go my naughty hand went up her dress behind and felt her warm, smooth buttocks. Ah, the poignancy of the ineffable sensations; her eyes smiled over her shoulder at me and she was gone – and the sunlight with her.

I still remember the sick disappointment as I sat in the boat alone. Life then, like school, had its chagrins, and as the pleasures were keener, the balks and blights were bitterer. For the first time in my life vague misgivings came over me, a heartshaking suspicion that everything delightful and joyous in life had to be paid for – I wouldn't harbour the fear. If I had to pay, I'd pay; after all, the memory of the ecstasy could never be taken away, while the sorrow was fleeting. And that faith I still hold.

Next day the chief steward allotted me a berth in a cabin with an English midshipman of seventeen going out to join his ship in the West Indies. William Ponsonby was not a bad sort, but he talked of nothing but girls from morning till night and insisted that Negresses were better than white girls: they were far more passionate, he said.

He showed me his sex; excited himself before me, while assuring me he meant to have a Miss Le Breton, a governess, who was going out to take up a position in Pittsburgh.

'But suppose you put her in the family way?' I asked.

'That's not my funeral,' was his answer, and seeing the cynicism shocked me, he went on to say there was no danger if you withdrew in time. Ponsonby never opened a book and was astoundingly ignorant: he didn't seem to care to learn anything that hadn't to do with sex. He introduced me to Miss Le Breton the same evening. She was rather tall, with fair hair and blue eyes, and she praised my reciting. To my wonder she was a woman and pretty, and I could see by the way she looked at Ponsonby that she was more than a little in love with him. He was above middle height, strong and good tempered, and that was all I could see in him.

Miss Jessie kept away the whole evening, and when I saw her father on the 'upper deck,' he glowered at me and went past without a word. That night I told Ponsonby my story, or part of it, and he declared he would find a sailor to carry a note to Jessie next morning if I'd write it.

Besides, he proposed we should occupy the cabin alternate afternoons; for example, he'd take it next day and I must not come near it, and if at any time one of us found the door locked, he was to respect his chum's privacy. I agreed to it all with enthusiasm and went to sleep in a fever of hope. Would Jessie risk her father's anger and come to me? Perhaps she would: at any rate I'd write and ask her and I did. In one hour the same sailor came back with her reply. It ran like this: 'Dear love, father is mad, we shall have to take great care for two or three days; as soon as it's safe, I'll come – your loving Jess,' with a dozen crosses for kisses.

That afternoon without thinking of my compact with Ponsonby, I went to our cabin and found the door locked: at once our compact came into my head and I went quickly away. Had he succeeded so quickly? And was she with him in bed? The half-certainty made my heart beat.

That evening Ponsonby could not conceal his success, but as he used it partly to praise his mistress, I forgave him.

'She has the prettiest figure you ever saw,' he declared, 'and is really a dear. We had just finished when you came to the door. I said it was some mistake and she believed me. She wants me to marry her, but I can't marry. If I were rich, I'd marry quick enough. It's better than risking some foul disease,' and he went on to tell about one of his colleagues, John Lawrence, who got black pox, as he called syphilis, caught from a Negress.

'He didn't notice it for three months,' Ponsonby went on, 'and it got into his system; his nose got bad and he was invalided home, poor devil. Those black girls are foul,' he continued; 'they give everyone the clap and that's bad enough, I can tell you; they're dirty devils.' His ruttish sorrows didn't interest me much, for I had made up my mind never at any time to go with any prostitute.

I came to several such uncommon resolutions on board that ship, and I may set down the chief of them here very briefly. First of all, I resolved that I would do every piece of work given to me as well as I could so that no one coming after me could do it better. I had found out at school in the last term that if you gave your whole mind and heart to anything, you learned it very quickly and thoroughly. I was sure even before the trial that my first job would lead me straight to fortune. I had seen men at work and knew it would be easy to beat any of them. I was only eager for the trial.

I remember one evening I had waited for Jessie and she never came, and just before going to bed, I went up into the bow of the ship where one was alone with the sea and sky, and swore to myself this great oath, as I called it in my romantic fancy: whatever I undertook to do, I would do it to the uttermost in me.

If I have had any successes in life or done any good work, it is due in great part to that resolution.

I could not keep my thoughts from Jessie; if I tried to put her out of my head, I'd get a little note from her, or Ponsonby would come, begging me to leave him the cabin the whole day: at length in despair I begged her for her address in New York, for I feared to lose her forever in that maelstrom. I added that I would always be in my cabin alone from one to half past, if she could ever come.

That day she didn't come and the old gentleman who said he would adopt me got hold of me, told me he was a banker and would send me to Harvard, the university near Boston; from what the doctor had said of me, he hoped I would do great things. He was really kind and tried to be sympathetic, but he had no idea that what I wanted chiefly was to prove myself, to justify my own high opinion of my powers in the open fight of life. I didn't want help and I absolutely resented his protective airs.

Next day in the cabin came a touch on the door and Jessie, all flustered, was in my arms. 'I can only stay a minute,' she cried. 'Father is dreadful, says you are only a child and won't have me engage myself and he watches me from morning to night. I could only get away now because he had to go down to the machine-room.'

Before she had finished, I locked the cabin door.

'Oh, I must go,' she cried. 'I must really; I only came to give you my address in New York; here it is,' and she handed me the paper that I put at once in my pocket. And then I put both my arms under her clothes and my hands were on her warm hips, and I was speechless with delight; in a moment my right hand came round in front and as I touched her sex our lips clung together and her sex opened at once, and my finger began to caress her and we kissed and kissed again. Suddenly her lips got hot and while I was still wondering why, her sex got wet and her eyes began to flutter and turn up. A moment or two later she tried to get out of my embrace.

'Really, dear, I'm frightened: he might come and make a noise and I'd die; please let me go now; we'll have lots of time in New York' – but I could not bear to let her go. 'He'd never come here where there are two men,' I said, 'never. He might find the wrong one,' and I drew her to me, but seeing she was only half-reassured, I said, while lifting her dress, 'Let mine just touch yours, and I'll let you go'; and the next moment my sex was against hers and almost in spite of herself she yielded to the throbbing warmth of it; but, when I pushed in, she drew away and down on it a little and I saw anxiety in her eyes that had grown very dear to me.

At once I stopped and put away my sex and let her clothes drop. 'You're such a sweet, Jess,' I said, 'who could deny you anything; in New York then, but now one long kiss.'

She gave me her mouth at once and her lips were hot. I learned that morning that, when a girl's lips grow hot, her sex is hot first and she is ready to give herself and ripe for the embrace.

★ ★ ★

A stolen kiss and fleeting caress as we met on the deck at night were all I had of Jessie for the rest of the voyage. One evening land lights flickering in the distance drew crowds to the deck; the ship began to slow down. The cabin passengers went below as usual, but hundreds of immigrants sat up as I did and watched the stars slide down the sky till at length dawn came with silver lights and startling revelations.

I can still recall the thrills that overcame me when I realized the great waterways of that land-locked harbour and saw Long Island Sound stretching away on one hand like a sea and the magnificent Hudson River with its palisades on the other, while before me was the East River, nearly a mile in width. What an entrance to a new world! A magnificent and safe ocean port which is also the meeting place of great water paths into the continent.

No finer site could be imagined for a world capital. I was entranced with the spacious grandeur, the manifest destiny of this Queen City of the Waters.

The Old Battery was pointed out to me and Governor's Island and the prison and where the bridge was being built to Brooklyn: suddenly Jessie passed on her father's arm and shot me one radiant, lingering glance of love and promise.

I remember nothing more till we landed and the old banker came up to tell me he had had my little box taken from the 'H's' where it belonged and put with his luggage among the 'S's.'

'We are going,' he added, 'to the Fifth Avenue Hotel a way uptown in Madison Square: we'll be comfortable there,' and he smiled self-complacently. I smiled too, and thanked him; but I had no intention of going in his company. I went back to the ship and thanked Doctor Keogh with all my heart for his great goodness to me; he gave me his address in New York, and incidentally I learned from him that if I kept the key of my trunk, no one could open it or take it away; it would be left in charge of the customs till I called for it.

In a minute I was back in the long shed on the dock and had wandered nearly to the end when I perceived the stairs. 'Is that the way into the town?' I asked and a man replied, 'Sure.' One quick glance around to see that I was not noticed and in a moment I was down the stairs and out in the street. I raced straight ahead of me for two or three blocks and then asked and was told that Fifth Avenue was right in front. As I turned up Fifth Avenue, I began to breathe freely; 'No more fathers for me.' The old greybeard who had bothered me was consigned to oblivion without regret. Of course, I know now that he deserved better treatment. Perhaps, indeed, I should have done better had I accepted his kindly, generous help, but I'm trying to set down the plain, unvarnished truth, and here at once I must say that children's affections are much slighter than most parents imagine. I never wasted a thought on my father; even my brother Vernon, who had always been kind to me and fed my inordinate vanity, was not regretted: the new life called me: I was in a flutter of expectancy and hope.

Some way up Fifth Avenue I came into the great square and saw the Fifth Avenue Hotel, but I only grinned and kept right on till at length I reached Central Park. Near it, I can't remember exactly where, but I believe it was near where the Plaza Hotel stands today, there was a small wooden house with an outhouse at the other end of the lot. While I stared a woman came out with a bucket and went across to the outhouse. In a few minutes she came back again and noticed me looking over the fence.

'Would you please give me a drink?' I asked. 'Sure I will,' she replied with a strong Irish brogue; 'come right in,' and I followed her into the kitchen.

'You're Irish,' I said, smiling at her. 'I am,' she replied, 'how did ye guess?' 'Because I was born in Ireland, too,' I retorted. 'You were not!' she cried emphatically, more for pleasure than to contradict. 'I was born in Galway,' I went on, and at once she became very friendly and poured me out some milk warm from the cow; and when she heard I had had no breakfast and saw I was hungry, she pressed me to eat and sat down with me and soon heard my whole story, or enough of it to break out in wonder again and again.

In turn she told me how she had married Mike Mulligan, a longshoreman who earned good wages and was a good husband but took a drop too much now and again, as a man will when tempted by one of 'thim saloons.' It was the saloons, I learned, that were the ruination of all the best Irishmen and 'they were the best men anyway, an' – an' – '; and the kindly, homely talk flowed on, charming me.

When the breakfast was over and the things cleared away, I rose to go with many thanks, but Mrs Mulligan wouldn't hear of it. 'Ye're a child,' she said, 'an' don't know New York; it's a terrible place and you must wait till Mike comes home an' – '

'But I must find some place to sleep,' I said. 'I have money.'

'You'll sleep here,' she broke in decisively, 'and Mike will put ye on yer feet; sure he knows New York like his pocket, an' yer as welcome as the flowers in May, an' – '

What could I do but stay and talk and listen to all sorts of stories about New York, and 'toughs' that were 'hard cases' and 'gunmen' and 'wimmin that were worse – bad scran to them.'

In due time Mrs Mulligan and I had dinner together, and after dinner I got her permission to go into the park for a walk, but 'mind now and be home by six or I'll send Mike after ye,' she added, laughing.

I walked a little way in the park and then started down town again to the address Jessie had given me near the Brooklyn Bridge. It was a mean street, I thought, but I soon found Jessie's sister's house and went to a nearby restaurant and wrote a little note to my love, that she could show if need be, saying that I proposed to call on the eighteenth, or two days after the ship we had come in was due to return to Liverpool. After that duty, which made it possible for me to hope all sorts of things on the eighteenth, nineteenth, or twentieth, I sauntered over to Fifth Avenue and made my way uptown again. At any rate I was spending nothing in my present lodging.

When I returned that night I was presented to Mike: I found him a big, good looking Irishman who thought his wife a wonder and all she did perfect. 'Mary,' he said, winking at me, 'is one of the best cooks in the wurrld and if it weren't that she's down on a man when he has a drop in him, she'd be the best gurrl on God's earth. As it is, I married her, and I've never been sorry, have I, Mary?' 'Ye've had no cause, Mike Mulligan.'

Mike had nothing particular to do next morning and so he promised he would go and get my little trunk from the custom house. I gave him the key. He insisted as warmly as his wife that I should stay with them till I got work: I told him how eager I was to begin and Mike promised to speak to his chief and some friends and see what could be done.

Next morning I got up at about five-thirty as soon as I heard Mike stirring, and went down Seventh Avenue with him till he got on the horse-car for down town and left me. About seven-thirty to eight o'clock a stream of people began walking down town to their offices. On several corners were bootblack shanties. One of them happened to have three customers in it and only one bootblack.

'Won't you let me help you shine a pair or two?' I asked. The bootblack looked at me. 'I don't mind,' he said and I seized the brushes and went to work. I had done the two just as he finished the first: he whispered to me 'halves' as the next man came in and he showed me how to use the polishing rag or cloth. I took off my coat and waistcoat and went to work with a will; for the next hour and a half we both had our hands full. Then the rush began to slack off, but not before I had taken just over a dollar and a half. Afterwards we had a talk, and Allison, the bootblack, told me he'd be glad to give me work any morning on the same terms. I assured him I'd be there and do my best till I got other work. I had earned three shillings and had found out I could get good board for three dollars a week, so in a couple of hours I had earned my living. The last anxiety left me.

Mike had a day off, so he came home for dinner at noon and he had great news. They wanted men to work under water in the iron caissons of Brooklyn Bridge and they were giving from five to ten dollars a day.

'Five dollars,' cried Mrs Mulligan. 'It must be dangerous or unhealthy or somethin' – sure, you'd never put the child to work like that.'

Mike excused himself, but the danger, if danger there was, appealed to me almost as much as the big pay: my only fear was that they'd think me too small or too young. I had told Mrs Mulligan I was sixteen, for I didn't want to be treated as a child, and now I showed her the eighty cents I had earned that morning bootblacking and she advised me to keep on at it and not go to work under the water; but the promised five dollars a day won me.

Next morning Mike took me to Brooklyn Bridge soon after five o'clock to see the contractor; he wanted to engage Mike at once but shook his head over me. 'Give me a trial,' I pleaded; 'you'll see I'll make good.' After a pause, 'O.K.,' he said; 'four shifts have gone down already underhanded: you may try.'

I've told about the work and its dangers at some length in my novel, *The Bomb*, but here I may add some details just to show what labour has to suffer.

In the bare shed where we got ready, the men told me no one could do the work for long without getting the 'bends'; the 'bends' were a sort of convulsive fit that twisted one's body like a knot and often made you an invalid for life. They soon explained the whole procedure to me. We worked, it appeared, in a huge bell-shaped caisson of iron that went to the bottom of the river and was pumped full of compressed air to keep the water from entering it from below: the top of the caisson is a room called the 'material chamber,' into which the stuff dug out of the river passes up and is carted away. On the side of the caisson is another room, called the 'air-lock,' into which we were to go to be 'compressed.' As the compressed air is admitted, the blood keeps absorbing the gases of the air till the tension of the gases in the blood becomes equal to that in the air; when this equilibrium has been reached, men can work in the caisson for hours without serious discomfort, if sufficient pure air is constantly pumped in. It was the foul air that did the harm, it appeared. 'If they'd pump in good air, it would be O.K.; but that would cost a little time and trouble, and men's lives are cheaper.' I saw that the men wanted to warn me thinking I was too young, and accordingly I pretended to take little heed.

When we went into the 'air-lock' and they turned on one air-cock after another of compressed air, the men put their hands to their ears and I soon imitated them, for the pain was very acute. Indeed, the drums of the ears are often driven in and burst if the compressed air is brought in too quickly. I found that the best way of meeting the pressure was to keep swallowing air and forcing it up into the middle ear, where it acted as an air-pad on the inner side of the drum and so lessened the pressure from the outside.

It took about half an hour or so to 'compress' us and that half an hour gave me lots to think about. When the air was fully compressed, the door of the air-lock opened at a touch and we all went down to work with pick and shovel on the gravelly bottom. My headache soon became acute. The six of us were working naked to the waist in a small iron chamber with a temperature of about 108° Fahrenheit: in five minutes the sweat was pouring from us, and all the while we were standing in icy water that was only kept from rising by the terrific air pressure. No wonder the headaches were blinding. The men didn't work for more than ten minutes at a time, but I plugged on steadily, resolved to prove myself and get constant employment; only one man, a Swede named Anderson, worked at all as hard. I was overjoyed to find that together we did more than the four others.

The amount done each week was estimated, he told me, by an inspector. Anderson was known to the contractor and received half a wage extra as head of our gang. He assured me I could stay as long as I liked, but he advised me to leave at the end of a month: it was too unhealthy: above all, I mustn't drink and should spend all my spare time in the open. He was kindness itself to me, as indeed were all the others. After two hours' work down below we went up into the air-lock room to get gradually 'decompressed,' the pressure of air in our veins having to be brought down gradually to the usual air pressure. The men began to put on their clothes and passed round a bottle of schnapps; but though I was soon as cold as a wet rat and felt depressed and weak to boot, I would not touch the liquor. In the shed above I took a cupful of hot cocoa with Anderson, which stopped the shivering, and I was soon able to face the afternoon's ordeal.

I had no idea one could feel so badly when being 'decompressed' in the air-lock, but I took Anderson's advice and got into the open as soon as I could, and by the time I had walked home in the evening and changed, I felt strong again; but the headache didn't leave me entirely and the earache came back every now and then, and to this day a slight deafness reminds me of that spell of work under water.

I went into Central Park for half an hour; the first pretty girl I met reminded me of Jessie: in one week I'd be free to see her and tell her I was making good and she'd keep her promise, I felt sure; the mere hope led me to fairyland. Meanwhile nothing could take away the proud consciousness that with my five dollars I had earned two weeks' living in a day: a month's work would make me safe for a year.

When I returned I told the Mulligans I must pay for my board, saying 'I'd feel better, if you'll let me,' and finally they consented, although Mrs Mulligan thought three dollars a week too much. I was glad when it was settled and went to bed early to have a good sleep. For three or four days things went fairly well with me, but on the fifth or sixth day we came on a spring of water, or 'gusher,' and were wet to the waist before the air pressure could be increased to cope with it. As a consequence, a dreadful pain shot through both my ears: I put my hands to them tight and sat still a little while. Fortunately, the shift was almost over and Anderson came with me to the horse-car. 'You'd better knock off,' he said. 'I've known 'em go deaf from it.'

The pain had been appalling, but it was slowly diminishing and I was resolved not to give in. 'Could I get a day off?' I asked Anderson. He nodded, 'Of course, you're the best in the shift, the best I've ever seen, a great little pony.'

Mrs Mulligan saw at once something was wrong and made me try her household remedy – a roasted onion cut in two and clapped tight on each ear with a flannel bandage. It acted like magic: in ten minutes I was free of pain; then she poured in a little warm sweet oil and in an hour I was walking in the park as usual. Still, the fear of deafness was on me and I was very glad when Anderson told me he had complained to the boss and we were to get an extra thousand feet of pure air. It would make a great difference, Anderson said, and he was right, but the improvement was not sufficient.

One day, just as the 'decompression' of an hour and a half was ending, an Italian named Manfredi fell down and writhed about, knocking his face on the floor till the blood spurted from his nose and mouth. When we got him into the shed, his legs were twisted like plaited hair. The surgeon had him taken to the hospital. I made up my mind that a month would be enough for me.

At the end of the first week, I got a note from Jessie saying that her father was going on board that afternoon and she could see me the next evening. I went and was introduced to Jessie's sister who, to my surprise, was tall and large but without a trace of Jessie's good looks.

'He's younger than you, Jess,' she burst out laughing. A week earlier I'd have been hurt to the soul, but I had proved myself, so I said simply, 'I'm earning five dollars a day, Mrs Plummer, and money talks.' Her mouth fell open in amazement. 'Five dollars,' she repeated, 'I'm so sorry, I – I – '

'There, Maggie,' Jessie broke in, 'I told you, you had never seen anyone like him; you'll be great friends yet. Now come and we'll have a walk,' she added, and out we went.

To be with her even in the street was delightful and I had a lot to say, but making love in a New York street on a summer evening is difficult and I was hungry to kiss and caress her freely. Jessie, however, had thought of a way: if her sister and husband had theatre tickets, they'd go out and we'd be alone in the apartment; it would cost two dollars, however, and she thought that a lot. I was delighted: I gave her the bills and arranged to be with her next night before eight o'clock. Did Jessie know what was going to happen? Even now I'm uncertain, though I think she guessed.

Next night I waited till the coast was clear and then hurried to the door. As soon as we were alone in the little parlor and I had kissed her, I said, 'Jessie, I want you to undress. I'm sure your figure is lovely, but I want to know it.'

'Not at once, eh?' she pouted. 'Talk to me first. I want to know how you are,' and I drew her to the big armchair and sat down with her in my arms. 'What am I to tell you?' I asked, while my hand went up her dress to her warm thighs and sex. She frowned, but I kissed her lips and with a movement or two stretched her out on me so that I could use my finger easily. At once, her lips grew hot and I went on kissing and caressing till her eyes closed and she gave herself to the pleasure. Suddenly she wound herself upon me and gave me a big kiss. 'You don't talk,' she said.

'I can't,' I exclaimed, making up my mind. 'Come,' and I lifted her to her feet and took her into the bedroom. 'I'm crazy for you,' I said; 'take off your clothes, please.' She resisted a little, but when I began loosening her dress, she helped me and took it off. Her knickers, I noticed, were new. They soon fell off and she stood in her chemise and black stockings.

'That's enough, isn't it,' she said, 'Mr Curious,' and she drew the chemise tight about her.

'No,' I cried, 'beauty must unveil, please!' The next moment the chemise, slipping down, caught for a moment on her hips and then slid circling round her feet.

Her nakedness stopped my heart; desire blinded me: my arms went round her, straining her soft form to me: in a moment I had lifted her on to the bed, pulling the bed clothes back at the same time. The foolish phrase of being in bed together deluded me: I had no idea that she was more in my power just lying on the edge of the bed; in a moment I had torn off my clothes and boots and got in beside her. Our warm bodies lay together, a thousand pulses beating in us; soon I separated her legs and, lying on her, tried to put my sex into hers, but she drew away almost at once. 'O-O, it hurts,' she murmured, and each time I tried to push my sex in her, her 'O's' of pain stopped me.

My wild excitement made me shiver; I could have struck her for drawing away; but soon I noticed that she let my sex touch her clitoris with pleasure and I began to use my cock as a finger, caressing her with it. In a moment or two I began to move it more quickly, and as my excitement grew to the height, I again tried to slip it into her pussy, and now, as her love-dew came, I got my sex in a little way, which gave me inexpressible pleasure; but when I pushed to go further, she drew away again with a sharp cry of pain. At the same moment my orgasm came on for the first time and seed like milk spirted from my sex. The pleasure-thrill was almost unbearably keen; I could have screamed with the pang of it, but Jessie cried out: 'Oh, you're wetting me,' and drew away with a frightened, 'Look, look!' And there, sure enough, on her round white thighs were patches of crimson blood. 'Oh! I'm bleeding,' she cried. 'What have you done?'

'Nothing,' I answered, a little sulky, I'm afraid, at having my indescribable pleasure cut short, 'Nothing'; and in a moment I had got out of bed, and taking my handkerchief soon wiped away the tell-tale traces.

But when I wanted to begin again, Jessie would not hear of it at first.

'No, no,' she said. 'You've really hurt me, Jim (my Christian name, I had told her, was James), and I'm scared; please be good.' I could only do her will until a new thought struck me. At any rate, I could see her now and study her beauties one by one, and so still lying by her I began kissing her left breast and soon the nipple grew a little stiff in my mouth. Why, I didn't know and Jessie said she didn't but she liked it when I said her breasts were lovely, and indeed they were, small and firm, while the nipples pointed straight out. Suddenly, the thought came, surprising me: it would have been much prettier if the circle surrounding the nipples had been rose-red, instead of merely amber-brown. I was thrilled by the bare idea. But her flanks and belly were lovely; the navel like a curled sea-shell, I thought, and the triangle of silky brown hairs on the Mount of Venus seemed to me enchanting, but Jessie kept covering her beauty-place. 'It's ugly,' she said, 'please boy,' but I went on caressing it and soon I was trying to slip my sex in again; though Jessie's 'O's' of pain began at once and she begged me to stop.

'We must get up and dress,' she said: 'they'll soon be back,' so I had to content myself with just lying in her arms with my sex touching hers. Soon she began to move against my sex, and to kiss me, and then she bit my lips just as my sex slipped into hers again; she left it in for a long moment and than as her lips grew hot: 'It's so big,' she said 'but you're a dear.' The moment after she cried: 'We must get up, boy! If they caught us, I'd die of shame.' When I tried to divert her attention by kissing her breasts, she pouted 'That hurts, too. Please, boy, stop and don't look,' she added as she tried to rise, covering her sex the while with her hand and pulling a frowning face. Though I told her she was mistaken and her sex was lovely, she persisted in hiding it, and in truth her breasts and thighs excited me more, perhaps because they were in themselves more beautiful.

I put my hand on her hip; she smiled, 'Please, boy,' and as I moved away to give her room, she got up and stood by the bed, a perfect little figure in rosy, warm outline. I was entranced, but the cursed critical faculty was awake. As she turned, I saw she was too broad for her height; her legs were too short, her hips too stout. It all chilled me a little. Should I ever find perfection?

Ten minutes later she had rearranged the bed and we were seated in the sitting room, but to my wonder Jessie didn't want to talk over our experience. 'What gave you the most pleasure?' I asked. 'All of it,' she said, 'you naughty dear; but don't let's talk of it.'

I told her I was going to work for a month, but I couldn't talk to her; my hand was soon up her clothes again, playing with her sex and caressing it, and we had to move apart hurriedly when we heard her sister at the door.

* * *

And now for a better and more memorable experience.

I had gone to balls twice or three times in the Heidelberg because a friend wished me to accompany him or to complete a gay party. I seldom went of my own accord because dancing made me excessively giddy, as I have already related. But at one ball I was introduced to a Miss Betsy C., an English girl of a good type, very well dressed and extraordinarily pretty, though very small. She stood out among the large German fräuleins like a moss-rose wrapped in a delicate greenery to heighten her entrancing colour, and at once I told her this and assured her that she had the most magnificent dark eyes I had ever seen; for bashfulness I had never felt, and I knew that praise was as the breath of life to every woman. We became friends at once, but to my disappointment, she told me she was going next day to Frankfort, where some friends would meet her the day after to accompany her back to England. Before I thought of what I was letting myself in for, I told her I would love to go to Frankfort with her and show her Goethe's birth-place and the Goethe-Haus; would she accept my escort? Would she? The great brown eyes danced with the thought of adventure and companionship – I was in for it – was this my next-born resolution of restraint? Was this my first essay in making an art of my life?

Yet I didn't even think of excusing myself: Bessie was too pretty and too alluring, with a quiet humour that appealed to me intensely. A big German girl passed us and Bessie, looking at her arms, said, 'I never knew what "mottled" was before. I've seen advertisements of "mottled soap"; but "mottled" arms! They're not pretty, are they?' Bessie was worse than pretty; under medium height but rounded in entrancing curves to beauty; her face piquant; the dark eyes now gleaming in malice, now deep in self-revealing; her arms exquisite and the small mounds of white breasts half hidden, half discovered by the lacy dress. No wonder I asked, 'What time is your train? Shall I take you to the *Bahnhof?*'

'We'll meet at the station,' she said, with a glint in her eye, 'but you must be very kind and good!' Had she ever given herself? Did this last admonition mean she would not yield to me? I was in a fever but resolved to be amiable as well as bold.

Next morning we met at the station and had a great talk; and at Frankfort I drove with her straight to the best hotel, walked boldly to the desk and ordered two good rooms communicating; and signed the register Mr. and Mrs. Harris.

We were shown rooms on the second floor: our English appearance had got us the best in the house, and as my luck would have it, the second smaller bedroom had the key and bolt, so that I could reckon at least on a fair chance. But at once I opened the door between the rooms and helped her with her outside wraps and then, taking her head in my hands, kissed her on the mouth. At once, almost, her lips grew warm, which seemed to me the best omen. I said to her, 'You'll knock when you're ready, won't you? Or come in to me?'

She smiled, reassured by my withdrawal, and nodded gaily, 'I'll call!'

I spent the whole day with her and talked my best, telling her of Goethe's many love affairs and of Gretchen-Frederika. After dinner we went out for a walk and then returned to the hotel and went up to our bedrooms.

I went into my room and closed the door, my heart throbbing heavily, my mouth all parched as in fever. I must cheat time, I said to myself, and so I put on my best suit of pyjamas, a sort of white stuff with threads of gold in it. And then I waited for the summons, but none came. I looked at my watch: it was twenty minutes since we parted; I must give her half an hour at least. 'Would she call me?' She had said she would. 'Would she yield easily?' Again, as my imagination recalled her wilful, mutinous face and lovely eyes, my heart began to thump! At last the half hour was up; should I go in? Yes, I would, and I walked over to the door and listened – not a sound. I turned the handle; the room was entirely in the dark. I moved quickly to the lights and turned them on: there she was in bed, with only her little face showing and the great eyes. In a second I was by her side.

'You promised to call me,' I said.

'Put out the light!' she begged. Without making any reply I pulled down the clothes and got in beside her. 'You'll be good!' she pouted.

'I'll try,' was my noncommittal answer, and I slipped my left arm under her and drew her lips to mine. I was thrilled by the slightness and warmth of her, and at first I just took her mouth and held her close to the heat of my body. In a moment or two her lips grew hot and I put my hand down to lift her nightie: 'No, no!' she resisted, pouting. 'You promised to be good.'

'There's nothing bad in this,' I said, persevering, and the next moment I had my hand on her sex. With a sigh she resigned herself and gave her lips. After caressing her for a minute or two her sex opened and I could move her legs apart, so at once I put her hand on my sex. My excitement was so intense that I felt a good deal of pain; but I was past caring for pain. In a moment I was between her legs with my sex caressing her sex; the great eyes closed, but as I sought to enter her she shrank back with a cry of pain: 'Oo, oo! It's terrible – please stop; oh, you said you'd be good.' Of course I kissed her, smiling, and went back to the caressing. Naturally, in a few minutes I was again trying to enter paradise; but at once the cries of pain began again and the entreaties to stop and be good and I'll love you so. She was so pretty in her entreating that I said: 'Let me see, and if I hurt you, I'll stop,' and drew down in the bed to look. The fools are always saying that one sex of a woman is very like another; it is absolutely false; they are as different as mouths and this I was looking at was one of the most lovely I had ever seen. As she lay there before me I could not help exclaiming, 'You dear, pocket Venus!' She was so dainty-small, but the damage done was undeniable; there was blood on her sex and a spot of blood on one lovely little round thigh; and at the same moment I noticed that my infernal prepuce had shrunk and now hurt me dreadfully, compressing my sex with a ring of iron. For some obscure reason, half of pity, half of affection for the little beauty, I moved and lay beside her as at first saying: 'I'll do whatever you wish; I love you so much, I hate to hurt you so.'

'Oh, you great dear,' she cried, and her arms went round my neck and she kissed me of her own accord a hundred times. A little later I lifted her upon me, naked body to naked body, and was ravished by the sheer beauty of her.

I must have spent an hour in fondling and caressing her; continually I discovered new beauties in her; time and again I pushed her nightie up to her neck, delighting in the plastic beauty of her figure; but Bessie showed no wish to see me or excite me. Why? Girls are a strange folk, I decided, but I soon found she was as greedy of praise as could be, so I told her what an impression she had made at the ball and how a dozen students had asked me to introduce them, saying she was the queen of the evening. At length she fell asleep in my arms and I must have slept, too, for it was four in the morning before I awoke, turned out the lights and crept to my own room. I had acted unselfishly, spared Bessie: to give her merely pain for my thrill of pleasure would not have been fair, I thought; I was rather pleased with myself.

When I awoke in the morning, I hastened to her, but found she was getting up and did not want to be disturbed; she'd be ready before me, she said, and she wished to see the town and shops before her friends came for her at two o'clock. I followed her wishes, bolted the door between our rooms, took her for a drive, gave her lunch, said 'Goodbye' afterwards. When I assured her that nothing had been done, she said that I was a darling, promised to write and kissed me warmly; but I felt a shade of reticence in her, a something of reserve too slight to be defined, and on the train back to Heidelberg I put my fears down to fancy. But though I wrote to her English address I received no answer. Had I lost her through sparing her? What a puzzle women were! Was Vergil right with his *spretae injuria formae*? the hatred that comes in them if their beauty is not triumphant? Do they forgive anything sooner than self-control? I was angry with myself and resolved not to be an unselfish fool next time.

* * *

I had been in the Hotel d'Athènes a week or so when I noticed a pretty girl on the stairs: she charmed my eyes. A chambermaid told me she was Mme. M— and had the next bedroom to mine. Then I discovered that her mother, a Mme. D—, had the big sitting-room on the first floor. I don't know how I made the mother's acquaintance, but she was kindly and easy of approach, and I found she had a son, Jacques D—, in the Corps des Pages, whom I came to know intimately in Paris some years later, as I shall relate in due course. The daughter and I soon became friends; she was a very pretty girl in the early twenties. The D—s were of pure Greek stock, but they came from Marseilles and spoke French as well as Modern Greek. The girl had been married to a Scot a couple of years before I met her; he was now in Britain somewhere, she said. She would hardly speak of her marriage; it was the mother who told me it had been a tragic failure.

In the freedom from fixed hours of study, my long habit of virtue weighed on me and Mme. M— was extraordinarily good looking: slight and rather tall with a Greek face of the best type, crowned with a mass of black hair. I have never seen larger or more beautiful dark eyes, and her slight figure had a lissom grace that was intensely provocative. Her name was Eirene, or 'Peace,' and she soon allowed me to use it. In three days I told her I loved her, and indeed I was taken as by storm. We went out together for long walks: one day we visited the Acropolis and she was delighted to learn from me all about the 'Altar of the Gods.' Another day we went down into the Agora, or market-place, and she taught me something of modern Greek life and customs. One day an old woman greeted us as lovers, and when Mme. M— shook her head and said, '*ouk éstiv*' (it is not so), she shook her finger and said, 'He's afire and you'll catch fire, too.'

At first Mme. M— would not yield to me at all, but after a month or so of assiduity and companionship, I was able to steal a kiss or an embrace and came slowly day by day, little by little, nearer to the goal. An accident helped me one day: shall I ever forget it? We had been all through the town together and only returned as the evening was drawing in. When we came to the first floor I opened the door of their sitting-room very quietly. As luck would have it, the screen before the door had been pushed aside and there on the sofa at the far side of the room I saw her mother in the arms of a Greek officer. I drew the door to slowly, so that the girl coming behind might see, and then closed it noiselessly.

As we turned off towards our bedrooms on the left, I saw that her face was glowing. At her door I stopped her. 'My kiss,' I said, and as in a dream she kissed me: *l'heure du berger* had struck.

'Won't you come to me tonight?' I whispered. 'That door leads into my room.' She looked at me with that inscrutable woman's glance, and for the first time her eyes gave themselves. That night I went to bed early and moved away the sofa, which on my side barred her door. I tried the lock but found it closed on her side, worse luck!

As I lay in bed that night about eleven o'clock, I heard and saw the handle of the door move. At once I blew out the light, but the blinds were not drawn and the room was alight with moonshine. 'May I come in?' she asked.

'May you?' I was out of bed in a jiffy and had taken her adorable soft round form in my arms. 'You adorable sweet,' I cried, and lifted her into my bed. She had dropped her dressing-gown, had only a nightie on, and in one moment my hands were all over her lovely body. The next moment I was with her in bed and on her, but she moved aside and away from me.

'No, let's talk,' she said.

I began kissing her, but acquiesced, 'Let's talk.'

To my amazement, she began: 'Have you read Zola's latest book, *Nana*?'

'Yes,' I replied.

'Well,' she said, 'you know what the girl did to Nana?'

'Yes,' I replied, with sinking heart.

'Well,' she went on, 'why not do that to me? I'm desperately afraid of getting a child; you would be too in my place; why not love each other without fear?' A moment's thought told me that all roads lead to Rome and so I assented and soon I slipped down between her legs. 'Tell me please how to give you most pleasure,' I said, and gently I opened the lips of her sex and put my lips on it and my tongue against her clitoris. There was nothing repulsive in it; it was another and more sensitive mouth. Hardly had I kissed it twice when she slid lower down in the bed with a sigh, whispering, 'That's it; that's heavenly!'

Thus encouraged I naturally continued: soon her little lump swelled out so that I could take it in my lips and each time I sucked it, her body moved convulsively, and soon she opened her legs further and drew them up to let me in to the uttermost. Now I varied the movement by tonguing the rest of her sex and thrusting my tongue into her as far as possible; her movements quickened and her breathing grew more and more spasmodic, and when I went back to the clitoris again and took it in my lips and sucked it while pushing my forefinger back and forth into her sex, her movements became wilder and she began suddenly to cry in French, 'Oh, c'est fou! Oh, c'est fou! Oh! Oh' And suddenly she lifted me up, took my head in both her hands, and crushed my mouth with hers, as if she wanted to hurt me.

The next moment my head was between her legs again and the game went on. Little by little I felt that my finger rubbing the top of her sex while I tongued her clitoris gave her the most pleasure, and after another ten minutes of this delightful practice, she cried: 'Frank, Frank, stop! Kiss me! Stop and kiss me, I can't stand any more, I am rigid with passion and want to bite or pinch you.'

Naturally I did as I was told and her body melted itself against mine while our lips met. 'You dear,' she said, 'I love you so, and oh how wonderfully you kiss.'

'You've taught me,' I said, 'I'm your pupil.'

While we were together my sex was against hers and seeking an entry; each time it pushed in, she drew away; at length she said: 'I'd love to give myself to you, dear, but I'm frightened.'

'You need not be,' I assured her. 'If you let me enter I'll withdraw before my seed comes and there'll be no danger.' But do what I would, say what I would, that first night she would not yield to me in the usual way.

I knew enough about women to know that the more I restrained myself and left her to take the initiative, the greater would be my reward. A few days later I took her up Mount Lycabettus and showed her 'all the kingdoms of the spirit,' as I used to call Athens and the surroundings. She wanted to know about ancient Greek literature. 'Was it better than modern French literature?'

'Yes and no; it was altogether different.'

She confessed she could not understand Homer, but when I recited choruses from the *Oedipus Rex*, she understood them; and the great oath in Demosthenes' speech, 'Not by those who first faced death at Marathon' – and the noble summing up brought tears to her eyes – 'Now by your judgment you will either drive our accusers out over land and over sea, houseless and homeless, or you will give to us a sure release from all danger in the peace of the eternal silence.' On hearing this, she kissed me of her own accord.

As we were walking that afternoon down the long slope of Lycabettus, 'You don't want me any more?' she said, suddenly. 'Men are such selfish creatures; if you don't do all they want at once, they draw away.'

'You don't believe a word of that,' I interrupted. 'When have I drawn away? I'm awaiting your good pleasure. I didn't want to bother you perpetually, that's all. If you could see me watching the handle of your door every night – '

'Some night soon it will turn,' she said, and slipped her hand through my arm. 'I don't like to decide important things when I am a quiver with feeling, but I've thought over all you said and I want to believe you, to trust you – see?' And her eyes were one promise.

Luckily, when the handle of her door did turn, I was on the watch and took her in my arms before she had crossed the threshold, and the love-game she had taught me went on for a long time. At length wearied and all dissolved in sensation, she lay in my arms and my sex throbbing hot was against hers, seeking, seeking its sheath. Luckily I did not force matters but let the contact plead for me. At length she whispered, 'I hate to deny you; will you do what you promised?'

'Surely,' I said.

'And there's no danger?'

'None,' I replied. 'I give you my word of honour,' and the next moment she relaxed in my arms and let me have my will. Slowly I penetrated, bit by bit, and she leaned to me with a greedy mouth, kissing me. It was divine, but oh, so brief: a few thrusts and I was compelled to withdraw to keep my word.

'Oh, it was heavenly,' she sighed as I took up my spirting semen on my handkerchief, 'but I like your mouth best: why is that? Your tongue excites me terribly: why?' she asked, and then, 'Let's talk!'

But I said, 'No dear! let's begin. Now there's no risk; I can go with you as much as we like without danger. I'll explain it to you afterwards, but take my word and let's enjoy ourselves.'

The next moment I was in her again and the great game went on with renewed vigour. Again and again she came to an ecstasy and at length as I mounted high up so as to excite her more, she suddenly cried out: 'Oh, oh, que c'est fou, fou, fou,' and she bit my shoulder and then burst into tears.

Naturally I took her in my arms and began to kiss her; our first great love-duet was over. From that night on she had no secrets from me, no reticences, and bit by bit she taught me all she felt in the delirium of love: she told me she could not tell which gave her most pleasure, but I soon learned that she preferred me to begin by kissing her sex for ten or fifteen minutes and then to complete the orgasm with my sex used rather violently.

All the English schoolboy stories of some fancied resemblance between the mouth and the sex of the women, and the nose and sex of the men, I found invariably false. Eirene had a rather large mouth and a very small pretty sex, whereas the girl with the largest sex and thickest lips I ever met had a small thin mouth. Similarly with the man. I'm sure there's no relation whatever between the sex and the feature of the face.

An exquisite mistress, Eirene, with a girl's body, small round breasts, and a mouth I never grew tired of. Often afterwards, instead of walks, we adjourned to my room and spent the afternoon in love's games.

Sometimes her mother came to her door and she would laugh and hug me; once or twice her brother came to mine, but we lay in each other's arms and let the foolish outside world knock. But we always practised the game she had been the first to teach me; for some reason or other I learned more about women through it and the peculiar ebb and flow of their sensuality than the natural love-play had taught me; it gives the key, so to speak, to a woman's heart and senses, and to the man this the chief reward, as wise old Montaigne knew, who wrote of 'standing at rack and manger before meal.'

I was always trying to win confessions from my girl friends about their first experiences in sensuality, but save in the case of some few Frenchwomen, actresses for the most part, I was not very successful. What the reason is, others must explain, but I found girls strangely reticent on the subject. Time and again when in bed with Eirene I tried to get her to tell me, and at long last she confessed to one adventure.

When she was about fifteen she had a French governess in Marseilles, and one day this lady came into the bathroom, telling her she had been a long time bathing, and offering to help her dry herself. 'I noticed,' said Eirene, 'that she looked at me intently and it pleased me. When I got out she wrapped the robe about me and then sat down to dry me. As she touched me often there I opened my legs and she touched me very caressingly, and then of a sudden she kissed me passionately on the mouth and left me. I liked her very much. She was a dear, really clever and kind.'

'Did she ever dry you again?' I asked.

Eirene laughed. 'You want to know too much, sir,' was all she would say.

When I returned to Athens at the end of the summer, I took rooms in the people's quarter and lived very cheaply. Soon Eirene came to visit me again and we went often to the Greek theatre and I read Theocritus with her on many afternoons; but she gave me nothing new and in the spring I decided to return by way of Constantinople and the Black Sea to Vienna, for I felt that my *Lehrjahre* – 'prentice-years' – were drawing to an end; and Paris beckoned, and London.

One of the last evenings we were together Eirene wanted to know what I liked best in her.

'You've a myriad good qualities,' I began. 'You are good tempered and reasonable always, to say nothing of your lovely eyes and lithe slight figure. But why do you ask?'

'My husband used to say I was bony,' she replied. 'He made me dreadfully unhappy, tho' I tried my best to please him. I didn't feel much with him at first and that word "bony" hurt terribly.'

'Don't you know,' I said '[on] one of our first meetings, when you got out of bed to go to your room, I lifted up your nightie and saw the outline of your curving thighs and hips; it has always seemed to me one of the loveliest contours I've ever seen. If I had been a sculptor I'd have modelled it long ago – "bony," indeed; the man didn't deserve you: put him out of your head.'

'I have,' she said, 'for we women have only room for one, and you've put yourself in my heart. I'm glad you don't think me bony, but fancy you caring for a curve of flesh so much. Men are funny things. No woman would so over-prize a mere outline – your praise and his blame both show the same spirit.'

'Yet desire is born of admiration,' I corrected.

'My desire is born of yours,' she replied. 'But a woman's love is better and different: it is of the heart and soul.'

'But the body gives the key,' I said, 'and makes intimacy divine!'

I found several unlooked for and unimaginable benefits in this mouth-worship. First of all, I could give pleasure to any extent without exhausting or even tiring myself. It thus enabled me to atone completely and make up for my steadily decreasing virility. Secondly, I discovered that by teaching me the most sensitive parts of the woman, I was able even in the ordinary way to give my mistress more and keener pleasure than ever before. I had all the joy of coming into a new kingdom of delight with increased vigour. Moreover, as I have said, it taught me to know every woman more intimately than I had known any up to that time, and I soon found that they liked me better than even in the first flush of inexhaustible youth.

Later I learned other devices but none so important as this first discovery which showed me once for all how superior art is to nature.

*   *   *

I was to meet my fate again and unexpectedly. It was in my second year as editor of the *Evening News* and I was so confident of ultimate success in my business as a journalist that I began to go into society more and more and extend my knowledge of that wonderful pulsing life in London.

One night I went to the Lyceum Theatre. I have forgotten what was on or why I went, but I had seen the whole play and was standing talking to Bram Stoker by the door when, in the throng of people leaving, I saw Laura Clapton and her fat mother coming down the steps. She smiled radiantly at me and again I was captivated: her height gave her presence, she carried herself superbly – she was the only woman in the world for me. I could tell myself that the oval of her face was a little round, as I knew her fingers were spatulate and ugly, but to me she was more than beautiful. I had seen more perfect women, women, too, of greater distinction, but she seemed made to my desire. She must be marvellously formed, I felt, from the way she moved; and her long hazel eyes, and masses of carelessly coiled chestnut hair, and the quick smile that lit up her face – all charmed me. I went forward at once and greeted her. Her mother was unusually courteous; in the crowd I could only be polite and ask them if they would sup with me at the Criterion, for the Savoy was not known then, as Ritz had not yet come and conquered London and made its restaurants the best in the world.

'Why have you never come to see me?' was her first question.

I could only reply, 'It was too dangerous, Laura.' The confession pleased her. Shall I ever forget that supper? Not so long as this machine of mine lasts. I was in love for the first time, on my knees in love, humble for the first time, and reverent in the adoration of true love.

I remember the first time I saw the beauty of flowers: I was thirteen and had been invited to Wynnstay. We had luncheon and Lady Watkin Wynn afterwards took me into the garden and we walked between two 'herbaceous borders,' as they're called, rows four and five yards deep of every sort of flower: near the path the small flowers, then higher and higher to very tall plants – a sloping bank of beauty. For the first time I saw the glory of their colouring and the exquisite fragility of the blossoms: my senses were ravished and my eyes flooded with tears!

So, overpowering was the sensation in the theatre: the appearance of Laura took my soul with admiration. But as soon as we were together, the demands of the mother in the cab began to cool me. 'Daughter, the window must be shut! Daughter, we mustn't be late: your father – ' and so forth. But after all, what did I care; my left foot was touching Laura's and I realized with a thrill that her right foot was on the other side of mine. If I could only put my knee between hers and touch her limbs: I would try as I got up to go out and I did and the goddess responded, or at least did not move away, and her smiling, kindly glance warmed my heart.

The supper was unforgettable, for Laura had followed my work and the subtle flattery enthralled me. 'Is May Fortescue really as pretty as you made out?'

'It was surely my cue to make her lovely,' I rejoined. Laura nodded with complete understanding. She enjoyed hearing the whole story; she was particularly interested in everything pertaining to the stage.

That evening everything went on velvet. The supper was excellent, the Perrier-Jouet of 1875 – the best wine chilled, not iced; and when I drove the mother and daughter home afterwards, while the mother was getting out Laura pressed her lips on mine and I touched her firm hips as she followed her mother. I had arranged too a meeting for the morrow for lunch at Kettner's of Soho in a private room.

I went home drunk with excitement. I had taken rooms in Gray's Inn and when I entered them that night, I resolved to ask Laura to come to them after lunch, for I had bought some Chippendale chairs and some pieces of table silver of the eighteenth century that I wanted her to see.

How did I come to like old English furniture and silver? I had got to know a man in Gray's Inn, one Alfred Tennyson, a son of Frederick Tennyson, the elder brother of the great poet, and he had taught me to appreciate the recondite beauty in everything one uses. I shall have much to tell of him in later volumes of this autobiography, for, strange to say, he is still my friend here in Nice forty-odd years later. Then he was a model of manliness and vigour; only medium height, but with good features and a splendidly strong figure. His love of poetry was the first bond between us. He was a born actor, too, and mimic; he had always wished to go on the stage – a man of cultivated taste and good company. Here I just wish to acknowledge his quickening influence: I only needed to be shown the right path.

Very soon I had read all I could find about the two Adam brothers who came to London from Scotland and dowered the capital in the latter half of the eighteenth century with their own miraculous sense of beauty. The Adelphi off the Strand was named after them: even in their own time they were highly appreciated. But I was genuinely surprised to find that almost every age in England had its own ideals of beauty, and that the silverware of Queen Anne was as fine in its way as that of the Adam Brothers; and the tables of William and Mary had their own dignity, while a hall chair of Elizabeth's time showed all the stateliness of courtly manners. I began to realize that beauty was of all times and infinitely more varied than I had ever imagined. And if it was of all times, beauty was assuredly of all countries, showing subtle race-characteristics that delighted the spirit. What could be finer than the silver and furniture of the First Empire in France? A sort of reflex of classic grace of form with super-abundance of ornament, as if flowered with pride of conquest. At length I had come into the very kingdom of man and discovered the proper nourishment for my spirit. No wonder I was always grateful to Alfred Tennyson, who had shown me the key, so to speak, of the treasure-house.

It was Alfred Tennyson, too, in his rooms in Gray's Inn, who introduced me to Carlo Pellegrini. Pellegrini was a little fat Italian from the Abruzzi and Tennyson's mother was also an Italian, and she had taught her son sympathy for all those of her race. At any rate, Tennyson knew Carlo intimately, and in the eighties Carlo was a figure of some note in London life. He was the chief cartoonist of *Vanity Fair* and signed his caricatures 'Ape.' They constituted a new departure in the art: he was so kindly that his caricatures were never offensive, even to his victims. He would prowl about the lobby of the House of Commons, taking notes, and a dozen of his caricatures are among the best likenesses extant. His comrade Leslie Ward, who signed 'Spy,' was nearly as successful. A better draftsman, indeed, but content with the outward presentment of a man, not seeking, as Pellegrini sought, to depict the very soul of the sitter.

Carlo confessed to being a homesexualist, flaunted his vice, indeed, and was the first to prove to me by example that a perverted taste in sex might go with a sweet and generous nature. For Carlo Pellegrini was one of nature's saints. One trait I must give: once every fortnight he went to the office of *Vanity Fair* in the Strand and drew twenty pounds for his cartoon. He had only a couple of hundred yards to go before reaching Charing Cross and usually owed his landlady five pounds; yet he had seldom more than five pounds left out of the twenty by the time he got to the end of the street. I have seen him give five pounds to an old prostitute and add a kindly word to the gift. Sometimes, indeed, he would give away all he had got and then say with a whimsical air of humility, '*Spero che* you will invite me to dine – eh, Frank-arris?'

The best thing I can say of the English aristocracy is that this member of it and that remained his friend throughout his career and supplied his needs time and again. Lord Roseberry was one of his kindliest patrons, my friend Tennyson was another, but it was in the nineties I learned to love him, so I'll keep him for my third volume. Here I only wish to remark that his frank confession of pederasty, of the love of a man for boys and youths, made me think and then question the worth of my instinctive, or rather unreasoned, prejudice. For on reflection I was forced to admit that paederastia was practised openly and without any condemnation – nay, was even regarded as a semi-religious cult by the most virile and most courageous Greeks, by the Spartans chiefly, at the highest height of their development in the seventh and sixth and fifth centuries before our era. And what was considered honourable by Aeschylus and Sophocles and Plato was not to be condemned lightly by any thinking person. Moreover, the passion was condemned in modern days merely because it was sterile, while ordinary sex-sensuality was permissible because it produced children. But as I practised Lesbianism, which was certainly sterile, I could not but see that my aversion to paederastia was irrational and illogical, a mere personal peculiarity. Boys might surely inspire as noble a devotion as girls, though for me they had no attraction. I learned too, from Carlo Pellegrini the entrancing, attractive power of sheer loving-kindness, for in person he was a grotesque caricature of humanity, hardly more than five feet two in height, squat and stout, with a face like a mask of Socrates, and always curiously ill-dressed; yet always and everywhere a gentleman – and to those who knew him, a good deal more.

Next day I was waiting at Kettner's when Laura drove up; I hastened to pay her cab and take her upstairs. She didn't even hesitate as she entered the private room, and she kissed me with unaffected kindness. There was a subtle change in her; what was it? 'Did she love anyone else?' I asked, and she shook her head.

'I waited for you,' she said, 'but the year ran out and five months more.'

'*Mea culpa*,' I rejoined, '*mea maxima culpa*, but forgive me and I'll try to make up – '

After we had lunched, and I had locked the door against any chance intrusion of waiter or visitor, she came and sat on my knees and I kissed and embraced her almost at will but – . 'What's the matter, Laura? The red of your lips is not uniform; what have you been doing with yourself?'

'Nothing,' she replied, with an air of bewilderment. 'What do you mean?'

'You've altered,' I persisted.

'We all alter in a year and a half,' she retorted. But I was not satisfied; once when I kissed the inside of her lips, she drew back questioning.

'How strangely you kiss.'

'Does it excite you?' I asked, and a pretty *moue* was all the answer I got in words. But soon under my kissings and caresses her lips grew hot and she did not draw away as she used to do a year and a half before; she gave her lips to me and her eyes too grew long in sensuous abandonment. I stopped, for I wanted to think, and above all, I wanted a memorable gift and not a casual conquest. 'I want to show you a lot of things, Laura,' I said. 'Won't you come to my rooms in Gray's Inn and have a great afternoon? Will you come tomorrow?' And soon we had made an appointment; and after some more skirmishing kisses I took her home.

Laura lunching with me in my rooms in Gray's Inn. The mere thought took my breath, set the pulses in my temples throbbing and parched my mouth. I had already discovered the Cafe Royal, at that time by far the best restaurant in London, thanks to the owner, M. Nichol, a Frenchman, who had come to grief twice in France because he wanted to keep a really good restaurant. But now Nichol was succeeding in London beyond his wildest hopes (London always wants the best) and was indeed already rich. Nichol's daughter married and the son-in-law was charged by Nichol with the purchase of wine for the restaurant. Of course he got a commission on all he purchased, and after five and twenty years was found to have bought and bought with rare judgment more than a million pounds worth of wine beyond what was necessary. In due time I may tell the sequel. But even in 1884 and 1885 the Cafe Royal had the best cellar in the world. Fifteen years later it was the best ever seen on earth.

Already I had got to know Nichol and more than once, being in full sympathy with his ideals, had praised him in the *Evening News*. Consequently, he was always willing to do better than his best for me. So now I ordered the best lunch possible: hors d'oeuvres with caviare from Nijni; a tail piece of cold salmon-trout; and a cold grouse, fresh, not high, though as tender as if it had been kept for weeks, as I shall explain later; and to drink, a glass of Chablis with the fish, two of Haut Brion of 1878 with the grouse, and a bottle of Perrier-Jouet of 1875 to go with the sweet that was indeed a *surprise* covering fragrant wild strawberries.

Nowhere could one have found a better lunch and Laura entered into the spirit of the whole ceremony. She came as the clock struck one and had a new hat and a new dress, and, looking her best, had also her most perfect manners. Did you ever notice how a woman's manners alter with her dress? Dressed in silk she is silky gracious, the queen in the girl conscious of the rustle of the silken petticoat. I had a kiss, of course, and many an embrace as I helped her to take off her wraps. Then I showed her the lunch and expatiated on the tablesilver of the Adam brothers.

When we had finished lunch, the water was boiling and I made the coffee and then we talked interminably, for I was jealously conscious of a change in her and determined to solve the mystery. But she gave me no clue – her reticence was a bad sign, I thought; she would not admit that she had any preferred cavalier in the long year of my absence, though I had seen her twice with the same man. Still, the proof was to come. About four I took her to my bedroom and asked her to undress. 'I'm frightened,' she said. 'You do care for me?'

'I love you,' I said, 'as I've never loved anyone in my life. I'm yours; do with me what you will!'

'That's a great promise?'

'I'll keep it,' I protested.

She accepted smiling: 'Go away, sir, and come back in ten minutes.'

When I returned I had only pyjamas on, and as I went hastily to the bed I was conscious of absolute reverence: if only the dreadful doubt had not been there, it would have been adoration. As I pushed back the clothes I found she had kept her chemise on. I lifted it up and pushed it round her neck to enjoy the sight of the most beautiful body I had ever seen. But adoring plastic beauty as I do, I could only give a glance to her perfections; the next moment I had touched her sex and soon I was at work: in a minute or two I had come but went on with the slow movement till she could not but respond, and then in spite of her ever-growing excitement, as I continued she showed surprise. 'Haven't you finished?' I shook my head and kissed her, tonguing her mouth and reveling the superb body that gave itself to my every movement. Suddenly her whole frame was shaken by a sort of convulsion; as if against her will, she put her legs about me and hugged me to her. 'Stop, please!' she gasped, and I stopped; but when I would begin again, she repeated, 'Please,' and I withdrew, still holding her in my arms.

A moment later, remembering her fear, I got out of bed and showed her in the next room the *bidet* and syringe. She went in at once, but as she passed me I lifted the chemise and had more than a glimpse of the most perfect hips and legs. She smiled indulgently and turning, kissed me and passed into the dressing-room.

I felt certain now that she had given herself in that d—d year and a half to someone else. She was not a virgin, nor at her first embrace, but she had not been used much. Why? Had she been *enceinte* and got rid of the coming child? That would explain her lips, poor dear girl. If she would trust me and tell me, I would marry her; if not –

When she returned she was all cold; I lifted her into bed, and after taking off her chemise covered her till she got warm, and then bit by bit studied her figure. It was not perfect, but the faults were all merits in my eyes. Her neck was a trifle too short, but her breasts were as small as a girl's of thirteen; her hips were perfect with [an] almost flat belly, long legs and the tiniest, best-kept sex in the world. It was always perfectly clean and sweet. I have never seen one more perfect. The clitoris was just a little mound and the inner lips were glowing crimson. I began to tongue the sensitive spot, and at once she began to move spasmodically. As I touched her just below the clitoris, she squirmed violently:

'What are you doing?' she cried, trying to lift my head.

'Wait and see,' I replied, 'it's even more intense there, the sensation, isn't it?' She nodded breathlessly, and I went on; in a little while she gave herself altogether to my lips and soon began to move convulsively and then: 'Oh, Frank, oh! It's too much. I can't stand it, oh, oh, oh!' – she tried to draw away: as I persisted, she said, 'I shall scream. I can't stand it – please stop,' and as I lifted my head I saw that her love-juice had come down all over her sex. I touched the little clitoris again with my lips but she lifted my head up for a kiss and putting her arms about me strained me to her madly. 'Oh you dear, dear, dear! I want you in me, your – , please.'

Of course I did as she requested and went on working till her eyes turned up and she grew so pale – I stopped. When she got her breath again – 'I would not have believed,' she said after a while, 'that one could feel so intensely. You took my breath and then my heart was in my throat, choking me – ' Those words were my reward. I had learned the way to her supreme moment.

How we dressed I don't know, but passing through the dining-room I found myself desperately hungry and Laura confessed to the same appetite, and once more we set to on the food.

Why was Laura to me different from any other woman? She did not give me as much pleasure as Topsy; indeed, already in my life there had been at least two superior to her in the list of love, and a couple also who had flattered me more cunningly and given me proofs of a more passionate affection. Her queenly personality, the sheer brains in her, may have accounted for part of the charm. She certainly found memorable words: this first day as we were leaving the bedroom, she stopped, and putting her hands on my shoulders she said, '*Non ti scordare di me*' (Don't forget me), and then, putting her arms round my neck, 'We were one, weren't we?' and she kissed me with clinging lips.

And if it wasn't a word that ravished me, it was a gesture of sacred boldness. As she gradually came to understand how her figure delighted me, she cast off shame and showed me that the Swedish exercises she practised day after day had given her lovely body the most astonishing flexibility. She could stand with her back to a wall and, leaning back, could kiss the wall with her head almost on a level with her hips, her backbone as flexible as a bow. To me she was the most fascinating mistress and companion with a thousand different appeals. To see her in her triumphant nakedness strike an attitude and recite three or four lines, and then take the ultra-modest pose of the Florentine Venus and cover her lovely sex with her hand was a revelation in mischievous coquetry.

But now and then she complained of pains in the lower body, and I became certain that her womb had been inflamed by a wilful miscarriage: she had given herself to my American rival. If she had only been frank and told me the whole truth, I'd have forgiven her everything and the last barrier between us would have fallen, but it was not to be. She was still doubtful, perhaps of my success in life, doubtful whether I would go from victory to victory. In the humility of love I wanted to show her the reasons of my success, told her how I had learnt from newsboys, foolishly forgetting that to women ignorant of life, results alone matter:

the outward and visible sign is everything to them. It took years for her to learn that I was able to win in life wherever I wished, on the stock exchange even more easily than in journalism. And her mother was always against me, as I learned later. 'He can talk, but so can other people,' she would say with a side glance at the Irish husband, whose talking was always unsuccessful. But though our immediate surroundings were unfavourable and doubtful, when we were together Laura and I lived golden hours; and now, when I think of her, I recall occasional phrases both of love's sweet spirit and poses of her exquisite body that made me shudder with delight.

Month in, month out, we met in private once at least a week, and once a fortnight or so I took mother and daughter to the theatre and supper afterwards. In that summer I bought a house in Kensington Gore opposite Hyde Park and only a few doors away from the mansion of the Sassoons, whom I came to know later. This little house gave me a place in London society. I gave occasional dinner parties in it, helped by Lord Folkestone and the Arthur Walters, and had a very real success. I remember Mrs Walter once advising me to invite a new pianist who was certain to make a great name for himself, and the first time I met him I arranged an evening for him: a hundred society people came to hear him and went away enthusiastic admirers. It was Paderewski on his first visit to London, and mine was the first house in which he played.

Of course I would have had Laura there to hear him, but it was difficult for her to go out in the evening without her mother, and I could not stand the mother.

She made herself the centre of every gathering by rudeness if in no other way, and Laura would not hear a word criticizing her. I remember saying once to her, 'You got all your beauty and grace from your father.'

She was annoyed immediately. 'I got my skin from my mother,' she retorted, 'and my hair as well and my heart, too, which is a good thing for you, Sir, as you may find out,' and she made a face at me of exquisite childishness that enchanted me as much as her loyalty. Girls nearly always prefer their mother to their father: why?

One evening Laura and her mother came to a small evening party I gave in Kensington Gore and Mrs Lynn Linton was there, who was by way of being a great admirer of mine and a great friend. Laura sang for us: she had been admirably trained by Lamperti of Milan, whom I knew well, but she had only a small voice and her singing was of the drawing-room variety. But afterwards, feeling that she was suffering through the failure of her song, I got her to act a scene from *Phèdre* and she astonished everyone: she was a born actress of the best! Everyone praised her most warmly in spite of the mother's pinched air of disapproval: she was always against Laura's acting. But Mrs Lynn Linton took me aside and advised me to get rid of the mother: 'She's impossible; the girl's a wonder and very good to look at, you Lothario! Or are you going to marry her?'

'Marry,' I replied, 'sure,' for Laura was within hearing.

'Get rid of the mother first,' advised Mrs Lynn Linton. 'She's no friend of yours, anyone can see that. How have you offended her?' I shrugged my shoulders; have likes and dislikes any avowable reason?

I found it difficult, not to say impossible, to get any sex knowledge from Laura. Like most girls with any Irish strain in them, she disliked talking of the matter at all. I asked her, 'When did you first come to realize the facts of sex?'

'I don't really know,' she'd say. 'Girls at school talk: some elder girl tells a younger one this or that and the younger one talks of the new discovery with her chums and so the knowledge comes.'

My reverence for her was so extraordinary that although I made up my mind a dozen times to ask her had she ever excited herself as a girl, I never could.

Often, indeed, when I asked her something intimate, she would take me in her arms and kiss me to silence while her eyes danced in amusement; and if I still persisted I'd get some phrase such as, 'You have me, Sir, body and soul; what more do you want?'

Once I asked her about dancing. I had grown jealous watching her: she was picked out by the best dancers at every party and the sensuous grace of her movements attracted universal admiration. Not that she exaggerated the sensuous abandonment; on the contrary, it was only indicated now and then. As a dancer she reminded me irresistibly of Kate Vaughan, whom I always thought incomparable, the most graceful dancer I ever saw on any stage. Laura moved with the same easy exquisite rhythm, a poem in motion. But she denied always that the dance excited her sensually. 'It's the music I love,' she would say, 'the rhythm, the swaying harmony of the steps. It's as near intoxication as sense-indulgence.'

'But again and again his leg was between yours,' I insisted. 'You must have felt the thrill.' She shrugged her shoulders and would not reply. Again I began. 'You know that even your little breasts are very sensitive; as soon as my lips touch them the nipples stand out firm and glowing red and your sex is still quicker to respond. You must feel the man's figure against your most sensitive part. I believe that now and again you take care his figure should touch you: that adds the inimitable thrill now and then to your grace of movement.'

At first she seemed to hesitate, then she said thoughtfully, 'That seems to me the great difference between the man and the woman in the way of love. From what you say, it is clear that touching a woman's legs or feeling her breast would excite you, even if you didn't care for her, perhaps even if you disliked her; but such a contact doesn't excite a woman in the least, unless she loves the man. And if she loves him as soon as he comes towards her, she's thrilled; when he puts his arms round her, she's shaken with emotion! With us women it's all a question of love; with you men, sensuality takes the place of love and often leads you to cheat yourselves and us.'

'That may indeed be the truth,' I replied. 'In any case, it's the deepest insight I've heard on the matter and I'm infinitely obliged to you for it. Love then intensifies your sensations whereas it is often the keenness of our sensations that intensifies our love.'

'You men, then,' she summed up, 'have surely the lower and more material nature.'

And in my heart I had to admit that she was right.

Whenever we had been long together, her attraction for me was so overpowering that it always excited suspicion in me. I don't know why; I state the fact: I was never sure of her love.

CHARLES DEVEREAUX

from
Venus in India

Venus in India or Love Adventures in Hindustan *was first published in Brussels in 1889 and is one of the best written Victorian erotic novels. Little is known about the author but it is presumed he was an army officer serving in India and if we are to believe him a sexual athlete.*

THE war in Afghanistan appeared to be coming to a close when I received sudden orders to proceed, at once, from England to join the First Battalion of my regiment, which was then serving there. I had just been promoted Captain and had been married about eighteen months. It pained me more than I care to express to part with my wife and baby girl, but it was agreed that it would be better for all of us, if their coming to India were deferred until it were certain where my regiment would be quartered, on its return to the fertile plains of Hindustan, from the stones and rocks of barren Afghanistan. Besides, it was very hot, being the height of the hot weather, when only those who were absolutely forced to do so went to India, and it was a time of year particularly unsuitable for a delicate woman and a babe to travel in so burning a climate. It was also not quite certain whether my wife would join me in India, as I had the promise of a staff appointment at home, but before I could enter upon that I had of necessity to join my own battalion, because it was at the seat of war. Thus it was annoying to have to go, all the same, as it was clear that the war was over, and that I should be much too late to participate in any of its rewards or glories, though it was quite possible I might come in for much of the hardship and experience of the sojourn, for a wild, and not to say rough and inhospitable country is Afghanistan; besides which it was quite possible for an Afghan knife to put an end to me, and that I might fall a victim to a common murder instead of dying a glorious death on the battlefield.

Altogether my prospects seemed by no means of a rosy colour, but there was nothing for it but to submit and go, which I did with the best grace possible but with a very heavy heart.

I will spare the readers the sad details of parting with my wife. I made no promise of fidelity, the idea seemed never to occur to her or to myself of there being any need for it, for although I had always been of that temperament so dear to Venus, and had enjoyed the pleasure of love with great good fortune before I married, yet I had, as I thought, quite steadied down into a proper married man, whose desires never wandered outside his own bed; for my passionate and loving spouse was ever ready to respond to my ardent caresses with caresses as ardent; and her charms, in their youthful beauty and freshness, had not only not palled upon me, but seemed to grow more and more powerfully attractive the more I revelled in their possession. For my dearest wife, gentle reader, was the life of passion; she was not one of those who coldly submit to their husbands' caresses because it is their duty to do so, a duty however not to be done with pleasure or joyfully, but more as a species of penance! No! With her it was not, 'Ah! no! let me sleep tonight, dear. I did it twice last night, and I really don't think you can want it again. You should be more chaste, and not try me as if I were your toy and plaything. No! take your hand away! Do leave my nightdress alone! I declare it is quite indecent the way you are behaving!' and so forth, until, worn out with her husband's pertinacity, she thinks the shortest way, after all, will be to let him have his way, and so grudgingly allows her cold slit to be uncovered, unwillingly opens her ungracious thighs, and lies a passionless log, insensible to her husband's endeavours to strike a spark of pleasure from her icy charms. Ah! no! With my sweet Louie it was far different; caress replied to caress, embrace to embrace. Each sweet sacrifice became sweeter than the one before, because she fully appreciated all the joy and delight of it! It is almost impossible to have too much of such a woman, and Louie seemed to think it quite impossible to have too much of me! It was, 'Once more my darling! Just one *little* more! I am sure it will do you good! and I should like it!' and it would be strange if the manly charm which filled her loving hand, were not once more raised in response to her caresses, and once again carrying rapturous delight to the deepest, richest depths of the trembling voluptuous charm, for the special benefit of which it was formed, a charm which was indeed the very temple of love.

Ah! My beloved Louie! Little did I think the last time I withdrew from thy tender passionate embrace, that between thy throbbing sheath and my sword there were waiting for me, in glowing India, all unknown and unsuspected, other voluptuous women, whose beautiful naked charms were to form my couch, and whose lovely limbs were to bind me in ecstatic embrace, before I should once more find myself again between thy tender, loving thighs! It is best too that thou should'st not know that so it was, for who is there that does not know the dire effects of green-eyed jealousy? Thanks be to tender Venus for having raised an imperious cloud, and hidden my sportings with my nymphs, as in olden days Great Jupiter was hidden from the sight of the Gods and men, when he revelled on the green mountain sides, with the lovely maidens, human or divine, whose beauteous charms formed the object of his passion.

But it is time to descend to earth again and to tell my tale in a manner more befitting this common-place world. Already, dear reader, I have, I fear, trespassed in so far that I have perhaps shocked your modest eyes with the name of that sweetest of feminine charms, which neither sculptor or painter will produce in their works, and which is seldom mentioned in public, except by the low and vulgar; yet I must crave your pardon, and beg you to permit me to offer it here of my pen, else I shall feel it difficult to describe, as I hope to all the full joys I so happily revelled in during the five happy years I spent in Hindustan. If you are wise, if you love to have your senses sweetly tickled, if the usually hidden scenes and secrets of delicious combats of love, of the fulfilment of hot desire, of the happy lovers, have any delight for you then simply imagine that your moist eyes see the charm, but not the name or action, and not the words by which I find it necessary to describe it.

It was in the middle of August when I landed in Bombay, that queenly capital of Western India. The voyage had been unimportant. Our passengers had been few and stupid, chiefly old Indian Civilians and officers returning unwillingly to the scenes of their labours in the hot country, after a short spell of life in England. It was not the season of the year when sprightly young ladies go out to India, each one with the fine hope in her heart that her rounded, youthful charms, her cheeks glowing with health, and her freshness might captivate a husband. We were a staid party; some like myself had left young wives at home; others were accompanied by theirs; all were of an age when time had softened down the burning ardours of passion, and when perhaps the last thought to enter their heads, on retiring at night to rest, was to take advantage of the ruined remains of beauty which reposed by their sides. Presently I landed feeling that all love, passion, desire and affection were left behind me, with my darling little wife in England, and that the all but naked, graceful charms of native girls carrying their water pots, could not but strike my eye when I first landed, no spark of desire for a moment made my blood run quicker, nor caused me for a moment to think that I could ever seek enjoyment in the embraces of any woman much less of a dusky maiden! And yet within only ten short days! Verily, the spirit is willing but the flesh is weak! But let us put it thus, the spirit may be willing, but when the flesh rises in all its vigorous power its strength is indomitable! or, so I found it to be! And now, gentle reader, I am sure you are curious and anxious to know who it was who raised my flesh, and whether I made that resistance of its impervious demands which a husband of such a Louie as mine, should, by right have made.

Having ascertained from the Adjutant General, that my destination was Cherat, a small camping ground, as I heard, on the top of a range of mountains forming the Southern Limit of the Valley of the Peshawar, and having received railroad warrants, via Allahabad, for the temporary station of Jhelum, and dak warrants from the spot to Cherat itself, I made my preparations for the long journey which still lay before me, and amongst other necessaries for mind and body I purchased some French novels. One of these was that masterpiece of drawing-room erotic literature, *Mademoiselle de Maupin*, by Theophile Gautier. But for the burning pictures of love and passion, drawn in the wonderful prose poem, perhaps I might have escaped from the nets in which love entangled me, for of a surety Mademoiselle de Maupin was a tempting bait which summoned my passions from the lethargy into which they had fallen since I had parted with my beloved, yet virtuous little wife, my adored Louie! I declare, dear reader, that I thought I had sown my wild oats, that I had become what the French call 'range' and that it lay not in the power of women to seduce me from the path of virtue, along which it seemed to me, and I believed firmly, that I was treading with certain steps, to the road to sanctity and heaven! So long as I had the protecting aegis of the beautiful and lovely charms of my darling little wife, I was, no doubt, quite safe, for frankly, now that I come to look over the past, I quite see why the tempter's darts fell all unheeded by me. Where could I find another girl, clothed or naked, who could compare with my Louie? She simply eclipsed all others. Like the full moon, shining on a cloudless night, she put out the light of the stars! Alas! when she was absent, the stars began to shine again to find places in my heart for admiration and adoration. I had not thought of this! Had my Louie? And oh! how tender, how passionately voluptuous had the last few weeks of my sojourn at home been! How many times had the fervent protestations of love and faith in one another's unspottable purity of affection been sealed by the rapturous blissful sacrifice, when clasped in one another's arms our bodies became as one, and the fountains of inexpressible bliss, set gushing by our voluptuous enlacements, we inundated one another with seas of enjoyment. These sacrifices, so exquisite, so full of fire and action, had undoubtedly, their aftereffects on me, for some few weeks Louie had, by the power of her never-dying charms, exhausted me of my present stock of that manly strength, that essence of my heart's blood, that marrow of my body, without which physical love is impossible, and it seemed to me that on leaving her I had left that power behind me; that all my desires, together with my manly vigour, were deposited for safe keeping in her exquisite grotto, and that I should not find them again until, once more with her I might seek them between her beloved thighs.

So I bought *Mademoiselle de Maupin* not caring whether it treated of passion or not, and all alone in my railway carriage I read *Mlle. de Maupin*, but alas! of human frailty! Desire, hot and burning desire, the power, and floods of hot, hot feeling came back to me! I drank the delicious poison of that matchless book, and as I drank I burnt! and yet I would not own to myself that in my deepest heart it was 'woman' I felt a raging thirst for. At present desire simply assumed the shadowy form, a kind of image of a woman the nearest approach to which was to be found in far off England, in the body of my own adored and beautiful little wife!

The route from Bombay via Allahabad to Peshawar runs almost entirely through a country as flat as a table. At the season of year, August, when I traversed it, the land dry, parching weather had apparently not been tempered by the rains, which usually fall between June and September. Here and there green waving crops, contrasted with the otherwise generally brown, burnt up soil, and there were few stretches of country which formed such attraction for the eyes as to call for mental appreciation, in comparison with the charms of the beautiful Mlle. De Maupin, especially as painted by Theophile Gautier, in that glowing chapter where she appears in all her glowing beauty, naked, and burning with tormenting desire, before the eyes of her enraptured lover! oh! Theophile! Why did you not allow your pen to describe, with a little more freedom, those undraped beauties? Why did you not permit us to do more than fancy the exquisite pleasures which the panting lovers experienced on their voluptuous couch? I felt that such minute painting was what was wanted to complete the rapturous sensations raised by that marvellous romance, and, gentle reader, I pray you not to exclaim and cry out, for in these pages I endeavour to avoid the one fault I find with Gautier. May Venus guide my pen and Eros hold the inkstand, and mayest thou, shade of the illustrious French poet and author, assist in these compilations of my reminiscences of the happy five years I spent in India.

Only once on this journey, about which I fear I may become so tedious did the tempter accost me, and then so clumsily as quite to prostrate his well-meant intentions. I had to make a few hours stay in Allahabad and to pass that away pleasantly I wandered about, examining the tombs of the kings and princes, who reigned in past times over the banks of the Ganges and the Jumna, and in seeing such sights as I could find to amuse and interest me.

As I was returning to my hotel a native accosted me in very good English.

'Like to have woman, Sahib? I got one very pretty little half-caste in my house, if master like to come and see!'

Oh! dear Mademoiselle de Maupin!

I felt no desire to see the pretty little half-caste! I put this self-abnegation down to virtue, and actually laughed, in my folly, at the idea that there existed, or could exist, a woman in India, who could raise even a ghost of desire in me!

The station beyond Jhelum is reached, I having but one mighty river to pass before I leave the bounds of India proper and tread the outskirts of Central Asia, in the valley of the Peshawar. But it took some two or three days and nights of continuous travel, in a dak gharry, before I reached Attock. The dak gharry is a fairly comfortable mode of conveyance, but one becomes tired of the eternal horizontal position which is the only one which gives any comfort to the weary traveller. Crossing the Indus in a boat rowed over a frightful torrent with the roar of the waters breaking on the rocks below the ferry, was a very exciting incident, especially as it happened at night, and the dark gloom added to its magnifying effect, to the roar of the suspected danger. Then again another dak gharry into which I got, lay down and went to sleep, not to waken until I reached Nowshera.

Ah! Mademoiselle de Maupin! What a lovely girl! Who can she be! She must I fancy, be the daughter of the Colonel commanding here, out for her morning walk, and perhaps, judging from the keen expectant glance shot in at me through the half-open sliding door of the gharry, she's expecting somebody, perhaps her fiancé; perhaps that is why she looked so eager and yet so disappointed!

Oh, dear reader! just as I opened my eyes I saw, through the half-open door a perfect figure of feminine beauty! A girl clothed in close-fitting grey-coloured dress with a Teria hat archly sloped on her lovely and well-shaped head! That beautiful face! How perfect the oval of it! Truly she must have aristocratic blood in her veins to be so daintily formed! What a rosebud of a mouth! What cherry lips! God! Jupiter! Venus! What a form! See those exquisite rounded shoulders, those full and beautiful arms, the shape of each can be so plainly seen so close does her dress fit her: and how pure, how virgin-like is that undulating bosom! See how proudly each swelling breast fills out her modest but still desire-provoking bodice! Ah! The little shell-like ears, fitting so close to the head! How I would like to have the privilege of gently pressing those tiny lobes! What a lovely creature she looks! How refined! How pure! How virginal! Ah! My Louie, like you this girl is not to be tempted, and long and arduous would be the chase before she could be compelled to own that her failing strength must yield her charms to the hands and lips of her panting pursuer! No! That girl, of all girls I have seen, struck me as one not to be seduced from the path of purity and honour.

And all these impressions flashed through my mind from a glimpse, a very vivid glimpse it is true, that I had of this lovely girl which I caught of her as my gharryman was urging his jaded steeds to a smart gallop, so that the Sahib might enter Nowshera in proper grand style!

The vision so short and so rapid, appeared to make but little impression on me, or rather, I should say, my sensations did not go beyond the sensations I have given above. Hot desire did not set my blood boiling or my heart and sense afire. I think it was rather the other way. I admired, indeed, as I might also admire a perfect Venus in marble. Shape and form pleased my eyes, and although the idea, that this lovely girl might be possessed some day by someone, did enter my head, it only entered in the same way as that the marble Venus might become flesh and blood and form the happy delight of some fortunate mortal. In other words, she seemed absolutely and completely removed from ordinary mankind, and I never dreamt that I should ever see her mound, as, according to my ideas, I was going to change horses at Nowshera, and proceed immediately to Cherat.

But on arriving at the post office, which was also the place for changing horses, the post master, a civil spoken Baboo, told me that he could give me horses only as far as Publi, a village about halfway between Nowshera and Peshawar, and that from that place I must make the best of my way to Cherat, for there was no road along which dak gharries could be driven, and my good Baboo added that the said interval between Publi and Cherat was dangerous for travellers, there being many lawless robbers. Moreover, he added, that the distance was a good fifteen miles. He advised me to put up at the Public Bungalow at Nowshera, until the Brigade Major could put me in the way of completing my journey.

This information was a great surprise and a great damper to me! How on earth was I to get to Cherat with my baggage if there was no road? How could I do fifteen miles under such circumstances? To think I had gone so many thousand miles, since I had left England, to be balked by a miserable little fifteen. However, for the present there seemed nothing to be done but to take the excellent Baboo's advice, put up at the Public Bungalow and see the Brigade Major.

The Public Bungalow stood in its own compound, a little distance from the high road, and to get back to it I had to drive back part of the road I had travelled. I dismissed my driver, and called the Khansamah, who informed me that the bungalow was full, and that there was no room for me! Here was a pretty state of affairs! but whilst I was speaking to the Khansamah, a pleasant-looking young officer, lifting the chick which hung over the entrance to his room, came out into the verandah, and told me that he had heard what I was saying, that he was only waiting for a gharry to proceed on his journey down country, and that my coming was as opportune for him, as his going would be for me. He had, he said, sent at once to secure my dak gharry, and if he could get it, he would give up his room to me, but anyhow, I should, if I did not dislike the idea, share his room which contained two bedsteads. Needless to say I was delighted to accept his kind offer, and I soon had my goods inside the room, and was enjoying that most essential and refreshing thing in India, a nice cool bath. My new friend had taken upon himself to order breakfast for me, and when I had completed my ablutions and toilet, we sat down together. Officers meeting in this manner, very quickly become like old friends. My new acquaintance told me all about himself, where he had been, where he was going to, and I reciprocated. Needless to say the war, which was now practically over, formed the great topic of our general conversation. Getting more intimate, we of course fell, as young men, or old too do, for the matter of that, to discussing about love and women, and my young friend told me that the entire British Army was just simply raging for women! That none were to be got in Afghanistan, and that, taking it as a general rule, neither officers nor men had had a woman for at least two years.

'By George!' he cried as he laughed, 'the Peshawar Polls are reaping a rich harvest! As fast as a regiment arrives from Afghanistan, the whole, boiling, rush off to bazaars, and you can see the Tommy Atkins waiting outside the knocking shops, holding their staffs in their hands, and roaring out to those having women to look sharp!'

This was of course an exaggeration, but not to so great an extent as my gentle reader may suppose.

We had just finished our cheroots after breakfast, when the young officer's servant drove up in the same dak gharry which had brought me in from Attock, and in a few minutes my cheerful host was shaking hands with me.

'There's somebody in there,' he said, pointing to the next room, 'to whom I must say goodbye, and then I'm off.'

He was not long absent, again shook my hands, and in another minute a sea of dust hid him and the gharry from my sight.

I felt quite lonely and sad, when he was gone, for, although the bungalow was full, I was left in a small portion of it walled off from the rest, so that I didn't see any of its other occupants, though I might occasionally hear them. I had forgotten to ask who my next door neighbour was, and indeed I did not much care. I was so bothered, wondering how I should get up to Cherat. It was now nearly ten o'clock, the sun was pouring sheets of killing rays of light on the parched plain in which Nowshera is situated, and the hot wind was beginning to blow, parching one up, and making lips and eyes quite sore as well as dry. I did not know what to do with myself. It was much too hot to think of going to the Brigade Major's, so I got another cheroot, and taking my delightful Mademoiselle de Maupin out of my bag, I went and sat behind a pillar on the verandah, to shelter myself from the full force of the blast and try to read; but even this most charming damsel failed to charm, and I sank back in my chair and smoked listlessly whilst my eyes wandered over the range of lofty mountains which I could just distinguish quivering through hot yellow-looking air. I did not know at the moment that I was looking at Cherat, and had I had a prescience of what was waiting for me there, I should certainly have gazed upon these hills with far greater interest than I did.

Reader dear, do you know what it is to feel that somebody is looking at you, though you may not be able to see him, nor are aware for a fact that somebody is looking at you? I am extremely susceptible to this influence. Whilst sitting thus idly looking at the most distant thing my eyes could find to rest upon, I began to feel that someone was near, and looking intently at me. At first I resisted the temptation to look round to see who it was. What with the hot wind, and what with the circumstances of the sudden halt I was compelled to make, I felt so irritable, that I resented, as an insult, the looking at me which I felt certain was going on; but at last this strange sensation added to my unrest and I half-turned my head to see whether it was reality or feverish fancy.

My surprise was unbounded when I saw the same lovely face, which I had caught a glimpse of that morning, looking at me from behind the slightly opened chick, of the room next to mine. I was so startled that instead of taking a good look at the lady I instantly gazed on the hills again, as if turning my head to look in her direction had been a breach of good manners on my part; but I felt she was still keeping her eyes fixed on me, and it amazed me that any one of the position which I imagined she held, for I was firmly convinced that I was right as to my surmise that my unknown beauty was a lady, and a Colonel's daughter, she should be guilty of such bad manners as to stare at a perfect stranger in this manner. I turned my head once more, and this time I looked at this lovely but strange girl a little more fixedly. Her eyes, large, lustrous, most beautiful, seemed to pierce mine, as though trying to read my thoughts. For a moment I fancied she must be a little off her head, when, apparently satisfied, with her reconnaissance, the fair creature let the chick fall once more against the side of the door and so was lost to my sight. From that moment my curiosity was greatly aroused. Who was she? Was she alone? Or was she with the unknown Colonel in that room? Why was she staring at me so hard? By Jove! There she is at it again! I could stand it no longer. I jumped up and went into my own room and called the Khansamah.

'Khansamah: who is in the room next to mine?' and I pointed to the door which communicated with the room the lady was in, and which was closed.

A Mem Sahib! Now I had been in India before, this was my second tour of service in the country, and I knew that a Mem Sahib meant a married lady. I was surprised, for had anyone asked me, I should have said that this lovely girl had never known a man, had never been had, and never would be had, unless she met the man of men who pleased her. It was extraordinary how this idea had taken root in my mind.

'Is the Sahib with her?'

'No, Sahib!'

'Where is he?'

'I don't know, Sahib.'

'When did the Mem Sahib come here, Khan?'

'A week or ten days ago, Sahib!'

'Is she going away soon?'

'I don't know, Sahib!'

It was plain I could get no information from this man, only one more question and I was done.

'Is the Mem Sahib quite alone, Khan?'

'Yes, Sahib: she has no one with her, not even an Ayah.'

Well! this is wonderful! How well did my young friend, who had only gone away this morning, know her? You, gentle reader, with experience, have no doubt your suspicions are that all was not right, but for the life of me I could not shake off the firm notion that this woman was not only a lady, but one exceptionally pure and highly connected.

I went back to my seat on the verandah, waiting to be looked at again, and I did not wait long. A slight rustle caught my ear, I looked around and there was my lovely girl showing more of herself. She still looked with the same eager gaze without the sign of a smile on her face. She appeared to be in her petticoats only, and her legs and feet, such lovely, tiny, beautiful feet, and such exquisitely turned ankles, were bare; she had not even a pair of slippers on. A light shawl covered her shoulders and bosom, but did not hide either her full well-shaped, white arms, her taper waist or her splendid and broad hips. These naked feet and legs inspired me with a sudden flow of desire, as much as her lovely face and its wonderful calm, yet her severe expression, had driven all such thoughts from my mind. Jacques Casanova, who certainly is a perfect authority on all that concerns women, declares that curiosity is the foundation on which desire is built, that, but for that, a man would be perfectly contented with one woman, since in the main all women are alike; yet from mere curiosity a man is impelled to approach a woman, and to wish for her possession. Something akin to this certainly influenced me. A devouring curiosity took possession of me. This exquisite girl's face inspired me to know how she could possibly be all alone here at Nowshera, in a public bungalow, and her lovely naked feet and legs, made me wonder whether her knees and thighs corresponded with them in perfect beauty, and my imagination painted to my mind a voluptuous motte and delicious slit, shaded by dark locks corresponding to the colour of the lovely eyebrows, which arched over those expressive orbs. I rose from my chair and moved towards her. She instantly withdrew and as instantly again opened the chick. For the first time I saw a smile wreathe her face. What a wonderfully different expression that smile gave it! Two lovely dimples appeared in her rounded cheeks, her rosy lips parted and displayed two rows of small perfectly even teeth, and those eyes which had looked so stern and almost forbidding, now looked all tenderness and softness.

'You must find it very hot out there in the verandah!' said she, in a low, musical voice, but with a rather vulgar, common accent which at first grated on my ear, 'and I know you are all alone! Won't you come into my room and sit down and chat? You will if you are a good fellow!'

'Thank you!' said I smiling and bowing, as I threw away my cheroot and entered whilst she held the chick so as to make room for me to pass. I caught the chick in my hand, but she still kept her arm raised, and extended; her shawl fell a little off her bosom which was almost entirely bare, and I saw not only two most exquisitely round, full and polished globes of ivory, but even the rosy coral marble which adorned the peak of one of them. I could see that she caught the direction of my glance, but she was in no hurry to lower her arm, and I judged, and rightly, that this liberal display of her charms was by no means unintentional.

'I have got two chairs in here,' said she, laughing such a sweet sounding laugh, 'but we can sit together on my bed, if you don't mind!'

'I shall be delighted,' said I, 'if sitting without a back to support you won't tire you!'

'Oh!' said she, in the most innocent manner, 'you just put your arm round my waist, and then I won't feel tired.'

Had it not been for the extraordinary innocent tone with which she said this, I think I should at once have lain her back and got on top of her, but a new idea struck me; could she be quite sane? And would not such an action be the very height of blackguardism?

However, I sat down, as she bade me do, and I slipped my left arm around her slender waist and gave her a little hug towards me.

'Ah!' she said, 'that's right! Hold me tight! I love being held tight!'

I found that she had no stays on at all. There was nothing between my hand and her smooth skin but a petticoat body, and a chemise of very light muslin. She felt so awfully nice! There's something so thrilling in feeling the warm, palpitating body of a lovely woman in one's arms, that it was only natural that not only did my blood run more quickly, but I began to feel what the French call the 'pricking of the flesh'. There she was, this really beautiful creature, half-naked and palpitating, her cheeks glowing with health, though paler than one is accustomed to see in our more temporate Europe, her lovely shining shoulders and bosom almost perfectly naked, and so exquisite! The nearer I got my eyes to the skin the better did I see how fine was its texture. The bloom of youth was on it. There were no ugly hollows to show where the flesh had receded and the bones projected. Her beautiful breasts were round, plump and firm looking. I longed to take possession of those lovely, lovely bubbies! To press them in my hand, to devour them and their rosy tips with my mouth! Her petticoats fell between her slightly parted thighs and showed their roundness and beautiful form perfectly as though to provoke my desire the more, desire she must have known was burning me, for she could feel the palpitating of my agitated heart, even if a glance of her eyes in another and lower direction did not betray to her the effect her touch and her beauty had on me, she held out one and then the other of her fairy feet, so white and perfect, as though to display them to my eager eyes. The soft and delicious perfume which only emanates from woman in her youth, stole in fragrant clouds over my face, and her abundant wavy hair felt like silk against my cheek.

Was she mad? That was the tormenting thought which would spring up between my hand and the glowing charms it longed to seize! For some few moments we sat in silence. Then I felt her hand creep up under my white jacket and toy with the buttons to which my braces were fastened behind. She undid one side of my brace and as she did so said:

'I saw you this morning! You were in a dak gharry and I just caught a glimpse of you.'

Her hand began to work at the other button. What the deuce was she up to?

'Oh yes!' I said, looking into her small eyes and returning the sharp glances which shot from them, 'and I saw you too! I had been fast asleep, and just as I opened my eyes my sight fell upon you! and I . . .'

She had unbuttoned my braces behind, and now stole her hand round and laid it, back up, on the top of my thigh.

'And you what?' said she, gently sliding her extended fingers down over the inside of my thigh: she was within a nail's breadth of the side of my rod which was now standing furiously!

'Oh!' I exclaimed, 'I thought I had never seen such a lovely face and figure in the world!'

The fingertips actually touched Johnnie! She slightly pressed them against him, and looking at me again with the sweetest smile, said:

'Did you really! Well! I'm glad you did, for do you know what I thought, when I saw you lying inside the gharry?'

'No, dear!'

'Well! I thought that I would not mind if I had been travelling with such a fine looking, handsome young man!'

Then after a short pause she continued, 'So you think me well made?' And she glanced down proudly on her swelling breast.

'Indeed then I do!' I exclaimed, quite unable to restrain myself any longer. 'I don't know when I ever saw such a lovely bosom as this, and such tempting, luscious bubbies!' and I slipped my hand into her bosom and seized a glowing globe and as I pressed it gently and squeezed the hard little nipples between my fingers, I kissed the lovely upturned mouth which was presented to me.

'Ah!' she cried, 'who gave you leave to do that? Well! Exchange is no robbery and I will have something nice of yours to feel for myself too!'

Her nimble fingers had my trousers unbuttoned, my braces undone in front too, and with a whisk of her hand she had my shirt out, and with it my burning, maddened stallion, of which she took immediate and instant possession.

'Ah!' she cried, 'Ah! oh! what a beauty! How handsome! bell topped! and so big! Isn't he just about stiff! He's like a bar of iron! and what fine big eggs you've got! My beautiful man! Oh! How I would like to empty them for you! Oh! you'll have me now! Won't you? do! do! oh! I feel that I could come so nicely if you only would!'

Would I have her? Why! Gods in Heaven! how could mortal man brimful of health, strength, youth and energy like myself, resist such an appeal to his ears and senses, and not comply, even if the fair petitioner were not half nor a quarter as beautiful as this lascivious and exquisite creature, whose hands were manipulating the most tenderly sensitive parts which man possesses! For all reply I gently pulled her on her back, she still kept a firm but voluptuous hold on her possessions, and I turned up her petticoat and chemise, and gliding my burning hand over the smooth surface of her ivory thigh, up to, I think, the most voluptuous bush I had ever seen or felt in my life! Never had my hand reposed on so voluptuous and full a motte. Never had my fingers probed charm so full of life and so soft outside, so smooth and velvety inside as it did now, that this most perfect place, and the domain around and above it, were in my possession! I was eager to get between her lovely thighs, and to snatch my almost painfully strained organ from her hands, and bury it up to its hilt, and further, in this melting charm, but she stopped me. With her face and bosom flushed, her eyes dancing in her head, and a voice choked with the greatest excitement she cried:

'Let us put on our skins first!'

I was standing before her, my sword at an angle of at least seventy degrees, my sack and groin arching, for the most vigorous action had set in, and my reservoirs had already been filled to the utmost they could hold. I felt I must either have this beautiful wild girl or burst!

'What do you mean?' I gasped.

'I'll show you! See!'

And in a moment she had, as it were, jumped out of her clothes, and stood, all naked and glowing, and radiant with beauty, real by all that is voluptuous and erotic before me.

In a moment or perhaps a little longer, for I had boots and socks as well as coat, shirt and trousers to take off, but at all events, in a brace of shakes, I was as naked as she! I can shut my eyes now and there before me I see this exquisitely formed creature, surely, quite the equal of the beautiful Mademoiselle de Maupin, standing in all her radiant nudity before me. That form so purely perfect so inimitably graceful, those matchless limbs! That bosom with its hills of living snow topped with rosy fire and that more than voluptuous motte, a perfect 'hill of Venus', clothed with the richest dark bushes of curly hair, sloping rapidly down, like a triangle standing on its point, until its two sides, folding in, form the deep soft-looking and inside line, which proclaimed the very perfection of a Goddess. The only thing which slightly marred this perfect galaxy of beauty was the occurrence of some slight wrinkles, which like fine lines crossed the otherwise perfect plain of her fair belly, that exquisite belly with its dimpling navel!

Gods! I rushed at this lovely creature, and in another moment I was on top of her, between her wide-opened thighs and resting on her beautiful bosom. How elastic did her beautiful bubbies feel against my chest! and how soft, how inexpressibly delicious, did her cavern feel, as inch by inch I buried Johnnie in it, until my motte jammed against hers, and my eggs hanging, or rather squeezed, against her lovely white bottom. I could get in no further. And what a woman to have! Every movement of mine brought forth an exclamation of delight from her! To hear her you would have imagined it was the very first time her senses had been powerfully excited from their very foundation! Her hands were never still, they promenaded over me, from the back of my head to the intimate limits of my body to which they could reach. She was simply perfect in the art of giving and receiving pleasure. Every transport of mine was returned with interest, every mad thrust met with a corresponding buck which had the effect of taking my engine into its extreme root! And she seemed to do nothing but 'come' or 'spend'! I had heard of a woman 'coming' thirteen or fourteen times during one session, but this woman seemed to do nothing else from beginning to end. But, it was not until I had arrived at the exciting, furious, ardent, almost violent short digs, that I knew to what an intense degree my Venus enjoyed pleasure! I thought she was in a fit! She almost screamed! She gurgled in her throat! She half-crushed me in her arms, and putting her feet on my behind, she pressed me to her motte, at the end, with a power I should never have thought she possessed. Oh! the relief! the exquisite delight of the spend on my part! I inundated her, and she felt the spouting torrents of my love darting in hot, quick jets, and striking against the deepest part of her almost maddened cleft! She seized my mouth with hers, and shot her tongue into it as far as she could, touching my palate, and pouring her hot, delicious breath down my throat whilst her whole body from head to heel literally quivered with the tremendous excitement she was in! Never in my life had I such a fling! Oh! why are there no better words to express what is really heaven upon earth?

The tempest past, we lay in one another's arms; tenderly gazing into one another's eyes. We were too breathless to speak at first. I could feel her belly heaving against mine, and her throbbing cunnie clasped my tool as though it had been another hand, whilst her motte leaped and bounded! I looked into that angelic-looking face, and drank in the intense beauty of it, nor could I believe it could be an abandoned woman, but rather Venus herself, whom I held thus clasped in my arms, and whose tender and voluptuous thighs encircled mine! I could have wished that she held her peace and let me dream that I was the much desired Adonis, and she my persistent, longing Venus, and that I had at length won her amorous wishes, and found the heaven in her arms of which, before I entered her matchless cleft, I had no notion. But my airy fancies were dispelled by her saying:

'You are a good poke and no mistake! Oh! You know how to do it! No fellow ever rams like that without he has been taught!'

'Yes!' I said, pressing her in my arms and kissing the ruby lips which had just spoken so coarsely but truly, and pointedly, 'I have been well trained! I had good lessons in my boyhood, and I have always tried to practise them as often as possible!'

'Ah!' she said. 'I thought so! You do the heel-and-toe better than any man I've ever had, and I've had, I dare say, many more men than you've had women!'

Frank and how!

'What do you mean by heel-and-toe, my pet!'

'Oh! Don't you know? You do it at any rate! And splendid! Heel-and-toe is to begin each stroke at the very beginning and end it at the very end. Just give me one long stroke now!' I did so. I withdrew until I was all but out of her panting orifice, and then gently but firmly drove it home, as far and as deep as I could, and then I rested again on her belly.

'There,' she cried, 'that's it! You almost pull it out, but not quite, and never stop short in your thrusts, but send it home, with a sharp rap of your cods against my bottom! and that's what's good!'

And she appeared to smack her lips involuntarily.

At length I withdrew, and my fairest nymph at once commenced a most minute examination of that part of me and its appendages which had pleased her so much. Everything was, according to her, absolutely perfect, and if I were to believe her there had not passed under her observation so noble and handsome an organ, and such beautiful, well balanced stones as I had and she was the mistress of! My stones especially pleased her! She said they were so big! She was sure they must be full of spend, and she intended, she told me, to empty them before she would consent to my leaving Nowshera!

This first sacrifice simply whetted our appetites, and still more inflamed with the minute examination of one another's charms, we fell to again, and writhed in the delicious agonies of another amorous combat! It was about two o'clock before I left her, and we had not been at any one time more than ten minutes 'out of action'. The more I had of this exquisite creature, the more I longed to have her. I was fresh, young, strong, vigorous, and it was nearly two months (a long time for me) since I had last indulged in the delights of Cyprian pleasures. No wonder my Venus was pleased with me, and called my performances a perfect feast.

They say that love destroys appetite for food. Perhaps it does when it is love unrequited, but I give you my word, dear reader, that I was ravenous for my tiffin after my morning's work. I was really glad to get something to eat, for what with the heat of the combats I had been through, and the parching effect of the terrible hot wind blowing, I was dried up, as far as my mouth was concerned, though far from being so as regards the proceeds of my sack. I never felt so fit for woman as I did that day, and I never probably have had so much joy with so little loss of physical force. Doubtless my steady married life with its regular hours, regular meals, and regular, never-excessive sacrifices on the altar of Venus had much to do with the steady power I felt so strong in me, but over and above that, was the fact of my new lady love being extraordinarily beautiful, and voluptuously lascivious, and the erotic excitement raised in me, was, of course, great in proportion to the cause which gave birth to it. In spite of my hunger for food, I would certainly have remained with her on that most genial of beds, and have revelled on in her joyous arms, and filled her with quintessence of my manly vigour, but she told me she always slept in the afternoon, was hungry herself, and, doubting my power, she wished me to reserve some good portions of my force to be expended between her lovely thighs that night and for the solace of her liveliest of crannies.

Whilst the Khansamah was laying the table I saw a note addressed to me, leaning against the wall, on the mantelpiece, (for in Northern India the winters are sharp enough to render a fire not only pleasant but sometimes quite necessary), and taking it and opening it, wondering who the writer could be, as I was perfectly unknown in this part of the world, I found it to be from my young officer friend who had quitted Nowshera this morning, it ran thus:

'Dear Devereaux: – In the room next to yours is one of the loveliest of women and best of pokes! Verbum Sap!*

Yours,
J.C.

P.S. – Don't offer her any rupees or you will offend her mortally, but if you are inclined to have her, and I think you will on seeing her, just tell her so and you won't have to ask twice.'

* Probably J.C. means to quote Terence, 'Dictum sapienti sat est'. (A word to the wise is sufficient.)

Ah! Dear young chap, now I understand why you were so reticent this morning and did not like to tell me that I had a lady for my next door neighbour! Well! Poor girl! I am afraid that you must be put down as one of the 'irregulars', although it is a shame to think ill of one who has given me the first few hours of real delight since I left home!

These thoughts naturally brought my beloved little wife into my recollection and I was somewhat staggered to feel I should so completely have forgotten her and my marital vows! But I was altogether too full of desire. Desire only just whetted and crying for more! More! I was in fact half mad with what some call lust and others love and, wife or no wife, nothing short of death would, or should, prevent my poking that heavenly girl again, and again, until I really could not raise a stand. Longed for evening. I burnt for night. I ate my tiffin like a ravenous tiger, hungry for food, but thirsting for the sweet savour of the blood of a victim he knew to be within easy reach. Tiffin put away, I lit a cheroot, and began wandering round and round my room, balancing impatiently at the door which closed the communication between it and that of my supposedly now sleeping Venus, and like Wellington wished and prayed for night or – not Blucher – her awakening! Suddenly it struck me as very funny that – supposing some catastrophe were to separate this girl and me, neither would be able to say who the other was! We had not exchanged names. My young friend the officer who signed his initials 'J.C.' had not told me. I did not even know his name, though he knew mine, probably from seeing it painted on my baggage. Of a surety this lovely Venus must have a history, and I resolved to try and get her to give me her version of it, from which no doubt I could make out what was true and what was invention, for that she would tell me the exact truth I hardly expected. Oh! when would she awake?

Should I go and peep and see? By Jupiter, I would . . .

Throwing away the fresh cheroot I had lighted I crept, in my stocking feet, to her chick, and pulled it slightly open, and there on the bed fast asleep, I saw my lovely enslaver. She had simply put on a petticoat and was lying on her back, with her hands clasped under her shapely head, her arms, bent in a charming position opened out, showing the little growth of hair under the arm pit next to me; hair the same in tint, but not so rich in colour, as that magnificent bush I had moistened so liberally, aided by her own offerings this morning; her bosom bare and naked, with its two priceless breasts, so beautifully placed, so round, polished and firm, and her entire body down to her slender waist, quite nude! One knee, that next to me, was bent, the small graceful foot planted on the bed clothes, each gem of a toe straight and just separated from its neighbour, a foot that would have charmed the most fastidious sculptor that ever lived, whilst the other leg, bare almost from the groin downwards, was extended at full length, the lovely foot, which terminated it, resting against the edge of the bed, so that her thighs, those lovely voluptuous and maddening thighs, were parted! Gods! could I remain outside while so much beauty was freely displayed, on which I could feast my burning eyes whilst its lovely owner slept? I went gently and noiselessly in, and passing round to the other side of the bed, so that my shadow might not fall on the exquisite form, and hide the light, already softened by the chick, from it, and gazed in silence on the beautiful girl who had made me enjoy the bliss of Mahomet's heaven in her voluptuous embraces that forenoon. How lovely was her sleep! Who, looking on that face so pure in all its lines, so innocent in all its expressions, could imagine that in that soul there burnt the fire of an unquenchable Cytherian furnace. Who, looking on those matchless breasts could imagine that lovers innumerable had pressed them with lascivious hand or lip and been supported by them when they trembled in the agonies and the delight of having her?

The fair broad plain of her belly was still hidden by the upper portion of her petticoats, but the fine lines, which I had noticed when she 'put on her skin', had told me the tale, that perhaps more than once it had been the breeding place of little beings, who, cast in such a beauteous mould, must needs be as beautiful as their lovely mother! I, who, looking at those virginal breasts which seemed as if they had never been disturbed by pent-up milk, and whose rosebud-like nipples seemed never to have been sucked, by the cherry lips of babies; who gazing in the girlish face, could connect such charms with the pains, the caress, and duties of maternity? No! surely, like the fair Houris of Mahomet's paradise, she must have been created for the fulfilment of the pleasure only, not for the consequences of the kiss of love! But the wrinkles told a different tale, and I should like to examine them more closely. It would be easy to do, if only they were naked, all but a small portion near the groin, and all that I had to do was to lift, gently, so as not to disturb her sleep, the part of her petticoat which still hid her there, and lay the garment back upon her waist.

With a hand trembling with excitement, I did so! lo! my nymph almost as naked as she was born! God of Gods! What a blaze of exciting beauty! I had uncovered the sweet belly to look at the wrinkles, but my eye was captured before it lifted its gaze so high! As the bird is caught in the snare surrounding the luscious bait exposed for it, so were my eyes entangled in the meshes of that glorious hair, which from the forest-like bush growing on that voluptuous motte, and shading the slit, the like of which for freshness, beauty, and all that excites desire, could not have existed in that to anybody but that of the great Mother of love, Venus herself. It seemed to me impossible that this beauteous portal to the realms of bliss, could have been invaded by so many worshippers as her speech of the morning had led me to believe. It looked far from having been hard used. What grand full lips it had. How sweetly it was placed. How pretty did the fine dark hairs, which crossed it look against the whiteness of the skin, whose infoldings formed that deep and perfect line. What a perfect forest overshadowed it, and how divine were the slopes of that glorious hill, the perfect little mountain, which led up the sweet descent to the deep vale between her thighs, and ended in that glowing grotto in which love delighted to hide his blushing head, and shed the hot tears of his exulting joy.

But what is that? What is that little ruby tip I see beginning to protrude, near the upper meeting of those exquisite lips? She moves. See! I think she must be dreaming! She slightly closes her bent leg towards that one outstretched! It is her most sensitive clitoris, as I live! See! It grows more and more! And by the Gods! it actually moves in little jerks, just like an excited stem standing stiff, and mad at the thought of hot desire!

I gazed at the tranquil face of the sleeping beauty, her lips moved and her mouth opened slightly showing the pearly teeth! Her bosom seemed to expand, her breasts to swell, they rose and fell more rapidly than they had been doing before this evident dream of love fulfilled or about to be, invaded the soft heart of this perfect priestess of Venus! Ah! Her bubbies do move! Their rosebuds swell out, they stand, each like an eager sentinel perched on the snowy tip of his own mountain, watching for the loving foe who is to invade this dreaming girl to the soft, and sharp and hot encounter.

Again those thighs close on one another. Heaven! again they open to show the domain of love, excited, moving, leaping, actually leaping! That glittering ruby clit is evidently striving to feel the manly staff of which my charmer dreams. Why not turn the dream into a sweet and luscious reality?

I do not hesitate. I swiftly strip and in a moment I am as naked as I had been that morning, but I would like to see whether I could actually get into this sleeping girl, before she woke to find me in her glowing orifice.

So I gently got over her thigh next me, and with knees between hers I supported myself upon my hands, one on each side of her and stretching out my legs backward, kept my eyes fixed on the sweet and burning cranny I intended to invade. I lowered my body until I brought the head and point of my agitated and jerking tool exactly opposite its lower half, and then I manoeuvred it in!

Gods! The voluptuousness of that moment! I could see myself penetrating that seat of love and luxury! I could feel the cap fall back from the tingling head of my member and fold behind its broad purple shoulder! For a moment I glanced at her face to see if she had perceived the gallant theft I was making of her secret jewel! No! She was asleep, but in the excitement of an erotic dream! Little by little I pressed further and further in, only withdrawing, to give her more pleasure. I am nearly all in – her thick and lofty bush hides the last inch or so of my spear from my eyes, our hairs co-mingle, my eggs touch her, and she wakes with a start!

In a moment her eyes met mine with that keen, almost wild glance, which had so impressed me when I saw her out of the gharry, but in a moment they changed and beamed with pleasure and affectionate caresses.

'Ah! Is it you?' she cried, 'I was dreaming of you! You darling man to wake me so sweetly!'

Some burning kisses, some close, close hugs, some little exclamations of delight, and then breast to breast, belly to belly, mouth to mouth, we play for the ninth or tenth time, I really don't know which, that same excited tune which had sounded all that morning so melodiously to our ravished senses. Heel-and-toe! as she called it: delicious movements mingling in every part, hot, quick, thrilling short digs, and then the torrents of two volcanoes of love burst forth simultaneously and mingled their lava floods in the hot recesses buried below the sylvan slopes of the Hill of Venus.

The gong on which the non-commissioned officer of the guard sounds the hour of the day in India, rang five o'clock. We had been in intense action nearly a whole hour, and my charming beauty was for the fifteenth time examining what she called, my 'wonderful' member and stones, wonderful, because the first showed no symptoms of fatigue, and the second no signs of exhaustion or depletion.

'I don't believe this can be a proper tool at all!' said she feeling it, pressing it, and kissing its impudent looking head, first on one side and then on the other.

'Why?' I asked laughing.

'Because it's always stiff as a poker – always standing!'

'That is because it admires your delicious cranny so much, my darling, that it is always in a hurry to get back into it after it has been taken out!'

'Well! I never saw one like it before! All other men that I have had always grew soft and limp, after the second go at any rate, and generally took a good deal of coaxing to get to stand again, unless one gives them lots of time! But yours! I never, never, met one like it! It will give me a lot of trouble, I can see, to take all the starch out of it!'

'Oh, but I can assure you my most lovely girl, that with ordinary women I am just as you describe the men you have known. I can assure you it must be your extraordinary beauty which has such a powerful effect upon me! Come!' I continued opening my arms and thighs. 'Come and lie on top of me and let me kiss you to death!'

Enraptured by the lavish, but not unmerited, praise of her beauty, she threw herself, with a cry of delight, on top of me, and my manhood found a sweet resting place between our respective bellies. She took and gave me the sweetest kisses, murmuring little words of love and passion like a cat purring, until I was just going to propose that she should put her thighs outside mine, and let me have her a la St. George, when a sudden idea seemed to strike her. She raised herself on her hand and asked me:

'I say! Have you reported your arrival to the Station Staff Officer?'

ANONYMOUS

from
The Cremorne

The Cremorne is a collection of some of the most sexually explicit stories of the nineteenth century. The name of the collection comes from Cremorne Gardens in Chelsea which was a well-known meeting place for young gentlemen on the look-out for carnal delights.

WITH the aid of Miss Fletcher's *Domestic Economy* purchased for one shilling and sixpence at the village bookshop, Katie and Penny were able, after one or two unsuccessful trial runs, to light the gas stove, boil the kettle and make their Mama the cup of tea she craved. They even managed to cut a loaf of bread and butter the slices as well as dividing a slab of Mrs Beaconsfield's famous Upside Down cake they found in the larder.

The servants might have walked out but the beds had been made, the house cleaned and Mrs Beaconsfield had cooked enough to provide a cold collation for supper that evening and luncheon the following day.

But what Katie did not and indeed could not have known was that she was seen and admired by Walter Stanton, a bright young spark who was browsing in the bookshop looking for a light novel with which to pass away the afternoon. Wally was staying in the village just a mile or so from the Arkley residence on a duty visit to his Uncle, the crusty old General Stanton who made Wally an annual allowance to supplement the relatively small amount provided by his worthy parents who alas had lost a great deal of cash through unwise speculation in Hudson's railway stock.

Walter was twenty-two years of age and supposedly spent his time in London studying as an articled clerk at Godfrey and Co, solicitors to the gentry, but the temptations of the capital city took their toll and one of the reasons why he did not begrudge the few days spent with his Uncle in the country was that here at least there were no gardens of pleasure such as The Cremorne where a young man could both be parted from his cash and joined in relationships which might be difficult out of which to disengage.

But, for a young man of Walter Stanton's spirit, the attractions of female flesh were never far from his thoughts. And when he glanced up from the book he was leafing through and saw the lovely Katie, her blonde hair tumbling down her shoulders, her pretty face with those large blue eyes, sparkling white teeth and charming dimples, he was irretrievably drawn as metal is to a magnet.

'Egad, what a stunner!' murmured Walter to himself as he looked upon Katie's merry face with unconcealed delight. To his eyes, the sweet girl was the very beau ideal of feminine beauty and after Katie and Penny had left the shop Walter hastened to the cash desk and purchased the novel he had been reading.

'That will be two shillings, sir,' said Mr Maher, wrapping the book in a brown paper bag.

'Oh, er, could you wrap it in coloured paper?' said Walter with a flash of inspiration.

'Certainly, sir, although that will cost an extra two pence,' said the bookseller. 'I hope you don't mind the small extra charge but in Beerstone's shop down the road coloured paper costs even more and they don't stock the range that we do.'

'No, no, don't worry, I don't mind the cost,' said Walter. 'But tell me, who are those two attractive girls who just left the premises?'

'Oh, you mean Lady Arkley's daughters, Miss Katie and Miss Penny. Miss Katie is the blonde-haired girl and I think that she is a year or two older than her sister.'

'Do they live near my Uncle, General Stanton?' Walter enquired, exchanging coins for the neatly-wrapped parcel.

'Oh, yes, not too far away, sir. Walk along the High Street for half a mile or so and then turn left into Titchfield Street and then right up Healy's Hill. It's probably less than a mile in all.'

After thanking the kind bookseller for his information Walter hurried home. At first he was minded to run after the sisters and present his compliments but he wisely decided to go home and change first and think of a suitable reason for his visiting their home. Such a reason was not hard to find and he smiled happily as he walked briskly back to Stanton Lodge where the General was snorting grumpily over a copy of *The Times*, a glass of whisky and soda on a table beside him.

'That you, Walter?' shouted the General who was inclined to deafness.

'Yes, I'm back, Uncle, but unless you have any objection I shall be going out again shortly.'

'Are you now? I thought you came to keep me company, young feller-me-lad. Where are you off to?'

'I shan't be long, Uncle,' said Walter trying to keep a note of convivial civility in his voice. 'One of our neighbours left a *book* she had purchased at Maher's and I thought I would walk down the road and return it to her.'

'Well, can't a servant take it round?' fretted the General. 'I want you to meet Colonel Bailstone and his niece who are dining with us tonight.'

'I won't be long,' promised his nephew. 'Don't worry, Uncle, I shall be back in good time.'

'Well see that you are,' said General Stanton, returning to the pages of his newpaper.

Walter rushed upstairs and ran a brisk if cool bath. He dried himself well and decided to shave for the second time that day. He was a handsome young rogue who was somewhat sallow in complexion with a dark growth of hair that often seemed to elude the strictest attempts at shaving. Certainly, he needed to run a razor over his face which he did carefully, for appearing before this delicious girl with a face covered in cuts was something he wished to avoid. He splashed on some *eau de cologne* – unlike many Englishmen he thoroughly approved of the Continental practice of masculine toiletries which perhaps accounted for his many successes with the fair sex. He changed into fresh clothes and after bidding his Uncle goodbye, set forth at a good stride to the Arkley residence, in happy anticipation of seeing the stunning Miss Katie again.

Young Walter – or Wally as he was known to his friends – walked as quickly as he could to *chez* Arkley. He did not run as the sun was now shining quite fiercely and he did not want to perspire. By the time he had reached his destination the girls had laid out a splendid tea for their Mama and partaken of the feast they had prepared. They were engaged in deciding how best to clean the cutlery and plates they had used when Walter rang the front door bell.

'Please answer the bell, somebody,' called out Lady Arkley. 'And remember, unless it is Reverend Tagholm or somebody important I am not at home.'

Katie marched out and opened the door herself. 'Good afternoon, Miss Arkley,' said the bold Wally, raising his hat. 'My name is Walter Stanton and I am staying with my Uncle, General Stanton at his home just down the hill.

'I do hope you will forgive my forwardness in speaking to you without an introduction but I saw you and your sister in Maher's bookshop this afternoon and I thought you might like to read this jolly little novel which I can recommend.'

Katie smiled and her dimples looked so kissable to the smitten Walter that he could scarcely keep his hands to his sides after passing the package wrapped in the coloured paper which had cost him an extra two pence to this lovely creature who stood before him.

'That is very kind of you, Mr Stanton,' said Katie. 'However, I regret that I cannot accept a present from a total stranger.'

'Oh, Miss Arkley, I do understand – but then if we were formally introduced I would no longer be a total stranger and then perhaps you could accept my little gift.'

'Yes, I suppose there is logic in your argument – but unfortunately there is no-one to introduce us.'

'Oh, yes there is,' broke in the cheerful voice of her young sister. 'Actually, although we have never met, Mr Stanton, I have been introduced to your Uncle, the General, by my mother with whom he is acquainted. Let me do the honours, starting perhaps with myself – I am Penelope Arkley and you are . . .'

'Walter Stanton, Miss Arkley, at your service,' murmured Wally gratefully.

'Very well. Mr Walter Stanton, I have the honour to introduce my sister Miss Katherine Arkley, but as my Mama has met your Uncle, do call us Penny and Katie.'

'And do call me Wally,' said the happy young man. 'Now, Katie, please do me the honour of accepting this little gift of a novel to while away a pleasant morning or two.'

'Thank you, Wally, I look forward to reading it. Look, do come in, we are in a bit of a mess just now as the servants have suddenly decamped but if you don't mind coming through into the kitchen for a moment whilst we clean up after tea – '

'It will be my pleasure. Do let me assist you,' said Walter. 'I live quite simply in town and am used to doing many of my own chores, which is perhaps as should be for an impoverished articled solicitor's clerk.'

'Golly, can you cook?' said Penny admiringly. 'How terribly clever you must be.'

'I can make a very passable omelette and prepare straightforward dishes like steak and chips,' said Walter modestly. 'I have a daily charwoman who comes in every morning but generally speaking I look after myself. Now, do let me help you with anything you need doing.'

It is strange how women of all ages and classes can divine when a man is interested either in themselves or another of the fair sex. Penny knew immediately of Walter's passion for her sister from the manner of his speech, how his words were spoken in her direction and in the way he looked as often as possible at Katie without staring in a vulgar fashion.

'If you two will excuse me, I have a slight headache coming on,' fibbed Penny. 'I hope you will not mind too much if I retired from the fray and went upstairs for a nap. Anyhow, you know the saying, too many cooks spoil the broth.' She almost spoiled the speech by adding 'and two is company but three is a crowd' but managed to restrain herself with a charming little giggle, closing the door behind her before either Katie or Walter could challenge her.

'That was very, very nice of your sister to leave us,' said Walter. 'She knew that we wanted to be by ourselves.'

Katie's pretty face coloured up as she looked down demurely at the floor.

'Now you must know what I mean,' continued Walter. 'Penny knows that I would love to be properly acquainted with you, Katie. I do hope you will let me be your friend.'

'You can be my friend if you will help me wash up,' said Katie quickly as she heard footsteps outside. 'And I do hope you can make as good an impression upon my Mama as you have done with Penny and myself, for otherwise all your words will count for nothing.'

'Never fear,' said Walter grandly as Lady Arkley entered the room. Luckily, Lady Arkley was in a mellow mood having partaken of tea and was easily flattered into accepting Walter into the family circle after he explained his relationship to General Stanton and that yes, indeed, he was one of the Gloucestershire Stantons and that on his mother's side he was a Hackney.

'Lady Arkley, I would be grateful if I could obtain your permission to take Katherine for a short walk after we have finished our domestic chores,' said the cunning Walter with his most practised dazzling smile.

'Certainly, Mr Stanton, it will do you both good. Do not forget to give the General my kindest regards when you return home,' said Lady Arkley graciously as she swept majestically out of the kitchen.

'Thank you, Lady Arkley,' said Walter happily to her disappearing back. 'Thank you very much indeed.'

And Katie, too, smiled with genuine delight.

So not long after this conversation Katie and Walter went off for a quiet stroll and came to a pretty stream where they sat down on the mossy bank to chat. But alas, just as Katie was taking off her shoe to take a pebble out of the heel, she saw a beetle on her leg which startled her and she dropped her shoe into the stream.

'Don't fret, Katie,' said Walter as he leaped up and cleverly fished out the dainty little shoe with the aid of a stick.

'Did ever Jove's tree drop such fruit?' he quoted as Katie hopped towards him.

Walter polished the patent leather inside and out with his handkerchief and offered it to her with a flourish. Katie sat down on the ground and, dimpling in the most distracting manner (there should be a law against that, thought Walter), said: 'Thank you so much, Walter, you really do seem to be my knight errant.'

'Don't put it on yet, Katie,' he said carefully. 'The shoe is still a little damp, so let's sit down here and rest for a few moments. Oh, I would so like to stay the evening with you but my dratted Uncle has invited guests to dine with us tonight so I shall have to take my leave of you within the hour.'

They chatted pleasantly about this and that until Katie's shoe was dry and then they set off home. But as the couple crossed Farmer Dawson's meadow they heard a muffled roar and saw a creature with tossing horns and waving tail making for them, head down, eyes flashing. Katie gave a shriek but luckily they happened to be near a pair of low bars and Walter had not been a college athlete for nothing. He swung Katie over the bars and jumped after her.

But she, not knowing in her fright where she was nor what she was doing, supposing also that the mad creature would still pursue her, flung herself bodily in his arms, crying: 'Walter! Walter! Save me!'

The young rascal needed no second invitation and proceeded to save her in the usual way by holding her close to his supple frame and kissing her boldly on the mouth, murmuring: 'You are safe, my darling. Not a hair of your precious head shall be hurt.'

'But what was it, Walter – I cannot help being so scared. Was it a dangerous bull?'

Walter looked up and saw the animal trotting off in the distance. It was that rare yet entirely possible thing – a sportive cow.

'Is he gone?' breathed Katie from his chest.

'Yes, the cow has gone and won't come back, darling,' smiled Walter. 'But you'd better not move just in case I'm wrong!'

'A cow?' exclaimed Katie. 'Oh Walter, I feel so ashamed. What a silly girl I've been, making all that fuss.'

'No, no, no,' said Walter quietly. 'I shall always be eternally grateful to the beast for enabling me to hold you in my arms in this lovely fashion.'

For a moment, they looked into each other's eyes as Katie lifted up her pretty face and then their mouths met in a most delicious kiss. They sank to the ground, clutching each other as Walter's tongue made an instant, darting journey of exploration inside the pretty girl's mouth.

She responded with avidity and did not repulse the handsome lad when his hand came up and touched her throat before moving slowly, lingeringly down towards the valley between her breasts, moulding the linen blouse against her skin.

Katie gasped with joy and the thought flashed through her mind that this must be how Tricia her cat must feel when she stroked her. His hand continued its journey, insistently, now, over the full twin curves of her rising breasts and she shivered with raw, unslaked desire.

'Oh, you are so beautiful,' murmured Walter as he eased her down on the dry grass and leaned over her. She hardly felt his swift fingers unbutton her blouse and slip the straps of her chemise down from her shoulders. He slid his palms over her breasts, feeling the rosy red nipples pouting hard against his hands. He dared venture further, moving his hand along her leg and under her skirt until he reached her thighs.

'Ah! Oh! Oh! Walter, don't!' she gasped, contracting her thighs around his fingers.

'I cannot resist you,' whispered Walter, smothering her with a renewed burst of kisses, thrusting the velvet tip of his tongue between her soft lips.

Katie sighed and relaxed her grip around his hand which proceeded to unbutton her drawers and work its way onto her mound of silky golden hair. Very soon, almost to her surprise, the lovely girl found that somehow Walter had slipped off all her clothes and she was lying quite naked on the grassy knoll as Walter's tongue explored her breasts, lingering over each nipple in turn as his fingers found their way through the triangle of golden hair nestling between her thighs. His wicked fingers stroked, probed and caressed her pussey which now dampened with her love juices and she cried out with pleasure at the joy it afforded her.

'Katie, Katie, feel here the staff of desire impatient to enter the divine lips of love between your thighs,' he whispered in her ear, pulling her half-resisting hand to the bulge in the front of his trousers. Now as aroused as he, Katie slid her hand to feel his stiff member as he wrenched off his belt and unbuttoned his fly. She assisted him to pull down his trousers and underpants in one fell swoop and she grasped his rampant penis. As his hand continued to plunge in and out between the lips of her pliant pussey, Katie jerked her hand up and down on the hot, velvet skin of Walter's swollen shaft, faster and faster until seconds later the white love juice gushed out of the purple bulb in a swift little fountain and a shuddering orgasm of pleasure flowed through his quivering body.

His lips remained glued to hers as her hand held his gushing rod in a convulsive grasp whilst his fingers continued to play with her clitty and cunney until Walter felt his hand deluged with her warm, juicy spend, spurting over his hand in loving sympathy.

'Katie, my darling! I must kiss your sweet pussey and taste the nectar of love!' exclaimed Walter, snatching his lips from hers and burying his face between her unresisting thighs. He licked up the luscious love juice that poured from her pussey lips and then his tongue found its way further till it tickled her sensitive little clitty which rose up to meet the welcome intruder. Katie moaned with passion as she twisted her legs over his head, squeezing it between her firm thighs in an ecstasy of delight.

'Mr Pego is now coming to meet you, darling,' panted Walter, his penis rising majestically upward as he went back to work titillating Katie's stiff little clitty, which worked her up to new paroxysms of desire. She now clutched at his rampant prick and rolled her tongue round the uncovered purple dome, licking and lapping in an acme of erotic enjoyment. She spent again in a second luscious flood whilst she felt his shaft swell and throb until with a shudder he sent a hot stream of creamy sperm into her mouth and she unthinkingly swallowed the veritable jet of love juice which had burst from Walter's excited engine of love.

They both nearly fainted from the excess of their emotions and lay quite exhausted for a few moments till Walter felt her sweet lips again sucking his still-erect cock.

'Oh, Katie, I must now position myself for the *coup de grâce*, the real stroke of love,' he said, his eyes shining brightly with desire as he parted the pretty girl's quivering thighs.

At first Katie made no resistance but then she struggled free and wriggled away from him. 'No, no, Walter, I am not ready yet for this. Please, please do not force me!' urged the lovely girl, covering her gorgeous naked body with her dress.

'You must forgive me, Walter, I got carried away but I will only make love when the time is right for me in both mind and body. Oh, my love, I do feel very much for you. Will you respect my feelings?'

Katie need not have worried her pretty little head about Walter's passion. For he was, after all, a gentleman who had been schooled at Nottsgrove Academy where the progressive views of the headmaster Doctor Simon White stressed the absolute necessity of always obeying your partner's wishes. 'When a girl says no she means no,' Doctor White declared to his Sixth Form again and again. 'Any man who forces a girl to submit to any intimacy to which she is not a willing partner deserves to have his testicles removed!'

So Walter immediately took a pace backwards and said: 'Of course I respect your feelings, Katie. I hope I always have and always will. Come, let us get dressed. Perhaps I may persuade you to change your mind at a another time and place.'

'If anyone will, you will, Walter,' said the grateful girl. 'I only wish all men were as kind and understanding as you. You aren't angry with me, are you?'

'No, no, of course not,' smiled Walter, kissing her on the tip of her elegant little nose. 'How could I be angry with such a beautiful creature like you?'

'Oh, Walter, you really are the nicest man I have ever met!'

They kissed again as they said their goodbyes and Walter made Katie promise that she would go out for another walk with him the next evening. She agreed and they waved farewell as Katie walked back home alone (as she had told Walter that she preferred to do) and the love-sick young man set off for Stanton Lodge. He looked at his pocket watch and noted that he was in good time – which was as well, for as he reached the road back to his Uncle's house he noticed a dark brown piece of leather lying on the grass. He picked it up and discovered that it was a pocket diary.

It was obviously a private diary, as opposed to one that simply recorded appointments, but Walter felt not unreasonably that he had to peer inside if for no other reason than to see who was the owner. He looked at the inside page and read the name 'Connie Chumbley' – a name that meant nothing to him although Katie could have enlightened him. For Connie was, until that morning, the Arkley family's maid and was one of the infamous trio – the other members being Formbey the butler and Mrs Beaconsfield the cook – who had walked out on Lady Arkley earlier that day.

The temptation to read the diary was too much for Walter and he had time on his hands before going back home and dressing for dinner. And when he found out almost immediately that he possessed the intimate diary of a young girl, wild horses would not have moved him from the wooden seat that had been thoughtfully placed at a pretty spot for pedestrians by a kindly old gentleman some five years previously.

Walter soon discovered by skimming through the first few paragraphs that Connie had been in service in India with Katie's uncle, Lord Daniel Arkley, and she had written of an encounter with a young lieutenant in the British Army in south India. Late one warm afternoon she had decided to wander down to the beach. His eyes widened and his heart began to beat a little faster as he read on:

★

'I drank in the solitude of the loveliness of it all. Though the sea sparkled benevolently, the golden-coloured sand somehow told me of being harried by the endless ebb and flow of storm-roused tides. Suddenly I was transfixed as an elephant apparently emerged from the shadows of a sandy grove. With some relief I realised that it was made from stone but the consummate skill of those Indian rock masons of long ago had for a moment scared me stiff!

'I turned away and yet another shock awaited me – there in the azure blue sea swimming lazily towards me was young Lieutenant Randolph Barnett of the Royal West Kents. Lieutenant Barnett was a liaison officer between the military authorities and the local Maharajah and as such had been summoned to several meetings with Lord Arkley. I had waited upon him and whilst passing round the tea and biscuits, I could not help but admire his handsome face, slim body and gracious manner.

'"Hello, there, I know you," he called out, "It's young Connie, Lord Arkley's maid, isn't it? Come on in for a dip, the water's warm yet so refreshing."

'I blushed but of course was quite delighted that the handsome young man had remembered me. "I can't come in, Lieutenant Barnett," I called back. "I don't have a bathing costume or a towel with me."

'"Don't worry about that," he replied. "I have a towel and as for a bathing costume, you don't need one. Come on in and swim without anything on – it's far, far nicer, Connie, I do assure you. Look, I haven't any clothes on! It feels so free to swim in the nude, do try it and you'll never want to put your costume on again!"

'I could hardly believe my ears but as if to prove that he was telling the truth, Lieutenant Barnett swam towards me until the water was too shallow to stay horizontal. He scrambled to his feet and to my astonishment I saw that the good-looking rogue had spoken naught but the truth! He paddled through the water towards me unashamedly naked and oh, diary! he looked a real Adonis, so well muscled in a manly fashion yet his face was totally smooth and free from any blemish. I admired the strength of his broad chest and the flatness of his belly. And of course I could not resist taking a demure look at the fine-looking penis that dangled saucily between his legs.

'"Come now, Connie, I promise you that you will enjoy yourself," urged my new companion.

'Suddenly a quotation from the book of sayings by the wise Indian sage Mustapha Pharte which I had been studying the previous evening came into my mind: "In our wild and dangerous world we must drink deeply from the cup of sensual joy lest it be suddenly dashed from our lips." In other words, enjoy yourself whilst you can, I thought and so I nodded my assent and kicked off my shoes. I unbuttoned my blouse and allowed Randolph (as he insisted I called him) to undo my skirt which I let fall onto the soft sand. I shrugged off my slips and pulled down my drawers leaving my naked body free to his gaze.

'"Gad, what a beautiful girl you are, Connie," he murmured, and I noticed that his cock twitched slightly as he spoke. "Can you swim? Yes? Good, let's strike out and then make for that deserted little cove over on our left. I've left my towel there together with a hamper."

'We stayed in the water for a quarter of an hour or so and I had to admit to Randolph that his comments about the joys of swimming in the nude were absolutely true – I did indeed revel in the glories of a sense of total freedom. I let myself wallow in a kind of sensuous joy, floating on my back and letting the gentle waves wash over me. Then I swam to Randolph's little cove and dabbed myself dry with the towel. It was hardly necessary to do so as the warm sun evaporated the moisture from my skin. Randolph had swum back for my clothes which he brought over to this pretty place which was hidden from general view. Randolph had prepared a fine feast of sandwiches and cake and had even brought a bottle of wine packed in crushed ice which was very welcome indeed.

'We lay naked on the sand and somehow it seemed the most natural thing in the world to be in Randolph's strong arms and exchanging the most passionate of kisses. My blood was now up and as our mouths crushed together I put my tongue in his mouth and explored the top half between teeth and lips with a long probing kiss. His hands descended to my full breasts and he squeezed my hard little nipples and my own left hand was suddenly pulled down to meet Randolph's rising shaft which fairly leaped into my grasp.

'My body was now on fire with unslaked desire – I whispered my wish to Randolph who smiled gently and murmured back "it will be my pleasure" as I lay back and opened my legs in preparation. I positioned Randolph on his knees in front of me so that he would have full view of my furry bush and pouting cunney lips. I took his hand and placed it on my already-dampening mound. His fingers splayed my outer lips and the fingers of his other hand ran down the length of my crack. I gently pushed the finger in as my hips rose up to meet the welcome visitor. Now I felt his lips part my cunney lips and I was soon in raptures as he found my excitable little clitty which sent waves of passion spilling all over me. My pussey was now spending freely under the voluptuous titillations of his velvety tongue. Aaah, the sweet memories of the moment make me ache with desire for another afternoon of love-making with dear randy Randolph!

'I clasped my legs around his head as he continued to lick and lap on my engorged clitty and I screamed with unalloyed joy as I reached the peak of pleasure. I released Randolph's head from between my thighs and pushed him firmly down on his back so that I could repay him for the joy he had given me. He had no protectives with him so I could not allow him to fuck me. However, I was determined to thrill him in another way that I knew he would find almost as exciting!

'He obeyed with alacrity my command to lie still and I smoothed my hand over his flat stomach and into the curly mass of pubic hair. I licked my lips with gusto when I looked at his thick shaft which was not fully erect but had that lovely, full, heavy look about it. I gently squeezed this huge pole and immediately his cock stood up in full erection, uncapping the delicious-looking purple knob. I grasped his shaft again, marvelling at the width of the monster – even bigger than that of Sir Leon Standlake, the scourge of every servant girl in Belgravia – and I could scarcely enclose it with my hand. My head now swooped down and I began to kiss and lick the red mushroom dome with my tongue. Then I began to suck greedily on this delicious-looking sweetmeat, dwelling around the ridge, up the underside and sucking up as much of the shaft as possible into my mouth. I pumped his prick firmly, keeping my lips taut on his length, kissing, sucking, licking and lapping as I took him fully into my mouth in long, rolling sucks. I continued to suck furiously until I felt the juices boil up inside that hot, hard shaft and then I knew he was about to spend which he did in long powerful squirts that I swallowed eagerly, milking his rod of every last drop of white love juice.

'To my amazement his shaft remained semi-erect and after I had rubbed it up and down for a minute or so it swelled up again as stiff as could be!

'"Goodness gracious, Randolph," I giggled. "You certainly have extraordinary powers of recovery."

'"I know," sighed the young rascal. "If only I could place my staff in your c—"

'I put my hand to his lips and murmured that today was too dangerous for a bareback ride but that next week he might be able to aim his charger at a wet and willing target. Still holding his magnificently thick tool, I sank down to the sand for a second helping as I kissed the ruby knob and then opened my lips to take it in my mouth. I sucked gently this time around, rolling my tongue over his knob, savouring the tangy taste of his juices. My tongue ran down his length and then ran back to the top to catch a sticky drip of spend that had formed around the "eye". I ran my lips around his noble cock, closing my lips firmly around the shaft as I squeezed his balls carefully to heighten his enjoyment.

'This caused Randolph to spend almost at once, sending a second stream of salty hot spunk down my throat. I swallowed to the final burning drops, smacking my lips with total abandon as, at last, Randolph's stand began to wilt and his shaft shrank down to its normal size.

'"Come on, Randolph," I said. "We must get dressed before we are discovered." We scrambled into our clothes and to my surprise I noticed that Randolph had been wearing his revolver belt.

'"Do you always wear a gun?" I asked.

'Randolph chuckled and said: "I'm glad it was you and not I that said 'gun', Connie."

'"Why?" I said with some puzzlement.

'"We don't use that word in the Army," he explained. "A pistol is a pistol, a revolver is a revolver and a rifle is a rifle. If a soldier says 'gun' instead of the noun of correct terminology, after morning drill he has to stand naked in the barrack square and with one hand holding, say, his pistol and the other holding his prick is forced to recite:

> *This is my pistol*
> *This is my gun*
> *This is for fighting*
> *And this is for fun*

'"Needless to say, not many recruits make this mistake more than once!"

'I laughed and we made our way back to Randolph's barracks where he showed me all round the camp and then entertained me to an early supper in his rooms. Later he drove me back to Lord Arkley's and I was hard put to keep my resolve not to let his stalwart pego enter its desired haven that night.'

Walter closed the diary and breathed heavily. Reading this erotic tale had excited him almost to a frenzy. His hand grasped his shaft which was as hard as a rock and threatened to burst out from the stretched material of his trousers. He took several deep breaths and forced himself into a calmer train of thought. He stuffed the diary into his pocket before marching purposefully back to Stanton Lodge, idly wondering whether Colonel Bailstone's niece would be of an age and of a kind that he would find attractive.

He arrived back in good time and after a brisk wash changed into evening dress.

Luckily the General was in better humour as he had received a telephone call from London in which his close friend Mr Roy St Clair had informed him that the tip they had received from their Club's head waiter had in fact 'turned up' – for as forecast the filly Amhurst Park had won the third race at Goodwood at odds of twelve to one. So the ten pound wager struck with the Cavalry Club's bookmaker would yield a handsome profit of one hundred and twenty pounds.

'Help yourself to a whisky and soda, my boy,' said General Stanton genially when Walter appeared in the drawing room. 'I don't expect Colonel Bailstone and his niece for another ten minutes or so. Sit yourself down and enjoy your drink.'

And the blessing of good fortune would have appeared to continue to hover over Stanton Lodge that evening, settling this time over young Wally's head for, to his absolute delight, Colonel Bailstone's niece, Louisa, turned out to be an extremely pretty girl of just eighteen years of age, as lithe and lovely as a fawn with masses of tawny brown hair and with a fine sense of mischief that sparkled in her large brown eyes.

On the other hand, Colonel Bailstone was a pompous old bore who liked nothing better than listening to the sound of his own voice. He was of a corpulent build and years of 'lifting the elbow', as the modern colloquialism has it, had no doubt added inches to his portly waistline as well as causing his face to flush a bright shade of red after only a glass or so of General Stanton's Bollinger '87 champagne.

The two old Army martinets were snorting their anger over a letter in *The Times* that day about the need to alleviate the sufferings of the poor.

'Just listen to this idiot,' grunted Colonel Bailstone, picking up the newspaper and reading aloud from the letter which had roused his ire. 'I can't believe that *The Times* would even deign publish such rot, Frederick, but it's all here in black and white – let me quote: "A way must be found of helping those thrifty working people who show no apparent evidence of dire want. At present it would appear that worthy working people who by industry and thrift have raised themselves above the brink of abject pauperism can make no further claim for assistance to lift the veil of greater want.

'"In addition of course we must also acknowledge the sad fact that people quickly forget that more than sympathy is needed to relieve those poor souls who have been brought to misfortune often through no fault of their own. There are far too many who in their professed detestation of roguery, supposed or real, forget that by a wholesale condemnation of charity and so-called demoralisation, they are running the risk of driving honest men to despair and peaceful folk to violence. Indeed, it may be wondered whether these comfortable wealthy people are in fact secret supporters of the Socialists for it is surely only in such interests that misery, hunger and social unrest should increase – I am, Sir, Yours Faithfully, Reverend T. H. Cooney, Vicar of Nayland, Colchester, Essex." So now we have padres writing this subversive kind of nonsense in *The Times* of all places – what is this country coming to?'

General Stanton nodded his agreement: 'I can't imagine what the twentieth century has in store for us. All we need to do is return to the good old military maxim of having a few people to give the orders and the rest to obey 'em, eh?'

'You dictatorial old fool,' muttered the delicious Louisa to Walter which startled the lad so much that he choked on a mouthful of apple flan.

'What did you say, Louisa?' snapped her uncle, fixing a gimlet eye upon her.

'Louisa asked me if we had any fish in our garden pool,' said Walter with commendable speed of thought.

General Stanton was a little hard of hearing but Louisa's uncle stared grimly at the young couple before deciding that it would be politic on this occasion to give his niece the benefit of the doubt.

Louisa sensed it was time to retreat in good order, to use an appropriate military metaphor and said: 'If you gentlemen would like to take your cigars and brandy in here, I will retire to the lounge. Would you mind if I took the opportunity of practising on your piano, General Stanton? I am due to play at a charity concert next Wednesday evening at the Wigmore Hall in London.'

'Of course, my dear, feel free. We will join you there later and perhaps we could be entertained by a short recital,' said General Stanton. 'Your uncle and I will join you in about half an hour.'

'With your permission, sir, I will escort Miss Bailstone to the lounge and take coffee with her there,' said Walter hopefully, rising from his seat.

'As you wish, my boy,' replied the General amiably, waving the young couple away as Cheetham the butler placed silver decanters of port and brandy upon the gleaming white tablecloth.

Once they were outside and Walter had closed the door, Louisa giggled and said: '*Tirez le rideau, la farce est jouée!*' Walter looked blankly for a moment and then returned her smile. 'That's Rabelais isn't it? Pull down the curtain the comedy is over,' he translated.

'Quite correct, and thank you so much for saving my bacon with your quick thinking just now. I really must learn to curb my tongue but Uncle, though a sweet man in many ways, is such an old reactionary when it comes to matters of social affairs that I just cannot keep quiet when he spouts such nonsense.'

'Are you a student of political economy?' asked Walter.

'Only in an amateur way,' dimpled the delicious girl. 'At the college I attend, Dame Bracknell's Academy for Young Ladies, we are taught by a daughter of Mrs Shackleton, the famous campaigner for women's rights and she has all the zeal of her mother when it comes to obtaining women such fundamental rights as the right to vote.'

'I haven't thought too much about votes for women,' Walter admitted. 'But of course all logic demands that men and women enjoy equal rights. After all, why should Dame Bracknell, for example, not be allowed to vote whilst her blacksmith may well possess the franchise?'

'Precisely, Walter,' she added. 'And I must tell you that in my opinion it is the Socialists who are showing us the way ahead, and soon the working people of this country will possess the full power of government through elective institutions to embody in law their rightful economic and social desires.'

Walter hardly heard her words, so dazzled was he by her pretty face and long hair which was worn simply, framing her attractive features and forming a level fringe on her forehead.

In the lounge, where Cheetham had set a pot of coffee bubbling cheerfully under a tiny gas light, Walter asked Louisa if he could turn the pages of her music.

'That's very kind of you, Walter,' she said, passing her tongue over her upper lip in a most sensuous fashion. 'But I was thinking of playing on some other instrument rather than General Stanton's piano.'

'Some other instrument, Louisa,' said the puzzled Walter, 'such as what?'

'How about the little piccolo down there?' said Louisa boldly. 'Gracious, it's more like a clarinet! Wally, have you something stuffed in your pocket or are you just glad to see me?'

Walter could not believe the evidence of his eyes and ears! But here was this lovely creature fondling his erect pego with one hand and unbuttoning her creamy Italian linen blouse with the other. The girl sensed his amazement and whispered: 'There is something else we learned in the Sixth Form at Dame Bracknell's Academy, Walter, best expressed perhaps in this little rhyme:

> *We may live without verses, music and art,*
> *We may live without conscience and live without heart,*
> *We may live without friends, we may live without luck,*
> *But life's mere existence without a good fuck!*

'This is a motto which the girls in my little circle there took to heart and with the aid of Doctor Coley's little book *The Young People's Guide to Procreation* to ensure the obtainment of the fullest joys without any accidents, we have discovered a very happy mode of living.'

Walter gulped and said: 'Do you mean you believe in free love?'

'Well, we don't charge for it nor do we expect to make payment to our partners,' said the delightful girl, stepping out of her drawers so that she stood completely nude in front of him. 'And of course we only pleasure ourselves with boys who we believe can match our standards in hygiene, ability and, above all, discretion.'

He stared in wonder and then with unabashed lust at her exquisitely-formed uptilted breasts each crowned by a rosy red nipple set in a large rounded areola, and her smooth white-skinned tummy below which twinkled a curly mass of fine brown hair.

Without further words they sank down to the floor, entwined in each other's arms, exchanging the most ardent of kisses as the hot-blooded Louisa unbuttoned Walter's trousers, releasing his straining shaft which sprang up like a flagpole between his thighs. She encircled his rigid member with her hand and planted a wet kiss on top of the uncovered red knob.

'My God, I didn't lock the door! Suppose someone comes in!' gasped Walter.

'No-one will come in, darling,' she whispered. 'I will confess to you however that covert intercourse does give me an added thrill. What a snub to the established order to enjoy the raw heat of ecstasy whilst everyone else is carrying on boring and being bored, totally oblivious to the intimacies taking place right under their silly noses!'

'If this is Socialism, I shall make a donation to the Party first thing tomorrow morning,' promised Walter.

'Never mind about a donation tomorrow, let us see if you can spend tonight,' said Louisa, diving down to wrap her lips around the swollen head of his rigid pole, taking as much of him as she could into her mouth. Her warm breath and moist mouth sent chills racing up and down his spine and her tongue slithering around his tingling rod soon brought him to the brink of orgasm. Louisa's delectable palating brought his truncheon past the point of no return and, as Walter began to spend, she gripped the base of his shaft, sucking him harder and harder until he felt his testicles hardening and he gasped a warning that his climax was near.

'I'm going to spend, Louisa!' he cried out, his penis jerking in and out of the sweet prison of her wet mouth.

But she made no move to extract his throbbing shaft from between her lips. She grasped the firm, muscular cheeks of his bottom, moving him backwards and forwards until with a final juddering throb he spurted a copious stream of spunk into her willing mouth. She swallowed his emission joyfully, smacking her lips as he quivered with convulsions of delight as they finished by wrapping their arms around each other and sealed their delight with a loving kiss.

Unlike earlier in the evening, Mr Pego could not be encouraged to remain at attention for there are limits to the stamina even of the most well-hung young gentlemen such as Walter. However, this did not preclude him from repaying his amorosa as she leaned back on the carpet with a cushion behind her head and another cushion stuffed underneath her delectable little bum. She spread her legs invitingly, affording Walter a bird's eye view of her silky-haired quim. His hands stroked her bare thighs and he moved higher to stroke her moist mons veneris, purring with sheer delight as he rubbed her furry little pussey.

She leaned forward to position Walter's head between her legs and he buried it in the hairs of her brown motte that covered her moist crack. It was delicious, divine. His heartbeat quickened with erotic excitement as his tongue raked her erect little clitoris then slipped down to probe inside her. Almost of their own volition her legs splayed even wider, bent at the knees as she sought to open herself even more to his questing tongue. He slurped lustily as he drew her cunney lips into his mouth, delighting in the taste of her flesh which he found clean and sweet to his tongue. Her hips thrust up in urgency, moaning and panting her pleasure as Walter lapped up the juices that were flowing freely from her cunney.

He was in the seventh heaven of delight as the unique feminine odour assailed his nose and he frantically attacked with his tongue the erect little clitty that trembled and twitched at his electric touch. This set Louisa off on her final journey to the highest hills of delight. She jerked her hips upwards as her stiff clitty was drawn further and further forward between his lips and her hands went down to clasp his head, pressing his mouth even more tightly against her. Her legs, folded across his shoulders, trembled as she cried: 'Walter, Walter, here I come! I can't stop now! Aaah! Aaah! Aaah!' She, too, spent profusely all over Walter's mouth and chin as she swam in a veritable sea of lubricity until she sank back exhausted and satiated by the delightful experience.

'What a superb *hors d'oeuvres* – now for the entrée!' enthused Louisa as, slowly at first, she gently stroked the underside of Walter's stiffening penis, allowing her fingers to trace a path around it and underneath his hairy ballsack which made his entire frame tingle with gratification. After a while she closed her finger and thumb around the shaft, sliding them along its length and easing down the foreskin, baring his purple knob as her head bobbed down and, like a lizard, her tongue slid around his rigid rod until it stood up firmly to attention.

As soon as it reached its fullest extent Louisa climbed on top of him with her knees on either side of his muscular trunk. The thick pile of the Turkish carpet acted as a mattress as she rubbed her pussey across the uncovered knob of his straining member. She smiled as she took hold of his prick and guided it slowly inside her. Walter could feel her cunney muscles contract and relax as she rocked up and down on his shaft, moving backwards and forwards in rhythm whilst Walter cupped her firm, uptilted breasts, flicking the rosy little nipples between his fingers and rubbing them against the palms of his hands.

Louisa bounced, shook and ground her hips and leaned first forwards and then right back so that his shaft was sliding deep in and then almost falling out – but never quite! Now their orgasms approached and the delectable girl drove down hard, spearing herself on his glistening cock as wave after wave of nervous spasms shot through her. Each spasm tightened her cunney muscles and then Walter began to jerk underneath her, thrusting up his hips to meet her pushes as their climaxes arrived simultaneously. Their hoarse cries of joy rang out as Walter pumped jets of salty spunk into her dark secret warmth whilst, with an immense shudder, Louisa's climax flowed and gradually subsided as her own love juices dribbled down the sides of her thighs.

She rolled off him and they lay panting with exhaustion until Louisa said: 'Walter, be a dear and pour some coffee. I think we both need a drink to revive us!'

'But of course, my love. What a terrible host I am not to have offered you something beforehand,' said Walter, rising to his feet and padding naked to the sideboard.

'I have no complaints about what I've eaten and drunk tonight,' murmured Louisa naughtily. 'But whilst you are up there, hadn't you better put on some clothes. After all, you know how traditional our two old uncles are about dressing for dinner!'

'Damnation, we'd better hurry!' exclaimed Walter, putting down his coffee cup and sorting through the pile of clothes for his underclothes.

They both dressed hastily and sat down on the couch to await the arrival of their avuncular fellow diners. Strangely, they waited in vain until Walter looked at his pocket watch and said: 'Do you know, it's almost an hour since we left the old boys. I think we'd better see what's going on.'

'Don't disturb them, perhaps they are in the middle of one of those interminable conversations about the Crimean campaigns,' advised Louisa, brushing the hair away from her eyes as they walked slowly back to the dining room.

So Walter opened the dining-room door – which was well away from the top of the table where dinner had been served – just a fraction and they popped their heads around just to see what was going on. Their mouths fell open when they saw that their uncles were engaged in activity with Nancy, the plump young kitchenmaid, which had little to do with military matters!

The table had been cleared but it was not empty, for lying across it, stark naked and flat on his back was Colonel Bailstone. His chest was covered with matted grey hair and his corpulent belly, without the restrictions imposed by a belt, sagged all over the place. But his member stood up smartly enough, a thick, twitching truncheon which was being manipulated with an expert hand by Nancy who was dressed, or rather half-undressed in her black maid's uniform. The Colonel, assisted no doubt by General Stanton, had undone all her top buttons and her large breasts were free of any covering and stood out naked and mouth-wateringly ripe for a touch of lips or fingers.

Nancy continued to rub her hand up and down his enormous shaft whilst the Colonel fondled her breasts. General Stanton muttered: 'A manoeuvre from the rear will win the battle,' as he undid the remaining buttons on the back of Nancy's blouse and slipped it off her. Her skirt and under-drawers soon followed along with the General's shirt, belt and trousers. He grunted with the effort of joining the pair already on the table but he made it without too much difficulty, panting 'Steady, the Buffs,' as he placed his hands on Nancy's bum cheeks. She had rich, sumptuous buttocks and as he prised open her legs the General and the prying eyes at the door were treated to a tantalizing glimpse of her furry pussey, a soft delicate purse waiting to be filled. She raised her buttocks slightly, showing herself wet and open, spread like a flower, inviting the General to plunge himself into her.

'Come on, sir, I'm ready for inspection,' cried Nancy but the General shook his head as he held his turgid penis and said apologetically: 'Sorry m'dear, my unit has surrendered without a fight. Gad, if I were twenty years younger!'

At the door, Louisa tapped Walter on the shoulder and said: 'Wally, in the name of social justice it is bounden upon you to fuck that poor girl immediately.'

'Do you really think I should?' said Walter whose bulging trousers showed how stimulated he had been by the wanton exhibition that was taking place on the dining-room table.

'Without any doubt,' said Louisa firmly. 'Go and do your duty at once.'

He needed no second bidding as he boldly marched forward and shucked off his clothes saying: 'Here comes the cavalry, Nancy!' as he leaped onto the rather crowded table behind her. She took one hand away from pumping Colonel Bailstone's tool and reached for Walter's rock hard shaft to guide it between her luscious bum cheeks. He was soon buried in her throbbing sheath as she thrust her bottom to and fro and Walter passed his hand round her waist to handle her luxuriously-covered mount quite freely, slipping two fingers inside to join his prick for her added enjoyment.

This was all too much for Colonel Bailstone who with a groan spent over Nancy's hand as she wriggled with glee for now she could concentrate on the velvety spear that was piercing her so engagingly from behind. She turned her head and exclaimed: 'Why Master Walter, fancy finding you here. Ooh! Ooh! Ooh! That's lovely, lovely. Now finish me off, sir, as I'm about to spend.'

She wriggled and worked her bottom cleverly so that Walter could embed even more of his thrusting shaft as her cunney magically expanded to receive it. How her bottom cheeks rotated as Walter's prick rammed in and out and his balls banged against her arse. Nancy screamed with happiness as Walter crashed down hard, pouring his frothy seed inside her in a tremendous gush just as her own explosion sent her over the edge into Nirvana.

Louisa had now walked into the room and on seeing her, the two uncles hastily pulled on their trousers, fumbling with red-faced embarrassment. However, the girl's eyes were fixed upon Walter and Nancy who had collapsed in a heap on the table.

With sublime coolness Louisa said that she hoped the copious libations of the love-making would not irretrievably stain the fine cotton tablecloth.

'Oh, no, miss, I find that a few dabs of Doctor Weston's Elixir will remove most stains from any material,' said Nancy, pulling on her drawers.

'Good heavens, I take a spoonful of Doctor Weston's Elixir to ease a cough,' said Walter.

'And I use it on my roses to keep the greenfly at bay,' confessed Colonel Bailstone, who may have held ridiculously reactionary political opinions but who possessed the saving grace of a sense of humour, which showed as he led the burst of laughter that followed his remark.

The party broke up shortly afterwards and nothing was mentioned then or ever afterwards about the goings-on in either the lounge or dining-room. Fortunately Cheetham had dozed off in the kitchen and was totally unaware as to what had taken place at Stanton Lodge – which was just as well for there are no bigger gossips than butlers.

Walter fell asleep that night almost as soon as his head touched the pillow, leaving the book he had purchased secretly at Hottens *An Introduction To The French Art of Fucking* by A Gentleman Much Experienced In These Arts unread. But before he drifted into the arms of Morpheus he suddenly thought of Katie Arkley for whose favours earlier that day he would have almost cheerfully laid down his life. He had been unfaithful to his would-be love not once but twice! He could not help smiling as John Gay's lines entered his mind:

> *How happy I could be with either*
> *Were t'other dear charmer away!*

I behaved like a cad, he told himself and resolved to continue wooing the lovely Katie at the first opportunity that presented itself. He closed his eyes and fell into a deep sleep, no doubt sated with all the pleasures that had been so freely and unexpectedly lavished upon him.

ANONYMOUS

from

The Voluptuous Night

The Voluptuous Night *was first published under the title,* The Voluptuous Night or the No Plus Ultra of Pleasure. *It is said that it is based on a translation of one of the numerous obscene pamphlets that were written about Marie Antoinette.*

AT the decease of my father, I came into the uncontrolled possession of a fortune which, though moderate, was yet sufficient to gratify my limited desires. That part of it which consisted of landed property, comprised, among other valuable estates, the ancient hereditary baronial domain of Bellesfesses, celebrated alike for fertility of its soil, the beauty of its scenery, the extent of its territory and the unbounded hospitality of its lords.

Three or four magnificent hotels at Paris, with about £400,000 in the funds, and £60,000 in ready cash at my bankers, constituted the remainder of my inheritance.

I was then but just turned of three-and-twenty. Weary of what appeared to my youthful and ardent mind the insipid monotony of a country life, I resolved to hasten to Paris, there to pursue the path of pleasure, ambition, or glory.

My reception at Court was highly gracious. The Monarch was pleased to eulogize the loyalty and bravery of my distinguished ancestors, and especially to pass strong ecomiums on the fealty and merits of my late father.

'That I may have the pleasure, sir,' continued his Majesty, 'of frequently seeing near me the representative of a friend I so highly esteemed, I appoint you to a Captaincy in my Body Guard.'

A reception so flattering, and an appointment that gave me immediate access to the Court and the highest circles, at once determined my wavering resolves.

Requesting, therefore, my banker to provide me with an establishment, I boldly entered the vortex of fashion and of pleasure.

Young, gay, of happy constitution, with an athletic yet symmetrically proportioned person – endowed with a lively imagination, having a reasonable share of good sense and good nature, tempered by as much knowledge as the generality of the best educated young men of that day, possessed with a disposition that led me always to do everything to please, and to abstain from everything that might offend those with whom I came in contact – I was esteemed and respected by men, and adored by the women.

Though there was scarcely any enjoyment beyond my reach, and although I tasted of pleasure in all its varied forms, yet the strongest penchant of my mind was to the delights that are derived from an amiable and intimate intercourse with the fair sex – the pleasures resulting from the lively and unrestrained discourse of a young, handsome and virtuous female, and the raptures experienced in the enjoyment of her person.

To these pleasures I was constitutionally biased, and by nature eminently gifted. They formed the ruling passion of my mind. My whole soul was indeed centred in them; and I permitted no opportunity of discreetly enjoying them to escape me.

Neither grossly and indiscriminately promiscuous, nor absurdly fastidious in my amours, the woman of fashion, the waiting maid, or the washerwoman, provided only that they possessed youth, beauty, and that happy plumpness of person and rotundity of limbs usually denominated *embonpoint*, were all equally loved, courted, and enjoyed by me.

Women in all ranks of life were adored by me; and frequently when lifting the cambric chemise of a marchioness, or the calico jupe of a milliner have I, as I intently surveyed the centre of bliss, dropped on my knees, and covering it with burning kisses, exclaimed, as I affectionately and tenderly compressed it with my hand:

> *'All glorious Cunt! through every land and clime,*
> *Thou reignest omnipotent, eternal, sublime!*
> *Sinner and saint alike thy empire own.*
> *And kneel uncovered fore thy joyous throne.'*

At my time of life, and with these sentiments, it will be easily imagined that I was not often without some love affair on my hands.

Madame d'Arbonne, so celebrated for her wit, beauty, and gallantry, was at that period the leader of the *ton*. A tender *liaison* existed between us; and I used frequently to assist at those delightful reunions which assembled at her house – all the rank, the beauty, and the talent of France.

It was on one of these occasions that I first beheld Madame Terville. She was in the flower of youth, handsome in her person, elegant in her manner, fascinating in her conversation, which, amidst all its gaiety and playfulness, was ever characterized by never exceeding the limits of the strictest propriety and decorum.

It was with surprise I learned her husband was so insensible to her charms that she was in a state of separation. The isolation of her worse than widowhood threw a touching interest around her. My senses also were powerfully influenced by her beauty, yet the delicacy of my sentiments, my connection with Madame d'Arbonne, who was her intimate friend, my aversion to inconstancy, and my knowledge that for a considerable time past a tender friendship had subsisted between her and the young Valsain induced me to stifle the first scintillations of passion, and to regard her only with a cold and decorous politeness.

But I could easily perceive these were not her sentiments. Her eyes perpetually sought mine, and tried, by their soft, penetrating, amorous glances, to read what was passing in my heart, and to reveal to me that state of hers. With this intent, she watched every opportunity of throwing herself in my way; but though her passion for me seemed daily to become more ardent, yet she did not permit it to compromise her dignity, or to infringe on that decorum to which, as will subsequently be seen, Madame Terville was scrupulously attached.

In this position of affairs, it chanced that on my going one evening to Madame d'Arbonne's opera box to await her arrival, I got there so unfashionably early as to put me quite out of countenance, the performance had not even commenced. Scarcely, however, had I entered, when I heard myself called to from the next box. It was the decorous Madame Terville who spoke to me.

'What,' said she 'can bring you here so early? Your time must hang very heavy on your hands. How solitary and lost you seem. Come and sit by me.'

I was far from imagining what extraordinary and romantic events this meeting would give rise to. But in woman that faculty is extremely lively, and Madame Terville instantly conceived a singular project.

'I must,' said she, 'save you from the ridicule which your being seen here so lonely and deserted would bring upon you. I must – the idea is a capital one; and as you are here, there is nothing more easy than for me to execute it. Some propitious deity has conducted you hither. Have you any engagements tonight? If you have, I apprise you that they will not be kept, I shall run away with you. Submit quietly; make no resistance; trust to Providence; call my people. You are a charming, delightful man.'

My entreaties to be excused were of no avail. She compelled me to call her servants. On their appearance:

'Go,' said she to one of them, 'to this gentleman's house, and acquaint his people that he will not be at home tonight.'

She then whispered something to him and dismissed him.

I attempted to speak; but the opera commenced, and she enjoined my silence. We listened, therefore, or at least pretended to listen to the performance. Scarcely however, was the first act over, when a note was handed to Madame Terville, and it was at the same time announced that everything was ready. She smiled, and taking me by the arm, descended to her carriage, caused me to enter it, gave her orders, and we were speedily out of town, without my being able to learn what were her intentions.

Whenever I attempted to question her on the subject, she burst into a loud laugh. If I had not been aware she was a woman of strong passions, and that she had at that very time an avowed attachment of which she could not suppose me ignorant, I should have been tempted to think she meant to make me a happy man.

On her part she was equally well acquainted with the state of my affections, for, as I have already stated, she was the intimate friend of Madame d'Arbonne. I dismissed, therefore, so presumptuous a supposition, and awaited as patiently as I could the *dénouement*.

We changed horses and again pursued our route without a moment's delay. The affair now seemed to be getting rather serious, I then asked, with some earnestness, where this whim of hers would terminate?

'It will terminate,' said she, 'in placing you in a delightful abode – but guess where? I will give you a thousand times to find out. Do you give it up? It is then to my husband's we are going. Are you acquainted with him?'

'Not at all.'

'No matter. I have a slight acquaintance with him, and I think you will like him. We have been reconciled now for these six months and during this month past we have been corresponding with each other. It is, I think very gallant in me to pay him the first visit.'

'It is so, but what, I beseech you, shall I do then? Of what service can I be?'

'That is my business. I dreaded the ennui of a *tête-à-tête*. You are an agreeable companion, and I am delighted at having you with me.'

'But it seems strange that you should choose the day of your reconciliation for my introduction to him. You would make me believe myself a mere cipher, if it was not impossible for a young man of five-and-twenty to be so. Consider also the restraint and embarrassment that always attend a first interview. Truly I see nothing pleasant to any one of us in the scheme you have formed.'

'Bah! no preaching, I beg of you. You mistake your errand. I want you to amuse, to divert, and not preach to me.'

Finding her so determined, I resolved to be equally decided. I began, therefore, to joke about the part I had to act. We became quite gay, and at last her project appeared to me not so very unreasonable.

We changed horses a second time. The mysterious lamp of night illumined a pure sky with a soft voluptuous light. We were approaching the spot where our *tête-à-tête* would finish. She made me at times admire the beauty of the landscape, the calmness of the night, the affecting silence of nature.

To admire this scene more perfectly, we leaned toward the window. In this situation the motion of the carriage caused Madame Terville's beautiful face frequently to come in contact with mine. The most delightful perfume exhaled from her rosy mouth, and thrilled my every vein. A sudden jolt made her grasp my hand; and I wishing to support her in my arms, by the merest accident in the world, placed one of my hands on a breast exquisitely firm and round. Thus reclining on each other, I know not what we looked at. I only remember that objects began rapidly to grow confused to my sight, and that at the delicate and divine lips of Madame Terville.

Suddenly she disengaged herself from me, and threw herself into a corner of the carriage. It was high time, for, to confess the truth the effects of this kiss had begun to work a strange revolution in my whole frame.

'Is it,' said she, after a deep reverie, 'your intention to convince me how imprudent a step I have taken?'

Her question perplexed me.

'My intention – with you – what a mockery! You are too clear-sighted for me to attempt – but accident, surprise – may – be – pardoned.'

'Yes,' replied she, 'you seem to have relied on accident and surprise.'

As we were discussing this point, we entered, without perceiving it, the court-yard of the chateau.

The mansion was illuminated throughout and everything wore the look of joy except the countenance of its proprietor. His languid air plainly evinced that family interests alone induced his reconciliation with his wife. Politeness however caused him to approach the coach door. On my being introduced to him, he offered me his hand, and I followed him into the house, thinking of the part I had to play, and delighted with the subtlety and agility of the mind and person of the beautiful and enchanting Madame Terville, whose charms were disturbing to my imagination and inflaming my blood.

I passed through several rooms, decorated with the utmost taste and magnificence, for the proprietor of the chateau carried luxury to its highest point of refinement, and sought to reanimate the powers of his exhausted constitution by the most attractive and voluptuous pictures. Not knowing what to say, I contented myself with merely admiring them.

The Goddess of the Temple hastened to do its honours, and to receive my compliments.

'You see nothing at present,' said she, 'I must show you the apartment of Monsieur.'

'Ah! Madame,' replied he, 'it is now five years since I unfurnished it.'

'Ha! ha!' returned she, wthout attending to what she said. I could scarce refrain from laughing when I saw how little she knew of what was passing in her own house.

At supper, she offered to help Monsieur to some pigeon en compote. 'Madame,' replied he, 'I have for these three years confined myself to a vegetable diet.' 'Ha! ha!' said she, again. Imagine to yourself what conversation could take place between three people so surprised to find themselves met together.

Supper over, I expected that we should retire early but my expectation was correct as regarded the husband only. On our return to the drawing room, 'Madame,' said he, 'I feel highly obliged at your having been so provident as to bring this gentleman with you. You thought that I was but a sorry companion for a night's rendez-vous, and you thought rightly, for I shall withdraw.' Then, turning to me, he said, with an air of irony: 'Monsieur will have the goodness to pardon me, and to make my peace with Madame.'

We looked at each other; and to divert the thoughts which this abrupt departure gave rise to, Madame Terville proposed that we should take a turn on the terrace until her people had finished their supper. Nothing could be more agreeable to me! but I dissembled the pleasure I felt, and offering her my arm, conducted to the garden this seducing lady of whom I had already had so delicious a foretaste.

The night was superb. The moon afforded an imperfect light, and seemed to veil objects only to give greater scope to the imagination. The mansion and gardens leaned against a mountain; and the latter stretched their long alleys to the banks of the Seine, which bounded them with its waters, whose numerous windings formed various rural and picturesque islands that diversified the scenery and augmented the beauty of the landscape.

It was in the longest of these alleys that we commenced our promenade. It was overhung with thickly leaved trees. The more we walked, the more forcibly my heart beat. She complained of the manner in which her husband had just been jeering her, and, as we strolled along, confided to me several little secrets. Confidence generates confidence, I entrusted to her several of my secrets, and our conversation became every instant more intimate and more interesting.

She had from the first given me her arm, the rotundity, whiteness, and firmness of which I could not help admiring. By degrees this arm entwined itself with mine until she leant so strongly on me that she scarcely touched the earth. This situation however did not prevent my active fingers from wandering over a breast that with a charming elasticity shrunk from and rebounded to my touch. It was a delightful position, but too fatiguing to be long continued, and we had still a great deal to say to each other.

A green and verdant bank presented itself and we sat down on it without changing our attitude. In this position, which caused me ardently to desire a still more interesting one, we began to extol friendship, and to praise the charms and delights of mutual confidence.

'Ah!' said she to me, 'who can enjoy them better than we, or with less dread of their consequences? I am well aware you are too strongly attached to another person for me to have anything to fear from you.'

Perhaps she wished the contrary, and excited as my desires were, I know not how I remained impassive. My blood was in a boil, I was wild to possess her, and yet I restrained myself. I am myself sincere, and this trait in my character has always caused me to detest affectation and coquettishness in women.

We were thus mutually persuaded that we could never be anything to each other but what we already were. This conviction, however, did not prevent me from surveying the beauties of one of the handsomest bosoms I ever had at my disposal. I endeavoured by gently squeezing two rose buds that delightfully repelled the pressure of my fingers, to awake desire in her palpitating heart.

'I was apprehensive,' said I, 'that my rashness just now in the carriage might have frightened you.'

'Oh! I am not so easily frightened.'

'I fear, however, it has offended you,' and in the meantime, my fingers, as though on the gamut of love, were incessantly playing with her heavenly breasts. 'Can I, by any means, reassure you?'

'It is in your power to do so.'

'In what manner?'

'Can you not guess?'

'But I wish to be told; I want to be certain that you have pardoned me.'

'How shall I convince you?'

'Grant me freely the kiss I accidentally snatched from you, and which appeared to displease you.'

'Why did you not speak plainly? I will grant it to you willingly. My refusal would make you too proud; your self-love would cause you to believe that I was afraid of you.'

She wished to prevent my so deceiving myself, and with that view repeatedly kissed me with ardour.

Heavens! what were my emotions when I felt her delicate tongue, as though darted by Love himself, gently open my glowing lips, insinuate itself like a flash of fire, and seeking my tongue, unite itself with and caress it! No, never can I describe the state into which this amorous and exciting tongue threw all my senses. I thought myself transported to the abodes of the Gods, or that in the Gardens of Imathonté, I was inhaling voluptuousness from the rosy mouth of the most enchanting of the Goddesses.

Kisses are like confidences – they attract, they excite additional ones. In fact, no sooner had she given me the first, than she followed it with a second still more tender – to which a third, yet warmer, succeeded. Our kisses, now mingled together, became so frequent and ardent as to interrupt – to discontinue our conversation, and at last, scarcely did they afford room for our amorous sighs. My breath grew shorter and shorter; the sight – the feel of her swelling breasts, which I covered with repeated and burning kisses – made me tremble with delight, and thrilled every vein with a gush of ecstatic joy.

A deep silence ensued. We heard it (for silence is sometimes audible). It terrified us. We rose without speaking and resumed our walk – he, disquieted, agitated; I, equally affected, but endeavouring, like Neptune, to calm the tempestuous waves, though my blood was so heated by our mutual caresses, that I could scarcely prevent emitting as we walked.

'We will return,' said she, 'the evening air is unpleasant.'

'I think,' said I, 'it will not affect you.'

'Oh!' replied she, 'I am not susceptible of its influence as many; but that is of no consequence, we will return.'

'It is, doubtless, from regard to me that – . You wish to preserve me from the impressions that a walk like this might make upon me – the fatal consequences to my happiness it might produce.'

'You assign a deal of delicacy to my motives; but I wish to return – I insist on it.'

How awkward is the conversation between two people who compel themselves to talk of every subject except that which they really wish to converse on! She forced me to retake the road of the chateau.

I know not, at least, I did not then know, if in this step she was doing violence to her own feelings, or if it proceeded from her having finally made up her mind, or if she was actuated to it by the mortification she mutually felt at a scene agreeably commenced having terminated so stupidly. However that was, our steps, by a species of instinct, reciprocally became slower, and we walked on, silent, melancholy, and dissatisfied with ourselves and with each other. We knew not how to act. We neither of us had a right to exact – to demand – anything of the other; we could not even have the consolation of mutual reproaches, so that our sentiments were confined to our own breasts. I should have been delighted with a quarrel, but how excite one? Meanwhile we approached the mansion, silently occupied in endeavouring to relieve ourselves from the conditions we had so unskilfully imposed on one another. All that I know is, that in spite of my fine theory on male coquetry I could not imagine how, after what had occurred between us, I could be such a Joseph.

We had reached the fatal door when at last Madame Terville spoke –

'I am not quite satisfied with you. After all the confidence I have shown you, you ought not to have withheld yours from me. During the whole time we have been together, you have not said a single word about Madame d'Arbonne, although it is so delightful to speak of those we love; and you cannot doubt but I should have heard you with interest. I could have done no less than be so complaisant, after having risked depriving you of her.'

'Cannot I reproach you with the same thing? Would not you have pretended much that has occurred if, instead of confiding to me the particulars of your reconciliation with your husband, you have spoken to me of a more suitable subject – of Valsain?'

'A moment's attention, if you please. Think how greatly the slightest suspicion hurts us. The little you know of women ought to make you aware that they will always choose their own time to confide their secrets. But to the point. On what terms are you with Madame d'Arbonne? Are you happy with her? Ah! I fear not; the thought afflicts me, for I feel great interest in your welfare. Yes, Sir, I am interested about you – far more than you may imagine.'

'But why then, Madame, adopt the rumour of a public prone to scandalize, to exaggerate, to invent, and believe that I am intimate with Madame d'Arbonne?'

'Spare yourself the dissimulation. I am thoroughly acquainted with the whole affair. Madame d'Arbonne is not so reserved as you are. Women like always to betray the secrets of their adorers, particularly when like you they maintain a discreet silence which might prevent their conquest being known. I am far from accusing her of coquetry; but a prude has as much vanity as a coquette.

'Tell me candidly, have you not frequently been the victim of this sort of character? Tell me — tell me – .'

'But Madame, you wished to re-enter the château, and the air – .'

'It has changed.'

She took my arm again, and we recommenced our walk, without my noticing what path we took. What she had said of the mistress she was aware I had – what she had said of the lover I knew she had – this journey in which I had met with so many delightful adventures – the scene in the carriage, that on the green bank, the situation, the hour – all these things perplexed me. I was by turns hurried away either by my self-love or by desires, and restored to myself by reflection, but I was too greatly agitated to form any plan or to make any decided resolutions.

Whilst I was thus a prey to contending emotions, she had not ceased speaking an instant; and her discourse ran entirely on Madame d'Arbonne, whilst my silence appeared to confirm everything she thought proper to say of her. Some sentiments which she dropped, recalled me, however, to my senses – or rather to her.

'How artful, but how graceful is she! A treachery in her hands seems nothing but a gaiety; infidelity appears to be an effort of the reason – a sacrifice to decorum; always amiable, rarely affectionate, never true, gallant from disposition, a prude from system – lively, skilful, prudent, rash, sensible, learned – a coquette and a philosopher – she is a Proteus in her forms, and a Grace in her manners – she entices, she eludes. How many parts have I seen her play! Between ourselves, with what dupes is she surrounded! What a laughing-stock she has made of Dormeuil; what tricks has she played with Belmont! When she formed a connection with you it was only to confound and mislead them. They had had time to observe her, and would have discovered her real character; to prevent this, she introduced you on the stage, roused their jealousy, excited them to fresh attempts – reduced you to despair, lamented you, consoled you, and finally rendered you all four perfectly contented. Ah! what power has an artful woman over you! and how happy is she, since at the game she has a chance of gaining everything whilst she takes nothing!'

Madame Terville accompanied this last sentence with a most expressive and insinuating sigh. It was a master stroke.

I felt that a bandage had been removed from my eyes, but I did not perceive that it had been replaced by another. My desires which my having carefully restrained them, only caused to inflame me more ardently, completed her triumph. I was struck with the fidelity of the picture she had drawn. Madame d'Arbonne seemed to me the falsest of women. I sighed, though without knowing wherefore, and without discovering whether it proceeded from regret or from hope. She seemed sorry at having disquieted me, and at having allowed herself to go rather too far in a sketch, which, being drawn by a female hand, might very possibly be doubted.

We continued our promenade; and after many ramblings she pointed out to me at the end of the terrace a pavilion that had witnessed her happiest moments. She described to me its situation, and the style in which it was fitted up. What a pity we had not the key! Whilst thus talking we approached it. By accident it was open. Nothing was wanting but daylight; darkness, however, might lend it some attractions. I knew also how heavenly was the object that was about to constitute its principal ornament.

We trembled as we entered. It was a sanctuary and that the sanctuary of love. The God took full possession of our knees – we lost every power and faculty but that of love. Our feeble arms entwined in each other, and we fell involuntarily on a sofa which was placed in a recess of the temple. The moon was on the point of setting, and the last of her rays presently stripped the veil from a modesty that was becoming rather annoying. Darkness confuses and confounds everything. My hands, more impatient than ever, one while roved over two charming globes, smooth and firm as marble, or toyed with albaster thighs, whose softness and plumpness delighted the touch! then they wandered to the centre of pleasure, the entrance to which seemed to be guarded by a profusion of curly hair, only to render it more attractive and exciting to the ardent lover; or played with buttocks whose elasticity, rotundity, and firmness could only be equalled by their fatness, their pliability and their happy adaptation for voluptuousness.

I felt everything – I rummaged everything – I wished to devour everything with my impatient tongue. But a hand repulsed or rather wished to repulse me. Then feeling how forcibly my heart beat she attempted to fly from me, but sank back more agitated, more impassioned than ever. An active and intelligent finger glided opportunely into the pavilion of pleasure, rendered her still more favourable to my wishes. As I titillated her clitoris, her thighs quivered with delight, half opened themselves – every part of her body trembled. I seized the propitious moment, and boldly penetrated to the very bottom of this sanctuary of love. A soft and stifled ejaculation announced her happiness.

Her deep drawn sighs – the wild movement of her loins, excited by my skilful fingers – only confirmed what her gestures and her voice had already clearly indicated until at last we sank in that delicious annihilation to which nothing but itself can be compared.

ANONYMOUS

from
Flossie

Flossie *is a masterpiece of Victorian erotica describing in intimate detail an older man's infatuation with a pretty, young girl who manages to combine naivety with just the right amount of sexual curiosity.*

'MY LOVE, SHE'S BUT A LASSIE YET.'

Towards the end of a bright sunny afternoon in June, I was walking in one of the quieter streets off Piccadilly, when my eye was caught by two figures coming in my direction. One was that of a tall, finely-made woman about 27, who would, under other circumstances, have received something more than an approving glance. But it was her companion that riveted my gaze of almost breathless admiration. This was a young girl of such astounding beauty of face and figure as I had never seen or dreamt of. Masses of bright, wavy, brown hair fell to her waist. Deep violet eyes looked out from under long curling lashes, and seemed to laugh in unison with the humorous curves of the full red lips. These and a thousand other charms I was to know by heart later on, but what struck me most at this first view, was the extraordinary size and beauty of the girl's bust, shown to all possible advantage by her dress which, in the true artistic French style, crept in between her breasts, outlining their full and perfect form with loving fidelity. Tall and lithe, she moved like a young goddess, her short skirt showing the action of a pair of exquisitely moulded legs, to which the tan-coloured openwork silk stockings were plainly designed to invite attention. Unable to take my eyes from this enchanting vision I was approaching the pair, when to my astonishment the elder lady suddenly spoke my name.

'You do not remember me, Captain Archer.' For a moment I was at a loss, but the voice gave me the clue.

'But I do,' I answered, 'you are Miss Letchford, who used to teach my sister.'

'Quite right. But I have given up teaching, for which fortunately there is no longer any necessity. I am living in a flat with my dear little friend here. Let me introduce you, – Flossie Eversley – Captain Archer.'

The violet eyes laughed up at me, and the red lips parted in a merry smile. A dimple appeared at the corner of the mouth. I was done for! Yes; at thirty-five years of age, with more than my share of experiences in every phase of love, I went down before this lovely girl with her childish face smiling at me above the budding womanhood of her rounded breasts, and confessed myself defeated!

A moment or two later I had passed from them with the address of the flat in my pocket, and under promise to go down to tea on the next day.

At midday I received the following letter:

Dear Captain Archer,

I am sorry to be obliged to be out when you come; and yet not altogether sorry, because I should like you to know Flossie very well. She is an orphan, without a relation in the world. She is just back from a Paris school. In years she is of course a child, but in tact and knowledge she is a woman; also in figure, as you can see for yourself! She is of an exceedingly warm and passionate nature, and a look that you gave her yesterday was not lost upon her. In fact, to be quite frank, she has fallen in love with you! You will find her a delightful companion. Use her *very* tenderly, and she will do anything in the world for you. Speak to her about her life in the French school; she loves to talk of it. I want her to be happy, and I think you can help.

Yours sincerely,
Eva Letchford.

I must decline any attempt to describe my feelings on receiving this remarkable communication. My first impulse was to give up the promised call at the flat. But the flower-like face, the soft red lips and the laughing eyes passed before my mind's eye, followed by an instant vision of the marvellous breasts and the delicate shapely legs in their brown silk stockings, and I knew that fate was too strong for me. For it was of course impossible to misunderstand the meaning of Eva Letchford's letter, and indeed when I reached the flat she herself opened the door to me, whispering as she passed out, 'Flossie is in there, waiting for you. You two can have the place to yourselves. One last word. You have been much in Paris, have you not? So has Flossie. She is *very* young – *and there are ways* – Good-bye.'

I passed into the next room. Flossie was curled up in a long chair, reading. Twisting her legs from under her petticoats with a sudden movement that brought into full view her delicately embroidered drawers she rose and came towards me, a rosy flush upon her cheeks, her eyes shining, her whole bearing instinct with an enchanting mixture of girlish coyness and anticipated pleasure. Her short white skirt swayed as she moved across the room, her breasts stood out firm and round under the close-fitting woven silk jersey; what man of mortal flesh and blood could withstand such allurements as these! Not I, for one! In a moment she was folded in my arms. I rained kisses on her hair, her forehead, her eyes, her cheeks, and then, grasping her body closer and always closer to me, I glued my lips upon the scarlet mouth and revelled in a long and maddeningly delicious kiss – a kiss to be ever remembered – so well remembered now, indeed, that I must make some attempt to describe it. My hands were behind Flossie's head, buried in her long brown hair. Her arms were round my body, locked and clinging. At the first impact her lips were closed, but a moment later they parted, and slowly, gently, almost as if in the performance of some solemn duty, the rosy tongue crept into my mouth, and bringing with it a flood of the scented juices from her throat, curled amorously round my own, whilst her hands dropped to my buttocks, and standing on tiptoe she drew me to her with such extraordinary force and vigour that our lower parts seemed to be already in conjunction. Not a word was spoken on either side – indeed under the circumstances speech was impossible, for our tongues had twined together in a caress of unspeakable sweetness, which neither would be the first to fore-go. At last the blood was coursing through my veins at a pace that became unbearable and I was compelled to unglue my mouth from hers. Still silent, but with love and longing in her eyes, she pressed me into a low chair, and seating herself on the arm passed her hand behind my head, and looking full into my eyes whispered my name in accents that were like the sound of a running stream. I kissed her open mouth again and again, and then feeling that the time had come for some little explanation: –

'How long will it be before your friend Eva comes back?' I asked.

'She has gone down into the country, and won't be here till late this evening.'

'Then I may stay with you, may I?'

'Yes, do, do, *do*, Jack. Do you know, I have got seats for an Ibsen play tonight. I was wondering . . . if . . . you would . . . take me!'

'Take *you* – to an Ibsen play – with your short frocks, and all that hair down your back! Why, I don't believe they'd let us in?'

'Oh, if *that's* all, wait a minute.'

She skipped out of the room with a whisk of her petticoats and a free display of brown silk legs. Almost before I had time to wonder what she was up to, she was back again. She had put on a long skirt of Eva's, her hair was coiled on the top of her head, she wore my 'billycock' hat and a pair of blue pince-nez, and carrying a crutch-handled stick, she advanced upon me with a defiant air, and glaring down over the top of her glasses she said in a deep masculine voice: –

'Now, sir, if, you're ready for Ibsen, *I* am. Or if your tastes are so *low* that you can't care about a play, I'll give you a skirtdance.'

As she said this she tore off the long dress, threw my hat on to a sofa, let down her hair with a turn of the wrist, and motioning me to the piano picked up her skirts and began to dance.

Enchanted as I was by the humour of her quick change to the 'Ibsen woman', words are vain to describe my feelings as I feebly tinkled a few bars on the piano and watched the dancer.

Every motion was the perfection of grace and yet no Indian Nautch-girl could have more skilfully expressed the idea of sexual allurement. Gazing at her in speechless admiration, I saw the violet eyes glow with passion, the full red lips part, the filmy petticoats were lifted higher and higher; the loose-frilled drawers gleamed white. At last breathless and panting, she fell back upon a chair, her eyes closed, her legs parted, her breasts heaving. A mingled perfume came to my nostrils – half '*odor di fæmina*', half the scent of white rose from her hair and clothes.

I flung myself upon her.

'Tell me, Flossie darling, what shall I do *first?*'

The answer came, quick and short.

'Kiss me – *between my legs!*'

In an instant I was kneeling before her. Her legs fell widely apart. Sinking to a sitting posture, I plunged my head between her thighs. The petticoats incommoded me a little, but I soon managed to arrive at the desired spot. Somewhat to my surprise instead of finding the lips closed and barricaded as is usual in the case of young girls, they were ripe, red and pouting, and as my mouth closed eagerly upon the delicious orifice and my tongue found and pressed upon the trembling clitoris I knew that my qualms of conscience had been vain. My utmost powers were now called into play and I sought by every means I possessed to let Flossie know that I was no half-baked lover. Passing my arms behind her I extended my tongue to its utmost length and with rapid agile movements penetrated the scented recesses. Her hands locked themselves under my head, soft gasps of pleasure came from her lips, and as I delivered a last and effective attack upon the erect clitoris, her fingers clutched my neck, and with a sob of delight she crossed her legs over my back, and pressing my head towards her held me with a convulsive grasp, whilst the aromatic essence of her being flowed softly into my enchanted mouth.

As I rose to my feet she covered her face with her hands and I saw a blue eye twinkle out between the fingers with an indescribable mixture of bashfulness and fun. Then as if suddenly remembering herself she sat up, dropped her petticoats over her knees, and looking up at me from under the curling lashes, said in a tone of profound melancholy:

'Jack, am I not a *disgraceful* child! All the same I wouldn't have missed *that* for a million pounds.'

'Nor would I, little sweetheart; and whenever you would like to have it again – '

'No, no, it is your turn now.'

'What! Flossie; you don't mean to say – '

'But I *do* mean to say it, and to *do* it, too. Lie down on that sofa at once, sir.'

'But, Flossie, I really – '

Without another word she leapt at me, threw her arms round my neck and fairly bore me down on to the divan. Falling on the top of me she twined her silken legs round mine and gently pushing the whole of her tongue between my lips, began to work her body up and down with a wonderful sinuous motion which soon brought me to a state of excitement bordering on frenzy. Then shaking a warning finger at me to keep still she slowly slipped to her knees on the floor.

In another moment I felt the delicate fingers round my straining yard. Carrying it to her mouth she touched it ever so softly with her tongue; then slowly parting her lips she pushed it gradually between them, keeping a grasp of the lower end with her hand which she moved gently up and down. Soon the tongue began to quicken its motion, and the brown head to work rapidly in a perpendicular direction. I buried my hands under the lovely hair, and clutched the white neck towards me, plunging the nut further and further into the delicious mouth until I seemed almost to touch the uvula. Her lips, tongue and hands now worked with redoubled ardour, and my sensations became momentarily more acute, until with a cry I besought her to let me withdraw. Shaking her head with great emphasis, she held my yard in a firmer grasp, and passing her disengaged hand behind me, drew me towards her face, and with an unspeakable clinging action of her mouth carried out the delightful act of love to its logical conclusion, declining to remove her lips until some minutes after the last remaining evidences of the late crisis had completely disappeared.

Then and not till then, she stood up, and bending over me as I lay kissed me on the forehead, whispering: –

'Then! Jack, now I love you twenty times more than ever.'*

I gazed into the lovely face in speechless adoration.

'Why don't you say something?' she cried. 'Is there anything else you want me to do?'

'Yes,' I answered, 'there *is*.'

'Out with it, then.'

'I am simply dying to see your breasts, naked.'

'Why, you darling, of course you shall! Stay there a minute.'

Off she whisked again, and almost before I could realize she had gone I looked up and she was before me. She had taken off everything but her chemise and stockings, the former lowered well beneath her breasts.

Any attempt to describe the beauties thus laid bare to my adoring gaze must necessarily fall absurdly short of the reality. Her neck, throat and arms were full and exquisitely rounded, bearing no trace of juvenile immaturity.

Her breasts, however, were of course the objects of my special and immediate attention.

For size, perfection of form and colour I had never seen their equals, nor could the mind of man conceive anything so alluring as the coral nipples, which stood out firm and erect, craving kisses. A wide space intervened between the two snowy hillocks, which heaved a little with the haste of her late exertions. I gazed a moment in breathless delight and admiration, then rushing towards her I buried my face in the enchanting valley, passed my burning lips over each of the neighbouring slopes and finally seized upon one after the other of the rosy nipples, which I sucked, mouthed and tongued with a frenzy of delight.

The darling little girl lent herself eagerly to my every action, pushing her nipples into my mouth and eyes, pressing her breasts against my face, and clinging to my neck with her lovely naked arms.

Whilst we were thus amorously employed my little lady had contrived dexterously to slip out of her chemise, and now stood before me naked but for her brown silk stockings and little shoes.

'There, Mr Jack, now you can see my breasts, and everything else

---

* This is a fact, as every girl knows who has ever gamahuched and been gamahuched by the man or boy she loves. As a *link*, it beats f . . . ing out of the field. I've tried both and I *know*.'

Flossie.

that you like of mine. In future this will be my full-dress costume for making love to you in. Stop, though; it wants just one touch,' and darting out of the room she came back with a beautiful chain of pearls round her neck, finishing with a pendant of rubies which hung just low enough to nestle in the Valley of Delight, between the wonderful breasts.

'I am now,' she said, 'the White Queen of the Gama Huchi Islands. My kingdom is bounded on this side by the piano, and on the other by the furthest edge of the bed in the next room. Any male person found wearing a *stitch* of clothing within those boundaries will be sentenced to lose his p. . . . But soft! who comes here?'

Shading her eyes with her hand she gazed in my direction: –

'Aha! a stranger; and, unless these royal eyes deceive us, a man! He shall see what it is to defy our laws! What ho! within there! Take this person and remove his p. . . .'

'Great Queen!' I said, in a voice of deep humility, 'if you will but grant me two minutes, I will make haste to comply with your laws.'

'And we, good fellow, will help you.'

(*Aside*).

'Methinks he is somewhat comely.'★

(*Aloud*).

'But first let us away with these leg garments, which are more than aught else a violation of our Gama Huchian Rules. Good! now the shirt. And what, pray, is *this*? We thank you, sir, but we are not requiring any *tent-poles* just now.'

'Then if your Majesty will deign to remove your royal fingers I will do my humble best to cause the offending pole to disappear. At present, with your Majesty's hand upon it – '

'Silence, sir! Your time is nearly up, and if the last garment be not removed in twenty seconds . . . So! you obey. 'Tis well! You shall see how we reward a faithful subject of our laws.'

And thrusting my yard between her lips the Great White Queen of the Gama Huchi Islands sucked in the whole column to the very root, and by dint of working her royal mouth up and down, and applying her royal fingers to the neighbouring appendages, soon drew into her throat a tribute to her greatness, which from its volume and the time it took in the act of payment, plainly caused her Majesty the most exquisite enjoyment. Of my own pleasure I will only say that it was

---

★ *Don't believe I ever said anything of the sort, but if I did, 'methinks' I'd better take this opportunity of withdrawing the statement.*

Flossie.

delirious, whilst in this as in all other love sports in which we indulged an added zest was given by the humour and fancy with which this adorable child-woman designed and carried out our amusements. In the present case the personating of the Great White Queen appeared to afford her especial delight, and going on with the performance, she took a long branch of pampas-grass from its place and waving it over my head, she said: –

'The next ceremony to be performed by a visitor to these realms will, we fear, prove somewhat irksome, but it must be gone through. We shall now place our royal person on this lofty throne. You, sir, will sit upon this footstool before us. We shall then wave our sceptre three times. At the third wave our knees will part and our guest will see before him the royal spot of love. This he will proceed to salute with a kiss which shall last until we are pleased to signify that we have had enough. Now, most noble guest, open your mouth, *don't* shut your eyes, and prepare! One, two, *three.*'

The pampas-grass waved, the legs parted, and nestling between the ivory thighs I saw the scarlet lips open to show the erected clitoris peeping forth from its nest below the slight brown tuft which adorned the base of the adorable belly. I gazed and gazed in mute rapture, until a sharp strident voice above me said: –

'Now then, there, move on, please; can't have you blocking up the road all day!' Then changing suddenly to her own voice: –

'Jack, if you don't kiss me at once I shall *die!*'

I pressed towards the delicious spot and taking the whole cunt into my mouth passed my tongue upwards along the perfumed lips until it met the clitoris, which thrust itself amorously between my lips, imploring kisses. These I rained upon it with all the ardour I could command, clutching the rounded bottom with feverish fingers and drawing the naked belly closer and ever closer to my burning face, whilst my tongue plunged deep within the scented cunt and revelled in its divine odours and the contraction of its beloved lips.

The Great White Queen seemed to relish this particular form of homage, for it was many minutes before the satin thighs closed, and with the little hands under my chin she raised my face and looking into my eyes with inexpressible love and sweetness shining from her own, she said simply: –

'Thank you, Jack. You're a darling!' –

By way of answer I covered her with kisses, omitting no single portion of the lovely naked body, the various beauties of which lent themselves with charming zest to my amorous doings. Upon the round and swelling breasts I lavished renewed devotion, sucking the rosy nipples with a fury of delight, and relishing to the full the quick movements of rapture with which the lithe clinging form was constantly shaken, no less than the divine aroma passing to my nostrils as the soft thighs opened and met again, the rounded arms rose and fell, and with this the faintly perfumed hair brushing my face and shoulders mingled its odour of tea-rose.

All this was fast exciting my senses to the point of madness, and there were moments when I felt that to postpone much longer the consummation of our amour would be impossible.

I looked at the throbbing breasts, remembered the fragrant lips below that had pouted ripely to meet my kisses, the developed clitoris that told of joys long indulged in. And then . . . And then . . . the sweet girlish face looked up into mine, the violet eyes seemed to take on a pleading expression, and as if reading my thoughts Flossie pushed me gently into a chair, seated herself on my knee, slipped an arm round my neck, and pressing her cheek to mine, whispered: –

'Poor, *poor* old thing! I know what it wants; and *I* want it too – badly, oh! so badly. But, Jack, you can't guess what a friend Eva has been to me, and I've promised her *not to!* You see I'm so very young, and . . . *the consequences!* There! don't let us talk about it. Tell me all about yourself, and then I'll tell you all about *myself*, and when you're tired of hearing me talk you shall stop my mouth with – well, whatever you like. Now sir, begin!'

I gave her a short narrative of my career from boyhood upwards, dry and dull enough in all conscience!

'Yes, yes, that's all very nice and prim and proper,' she cried. 'But you haven't told me the principal thing of all, – when you first began to be – naughty, and with whom?'

I invented some harmless fiction which I saw the quickwitted little girl did not believe, and begged her to tell me her own story which she at once proceeded to do. I shall endeavour to transcribe it, though it is impossible to convey any idea of the humour with which it was delivered, still less of the irrepressible fun which flashed from her eyes at the recollection of her schoolgirl pranks and amourettes. There were, of course, many interruptions,* for most of which I was probably responsible; but, on the whole, in the following chapter will be found a fairly faithful transcript of Flossie's early experiences. Some at least of these I am sanguine will be thought to have been of a sufficiently appetizing character.

---

* The first of these is a really serious one, but for this the impartial reader will see that the responsibility was divided.

'HOW FLOSSIE ACQUIRED THE FRENCH TONGUE.'

'Before I begin, Jack, I should like to hold something nice and solid in my hand, to sort of give me confidence as I go on. Have you got anything about you that would do?'

I presented what seemed to me the most suitable article 'in stock' at the moment.

'Aha!' said Flossie in an affected voice, 'the very thing! How *very* fortunate that you should happen to have it ready!'

'Well, madam, you see it is an article we are constantly being asked for by our lady-customers. It is rather an expensive thing – seven pound ten – '

'Yes. It's rather stiff. Still, if you can assure me that it will always keep in its present condition, I shouldn't mind spending a good deal upon it.'

'You will find, madam, that anything you may spend upon it will be amply returned to you. Our ladies have always expressed the greatest satisfaction with it.'

'Do you mean that you find they come more than once? If so, I'll take it now.'

'Perhaps you would allow me to bring it myself – ?'

'Thanks, but I think I can hold it quite well in my hand. It won't go off suddenly, will it?'

'Not if it is kept in a cool place, madam.'

'And it mustn't be shaken, I suppose, like *that*, for instance?' (*shaking it*)

'For goodness gracious sake, take your hand away, Flossie, or there'll be a catastrophe.'

'That is a good word, Jack! But do you suppose that if I saw a "catastrophe" coming I shouldn't know what to do with it?'

'*What* should you do?'

'Why, what *can* you do with a catastrophe of that sort but *swallow it*?'

The effect of this little interlude upon us both was magnetic. Instead of going on with her story Flossie commanded me to lie upon my back on the divan, and having placed a couple of pillows under my neck, knelt astride of me with her face towards my feet. With one or two caressing movements of her bottom she arranged herself so that the scarlet vulva rested just above my face. Then gently sinking down she brought her delicious cunt full upon my mouth from which my tongue instantly darted to penetrate the adorable recess. At the same moment I felt the brown hair fall upon my thighs, my straining prick plunged between her lips, and was engulfed in her velvet mouth to the very root, whilst her hands played with feverish energy amongst the surrounding parts, and the nipples of her breasts rubbed softly against my belly.

In a very few moments I had received into my mouth her first tribute of love and was working with might and main to procure a second, whilst she in her turn, wild with pleasure my wandering tongue was causing her, grasped my yard tightly between her lips, passing them rapidly up and down its whole length, curling her tongue round the nut, and maintaining all the time an ineffable sucking action which very soon produced its natural result. As I poured a torrent into her eager mouth I felt the soft lips which I was kissing contract for a moment upon my tongue and then part again to set free the aromatic flood to which the intensity of her sensations imparted additional volume and sweetness.

The pleasure we were both experiencing from this the most entrancing of all the reciprocal acts of love was too keen to be abandoned after one effort. Stretching my hands upwards to mould and press the swelling breasts and erected nipples, I seized the rosy clitoris anew between my lips, whilst Flossie resumed her charming operations upon my instrument which she gamahuched with ever increasing zest and delight, and with a skill and variety of action which would have been marvellous in a woman of double her age and experience. Once again the fragrant dew was distilled upon my enchanted tongue, and once again the velvet mouth closed upon my yard to receive the results of its divinely pleasurable ministrations.

Raising herself slowly and almost reluctantly from her position Flossie laid her naked body at full length upon mine and after many kisses upon my mouth, eyes and cheeks said, 'Now you may go and refresh yourself with a bath while I dress for dinner.'

'But where are we going to dine?' I asked.

'You'll see presently. *Go* along, there's a good boy!'

I did as I was ordered and soon came back from the bath-room, much refreshed by my welcome ablutions.

Five minutes later Flossie joined me, looking lovelier than ever, in a short-sleeved pale blue muslin frock, cut excessively low in front, black open work silk stockings and little embroidered shoes.

'Dinner is on the table,' she said, taking my arm and leading me into an adjoining room where an exquisite little cold meal was laid out, to which full justice was speedily done, followed by coffee made by my hostess, who produced some Benedictine and a box of excellent cigars.

'There, Jack, if you're quite comfy I'll go on with my story. Shall I stay here, or come and sit on your knee?'

'Well, as far as getting on with the story goes, I think you are better in that chair, Flossie – '

'But I told you I must have something to hold.'

'Yes, you *did*, and the result was that we didn't get very far with the story, if you remember – '

'Remember! As if I was likely to forget. But look at this,' holding up a rounded arm bare to the shoulder. 'Am I to understand that you'd rather not have this round your neck?'

Needless to say she was to understand nothing of the sort, and a moment later she was perched upon my knee and having with deft penetrating fingers found her way to the support she required, 'solid' enough under her magic touch, began her narrative.

'I don't think there will be much to tell you until my school life at Paris begins. My father and mother both died when I was quite small; I had no brothers or sisters, and I don't believe I've got a relation in the world. You mustn't think I want to swagger, Jack, but I am rather rich. One of my two guardians died three years ago and the other is in India and doesn't care a scrap about me. Now and then he writes and asks how I am getting on, and when he heard I was going to live with Eva (whom he knows quite well) he seemed perfectly satisfied. Two years ago he arranged for me to go to school in Paris.

'Now I must take great care not to shock you, but there's nothing for it but to tell you that about this time I began to have the most wonderful feelings all over me – a sort of desperate longing for something, – I didn't know what – which used to become almost unbearable when I danced or played any game in which a boy or man was near me. At the Paris school was a very pretty girl, named Ylette de Vespertin, who, for some reason I never could understand, took a fancy to me. She was two years older than I, had several brothers and boy cousins at home, and being up to every sort of lark and mischief, was just the girl I wanted as a confidante. Of course she had no difficulty in explaining the whole thing to me, and in the course of a day or two I knew everything there was to know. On the third day of our talks Ylette slipped a note into my hand as I was going up to bed. Now, Jack, you must really go and look out of the window while I tell you what it said:

'"Chérie,
'"Si tu veux te faire sucer la langue, les seins et le con, viens dans mon lit toute nue ce soir. C'est moi qui te ferai voir les anges.
'"Viens de suite à ton
'"Ylette."

'I have rather a good memory, and even if I hadn't, I don't think I could ever forget the words of that note, for it was the beginning of a most delicious time for me.

'I suppose if I had been a well-regulated young person, I should have taken no notice of the invitation. As it was I stripped myself naked in a brace of shakes, and flew to Ylette's bedroom which was next door to the one I occupied. I had not realized before what a beautifully made girl she was. Her last garment was just slipping from her as I came in, and I stared in blank admiration at her naked figure which was like a statue in the perfection of its lines. A furious longing to touch it seized me and springing upon her I passed my hands feverishly up and down her naked body, until grasping me round the waist she half dragged half carried me to the bed, laid me on the edge of it, and kneeling upon the soft rug plunged her head between my legs, and bringing her lips to bear full upon the *other* lips before her, parted them with a peculiar action of the mouth and inserted her tongue with a sudden stroke which sent perfect waves of delight through my whole body, followed by still greater ecstasy when she went for the particular spot *you* know of, Jack – the one near the top, I mean – and twisting her tongue over it, under it, round it and across it soon brought about the result she wanted, and in her own expressive phrase "me faisait voir les anges".

'Of course I had had no experience, but I did my best to repay her for the pleasure she had given me, and as I happen to possess an extremely long and pointed tongue, and Ylette's cunt – oh Jack, *I've said it at last!* Go and look out of the window again; or better still, come and stop my naughty mouth with – I *meant* your tongue, but this will do better still. The wicked monster, what a size he is! Now put both your hands behind my head, and push him in till he touches my throat. Imagine he is *somewhere else*, work like a demon and for your life don't stop until the very end of all things. Ah! the dear, darling, delicious thing! How he throbs with excitement! I believe he can *see* my mouth waiting for him. Come, Jack, my darling, my beloved, let me gamahuche you. I want to feel this heavenly prick of yours between my lips and against my tongue so that I may suck it and drain every drop that comes from it into my mouth. Now, Jack *now* . . .'

The red lips closed hungrily upon the object of their desire, the rosy tongue stretched itself amorously along the palpitating yard, and twice the tide of love poured freely forth to be received with every sign of delight into the velvet mouth.

Nothing in my experience had ever approached the pleasure which I derived from the intoxicating contact of this young girl's lips and tongue upon my most sensitive parts, enhanced as it was by my love for her, which grew apace, and by her own intense delight in the adorable pastime. So keen indeed were the sensations she procured me that I was almost able to forget the deprivation laid upon me by Flossie's promise to her friend. Indeed, when I reflected upon her youth, and the unmatched beauty of her girlish shape with its slender waist, smooth satin belly and firm rounded breasts, the whole seemed too perfect a work of nature to be marred – at least as yet – by the probable consequences of an act of coition carried to its logical conclusion by a pair of ardent lovers.

So I bent my head once more to its resting-place between the snowy thighs, and again drew from my darling little mistress the fragrant treasures of love's sacred storehouse, lavished upon my clinging lips with gasps and sighs and all possible tokens of enjoyment in the giving.

After this it was time to part, and at Flossie's suggestion I undressed her, brushed out her silky hair and put her into bed. Lying on her white pillow she looked so fair and like a child that I was for saying goodnight with just a single kiss upon her cheek. But this was not in accordance with her views on the subject. She sat up in bed, flung her arms round my neck, nestled her face against mine and whispered in my ear:

'I'll never give a promise again as long as I live.'

It was an awful moment and my resolution all but went down under the strain. But I just managed to resist, and after one prolonged embrace, during which Flossie's tongue went twining and twisting round my own with an indescribably lascivious motion, I planted a farewell kiss full upon the nipple of her left breast, sucked it for an instant and fled from the room.

On reaching my own quarters I lit a cigar and sat down to think over the extraordinary good fortune by which I had chanced upon this unique liaison. It was plain to me that in Flossie I had encountered probably the only specimen of her class. A girl barely adult with all the fresh charm of that beautiful age united to the fascination of a passionate and amorous woman. Add to these a finely-strung temperament, a keen sense of humour, and the true artist's striving after thoroughness in all she did, and it will be admitted that all these qualities meeting in a person of quite faultless beauty were enough to justify the self-congratulations with which I contemplated my present luck, and the rosy vision of pleasure to come which hung about my waking and sleeping senses till the morning.

About midday I called at the flat. The door was opened to me by Eva Letchford.

'I am so glad to see you,' she said. 'Flossie is out on her bicycle, and I can say what I want to.'

As she moved to the window to draw up the blind a little, I had a better opportunity of noticing into what a really splendid woman she had developed. Observing my glances of frank admiration she sat down in a low easy chair opposite to me, crossed her shapely legs, and looking over at me with a bright pleasant smile, said,

'Now, Jack – I may call you Jack, of course, because we are all three going to be great friends – you had my letter the other day. No doubt you thought it a strange document, but when we know one another better you will easily understand how I came to write it.'

'My dear girl, I understand it already. You forget I have had several hours with Flossie. It was her happiness you wanted to secure, and I hope she will tell you your plan was successful!'

'Flossie and I have no secrets. She has told me everything that passed between you. She has also told me what did *not* pass between you, and how you did not even try to make her break her promise to me.'

'I should have been a brute if I had – '

'Then I am afraid nineteen men out of twenty are brutes – but that's neither here nor there. What I want you to know is that I appreciate your nice feeling, and that some day soon I shall with Flossie's consent take an opportunity of shewing that appreciation in a practical way.' Here she crossed her right foot high over the left knee and very leisurely removed an imaginary speck of dust from the shotsilk stocking.

'Now I must go and change my dress. You'll stay and lunch with us in the coffee-room won't you? – that's right. This is my bedroom. I'll leave the door open so that we can talk till Flossie comes. She promised to be in by one o'clock.'

We chatted away on indifferent subjects whilst I watched with much satisfaction the operations of the toilette in the next room.

Presently a little cry of dismay reached me: –

'Oh dear, oh dear! do come here a minute, Jack. I have pinched one of my breasts with my stays and made a little red mark. Look! *Do* you think it will show in evening dress?'

I examined the injury with all possible care and deliberation.

'My professional opinion is, madam, that as the mark is only an inch above the nipple we may fairly hope – '

'*Above* the nipple! then I'm afraid it will be a near thing,' said Eva with a merry laugh.

'Perhaps a little judicious stroking by an experienced hand might – '

'Naow then there, Naow then!' suddenly came from the door in a hoarse cockney accent. 'You jest let the lydy be, or oi'll give yer somethink to tyke 'ome to yer dinner, see if oi don't!'

'Who is this person?' I asked of Eva, placing my hands upon her two breasts as if to shield them from the intruder's eyes.

'Person yerself!' said the voice, 'Fust thing *you've* a-got ter do is ter leave 'old of my donah's breasties and then oi'll *tork* to yer!'

'But the lady has hurt herself, sir, and was consulting me professionally.'

There was a moment's pause, during which I had time to examine my opponent whom I found to be wearing a red Tam-o'-Shanter cap, a close fitting knitted silk blouse, a short white flannel skirt, and scarlet stockings. This charming figure suddenly threw itself upon me open-armed and open-mouthed and kissed me with delightful abandon.

After a hearty laugh over the success of Flossie's latest 'impersonation', Eva pushed us both out of the room, saying, 'Take her away, Jack, and see if *she* has got any marks. Those bicycle saddles are rather trying sometimes. We will lunch in a quarter of an hour.'

I bore my darling little mistress away to her room, and having helped her to strip off her clothes, I inspected on my knees the region where the saddle might have been expected to gall her, but found nothing but a fair expanse of firm white bottom which I saluted with many lustful kisses upon every spot within reach of my tongue. Then I took her naked to the bath-room, and sponged her from neck to ankles, dried her thoroughly, just plunged my tongue once deep into her cunt, carried her back to her room, dressed her and presented her to Eva within twenty minutes of our leaving the latter's bedroom.

Below in the coffee-room a capitally served luncheon awaited us. The table was laid in a sort of little annexe to the principal room and I was glad of the retirement, since we were able to enjoy to the full the constant flow of fun and mimicry with which Flossie brought tears of laughter to our eyes throughout the meal. Eva, too, was gifted with a fine sense of the ridiculous, and as I myself was at least an appreciative audience, the ball was kept rolling with plenty of spirit.

After lunch Eva announced her intention of going to a concert in Piccadilly, and a few minutes later Flossie and I were once more alone.

'Jack,' she said, 'I feel thoroughly and hopelessly naughty this afternoon. If you like I will go on with my story while you lie on the sofa and smoke a cigar.'

This exactly suited my views and I said so.

'Very well, then. First give me a great big kiss with all the tongue you've got about you . . . Ah! that was good! Now I'm going to sit on this footstool beside you, and I *think* one or two of these buttons might be unfastened, so that I can feel whether the story is producing any effect upon you. Good gracious! why, it's as hard and stiff as a poker already. I really *must* frig it a little – '

'Quite gently and slowly then, *please* Flossie, or – '

'Yes, quite, *quite* gently and slowly, so – Is that nice, Jack?'

'Nice is not the word, darling!'

'Talking of words, Jack, I am afraid I shall hardly be able to finish my adventures without occasionally using a word or two which you don't hear at a Sunday School Class. Do you mind, very much? Of course you can always go and look out of the window, can't you!'

'My dearest little sweetheart, when we are alone together like this, and both feeling extremely naughty, as we do now, any and every word that comes from your dear lips sounds sweet and utterly void of offence to me.'

'Very well, then; that makes it ever so much easier to tell my story, and if I *should* become too shocking – well, you know how I *love* you to stop my mouth, don't you Jack!'

A responsive throb from my imprisoned member gave her all the answer she required.

'Let me see,' she began, 'where was I? Oh, I remember, in Ylette's bed.'

'Yes, she had gamahuched you, and you were just performing the same friendly office for her.'

'Of course: I was telling you how the length of my tongue made up for the shortness of my experience, or so Ylette was kind enough to say. I think she meant it too: at any rate she spent several times before I gave up my position between her legs. After this we tried the double gamahuche, which proved a great success because, although she was, as I have told you, two years older than I, we were almost exactly of a height, so that as she knelt over me her cunt came quite naturally upon my mouth, and her mouth upon my cunt, and in this position we were able to give each other an enormous amount of pleasure.'

At this point I was obliged to beg Flossie to remove her right hand from the situation it was occupying.

'What I cannot understand about it,' she went on, 'is that there are any number of girls in France, and a good many in England too, who after they have once been gamahuched by another girl don't care about anything else. Perhaps it means that they have never been really in love with a man, because to *me* one touch of your lips in that particular neighbourhood is worth ten thousand kisses from anybody else, male or female and when I have got your dear darling, delicious prick in my mouth, I want nothing else in the whole wide world except to give you the greatest possible amount of pleasure and to make you spend down my throat in the quickest possible time – '

'If you really want to beat the record, Flossie, I think there's a good chance now – '

Almost before the words had passed my lips the member in question was between *hers*, where it soon throbbed to the crisis in response to the indescribable sucking action of mouth and tongue of which she possessed the secret.

On my telling her how exquisite were the sensations she procured me by this means she replied:

'Oh, you have to thank Ylette for that! Just before we became friends she had gone for the long holidays to a country house belonging to a young couple who were great friends of hers. There was a very handsome boy of eighteen or so staying in the house. He fell desperately in love with Ylette and she with him, and he taught her exactly how to gamahuche him so as to produce the utmost amount of pleasure. As she told me afterwards, "Every day, every night, almost every hour, he would bury his prick in my mouth, frig it against my tongue, and fill my throat with a divine flood. With a charming amiability he worked incessantly to show me every kind of gamahuching, all the possible ways of sucking a man's prick. Nothing, said he, should be left to the imagination, which, he explained, can never produce such good results as a few practical lessons given in detail upon a real standing prick, plunged to the very root in the mouth of the girl pupil, to whom one can thus describe on the spot the various suckings, hard, soft, slow or quick, of which it is essential she should know the precise effect in order to obtain the quickest and most copious flow of the perfumed liquor which she desires to draw from her lover.

'"I suppose," Ylette went on, "that one invariably likes what one can do well. Anyhow, my greatest pleasure in life is to suck a good-looking boy's prick. If he likes to slip his tongue into my cunt at the same time, *tant mieux*."

'Unfortunately this delightful boy could only stay a fortnight, but as there were several other young men of the party, and as her lover was wise enough to know that after his recent lessons in the art of love Ylette could not be expected to be an abstainer, he begged her to enjoy herself in his absence, with the result, as she said that "au bout d'une semaine il n'y avait pas un vit dans la maison qui ne m'avait tripoté la luette,* ni une langue qui n'était l'amie intime de mon con."

'Every one of these instructions Ylette passed on to me, with practical illustrations upon my second finger standing as substitute for the real thing, which, of course, was not to be had in the school at – least not just then.

'She must have been an excellent teacher for I have never had any other lessons than hers, and yours is the first and only staff of love that I have ever had the honour of gamahuching. However, I mean to make up now for lost time, for I would have you to know, my darling, that I am madly in love with every bit of your body, and that most of all do I

---

* Uvula

adore your angel prick with its coral head that I so love to suck and plunge into my mouth. Come, Jack. Come! let us have one more double gamahuche. One moment! There! now I am naked. I am going to kneel over your face with my legs wide apart and my cunt kissing your mouth. Drive the whole of your tongue into it, won't you, Jack, and make it curl round my clitoris. Yes! that's it – just like that. Lovely! Now I can't talk any more, because I am going to fill my mouth with the whole of your darling prick; push it down my throat, Jack, and when the time comes spend your very longest and most. I'm going to frig you a little first and rub you under your balls. Goodness! how the dear thing is standing. In he goes now . . . m . . . m . . . m.m.m.m . . .'

A few inarticulate gasps and groans of pleasure were the only sounds audible for some minutes during which each strove to render the sensations of the other as acute as possible. I can answer for it that Flossie's success was complete, and by the convulsive movements of her bottom and the difficulty I experienced in keeping the position of my tongue upon her palpitating clitoris, I gathered that my operations had not altogether failed of their object. In this I was confirmed by the copious and protracted discharge which the beloved cunt delivered into my throat at the same instant as the incomparable mouth received my yard to the very root, and a perfect torrent rewarded her delicious efforts for my enjoyment.

'Ah, Jack! that was just heavenly,' she sighed, as she rose from her charming position. '*How* you did spend, that time, you darling old boy, and so did I, eh, Jack?'

'My little angel, I thought you would never have finished,' I replied.

'Do you know, Jack, I believe you really did get a little way down my throat, then! At any rate you managed the "tripotage de luette" that Ylette's friend recommended so strongly!'

'And I don't think I ever got quite so far into your cunt, Flossie.'

'That's quite true; I felt your tongue touch a spot it had never reached before. And just wasn't it lovely when you got there! It almost makes me spend again to think of it! But I am not going to be naughty any more. And to show you how truly virtuous I am feeling I'll continue my story if you like. I want to get on with it, because I know you must be wondering all the time how a person of my age can have come to be so . . . what shall we say, Jack?'

'Larky,' I suggested.

'Yes, "larky" will do. Of course I have always been "older than my age" as the saying goes, and my friendship with Ylette and all the lovely things she used to do to me made me "come on" much faster than most girls. I ought to tell you that I got to be rather a favourite at school, and after it came to be known that Ylette and I were on gamahuching terms, I used to get little notes from almost every girl in the school, imploring me to sleep with her. One dear little thing even went so far as to give me the measurements of her tongue, which she had taken with a piece of string.'

'Oh, I say, Flossie, *come now* – I can swallow a good deal but – '

'You can indeed, Jack, as I have good reason to know! But all the same it's absolutely true. You can't have any conception what French school-girls of a certain age are like. There is nothing they won't do to get themselves gamahuched, and if a girl is pretty or fascinating or has particularly good legs, or specially large breasts, she may, if she likes, have a fresh admirer's head under her petticoats every day in the week. Of course it's all very wrong and dreadful, I know, but what else can you expect? In France gamahuching between grown-up men and women is a recognized thing – '

'Not only in France, *nowadays*,' I put in.

'So I have heard. But at any rate in France every body does it. Girls at school naturally know this, as they know most things. At that time of life – at *my* time of life, if you like – a girl thinks and dreams of nothing else. She cannot, except by some extraordinary luck, find herself alone with a boy or man. One day her girl chum at school pops her head under her petticoats and gamahuches her deliciously. How can you wonder if from that moment she is ready to go through fire and water to obtain the same pleasure?'

'Go on, Flossie. You are simply delicious to-day!'

'Don't laugh, Jack. I am very serious about it. I don't care how much a girl of SAY my age longs for a boy to be naughty with – it's perfectly right and natural. What I think is bad is that she should *begin* by having a liking for a girl's tongue inculcated into her. I should like to see boys and girls turned loose upon one another once a week or so at authorized gamahuching parties, which should be attended by masters and governesses (who would have to see that the *other* thing was not indulged in, of course). Then the girls would grow up with a good healthy taste for the other sex, and even if they did do a little gamahuching amongst themselves between whiles, it would only be to keep themselves going till the next "party". By my plan a boy's prick would be the central object of their desires, as it ought to be. Now *I* think that's a very fine scheme, Jack, and as soon as I am a little older, I shall go to Paris and put it before the Minister of Education!'

'But why wait, Flossie? Why not go now?'

'Well, you see, if the old gentleman (I suppose he *is* old, isn't he, or he wouldn't be a minister?) – if he saw a girl in short frocks, he would think she had got some private object to serve in regard to the gamahuching parties. Whereas a grown-up person who had plainly left school might be supposed to be doing it unselfishly for the good of the rising generation.'

'Yes, I understand that. But when you *do* go, Flossie, please take me or some other respectable person with you, because I don't altogether trust that Minister of Education, and whatever the length of your frocks might happen to be at the time, I feel certain that, old or young, the moment you had explained your noble scheme, he would be wanting some practical illustrations on the office armchair!'

'How dare you suggest such a thing, Jack! You are to understand, sir, that from henceforth my mouth is reserved for three purposes, to eat with, to talk with, and to kiss you with on whatever part of your person I may happen to fancy at the moment. By the way you won't mind my making just one exception in favour of Eva, will you? She loves me to make her nipples stand with my tongue; occasionally, too, we perform the "*soixante-neuf.*"'

'When the next performance takes place, may I be there to see?' I ejaculated fervently.

'Oh, Jack, how shocking!'

'Does it shock you, Flossie? Very well. Then I withdraw it, and apologise.'

'You cannot withdraw it now. You have distinctly stated that you would like to be there when Eva and I have our next gamahuche.'

'Well, I suppose I *did* say – '

'Silence, sir,' said Flossie in a voice of thunder, and shaking her brown head at me with inexpressible ferocity. 'You have made a proposal of the most indecent character, and the sentence of the Court is that at the first possible opportunity you shall be *held to that proposal*. Meanwhile, the Court condemns you to receive 250 kisses on various parts of your body, which it will at once proceed to administer. Now, sir, off with your clothes!'

'Mayn't I keep my – '

'No, sir, you may *not!*'

The sentence of the Court was accordingly carried out to the letter, somewhere about three-fourths of the kisses being applied upon one and the same part of the prisoner to which the Court attached its mouth with extraordinary gusto.

NOX AMBROSIANA.

My intercourse with the tenants of the flat became daily more intimate and more frequent. My love for Flossie grew intensely deep and strong as opportunities increased for observing the rare sweetness and amiability of her character, and the charm which breathed like a spell over everything she said and did. At one moment, so great was her tact and so keen her judgement, I would find myself consulting her on a knotty point with the certainty of getting sound advice; at another the child in her would suddenly break out and she would romp and play about like the veriest kitten. Then there would be yet another reaction, and without a word of warning she would become amorous and caressing and seizing upon her favourite plaything, would push it into her mouth and suck it in a perfect frenzy of erotic passion. It is hardly necessary to say that these contrasts of mood lent an infinite zest to our liaison and I had almost ceased to long for its more perfect consummation. But one warm June evening allusion was again made to the subject by Flossie, who repeated her sorrow for the deprivation she declared I must be feeling so greatly.

I assured her that it was not so.

'Well, Jack, if you aren't, *I* am,' she cried. 'And what is more there is some one else who is "considerably likewise" as our old gardener used to say.'

'What *do* you mean, child?'

She darted into the next room and came back almost directly.

'Sit down there and listen to me. In that room lying asleep on her bed is the person whom, after you, I love best in the world. There is nothing I wouldn't do for her, and I'm sure you'll believe this when I tell you that I am going to beg you on my knees, to go in there and do to Eva what my promise to her prevents me from letting you do to me. Now, Jack, I know you love me and you know how *dearly* I love you. Nothing can alter *that*. Well, Jack, if you will go into Eva, gamahuche her well and let her gamahuche you (she *adores* it), and then *have* her thoroughly and in all positions – I shall simply love you a thousand times better than ever.'

'But Flossie, my darling, Eva doesn't – '

'Oh, doesn't she! Wait till you get between her legs, and see! Come along: I'll just put you inside the room and then leave you. She is lying outside her bed for coolness – on her side. Lie down quietly *behind* her. She will be almost sure to think it's me, and perhaps you will hear – something interesting. Quick's the word! Come!'

The sight which met my eyes on entering Eva's bedroom was enough to take one's breath away. She lay on her side with her face towards the door, stark naked, and fast asleep. I crept noiselessly towards her and gazed upon her glorious nudity in speechless delight. Her dark hair fell in a cloud about her white shoulders. Her fine face was slightly flushed, the full red lips a little parted. Below, the gleaming breasts caught the light from the shaded lamp at her bedside, the pink nipples rising and falling to the time of her quiet breathing. One fair round arm was behind her head, the other lay along the exquisitely turned thigh. The good St. Antony might have been pardoned for owning himself defeated by such a picture!

As is usual with a sleeping person who is being looked at, Eva stirred a little, and her lips opened as if to speak. I moved on tiptoe to the other side of the bed and stripping myself naked lay down beside her.

Then without turning round a sleepy voice said, 'Ah, Flossie, are you there? What have you done with Jack? (*a pause*) When are you going to lend him to me for a night Flossie? I wish I'd got him here now, between my legs – betwe-e-e-n m-y-y-y le-egs! Oh dear! how randy I do feel tonight. When I *do* have Jack for a night, Flossie, may I take his prick in my mouth before we do the other thing? Flossie – Floss*ee* – why don't you answer? Little darling! I expect she's tired out, and no wonder! Well, I suppose I'd better put something on me and go to sleep too!'

As she raised herself from the pillow her hand came in contact with my person.

'Angels and Ministers of Grace defend us! What's this? *You*, Jack! *And you've heard what I've been saying?*'

'I'm afraid I have, Eva.'

'Well, it doesn't matter: I meant it all, and more besides! Now before I do anything else I simply must run in and kiss that darling Floss for sending you to me. It is just like her, and I can't say anything stronger than *that!*'

'Jack,' she said on coming back to the room. 'I warn you that you are going to have a stormy night. In the matter of love I've gone starving for many months. Tonight I'm fairly roused and when in that state I believe I am about the most erotic bed-fellow to be found anywhere. Flossie has given me leave to *say* and *do* anything and everything to you, and I mean to use the permission for all its worth. Flossie tells me that you are an absolutely perfect gamahucher. Now I adore being gamahuched. Will you do that for me, Jack?'

'My dear girl, I should rather think so!'

'Good! But it is not to be all on one side. I shall gamahuche you, too, and you will have to own that I know something of the art. Another thing you may perhaps like to try is what the French call "*fouterie aux seins.*"'

'I know all about it, and if I may insert monsieur Jacques between those magnificent breasts of yours, I shall die of the pleasure.'

'Good again. Now we come to the legitimate drama from which you and Floss have so nobly abstained. I desire to be thoroughly and comprehensively fucked tonight – sorry to have to use the word, Jack, but it is the only one that expresses my meaning.'

'Don't apologise, dear. Under present circumstances all words are allowable.'

'Glad to hear you say that because it makes conversation so much easier. Now let me take hold of your prick, and frig it a little, so that I may judge what size it attains in full erection. So! He's a fine boy, and I think he will fit my cunt to a turn. I must kiss his pretty head, it looks so tempting. Ah! delicious! See here, Jack, I will lie back with my head on the pillow, and you shall just come and kneel over me and have me in the mouth. Push away gaily, just as if you were fucking me, and when you are going to spend slip one hand under my neck and drive your prick down my throat, and do not *dare* to withdraw it until I have received all you have to give me. Sit upon my chest first for a minute and let me tickle your prick with the nipples of my breasts. Is that nice? Ah! I thought you would like it! *Now* kneel up to my face, and I will suck you.'

With eagerly pouting lips and clutching fingers she seized upon my straining yard, and pressed it into her soft mouth. Arrived there, it was saluted by the velvet tongue which twined itself about the nut in a thousand lascivious motions.

Mindful of Eva's instructions I began to work the instrument as if it was in another place. At once she laid her hands upon my buttocks and regulated the time of my movements, assisting them by a corresponding action of her head. Once, owing to carelessness on my part, her lips lost their hold altogether; with a little cry she caught my prick in her fingers and in an instant it was again between her lips and revelling in the adorable pleasure of their sucking.

A moment later and my hands were under her neck, for the signal, and my very soul seemed to be exhaled from me in response to the clinging of her mouth as she felt my prick throb with the passage of love's torrent.

After a minute's rest, and a word of gratitude for the transcendent pleasure she had given me, I began a tour of kisses over the enchanting regions which lay between her neck and her knees, ending with a protracted sojourn in the most charming spot of all. As I approached this last, she said:

'Please to begin by passing your tongue slowly round the edges of the lips, then thrust it into the lower part at full length and keep it there, working it in and out for a little. Then move it gradually up to the top and when there press your tongue firmly against my clitoris a minute or so. Next take the clitoris between your lips and suck it *furiously*, bite it gently, and slip the point of your tongue underneath it. When I have spent twice, which I am sure to do in the first three minutes, get up and lie between my legs, drive the whole of your tongue into my mouth, and the whole of your prick into my cunt, and fuck me with all your might and main!'

I could not resist a smile at the naiveté of these circumstantial directions. My amusement was not lost upon Eva, who hastened to explain, by reminding me again that it was 'ages' since she had been touched by a man. 'In gamahuching,' she said, 'the *details* are everything. In copulation they are not so important, since the principal things that increase one's enjoyment – such as the quickening of the stroke towards the end by the man, and the knowing exactly how and when to apply the *nipping* action of the cunt by the woman – come more or less naturally, especially with practice. But now, Jack, I want to be gamahuched, please.'

'And I'm longing to be at you, dear. Come and kneel astride of me, and let me kiss your cunt without any more delay.'

Eva was pleased to approve of this position and in another moment I was slipping my tongue into the delicious cavity which opened wider and wider to receive its caresses and to enable it to plunge further and further into the perfumed depths. My attentions were next turned to the finely developed clitoris which I found to be extraordinarily sensitive. In fact Eva's own time-limit of three minutes had not been reached when the second effusion escaped her, and a third was easily obtained by a very few more strokes of the tongue. After this she laid herself upon her back, drew me towards her and, taking hold of my prick, placed it tenderly between her breasts and pressing them together with her hands urged me to enjoy myself in this enchanting position. The length and stiffness imparted to my member by the warmth and softness of her breasts delighted her beyond measure, and she implored me to fuck her without any further delay. I was never more ready or better furnished than at that moment, and after she had once more taken my prick into her mouth for a moment, I slipped down to the desired position between her thighs which she had already parted to their uttermost to receive me. In an instant she had guided the staff of love to the exact spot, and with a heave of her bottom, aided by an answering thrust from me, had buried it to the root within the soft folds of its natural covering.

Eva's description of herself as an erotic bed-fellow had hardly prepared me for the joys I was to experience in her arms. From the moment the nut of my yard touched her womb, she became as one possessed. Her eyes were turned heavenwards, her tongue twined round my own in rapture, her hands played about my body, now clasping my neck, now working feverishly up and down my back and ever and again creeping down to her lower parts where her first and second finger would rest compass-shaped upon the two edges of her cunt, pressing themselves upon my prick as it glided in and out and adding still further to the maddening pleasure I was undergoing. Her breath came in short quick gasps, the calves of her legs sometimes lay upon my own but more often were locked over my loins or buttocks, thus enabling her to time to a nicety the strokes of my body, and to respond with accurately judged thrusts from her own splendid bottom. At last a low musical cry came from her parted lips, she strained me to her naked body with redoubled fury and driving the whole length of her tongue into my mouth she spent long and deliciously, whilst I flooded her clinging cunt with a torrent of unparalleled volume and duration.

'Jack,' she whispered, 'I have never enjoyed anything half so much in my life before. I hope you liked it too?'

'I don't think you can expect anyone to say that he "liked" fucking *you*, Eva! One might "like" kissing your hand, or helping you on with an opera cloak or some minor pleasure of that sort. But to lie between a pair of legs like yours, cushioned on a pair of breasts like yours, with a tongue like yours down one's throat, and one's prick held in the soft grip of a cunt like yours, is to undergo a series of sensations such as don't come twice in a lifetime.'

Eva's eyes flashed as she gathered me closer in her naked arms and said,

'*Don't* they, though! In this particular instance I am going to see that they come twice *within half an hour!*'

'Well, *I*'ve come twice in less than half an hour and – '

'Oh! I know what you are going to say, but we'll soon put that all right.'

A careful examination of the state of affairs was then made by Eva who bent her pretty head for the purpose, kneeling on the bed in a position which enabled me to gaze at my leisure upon all her secret charms.

Her operations meanwhile were causing me exquisite delight. With an indescribable tenderness of action, soft and caressing as that of a young mother tending her sick child, she slipped the fingers of her left hand under my balls while the other hand wandered luxuriously over the surrounding country and finally came to an anchor upon my prick, which not unnaturally began to show signs of returning vigour. Pleased at the patient's improved state of health she passed her delicious velvet tongue up and down and round and round the whole length, when hey!

presto he had leapt into a standing position! This sudden and satisfactory result of her ministrations so excited her that, without letting go of her prisoner, she cleverly passed one leg over me as I lay, and behold us in the traditional attitude of the *gamahuche à deux*! I now for the first time looked upon Eva's cunt in its full beauty, and I gladly devoted a moment to the inspection before plunging my tongue between the rich red lips which seemed to kiss my mouth as it clung in ecstasy to their luscious folds. I may say here that in point of colour, proportion, and beauty of outline Eva Letchford's cunt was the most perfect I had ever seen or gamahuched, though in after years my darling little Flossie's displayed equal faultlessness, and, as being the cunt of my beloved little sweetheart, whom I adored, it was entitled to and received from me a degree of homage never accorded to any other before or since.

The particular part of my person to which Eva was paying attention soon attained in her mouth a size and hardness which did the highest credit to her skill. With my tongue revelling in its enchanted resting-place, and my prick occupying what a house-agent might truthfully describe as 'this most desirable site', I was personally content to remain as we were, whilst Eva, entirely abandoning herself to her charming occupation, had apparently forgotten the object with which she had originally undertaken it. Fearing therefore lest the clinging mouth and delicately twining tongue should bring about the crisis which Eva had designed should take place elsewhere, I reluctantly took my lips from the clitoris they were enclosing at the moment, and called to its owner to stop.

'But Jack, you're just going to spend!' was the plaintive reply.

'Exactly, dear! And how about that "twice in half an hour".'

'Oh! of course. You were going to fuck me again, weren't you! Well, you'll find Massa Johnson in pretty good trim for the fray,' and she laughingly held up my prick, which was really of enormous dimensions, and pulling it downwards let it rebound with a loud report against my belly.

This appeared to delight her, for she repeated it several times. Each time the elasticity seemed to increase and the force of the recoil to become greater.

'The darling! she cried, as she kissed the coral head. 'He is going to his own chosen abiding-place. Come! come! blessed, *blessed* prick! Bury yourself in this loving cunt which longs for you; frig yourself deliciously against the lips which wait to kiss you; plunge into the womb which yearns to receive your life-giving seed; pause as you go by to press the clitoris that loves you. Come, divine, adorable prick! fuck me, fuck me, fuck me! fuck me long and hard: fuck and spare not! – Jack, you are into me, my cunt clings to your prick, do you feel how it nips you? Push, Jack, further, further; now your balls are kissing my bottom. That's lovely! Crush my breasts with your chest, *cr-r-r-ush* them, Jack. Now go slowly a moment, and let your prick gently rub my clitoris. So . . . o . . . o . . . o. Now faster and harder – faster still – now your tongue in my mouth, and dig your nails into my bottom. I'm going to spend: fuck, Jack, fuck me, fuck me, fu-u-u-ck me! Heavens! what bliss it is! Ah! you're spending too! bo . . . o . . . o . . . th together, both toge . . . e . . . e . . . ther. Pour it into me, Jack. Flood me, drown me, fill my womb. God! what rapture. Don't stop. Your prick is still hard and long. Drive it into me – touch my navel. Let me get my hand down to frig you as you go in and out. The sweet prick! He's stiffer than ever. How splendid of him! Fuck me again, Jack. Ah! fuck me till tomorrow! fuck me till I die!'

I fear that this language in the cold form of print may seem more than a little crude. Yet those who have experience of a beautiful and refined woman, abandoning herself in moments of passion to similar freedom of speech, will own the stimulus thus given to the sexual powers. In the present instance its effect, joined to the lascivious touches and never ceasing efforts to arouse and increase desire of this deliciously lustful girl, was to impart an unprecedented stiffness to my member which throbbed almost to bursting within the enclosing cunt and pursued its triumphant career to such lengths that even the resources of the insatiable Eva gave out at last, and she lay panting in my arms, where soon afterwards she passed into a quiet sleep. Drawing a silken coverlet over her I rose with great caution, slipped on my clothes, and in five minutes was on my way home.

MORE OF FLOSSIE'S SCHOOL-LIFE; AND OTHER MATTERS.

'Good morning, Captain Archer, I trust that you have slept well?' said Flossie on my presenting myself at the flat early the next day. 'My friend Miss Letchford,' she went on, in a prim middle-aged tone of voice, 'has not yet left her apartment. She complains of having passed a somewhat disturbed night owing to – ahem!'

'Rats in the wainscot?' I suggested.

'No, my friend attributes her sleepless condition to a severe irritation in the – forgive the immodesty of my words – lower part of her person, followed by a prolonged pricking in the same region. She is still feeling the effects, and I found her violently clasping a pillow between her – ahem! – legs, with which she was apparently endeavouring to soothe her feelings.'

'Dear me! Miss Eversley, do you think I could be of any assistance?' (*stepping towards Eva's door*).

'You are *most* kind, Captain Archer, but I have already done what I could in the way of friction and – other little attentions, which left the poor sufferer somewhat calmer. Now, Jack, you wretch! you haven't kissed me yet . . . That's better! You will not be surprised to hear that Eva has given me a full and detailed description of her sleepless night, in her own language, which, I have no doubt you have discovered, is just a bit *graphic* at times.'

'Well, my little darling, I did my best, as I knew you would wish me to do. It wasn't difficult with such a bed-fellow as Eva. But charming and amorous as she is, I couldn't help feeling all the time "if it were only my little Flossie lying under me now!" By the way how utterly lovely you are this morning, Floss.'

She was dressed in a short sprigged cotton frock, falling very little below her knees, shot pink and black stockings, and low patent leather shoes with silver buckles. Her long waving brown hair gleamed gold in the morning light, and the deep blue eyes glowed with health and love and now and again flashed with merriment. I gazed upon her in rapture at her beauty.

'Do you like my frock, Jack? I'm glad. It's the first time I've had it on. It's part of my trousseau.'

'Your *what*, Flossie?' I shouted.

'I said my trousseau,' she repeated quietly, but with sparks of fun dancing in her sweet eyes. 'The fact is, Jack, Eva declared the other day that though I am not married to you, you and I are really on a sort of honeymoon. So as I have just had a good lot of money from the lawyers she made me go with her and buy everything new. Look here' (*unfastening her bodice*) 'new stays, new chemise, new stockings and oh! Jack, *look!* such *lovely* new drawers – none of your horrid vulgar knickerbockers, but real drawers, with Madeira embroidery trimmings and lovely little tucks all the way up, and quite wide open in front for . . . ventilation I suppose! Feel what soft stuff they are made of! Eva was awfully particular about these drawers. She is always so practical, you know.'

'Practical!' I interrupted.

'Yes. What she said was that you would often be wanting to kiss me between my legs when there wasn't time to undress and be naked together, so that I must have drawers made of the finest and most delicate stuff to please you, and with the opening cut extra wide so as not to get in the way of your tongue! Now don't you call that practical?'

'I do indeed! Blessed Eva, that's another good turn I owe her!'

'Well, for instance, there isn't time to undress *now*, Jack, and – '

She threw herself back in her chair and in an instant I had plunged under the short rose-scented petticoats and had my mouth glued to the beloved cunt once more. In the midst of the delicious operation, I fancied I heard a slight sound from the direction of Eva's door and just then Flossie locked her hands behind my head and pressed me to her with even more than her usual ardour; a moment later deluging my throat with the perfumed essence of her being.

'You darling old boy, how you *did* make me spend that time! I really think your tongue is longer than it was. Perhaps the warmth of Eva's interior has made it grow! Now I must be off to the dressmaker's for an hour or so. By the way, she wants to make my frocks longer. She declares people can see my drawers when I run upstairs.'

'Don't you let her do it, Floss.'

'*Rather not!* What's the use of buying expensive drawers like mine if you can't show them to a pal! *Good* morning, Capting. Sorry I can't stop. While I'm gone you might just step in and see how my lydy friend's gettin' on. Fust door on the right. *Good* morning!'

For a minute or two I lay back in my chair and wondered whether I would not take my hat and go. But a moment's further reflection told me that I must do as Flossie directed me. To this decision, I must own, the memory of last night's pleasure and the present demands of a most surprising erection contributed in no small degree. Accordingly I tapped at Eva's bedroom door.

She had just come from her bath and wore only a peignoir and her stockings. On seeing me she at once let fall her garment and stood before me in radiant nakedness.

'Look at this,' she said, holding out a half-sheet of notepaper. 'I found it on my pillow when I woke an hour ago.

> '"If Jack comes this morning I shall send him in to see you while I go to Virginie's. Let him – *anything beginning with 'f' or 's' that rhymes with* luck – you. 'A hair of the dog' etc. will do you both good. *My time will come. Ha! Ha!*
>
> FLOSS."

'Now I ask you, Jack, was there ever such an adorable little darling?'

My answer need not be recorded.

Eva came close to me and thrust her hand inside my clothes.

'Ah! I see you are of the same way of thinking as myself,' she said, taking hold of my fingers and carrying them to her cunt, which pouted hungrily. 'So let us have one good royal fuck and then you can stay here with me while I dress, and I'll tell you anything that Flossie may have left out about her school-life in Paris. Will that meet your views?'

'Exactly,' I replied.

'Very well then. As we are going to limit ourselves to *one*, would you mind fucking me *en levrette?*'

'Any way you like, most puissant and fucksome of ladies!'

I stripped off my clothes in a twinkling and Eva placed herself in position, standing on the rug and bending forwards with her elbows on the bed. I reverently saluted the charms thus presented to my lips, omitting none, and then rising from my knees, advanced weapon in hand to storm the breach. As I approached Eva opened her legs to their widest extent, and I drove my straining prick deep into the mellow cunt, fucking it with unprecedented vigour and delight as the lips alternately parted and contracted, nipping me with an extraordinary force in response to the pressure of my right forefinger upon the clitoris and of my left upon the nipples of the heaving breasts. Keen as was the enjoyment we were both experiencing the fuck – as is invariably the case with a morning performance – was of very protracted duration, and several minutes had elapsed before I dropped my arms to Eva's thighs and with my belly glued against her bottom and my face nestling between her shoulder blades, felt the rapturous throbbing of my prick as it discharged an avalanche into the innermost recesses of her womb.

'Don't move, Jack, for Heaven's sake,' she cried.

'Don't want to, Eva, I'm quite happy where I am, thank you!'

Moving an inch or two further out from the bed so as to give herself more 'play', she started an incredibly provoking motion of her bottom, so skilfully executed that it produced the impression of being almost *spiral*. The action is difficult to describe, but her bottom rose and fell, moved backwards and forwards, and from side to side in quick alternation, the result being that my member was constantly in contact with, as it were, some fresh portion of the embracing cunt, the soft folds of which seemed by their varied and tender caresses to be pleading to him to emerge from his present state of partial apathy and resume the proud condition he had displayed before.

'Will he come up this way, Jack, or shall I take the dear little man in my mouth and suck him into an erection?'

'I think he'll be all right as he is, dear. Just keep on nipping him with your cunt and push your bottom a little closer to me so that I may feel your naked flesh against mine . . . *that's* it!'

'Ah! the darling prick, he's beginning to swell! he's going to fuck me directly, I know he is! Your finger on my cunt in front, please Jack, and the other hand on my nipples. So! *that's* nice. Oh dear! how I *do* want your tongue in my mouth, but that can't be. Now begin and fuck me slowly at first. Your *second* finger on my clitoris, please, and frig me in time to the motion of your body. Now fuck faster a little, and deeper into me. Push, dear, push like a demon. Pinch my nipple; a little faster on the clitoris. I'm spending! I'm dying of delight! Fuck me, Jack, keep on fucking me. Don't be afraid. Strike against my bottom with all your strength, harder still, harder! Now put your hands down to my thighs and *drag* me on to you. Lovely! grip the flesh of my thighs with your fingers and fuck me to the very womb.'

'Eva, look out! I'm going to spend!'

'So am I, Jack. Ah! how your prick throbs against my cunt! Fuck me, Jack, to the last moment, spend your last drop, as I'm doing. One last push up to the hilt – there, keep him in like that and let me have a deluge from you. How exquisite! how adorable to spend together! *One* moment more before you take him out, and let me kiss him with my cunt before I say good-bye.'

'What a nip that was, Eva, it felt more like a hand on me than a – '

'Yes,' she interrupted, turning round and facing me with her eyes languorous and velvety with lust, 'that is my only accomplishment, and I must say I think it's a valuable one! In Paris I had a friend – but no matter. I'm not going to talk about myself, but about Flossie. Sit down in that chair, and have a cigarette while I talk to you. I'm going to stay naked if you don't mind. It's so hot. Now if you're quite comfy, I'll begin.'

She seated herself opposite to me, her splendid naked body full in the light from the window near her.

'There is a part of Flossie's school story,' began Eva, 'which she has rather shrunk from telling you, and so I propose to relate the incident, in which I am sure you will be sufficiently interested. For the first twelve months of her school days in Paris, nothing very special occurred to her beyond the cementing of her friendship with Ylette Vespertin. Flossie was a tremendous favourite with the other girls on account of her sweet nature and her extraordinary beauty, and there is no doubt that a great many curly heads were popped under her petticoats at one time and another. All these heads, however, belonged to her own sex, and no great harm was done. But at last there arrived at the convent a certain Camille de Losgrain, who, though by no means averse to the delights of gamahuche, nursed a strong preference for male, as against female, charms. Camille speedily struck up an alliance with a handsome boy of seventeen who lived in the house next door. This youth had often seen Flossie and greatly desired her acquaintance. It seems that his bedroom window was on the same level as that of the room occupied by Flossie, Camille and three other girls, all of whom knew him by sight and had severally expressed a desire to have him between their legs. So it was arranged one night that he was to climb on to a buttress below his room, and the girls would manage to haul him up into theirs. All this had to be done in darkness as of course no light could be shown. The young gentleman duly arrived on the scene in safety – the two eldest girls divested him of his clothes, and then, according to previous agreement, the five damsels sat naked on the edge of the bed in the pitch-dark room, and Master Don Juan was to decide by passing his hands over their bodies which of the five should be favoured with his attentions. No one was to speak, to touch his person or to make any sign of interest. Twice the youth essayed this novel kind of ordeal by touch, and after a moment's profound silence he said, "J'ai choisi, c'est la troisième." "La troisième" was no other than Flossie, the size of whose breasts had at once attracted him as well as given a clue to her identity. And now, Jack, I hope the sequel will not distress you. The other girls accepted the decision most loyally, having no doubt anticipated it. They laid Flossie tenderly on the bed and lavished every kind of caress upon her, gamahuching her with especial tenderness so as to open the road as far as possible to the invader. It fortunately turned out to be the case that the boy's prick was not by any means of abnormal size, and as the dear little maidenhead had been already subjected to very considerable wear and tear of fingers and tongues the entrance was, as she told me herself, effected with a minimum of pain and discomfort, hardly felt indeed in the midst of the frantic kisses upon mouth, eyes, nipples, breasts and buttocks which the four excited girls rained upon her throughout the operation. As for the boy his enjoyment knew no bounds, and when his allotted time was up could hardly be persuaded to make the return voyage to his room. This, however, was at last accomplished, and the four virgins hastened to hear from their ravished friend the full true and particular account of her sensations. For several nights after this the boy made his appearance in the room, where he fucked all the other four in succession, and pined openly for Flossie, who, however, regarded him as belonging to Camille and declined anything beyond the occasional service of his tongue which she greatly relished and which he, of course, as gladly put at her disposal.

'All this happened before my time and was related to me afterwards by Flossie herself. It is only just a year ago that I was engaged to teach English at the convent. Like everyone else who is brought in contact with her, I at once fell in love with Flossie and we quickly became the greatest of friends. Six months ago came a change of fortune for me, an old bachelor uncle dying suddenly and leaving me a competence. By this time the attachment between Flossie and myself had become so deep that the child could not bear the thought of parting from me. I too was glad enough of the excuse thus given for writing to Flossie's guardian – who has never taken more than a casual interest in her – to propose her returning to England with me and the establishment of a joint menage. My "references" being satisfactory, and Flossie having declared herself to be most anxious for the plan, the guardian made no objection and in short – here we are!'

'Well, that's a very interesting story, Eva. Only – *confound* that French boy and his buttress!'

'Yes, you would naturally feel like that about it, and I don't blame you. Only you must remember that if it hadn't been for the size of Flossie's breasts, and its being done in the dark, and . . .'

'But Eva, you don't mean to tell me the young brute wouldn't have chosen her out of the five if there had been a *light*, do you!'

'No, of course not. What I *do* mean is that it was all a sort of fluke, and that Flossie is really, to all intents and purposes . . .'

'Yes, yes, I know what you would like to say, and I entirely and absolutely agree with you. I *love* Flossie with all my heart and soul and . . . well, that French boy can go to the devil!'

'Miss Eva! Miss Eva!' came a voice outside the door.

'Well, what is it?'

'Oh, if you please, Miss, there's a young man downstairs called for his little account. Says 'e's the coals, Miss. I *towld* him you was engyged, Miss?'

'Did you – and what did he say?'

'"Ow!" 'e sez, "engyged, *is* she," 'e sez – "well, you tell 'er from me confidential-like, as it's 'igh time she was *married*," 'e sez!'

Our shouts of laughter brought Flossie scampering into the room, evidently in the wildest spirits.

'Horful scandal in 'igh life,' she shouted. 'A genl'man dish-covered in a lydy's aportments! 'arrowin' details. Speshul! Pyper! Speshul! – Now then, you two, what have you been doing while I've been gone? Suppose you tell me exactly what you've done and I'll tell you exactly what *I've* done!' – then in a tone of cheap melodrama – 'Aha! 'ave I surproised yer guilty secret? She winceth! likewise '*e* winceth! in fact they both winceth! Thus h'am I avenged upon the pair!' And kneeling down between us she pushed a dainty finger softly between the lips of Eva's cunt, and with her other hand took hold of my yard and tenderly frigged it, looking up into our faces all the time with inexpressible love and sweetness shining from her eyes.

'You *dears*!' she said. 'It *is* nice to have you two naked together like this!'

A single glance passed between Eva and me, and getting up from our seats we flung ourselves upon the darling and smothered her with kisses. Then Eva with infinite gentleness and many loving touches proceeded to undress her, handing the dainty garments to me one by one to be laid on the bed near me. As the fair white breasts came forth from the corset, Eva gave a little cry of delight, and pushing the lace-edged chemise below the swelling globes, took one erect and rosy nipple into her mouth and putting her hand behind my neck motioned me to take the other. Shivers of delight coursed one another up and down the shapely body over which our fingers roamed in all directions. Flossie's remaining garments were soon allowed to fall by a deft touch from Eva, and the beautiful girl stood before us in all her radiant nakedness. We paused a moment to gaze upon the spectacle of loveliness. The fair face flushed with love and desire; the violet eyes shone; the full rounded breasts put forth their coral nipples as if craving to be kissed again; below the smooth satin belly appeared the silken tuft that shaded without concealing the red lips of the adorable cunt; the polished thighs gained added whiteness by contrast with the dark stockings which clung amorously to the finely moulded legs.

'Now, Jack, *both together*,' said Eva, suddenly.

I divined what she meant and arranging a couple of large cushions on the wide divan, I took Flossie in my arms and laid her upon them, her feet upon the floor. Her legs opened instinctively and thrusting my head between her thighs I plunged my tongue into the lower part of the cunt, whilst Eva, kneeling over her upon the divan, attacked the developed clitoris. Our mouths thus met upon the enchanted spot and our tongues filled every corner and crevice of it. My own, I must admit, occasionally wandered downwards to the adjacent regions, and explored the valley of delight in that direction. But wherever we went and whatever we did, the lithe young body beneath continued to quiver from head to foot with excess of pleasure, shedding its treasures now in Eva's mouth, now in mine and sometimes in both at once! But vivid as were the delights she was experiencing, they were of a passive kind only, and Flossie was already artist enough to know that the keenest enjoyment is only obtained when giving and receiving are equally shared. Accordingly I was not surprised to hear her say,

'Jack, could you come up here to me now, please?'

Signing to me to kneel astride of her face she seized my yard, guided it to her lips and then locking her hands over my loins, she alternately tightened and relaxed her grasp signifying that I was to use the delicious mouth freely as a substitute for the interdicted opening below. The peculiar sucking action of her lips, of which I have spoken before, bore a pleasant resemblance to the nipping of an accomplished cunt, whilst the never-resting tongue, against whose soft fold M. Jacques frigged himself luxuriously in his passage between the lips and throat, added a provocation to the lascivious sport not to be enjoyed in the ordinary act of coition. Meanwhile Eva had taken my place between Flossie's legs and was gamahuching the beloved cunt with incredible ardour. A sloping mirror on the wall above enabled me to survey the charming scene at my leisure, and to observe the spasms of delight which from time to time shook both the lovely naked forms below me. At last my own time arrived, and Flossie, alert as usual for the signs of approaching crisis, clutched my bottom with convulsive fingers and held me close-pressed against her face, whilst I flooded her mouth with the stream of love that she adored. At the same moment the glass told me that Eva's lips were pushing far into the vulva to receive the result of their amorous labours, the passage of which from cunt to mouth was accompanied by every token of intense enjoyment from both the excited girls.

Rest and refreshment were needed by all three after the strain of our morning revels, and so the party broke up for the day after Flossie had mysteriously announced that she was designing something 'extra special', for the morrow.

BIRTHDAY FESTIVITIES.

The next morning there was a note from Flossie asking me to come as soon as possible after receiving it.

I hurried to the flat and found Flossie awaiting me, and in one of her most enchanting moods. It was Eva's birthday, as I was now informed for the first time, and to do honour to the occasion Flossie had put on a costume in which she was to sell flowers at a fancy bazaar a few days later. It consisted of a white Tam-o'-Shanter cap with a straight upstanding feather – a shirt of the thinnest and gauziest white silk falling open at the throat and having a wide sailor collar – a broad lemon-coloured sash, a very short muslin skirt, lemon-coloured silk stockings and high-heeled brown shoes. At the opening of the shirt a bunch of flame-coloured roses nestled between the glorious breasts, to the outlines of which all possible prominence was given by the softly clinging material. As she stood waiting to hear my verdict, her red lips slightly parted, a rosy flush upon her cheeks, and love and laughter beaming from the radiant eyes, the magic of her youth and beauty seemed to weave a fresh spell around my heart and a torrent of passionate words burst from my lips as I strained the lithe young form to my breast and rained kisses upon her hair, her eyes, her cheeks and mouth.

She took my hand in hers and quietly led me to my favourite chair, and then seating herself on my knee nestled her face against my cheek and said,

'Oh, Jack, Jack, my darling boy, how can you possibly love me like that!' The sweet voice trembled and a tear or two dropped softly from the violet eyes whilst an arm stole round my neck and the red lips were pressed in a long intoxicating kiss upon my mouth.

We sat thus for some time when Flossie jumped from my knee, and said, 'We are forgetting all about Eva. Come in to her room and see what I have done.'

We went hand in hand into the bedroom and found Eva still asleep. On the chairs were laid her dainty garments, to which Flossie silently drew my attention. All along the upper edge of the chemise and corset, round the frills of the drawers and the hem of the petticoat Flossie had sewn a narrow chain of tiny pink and white rosebuds, as a birthday surprise for her friend. I laughed noiselessly, and kissed her hand in token of my appreciation of the charming fancy.

'Now for Eva's birthday treat,' whispered Flossie in my ear. 'Go over into that corner and undress yourself as quietly as you can. I will help you.'

Flossie's 'help' consisted chiefly in the use of sundry wiles to induce an erection. As these included the slow frigging in which she was such an adept, as well as the application of her rosy mouth and active tongue to every part of my prick, the desired result was rapidly obtained.

'Now, Jack, you are going to have Eva whilst I look on. *Some* day, my turn will come, and I want to see exactly how to give you the greatest possible amount of pleasure. Come and stand here by me, and we'll wake her up.'

We passed round the bed and stood in front of Eva, who still slept on unconscious.

'Ahem!' from Flossie.

The sleeping figure turned lazily. The eyes unclosed and fell upon the picture of Flossie in her flower-girl's dress, standing a little behind me and with her right hand passed in front of me vigorously frigging my erected yard, whilst the fingers of the other glided with a softly caressing motion over and under the attendant balls.

Eva jumped up, flung off her nightdress and crying to Flossie '*Don't leave go!*' fell on her knees, seized my prick in her mouth and thrust her hand under Flossie's petticoats. The latter, obeying Eva's cry, continued to frig me deliciously from behind whilst Eva furiously sucked the nut and upper part and passing her disengaged hand round my bottom, caused me a new and exquisite enjoyment by inserting a dainty finger into the aperture thus brought within her reach. Flossie now drew close up to me and I could feel the swelling breasts in their thin silken covering pressed against my naked back, whilst her hand quickened its maddeningly provoking motion upon my prick and Eva's tongue pursued its enchanted course with increasing ardour and many luscious convolutions. Feeling I was about to spend Flossie slipped her hand further down towards the root so as to give room for Eva's mouth to engulf almost the whole yard, a hint which the latter was quick to take, for her lips at once pressed close down to Flossie's fingers and with my hands behind my fair gamahucher's neck, I poured my very soul into her waiting and willing throat.

During the interval which followed I offered my congratulations to Eva and told her how sorry I was not to have known of her birthday before, so that I might have presented a humble gift of some sort. She hastened to assure me that nothing in the world that I could have brought would be more welcome than what I had just given her!

Eva had not yet seen her decorated underclothes and these were now displayed by Flossie with countless merry jokes and quaint remarks. The pretty thought was highly appreciated and nothing would do but our dressing Eva in the flowery garments. When this was done Flossie suggested a can-can, and the three of us danced a wild *pas-de-trois* until the breath was almost out of our bodies. As we lay panting in various unstudied attitudes of exhaustion, a ring was heard at the door and Flossie, who was the only presentable one of the party went out to answer the summons. She came back in a minute with an enormous basket of Neapolitan violets. Upon our exclaiming at this extravagance Flossie gravely delivered herself of the following statement.

'Though not in a position for the moment to furnish chapter and verse I am able to state with conviction that in periods from which we are only separated by some twenty centuries or so it was customary for ladies and gentlemen of the time to meet and discuss the business or pleasure of the hour without the encumbrance of clothes upon their bodies. The absence of *arrière pensée* shown by this commendable practice might lead the superficial to conclude that these discussions led to no practical results. Nothing could be further from the truth. The interviews were invariably held upon a Bank of Violets (so the old writers tell us), and at a certain point in the proceedings the lady would fall back upon this bank with her legs spread open at the then equivalent to an angle of forty-five. The gentleman would thereupon take in his right (or dexter) hand the instrument which our modern brevity of speech has taught us to call his prick. This, with some trifling assistance on her part, he would introduce into what the same latter-day rage for conciseness of expression leaves us powerless to describe otherwise than as her cunt. On my right we have the modern type of the lady; on my left, that of the gentleman. In the middle, the next best thing to a bank of violets. Ha! you take me at last! Now I'm going to put them all over the bed, and when I'm ready, you, Eva, will kindly oblige by depositing your snowy bottom in the middle, opening your legs and admitting Mr Jack to the proper position between them.'

While delivering this amazing oration Flossie had gradually stripped herself entirely naked. We both watched her movements in silent admiration as she strewed the bed from end to end with the fragrant blossoms, which filled the room with their delightful perfume. When all was ready, she beckoned to Eva to lay herself on the bed, whispering to her, though not so low but that I could hear,

'Imagine you are Danaë. I'll trouble you for the size of Jupiter's prick. Just look at it' – then much lower, but still audibly – 'You're going to be fucked, Eva darling, jolly well fucked! and I'm going to *see* you – *Lovely!*'

The rose-edged chemise and drawers were once more laid aside and the heroine of the day stretched herself voluptuously on the heaped-up flowers, which sent forth fresh streams of fragrance in response to the pressure of the girl's naked body.

'Ah, a happy thought!' cried Flossie. If you would lie *across* the bed with your legs hanging down, and Jack wouldn't mind standing up to his work, I think I could be of some assistance to you both.'

The change was quickly made, a couple of pillows were slipped under Eva's head, and Flossie, kneeling across the other's face, submitted her cunt to be gamahuched by her friend's tongue which at once darted amorously to its place within the vulva. Flossie returned the salutation for a moment and then resting her chin upon the point just above Eva's clitoris, called to me to 'come on'. I placed myself in position and was about to storm the breach when Flossie found the near proximity of my yard to be too much for her feelings and begged to be allowed to gamahuche me for a minute.

'After that, I'll be quite good,' she added to Eva, 'and will only *watch.*'

Needless to say I made no objection. The result, as was the case with most of Flossie's actions, was increased pleasure to everybody concerned and to Eva as much as anyone inasmuch as the divine sucking of Flossie's rosy lips and lustful tongue produced a sensible hardening and lengthening of my excited member.

After performing this delightful service, she was for moving away, but sounds of dissent were heard from Eva who flung her arms round Flossie's thighs and drew her cunt down in closer contact with the caressing mouth.

From my exalted position I could see all that was going on and this added enormously to the sensations I began to experience when Flossie, handling my yard with deft fingers, dropped a final kiss upon the nut, and then guided it to the now impatient goal. With eyes lit up with interest and delight she watched it disappear within the soft red lips whose movements she was near enough to follow closely. Under these conditions I found myself fucking Eva with unusual vigour and penetration, whilst she on her part returned my strokes with powerful thrusts of her bottom and exquisitely pleasurable contractions of her cunt upon my prick.

Flossie taking in all this with eager eyes, became madly excited, and at last sprang from her kneeling position on the bed, and taking advantage of an *outward* motion of my body, bent down between us and pushing the point of her tongue under Eva's clitoris insisted on my finishing the performance with this charming incentive added. Its effect upon both Eva and myself was electric and as her clitoris and my prick shared equally in the contact of the tongue we were not long in bringing the entertainment to an eminently satisfactory conclusion.

The next item in the birthday programme was the exhibition of half a dozen cleverly executed pen and ink sketches – Flossie's gift to Eva – showing the three of us in attitudes not to be found in the illustrations of the 'Young Ladies' Journal'. A discussion arose as to whether Flossie had not been somewhat flattering to the longitudinal dimensions of the present writer's member. She declared that the proportions were 'according to *Cocker*' – obviously, as she wittily said, the highest authority on the question.

'Anyhow, I'm going to take measurements and then you'll see I'm right! In the picture the length of Jack's prick is exactly one-third of the distance from his chin to his navel. Now measuring the real article – Hullo! I *say*, Evie, what *have* you done to him!'

In point of fact the object under discussion was feeling the effects of his recent exercise and had drooped to a partially recumbent attitude.

Eva, who was watching the proceedings with an air of intense amusement called out,

'Take it between your breasts, Flossie; you'll soon see a difference then!'

The mere prospect of such a lodging imparted a certain amount of vigour to Monsieur Jacques, who was thereupon introduced into the delicious cleft of Flossie's adorable bosom, and in rapture at the touch of the soft flesh on either side of him at once began to assume more satisfactory proportions.

'But he's not up to his full height yet,' said Flossie. 'Come and help me, Evie dear; stand behind Jack and frig him whilst I gamahuche him in front. *That's* the way to get him up to concert pitch! When I feel him long and stiff enough in my mouth, I'll get up and take his measure.'

The success of Flossie's plan was immediate and complete, and when the measurements were made the proportions were found to be exactly twenty-one and seven inches respectively, whilst in the drawing they were three inches to one inch. Flossie proceeded to execute a wild war-dance of triumph over this signal vindication of her accuracy, winding up by insisting on my carrying her pick-a-back round the flat. Her enjoyment of this ride was unbounded, as also was mine, for besides the pleasure arising from the close contact of her charming body, she contrived to administer a delicious friction to my member with the calves of her naked legs.

On our return to the bedroom Eva was sitting on the edge of the low divan.

'Bring her to me here,' she cried.

I easily divined what was wanted, and carrying my precious burden across the room, I faced round with my back to Eva. In the sloping glass to the left I could see her face disappear between the white rounded buttocks, at the same moment that her right hand moved in front of me and grasped my yard which it frigged with incomparable tenderness and skill. This operation was eagerly watched by Flossie over my shoulder while she clung to me with arms and legs and rubbed herself against my loins with soft undulating motions like an amorous kitten, the parting lips of her cunt kissing my back and her every action testifying to the delight with which she was receiving the attentions of Eva's tongue upon the neighbouring spot.

My feelings were now rapidly passing beyond my control, and I had to implore Eva to remove her hand, whereupon Flossie, realising the state of affairs, jumped down from her perch, and burying my prick in her sweet mouth sucked and frigged me in such a frenzy of desire that she had very soon drawn from me the last drop I had to give her.

A short period of calm ensued after this last ebullition, but Flossie was in too mad a mood today to remain long quiescent.

'Eva,' she suddenly cried, 'I believe I am as tall as you nowadays, and I am *quite sure* my breasts are as large as yours. I'm going to measure and see!'

After Eva's height had been found to be only a short inch above Flossie's the latter proceeded to take the most careful and scientific measurements of the breasts. First came the circumference, then the diameter *over* the nipples, then the diameter omitting the nipples, then the distance from the nipple to the upper and lower edges of the hemispheres, and so on. No dry-as-dust old savant, staking his reputation upon an absolutely accurate calculation of the earth's surface, could have carried out his task with more ineffable solemnity than did this merry child who one knew was all the time secretly bubbling over with the fun of her quaint conceit.

The result was admitted to be what Flossie called it – 'a moral victory' for herself, inasmuch as half a square inch, or as Flossie declared, 'fifteen thirty-*two-ths*', was all the superiority of area that Eva could boast.

'There's one other measurement I *should* like to have taken,' said Eva, 'because in spite of my ten years "*de plus*" and the fact that my cunt is not altogether a stranger to the joys of being fucked, I believe that Flossie would win *that* race, and I should like her to have one out of three!'

'*Lovely!*' cried Flossie. 'But Jack must be the judge. Here's the tape, Jack: fire away. Now, Evie, come and lie beside me on the edge of the bed, open your legs, and swear, to abide by the verdict!'

After a few minutes fumbling with the tape and close inspection of the parts in dispute I retired to a table and wrote down the following, which I pinned against the window-curtain.

Letchford v. Eversley.

Mesdames,

In compliance with your instructions I have this day surveyed the private premises belonging to the above parties, and have now the honour to submit the following report, plan, and measurements.

As will be seen from the plan, Miss Letchford's cunt is exactly $3\frac{1}{16}$ inches from the underside of clitoris to the base of vulva. Miss Eversley's cunt, adopting the same line of measurement, gives $3\frac{5}{8}$ inches.

I may add that the premises appear to me to be thoroughly desirable in both cases, and to a good, upright and painstaking tenant would afford equally pleasant accommodation in spring, summer, autumn or winter.

A small but well-wooded covert is attached to each, whilst an admirable dairy is in convenient proximity.

With reference to the Eversley property I am informed that it has not yet been occupied, but in view of its size and beauty, and the undoubted charms of the surrounding country I confidently anticipate that a permanent and satisfactory tenant (such as I have ventured to describe above), will very shortly be found for it. My

opinion of its advantages as a place of residence may, indeed, be gathered from the fact that I am greatly disposed to make an offer in my own person.
Yours faithfully
J Archer.
(Captain 174 th Regt.)

As the two girls stood with their hands behind their backs reading my ultimatum, Flossie laughed uproariously, but I noticed that Eva looked grave and thoughtful.

Had I written anything that annoyed her? I could hardly think so, but while I was meditating on the possibility, half resolved to put it to the test by a simple question, Eva took Flossie and myself by the hand, led us to the sofa and sitting down between us, said,

'Listen to me, you two dears! You, Flossie, are my chosen darling, and most beloved little friend. You Jack, are Flossie's lover, and for her sake as well as for your own I have the greatest affection for you. You both know all this. Well, I have not the heart to keep you from one another any longer. Flossie, dear, I hereby absolve you from your promise to me. Jack, you have behaved like a brick, as you are. Come here tomorrow at your usual time and I think we shall be able to agree upon *"a tenant for the Eversley property"*.'

This is not a novel of sentiment, and a description of what followed would therefore be out of place. Enough to say that after one wild irrepressible shriek of joy and gratitude from Flossie, the conversation took a sober and serious turn, and soon afterwards we parted for the day.

THE TENANT IN POSSESSION

The next morning's post brought me letters from both, Eva and Flossie.

'My dear Jack (wrote the former),

'Tomorrow will be a red-letter day for you two! and I want you both to get the utmost of delight from it. So let no sort of scruple or compunction spoil your pleasure. Flossie is, in point of physical development, a woman. As such she longs to be fucked by the man she loves. Fuck her therefore with all and more than all the same skill and determination you displayed in fucking me. She can think and talk of nothing else. Come early tomorrow and bring your admirable prick in its highest state of efficiency and stiffness!

'Yours

'Eva.'

Flossie wrote:

'I cannot sleep a wink for thinking of what is coming to me tomorrow. All the time I keep turning over in my mind how best to make it nice for you. I am practising Eva's "nip". I *feel* as if I could do it, but nipping *nothing* is not really practice, is it, Jack? My beloved, I kiss your prick, in imagination. Tomorrow I will do it in the flesh, for I warn you that nothing will ever induce me to give up *that*, nor will even the seven inches which I yearn to have in my cunt ever bring me to consent to being deprived of the sensation of your dear tongue when it curls between the lips and pays polite little attentions to my clitoris! But you shall have me as you like tomorrow, and all days to follow. I am to be in future

'Yours, body and soul
'FLOSSIE.'

When I arrived at the flat I found Flossie had put on the costume in which I had seen her the first day of our acquaintance. The lovely little face wore an expression of gravity, as though to show me she was not forgetting the importance of the occasion. I am not above confessing that, for my part, I was profoundly moved.

We sat beside one another, hardly exchanging a word. Presently Flossie said,

'Whenever you are *ready*, Jack, I'll go to my room and undress.'

The characteristic naiveté of this remark somewhat broke the spell that was upon us, and I kissed her with effusion.

'Shall it be . . . *quite* naked, Jack?'

'Yes, darling, if *you* don't mind.'

'All right. When I am ready I'll call to you.'

Five minutes later I heard the welcome summons.

From the moment I found myself in her room all sense of restraint vanished at a breath. She flew at me in a perfect fury of desire, pushed me by sheer force upon my back on the bed, and lying at full length upon me with her face close to mine, she said,

'Because I was a girl and not a woman, Jack, you have never fucked me. But you are going to fuck me now, and I shall be a woman. But first I want to be a girl to you still for a few minutes only. I want to have your dear prick in my mouth again; I want you to kiss my cunt in the old delicious way; I want to lock my naked arms round your naked body; and hold you to my face, whilst I wind my tongue round your prick until you spend. Let me do all this, Jack, and then you shall fuck me till the skies fall.'

Without giving me time to reply to this frenzied little oration, Flossie had whisked round and was in position for the double gamahuche she desired. Parting her legs to their widest extent on each side of my face, she sank gently down until her cunt came full upon my open mouth. At the same moment I felt my prick seized and plunged deep into her mouth with which she at once commenced the delicious sucking action I knew so well. I responded by driving my tongue to the root into the rosy depths of her perfumed cunt, which I sucked with ever increasing zest and enjoyment, drawing fresh treasures from its inner recesses at every third or fourth stroke of my tongue. Words fail me to describe the unparalleled vigour of her sustained attack upon my erected prick, which she sucked, licked, tongued and frigged with such a furious *abandon* and at the same time with such a subtle skill and knowledge of the sublime art of gamahuching that the end came with unusual rapidity, and wave after wave of the sea of love broke in ecstasy upon the 'coral strand' of her adorable mouth. For a minute or two more her lips retained their hold and then leaving her position she came and lay down beside me, nestling her naked body against mine, and softly chafing the lower portion of my prick whilst she said,

'Now, Jack darling, I am going to talk to you about the different ways of fucking, because of course you will want to fuck me, and I shall want to be fucked, in every possible position, and in every single part of my body where a respectable young woman may reasonably *ask* to be fucked.'

The conversation which followed agreeably filled the intervening time before the delicate touches which Flossie kept constantly applying to my prick caused it to raise its head to a considerable altitude, exhibiting a hardness and rigidity which gave high promise for the success of the coming encounter.

'Good Gracious!' cried Flossie, 'do you think I shall ever find room for all that, Jack?'

'For that, and more also, sweetheart,' I replied.

'*More*! Why, *what* more are you going to put into me?'

'This is the only article I propose to introduce at present, Floss. But I mean that when Monsieur Jacques finds himself for the first time with his head buried between the delicious cushions in *there*' (*touching her belly*) 'he will most likely beat his own record in the matter of length and stiffness.'

'Do you mean, Jack, that he will be bigger with me than he was with Eva?' said Flossie with a merry twinkle.

'Certainly I mean it,' was my reply. 'To fuck a beautiful girl like Eva must always be immensely enjoyable, but to fuck a young Venus, who besides being the perfection of mortal loveliness, is also one's own chosen and adorable little sweetheart – *that* belongs to a different order of pleasure altogether.'

'And I suppose, Jack, that when the Venus is simply dying to be fucked by her lover, as I am at this moment, the chances are that she may be able to make it rather nice for him, as well as absolutely heavenly for herself. Now I can wait no longer. "First position" at once, please, Jack. Give me your prick in my hand and I will direct his wandering footsteps.'

'He's at the door, Flossie; shall he enter?'

'Yes. Push him in slowly and fuck gently at first, so that I may find out by degrees how much he's going to hurt me. A little further, Jack. Why, he's more than half way in already! Now you keep still and I'll thrust a little with my bottom.'

'Why, Floss, you darling, you're nipping me deliciously!'

'Can you feel me Jack? How lovely! Fuck me a little more, Jack, and get in deeper, that's it! now faster and harder. What glorious pleasure it is!'

'And no pain, darling?'

'Not a scrap. One more good push and he'll be in up to the hilt, won't he? Eva told me to put my legs over your back. Is that right?'

'Quite right, and if you're sure I'm not hurting you, Floss, I'll really begin now and fuck you in earnest.'

'That's what I'm here for, Sir,' she replied with a touch of her never absent fun even in this supreme moment.

'Here goes, then!' I answered Having once made up her mind that she had nothing to dread, Flossie abandoned herself with enthusiasm to the pleasures of the moment. Locking her arms round my neck and her legs round my buttocks, she cried to me to fuck her with all my might.

'Drive your prick into me again and again, Jack. Let me feel your belly against mine. Did you feel my cunt nip you then? Ah! how you are fucking me now! – fucking me, fu . . . u . . . ucking me!'

Her lovely eyes turned to heaven, her breath came in quick short gasps, her fingers wandered feverishly about my body. At last with a cry she plunged her tongue into my mouth and with convulsive undulations of the lithe body let loose the floods of her being to join the deluge which, with sensations of exquisite delight, I poured into her burning cunt.

The wild joy of this our first act of coition was followed by a slight reaction, and with a deep sigh of contentment Flossie fell asleep in my arms, leaving my prick still buried in its natural resting-place. Before long my own eyelids closed and for an hour or more we lay thus gaining from blessed sleep fresh strength to enter upon new transports of pleasure.

Flossie was the first to awake, stirred no doubt by the unaccustomed sensations of a swelling prick within her. I awoke to find her dear eyes resting upon my face, her naked arms round my neck and her cunt enfolding my yard with a soft and clinging embrace.

Her bottom heaved gently, and accepting the invitation thus tacitly given, I turned my little sweetheart on her back and lying luxuriously between her widely parted legs once more drove my prick deep into her cunt and fucked her with slow lingering strokes, directed upwards so as to bring all possible contact to bear upon the clitoris.

This particular motion afforded her evident delight and the answering thrusts of her bottom were delivered with ever increasing vigour and precision, each of us relishing to the full the efforts of the other to augment the pleasure of the encounter. With sighs and gasps and little cries of rapture Flossie strained me to her naked breasts, and twisting her legs tightly round my own, cried out that she was spending and implored me to let her feel my emission mix with hers. By dint of clutching her bottom with my hands and driving the whole length of my tongue into her mouth I was just able to manage the simultaneous discharge she coveted, and once more I lay upon her in a speechless ecstasy of consummated passion.

Anyone of my readers who has had the supreme good fortune to fuck the girl of his heart will bear me out in saying that the lassitude following upon such a meeting is greater and more lasting than the mere weariness resulting from an ordinary act of copulation 'where love is not'.

Being well aware of this fact, I resolved that my beloved little Flossie's powers should not be taxed any further for the moment, and told her so.

'But Jack,' she cried, almost in tears, 'we've only done it *one* way, and Eva says there are at least *six*! And oh, I do *love* it so!'

'And so do I, little darling. But also I love *you*, and I'm not going to begin by giving you and that delicious little caressing cunt of yours more work than is good for you both.'

'Oh, dear! I suppose you're right, Jack.'

'Of course I'm right, darling. Tomorrow I shall come and fuck you again, and the next day, and the next, and many days after that. It will be odd if we don't find ourselves in Eva's six different positions before we've done!'

At this moment Eva herself entered the room.

'Well, Flossie . . .?' she said.

'Ask Jack!' replied Flossie.

'Well, Jack, then . . .?' said Eva.

'Ask Flossie!' I retorted, and fled from the room.

The adventures I have, with many conscious imperfections, related in the foregoing pages were full of interest to me, and were, I am disposed to think, not without their moments of attraction for my fellow-actors in the scenes depicted.

It by no means necessarily follows that they will produce a corresponding effect upon the reading public, who in my descriptions of Flossie and her ways may find only an ineffectual attempt to set forth the charms of what appears to me an absolutely unique temperament. If haply it should prove to be otherwise, I should be glad to have the opportunity of continuing a veritable labour of love by recounting certain further experiences of Eva, Flossie and

Yours faithfully
'Jack'.

SIR RICHARD BURTON

from
The Perfumed Garden

The Perfumed Garden *dates from the sixteenth century but it is known to the English-speaking world through Sir Richard Burton's translation published privately in 1886. It is described on the title page as being by 'Shaykh Umar ibn Muhammed al-Nefzawi' and is a treastise on sexual pleasure. Its tone is objective, its design seems to be educational and it is the first survey of sexual behaviour. No modern survey is more explicit.*

General Remarks About Coition

Praise be given to God, who has placed man's greatest pleasure in the natural parts of woman, and has destined the natural parts of man to afford the greatest enjoyment to woman.

He has not endowed the parts of woman with any pleasurable or satisfactory feeling until the same have been penetrated by the instrument of the male; and likewise the sexual organs of man know neither rest nor quietness until they have entered those of the female.

Hence the mutual operation. There takes place between the two actors wrestling, intertwinings, a kind of animated conflict. Owing to the contact of the lower parts of the two bellies, the enjoyment soon comes to pass. The man is at work as with a pestle, while the woman seconds him by lascivious movements; finally comes the ejaculation.

The kiss on the mouth, on the two cheeks, upon the neck, as well as the sucking up of fresh lips, are gifts of God, destined to provoke erection at the favourable moment. God also was it who has embellished the chest of the woman with breasts, has furnished her with a double chin, and has given brilliant colours to her cheeks.

He has also gifted her with eyes that inspire love, and with eyelashes like polished blades.

He has furnished her with a rounded belly and a beautiful navel, and with a majestic crupper; and all these wonders are borne up by the thighs. It is between these latter that God has placed the arena of the combat; when the same is provided with ample flesh, it resembles the head of a lion. It is called *vulva*. Oh! how many men's deaths lie at her door? Amongst them how many heroes!

God has furnished this object with a mouth, a tongue,* two lips; it is like the impression of the hoof of the gazelle in the sands of the desert.

The whole is supported by two marvellous columns, testifying to the might and the wisdom of God; they are not too long nor too short; and they are graced with knees, calves, ankles, and heels, upon which rest precious rings.

Then the Almighty has plunged woman into a sea of splendours, of voluptuousness, and of delights, and covered her with precious vestments, with brilliant girdles and provoking smiles.

So let us praise and exalt him who has created woman and her beauties, with her appetising flesh; who has given her hairs, a beautiful figure, a bosom with breasts which are swelling, and amorous ways, which awaken desires.

The Master of the Universe has bestowed upon them the empire of seduction; all men, weak or strong, are subjected to the weakness for the love of woman. Through woman we have society or dispersion, sojourn or emigration.

The state of humility in which are the hearts of those who love and are separated from the object of their love, makes their hearts burn with love's fire; they are oppressed with a feeling of servitude, contempt and misery; they suffer under the vicissitudes of their passion: and all this as a consequence of their burning desire of contact.

I, the servant of God, am thankful to him that no one can help falling in love with beautiful women, and that no one can escape the desire to possess them, neither by change, nor flight, nor separation.

I testify that there is only one God, and that he has no associate. I shall adhere to this precious testimony to the day of the last judgment.

I likewise testify as to our lord and master, Mohammed, the servant and ambassador of God, the greatest of the prophets (the benediction and pity of God be with him and with his family and disciples!). I keep prayers and benedictions for the day of retribution, that terrible moment.

The Origin of this Work

I have written this magnificent work after a small book called *The Torch of the World*, which treats of the mysteries of generation.

* Meaning the clitoris.

This latter work came to the knowledge of the Vizir of our master Abd-el-Aziz, the ruler of Tunis.

This illustrious Vizir was his poet, his companion, his friend and private secretary. He was good in council, true, sagacious and wise, the best learned man of his time, and well acquainted with all things. He called himself Mohammed ben Ouana ez Zonaoui, and traced his origin from Zonaoua. He had been brought up at Algiers, and in that town our master Abd-el-Aziz el Hafsi had made his acquaintance.

On the day when Algiers was taken, that ruler took flight with him to Tunis (which land may God preserve in his power till the day of resurrection), and named him his Grand Vizir.

When the above mentioned book came into his hands, he sent for me, and invited me pressingly to come and see him. I went forthwith to his house, and he received me most honorably.

Three days after he came to me, and showing me my book, said, 'This is your work.' Seeing me blush, he added, 'You need not be ashamed; everything you have said in it is true; no one need be shocked at your words. Moreover, you are not the first who has treated of this matter; and I swear by God that it is necessary to know this book. It is only the shameless bore and the enemy of all science who will not read it, or make fun of it. But there are sundry things which you will have to treat about yet.' I asked him what these things were, and he answered, 'I wish that you would add to the work a supplement, treating of the remedies of which you have said nothing, and adding all the facts appertaining thereto, omitting nothing. You will describe in the same the motives of the act of generation, as well as the matters that prevent it. You will mention the means for undoing spells (aiguillette), and the way to increase the size of the virile member, when too small, and to make it resplendent. You will further cite those means which remove the unpleasant smells from the armpits and the natural parts of women, and those which will contract those parts. You will further speak of pregnancy, so as to make your book perfect and wanting in nothing. And, finally, you will have done your work, if your book satisfy all wishes.'

I replied to the Vizir: 'Oh, my master, all you have said here is not difficult to do, if it is the pleasure of God on high.'

I forthwith went to work with the composition of this book, imploring the assistance of God (may he pour his blessing on his prophet, and may happiness and pity be with him).

I have called this work *The Perfumed Garden for the Soul's Recreation (Er Roud el Âater p'nezaha el Khater).*

And we pray to God, who directs everything for the best (and there is no other God than He, and there is nothing good that does not come from Him), to lend us His help, and lead us in good ways; for there is no power nor joy but in the high and mighty God.

I have divided this book into twenty-one chapters, in order to make it easier reading for the *taleb* (student) who wishes to learn, and to facilitate his search for what he wants. Each chapter relates to a particular subject, be it physical, or anecdotal, or treating of the wiles and deceits of women.

Concerning Praiseworthy Men

Learn, O Vizir (God's blessing be upon you), that there are different sorts of men and women; that amongst these are those who are worthy of praise, and those who deserve reproach.

When a meritorious man finds himself near to women, his member grows, gets strong, vigorous and hard; he is not quick to discharge, and after the trembling caused by the emission of the sperm, he is soon stiff again.

Such a man is liked and appreciated by women; this is because the woman loves the man only for the sake of coition. His member should, therefore, be of ample dimensions and length. Such a man ought to be broad in the chest, and heavy in the crupper; he should know how to regulate his emission, and be ready as to erection; his member should reach to the end of the canal of the female, and completely fill the same in all its parts. Such an one will be well beloved by women, for, as the poet says:

> I have seen women trying to find in young men
> The durable qualities which grace the man of full power,
> The beauty, the enjoyment, the reserve, the strength,
> The full-formed member providing a lengthened coition,
> A heavy crupper, a slowly coming emission,
> A lightsome chest, as it were floating upon them;
> The spermal ejaculation slow to arrive, so as
> To furnish forth a long drawn-out enjoyment.
> His member soon to be prone again for erection,
> To ply the plane again and again and again on their vulvas,
> Such is the man whose cult gives pleasure to women,
> And who will ever stand high in their esteem.

Qualities which Women are looking for in Men

The tale goes, that on a certain day, Abd-el-Melik ben Merouane, went to see Leilla, his mistress, and put various questions to her. Amongst other things, he asked her what were the qualities which women looked for in men.

Leilla answered him: 'Oh, my master, they must have cheeks like ours.' 'And what besides?' said Ben Merouane. She continued: 'And hairs like ours; finally they should be like to you, O prince of believers, for, surely if a man is not strong and rich he will obtain nothing from women.'

Various Lengths of the Virile Member

The virile member, to please women, must have at most a length of the breadth of twelve fingers, or three hand-breadths, and at least six fingers, or a hand and a half breadth.

There are men with members of twelve fingers, or three hand-breadths; others of ten fingers, or two and a half hands. And others measure eight fingers, or two hands. A man whose member is of less dimensions cannot please women.

The use of Perfumes in Coition. The History of Moçailama

The use of perfumes, by man as well as by woman, excites to the act of copulation. The woman, inhaling the perfumes employed by the man, becomes intoxicated; and the use of scents has often proved a strong help to man, and assisted him in getting possession of a woman.

On this subject it is told of Moçailama, the imposter, the son of Kaiss (whom God may curse!), that he pretended to have the gift of prophecy, and imitated the Prophet of God (blessings and salutations to him). For which reasons he and a great number of Arabs have incurred the ire of the Almighty.

Moçailama, the son of Kaiss, the impostor, misconstrued likewise the Koran by his lies and impostures; and on the subject of a chapter of the Koran, which the angel Gabriel (Hail be to him) had brought to the Prophet (the mercy of God and hail to him), people of bad faith had gone to see Moçailama, who had told them, 'To me also has the angel Gabriel brought a similar chapter.'

He derided the chapter headed 'The Elephant', saying, 'In this chapter of the Elephant I see the elephant. What is the elephant? What does it mean? What is this quadruped? It has a tail and a long trunk. Surely it is a creation of our God, the magnificent.'

The chapter of the Koran named the *Kouter* was also an object of controversy. He said, 'We have given you precious stones for yourself, and preference to any other man, but take care not to be proud of them.'

Moçailama thus perverted sundry chapters in the Koran by his lies and his impostures.

He had been at his work when he heard the Prophet (the salutation and mercy of God be with him) spoken of. He heard that after he had placed his venerable hands upon a bald head, the hair had forthwith sprung up again; that when he spat into a pit, the water came in abundantly, and that the dirty water turned at once clean and good for drinking; that when he spat into an eye that was blind or obscure, the sight was at once restored to it, and when he placed his hands upon the head of a child, saying, 'Live for a century,' the child lived to be a hundred years old.

When the disciples of Moçailama saw these things or heard speak of them, they came to him and said, 'Have you no knowledge of Mohammed and his doings?' He replied, 'I shall do better than that.'

Now, Moçailama was an enemy of God, and when he put his luckless hand on the head of someone who had not much hair, the man was at once quite bald; when he spat into a well with a scanty supply of water, sweet as it was, it was turned dirty by the will of God; if he spat into a suffering eye, that eye lost its sight at once, and when he laid his hand upon the head of an infant, saying, 'Live a hundred years,' the infant died within an hour.

Observe, my brethren, what happens to those whose eyes remain closed to the light, and who are deprived of the assistance of the Almighty!

And thus acted that woman of the Beni-Temim, called *Chedjâ el Temimia*, who pretended to be a prophetess. She had heard of Moçailama, and he likewise of her.

This woman was powerful, for the Beni-Temim form a numerous tribe. She said, 'Prophecy cannot belong to two persons. Either he is a prophet, and then I and my disciples will follow his laws, or I am a prophetess, and then he and his disciples will follow my laws.'

This happened after the death of the Prophet (the salutation and mercy of God be with him).

Chedjâ then wrote to Moçailama a letter, in which she told him, 'It is not proper that two persons should at one and the same time profess prophecy; it is for one only to be a prophet. We will meet, we and our disciples, and examine each other. We shall discuss about that which has come to us from God (the Koran), and we will follow the laws of him who shall be acknowledged as the true prophet.'

She then closed her letter and gave it to a messenger, saying to him:

'Betake yourself, with this missive, to Yamama, and give it to Moçailama ben Kaiss. As for myself, I follow you, with the army.'

Next day the prophetess mounted horse, with her *goum*, and followed the spoor of her envoy. When the latter arrived at Moçailama's place, he greeted him and gave him the letter.

Moçailama opened and read it, and understood its contents. He was dismayed, and began to advise with the people of his *goum*, one after another, but he did not see anything in their advice or in their views that could rid him of his embarrassment.

While he was in this perplexity, one of the superior men of his *goum* came forward and said to him: 'Oh, Moçailama, calm your soul and cool your eyes. I will give you the advice of a father to his son.'

Moçailama said to him: 'Speak, and may thy words be true.'

And the other one said: 'Tomorrow morning erect outside the city a tent of coloured brocades, provided with silk furniture of all sorts. Fill the tent afterwards with a variety of different perfumes, amber, musk, and all sorts of scents, as rose, orange flowers, jonquils, jessamine, hyacinth, carnation and other plants. This done, have then placed there several gold censers filled with green aloes, ambergris, *nedde* and so on. Then fix the hangings so that nothing of these perfumes can escape out of the tent. Then, when you find the vapour strong enough to impregnate water, sit down on your throne, and send for the prophetess to come and see you in the tent, where she will be alone with you. When you are thus together there, and she inhales the perfumes, she will delight in the same, all her bones will be relaxed in a soft repose, and finally she will be swooning. When you see her thus far gone, ask her to grant you her favours; she will not hesitate to accord them. Having once possessed her, you will be freed of the embarrassment caused to you by her and her *goum*.'

Moçailama exclaimed: 'You have spoken well. As God lives, your advice is good and well thought out.' And he had everything arranged accordingly.

When he saw that the perfumed vapour was dense enough to impregnate the water in the tent he sat down upon his throne and sent for the prophetess. On her arrival he gave orders to admit her into the tent; she entered and remained alone with him. He engaged her in conversation.

While Moçailama spoke to her she lost all her presence of mind, and became embarrassed and confused.

When he saw her in that state he knew that she desired cohabitation, and he said: 'Come, rise and let me have possession of you; this place has been prepared for that purpose. If you like you may lie on your back, or you can place yourself on all fours, or kneel as in prayer, with your brow touching the ground, and your crupper in the air, forming a tripod. Whichever position you prefer, speak, and you shall be satisfied.'

The prophetess answered, 'I want it done in all ways. Let the revelation of God descend upon me, O Prophet of the Almighty.'

He at once precipitated himself upon her, and enjoyed her as he liked. She then said to him, 'When I am gone from here, ask my *goum* to give me to you in marriage.'

When she had left the tent and met her disciples, they said to her, 'What is the result of the conference, O prophetess of God?' and she replied, 'Moçailama has shown me what has been revealed to him, and I found it to be the truth, so obey him.'

The Moçailama asked her in marriage from the *goum*, which was accorded to him. When the *goum* asked about the marriage-dowry of his future wife, he told them, 'I dispense you from saying the prayer "*aceur*"' (which is said at three or four o'clock). Ever from that time the Beni-Temim do not pray at that hour; and when they are asked the reason, they answer, 'It is on account of our prophetess; she only knows the way to the truth.' And, in fact, they recognized no other prophet.

On this subject a poet has said:

> *For us a female prophet has arisen;*
> *Her laws we follow; for the rest of mankind*
> *The prophets that appeared were always men.*

The death of Moçailama was foretold by the prophecy of Abou Beker (to whom God be good). He was, in fact, killed by Zeid ben Khettab. Other people say it was done by Ouhcha, one of his disciples. God only knows whether it was Ouhcha. He himself says on this point, 'I have killed in my ignorance the best of men, Haman ben Abd el Mosaleb, and then I killed the worst of men, Moçailama. I hope that God will pardon one of these actions in consideration of the other.'

The meaning of these words, 'I have killed the best of men' is, that Ouhcha, before having yet known the prophet, had killed Hamza (to whom God be good), and having afterwards embraced Islamism, he killed Moçailama.

As regards Chedjâ el Temimia, she repented by God's grace, and took to the Islamitic faith; she married one of the Prophet's followers (God be good to her husband).

Thus finishes the story.

The man who deserves favours is, in the eyes of women, the one who is anxious to please them. He must be of good presence, excel in beauty those around him, be of good shape and well-formed proportions; true and sincere in his speech with women; he must likewise be generous and brave, not vainglorious, and pleasant in conversation. A slave to his promise, he must always keep his word, ever speak the truth, and do what he has said.

The man who boasts of his relations with women, of their acquaintance and good will to him, is a dastard. He will be spoken of in the next chapter.

There is a story that once there lived a king named Mamoum, who had a court fool of the name of Bahloul, who amused the princes and Vizirs.

One day this buffoon appeared before the King, who was amusing himself. The King bade him to sit down, and then asked him, turning away, 'Why hast thou come, O son of a bad woman?'

Bahloul answered, 'I have come to see what has come to our Lord, whom may God make victorious.'

'And what has come to thee?' replied the King, 'and how art thou getting on with thy new and with thy old wife?' For Bahloul, not content with one wife, had married a second one.

'I am not happy,' he answered, 'neither with the old one, nor with the new one; and moreover poverty over-powers me.'

The King said, 'Can you recite any verses on this subject?'

The buffoon having answered in the affirmative, Mamoum commanded him to recite those he knew, and Bahloul began as follows:

> *Poverty holds me in chains; misery torments me:*
> *I am being scourged with all misfortunes;*
> *Ill luck has cast me in trouble and peril,*
> *And has drawn upon me the contempt of man.*
> *God does not favour a poverty like mine;*
> *That is opprobrius in every one's eyes.*
> *Misfortune and misery for a long time*
> *Have held me tightly; and no doubt of it*
> *My dwelling house will soon not know me more.*

Mamoum said to him, 'Where are you going to?'

He replied, 'To God and his Prophet, O prince of the believers.'

'That is well' said the King; 'those who take refuge in God and his Prophet, and then in us, will be made welcome. But can you now tell me some more verses about your two wives, and about what comes to pass with them?'

'Certainly,' said Bahloul.
'Then let us hear what you have to say!'
Bahloul then began thus with poetical words:

> *By reason of my ignorance I have married two wives –*
> *And why do you complain, O husband of two wives?*
> *I said to myself, I shall be like a lamb between them;*
> *I shall take my pleasure upon the bosoms of my two sheep,*
> *And I have become like a ram between two female jackals,*
> *Days follow upon days and nights upon nights,*
> *And their yoke bears me down during both days and nights.*
> *If I am kind to one, the other gets vexed.*
> *And so I cannot escape from these two furies.*
> *If you want to live well and with a free heart,*
> *And with your hands unclenched, then do not marry.*
> *If you must wed, then marry one wife only:*
> *One alone is enough to satisfy two armies.*

When Mamoum heard these words he began to laugh, till he nearly tumbled over. Then, as a proof of his kindness, he gave to Bahloul his golden robe, a most beautiful vestment.

Bahloul went in high spirits towards the dwelling of the Grand Vizir. Just then Hamdonna looked from the height of her palace in that direction, and saw him. She said to her negress, 'By the God of the temple of Mecca! There is Bahloul dressed in a fine gold-worked robe! How can I manage to get possession of the same?'

The negress said, 'Oh, my mistress, you would not know how to get hold of that robe.'

Hamdonna answered, 'I have thought of a trick whereby to achieve my ends, and I shall get the robe from him.'

'Bahloul is a sly man,' replied the negress. 'People think generally that they can make fun of him; but, for God, it is he who really makes fun of them. Give up the idea, mistress mine, and take care that you do not fall into the snare which you intend setting for him.'

But Hamdonna said again, 'It must be done!' She then sent her negress to Bahloul, to tell him that he should come to her.

He said, 'By the blessing of God, to him who calls you, you shall make answer,' and went to Hamdonna.

Hamdonna welcomed him and said: 'Oh, Bahloul, I believe you come to hear me sing.' He replied: 'Most certainly, oh, my mistress! You have a marvellous gift for singing.'

'I also think that after having listened to my songs, you will be pleased to take some refreshments.'

'Yes,' said he.

Then she began to sing admirably, so as to make people who listened die with love.

After Bahloul had heard her sing, refreshments were served; he ate, and he drank. Then she said to him: 'I do not know why, but I fancy you would gladly take off your robe, to make me a present of it.' And Bahloul answered: 'Oh, my mistress! I have sworn to give it to her to whom I have done as a man does to a woman.'

'Do you know what that is, Bahloul?' said she.

'Do I know it?' replied he. '*I*, who am instructing God's creatures in that science? It is I who make them copulate in love, who initiate them in the delights a female can give, show them how one must caress a woman, and what will excite and satisfy her. Oh, my mistress, who should know the art of coition if it is not I?'

Hamdonna was the daughter of Mamoum, and the wife of the Grand Vizir. She was endowed with the most perfect beauty; of a superb figure and harmonious form. No one in her time surpassed her in grace and perfection. Heroes on seeing her became humble and submissive, and looked down to the ground for fear of temptation, so many charms and perfections had God lavished on her. Those who looked steadily at her were troubled in their mind, and oh! how many heroes imperilled themselves for her sake. For this very reason Bahloul had always avoided meeting her for fear of succumbing to the temptation; and, apprehensive for his peace of mind, had never, until then, been in her presence.

Bahloul began to converse with her. Now he looked at her and anon bent his eyes to the ground, fearful of not being able to command his passion. Hamdonna burnt with desire to have the robe, and he would not give it up without being paid for it.

'What price do you demand,' she asked. To which he replied, 'Coition, O apple of my eye.'

'You know what that is, O Bahloul?' said she.

'By God,' he cried; 'no man knows women better than I; they are the occupation of my life. No one has studied all their concerns more than I. I know what they are fond of; for learn, oh, lady mine, that men choose different occupations according to their genius and their bent. The one takes, the other gives; this one sells, the other buys. My only thought is of love and of the possession of beautiful women. I heal those that are lovesick, and carry a solace to their thirsting vaginas.'

Hamdonna was surprised at his words and the sweetness of his language. 'Could you recite me some verses on this subject?' she asked.

'Certainly,' he answered.

'Very well, O Bahloul, let me hear what you have to say.'
Bahloul recited as follows:

> Men are divided according to their affairs and doings;
> Some are always in spirits and joyful, others in tears.
> There are those whose life is restless and full of misery,
> While, on the contrary, others are steeped in good fortune,
> Always in luck's happy way, and favoured in all things.
> I alone am indifferent to all such matters.
> What care I for Turkomans, Persians, and Arabs?
> My whole ambition is in love and coition with women,
> No doubt nor mistake about that!
> If my member is without vulva, my state becomes frightful,
> My heart then burns with a fire which cannot be quenched.
> Look at my member erect! There it is – admire its beauty!
> It calms the heat of love and quenches the hottest fires
> By its movement in and out between your thighs.
> Oh, my hope and my apple, oh, noble and generous lady,
> If one time will not suffice to appease thy fire,
> I shall do it again, so as to give satisfaction;
> No one may reproach thee, for all the world does the same.
> But if you choose to deny me, then send me away!
> Chase me away from thy presence without any fear or remorse!
> Yet bethink thee, and speak and augment not my trouble,
> But, in the name of God, forgive me and do not reproach me.
> While I am here let thy words be kind and forgiving.
> Let them not fall upon me like sword-blades, keen and cutting!
> Let me come to you and do not repel me.
> Let me come to you like one that brings drink to the thirsty;
> Hasten and let my hungry eyes look at thy bosom.
> Do not withhold from me love's joys, and do not be bashful,
> Give yourself up to me – I shall never cause you trouble,
> Even were you to fill me with sickness from head to foot.
> I shall always remain as I am, and you as you are,
> Knowing that I am the servant, and you are the mistress ever.
> Then shall our love be veiled? It shall be hidden for all time,
> For I keep it a secret and I shall be mute and muzzled.
> It is by God's will that everything happens,
> And he has filled me with love; but today my luck is ill.

While Hamdonna was listening she nearly swooned, and set herself to examine the member of Bahloul, which stood erect like a column between his thighs. Now she said to herself: 'I shall give myself up to him,' and now, 'No I will not.' During this uncertainty she felt a yearning for pleasure deep within her parts privy; and Eblis made flow from her natural parts a moisture, the fore-runner of pleasure. She then no longer combated her desire to cohabit with him, and reassured herself by the thought: 'If this Bahloul, after having had his pleasure with me, should divulge it no one will believe his words.'

She requested him to divest himself of his robe and to come into her room, but Bahloul replied: 'I shall not undress till I have sated my desire, O apple of my eye.'

Then Hamdonna rose, trembling with excitement for what was to follow; she undid her girdle, and left the room, Bahloul following her and thinking: 'Am I really awake or is this a dream?' He walked after her till she had entered her boudoir. Then she threw herself on a couch of silk, which was rounded on the top like a vault, lifted her clothes up over her thighs, trembling all over, and all the beauty which God had given her was in Bahloul's arms.

Bahloul examined the belly of Hamdonna, round like an elegant cupola, his eyes dwelt upon a navel which was like a pearl in a golden cup; and descending lower down there was a beautiful piece of nature's workmanship, and the whiteness and shape of her thighs surprised him.

Then he pressed Hamdonna in a passionate embrace, and soon saw the animation leave her face; she seemed almost unconscious. She had lost her head; and holding Bahloul's member in her hands, excited and fired him more and more.

Bahloul said to her: 'Why do I see you so troubled and beside yourself?' And she answered: 'Leave me, O son of a debauched woman! By God, I am like a mare in heat, and you continue to excite me still more with your words, and what words! They would set any woman on fire, if she was the purest creature in the world. You will insist in making me succumb by your talk and your verses.'

Bahloul answered: 'Am I then not like your husband?' 'Yes,' she said, 'but a woman gets heat on account of the man, as a mare on account of the horse, whether the man be the husband or not; with this difference, however, that the mare gets lusty only at certain periods of the year, and only then receives the stallion, while a woman can always be made rampant by words of love. Both these dispositions have met within me, and, as my husband is absent, make haste, for he will soon be back.'

Bahloul replied: 'Oh, my mistress, my loins hurt me and prevent me mounting upon you. You take the man's position, and then take my robe and let me depart.'

Then he laid himself down in the position the woman takes in receiving a man; and his verge was standing up like a column.

Hamdonna threw herself upon Bahloul, took his member between her hands and began to look at it. She was astonished at its size, strength and firmness, and cried: 'Here we have the ruin of all women and the cause of many troubles. O Bahloul! I never saw a more beautiful dart than yours!' Still she continued keeping hold of it, and rubbed its head against the lips of her vulva till the latter part seemed to say: 'O member, come into me.'

Then Bahloul inserted his member into the vagina of the Sultan's daughter, and she, settling down upon his engine, allowed it to penetrate entirely into her furnace till nothing more could be seen of it, not the slightest trace, and she said: 'How lascivious has God made woman, and how indefatigable after her pleasures.' She then gave herself up to an up-and-down dance, moving her bottom like a riddle; to the right and left, and forward and backward; never was there such a dance as this.

The Sultan's daughter continued her ride upon Bahloul's member till the moment of enjoyment arrived, and the attraction of the vulva seemed to pump the member as though by suction: just as an infant sucks the teat of the mother. The acme of enjoyment came to both simultaneously, and each took the pleasure with avidity.

Then Hamdonna seized the member in order to with-draw it, and slowly, slowly she made it come out, saying: 'This is the deed of a vigorous man.' Then she dried it and her own private parts with a silken kerchief, and rose.

Bahloul also got up and prepared to depart, but she said, 'And the robe?'

He answered, 'Why,. O mistress! You have been riding me, and still want a present?'

'But,' said she, 'did you not tell me that you could not mount me on account of the pains in your loins?'

'It matters but little,' said Bahloul. 'The first time it was your turn, the second will be mine, and the price for it will be the robe, and then I will go.'

Hamdonna thought to herself, 'As he began he may now go on; afterwards he will go away.'

So she laid herself down, but Bahloul said, 'I shall not lie with you unless you undress entirely.'

Then she undressed until she was quite naked, and Bahloul fell into an ecstasy on seeing the beauty and perfection of her form. He looked at her magnificent thighs and rebounding navel, at her belly vaulted like an arch, her plump breasts standing out like hyacinths. Her ncek was like a gazelle's, the opening of her mouth like a ring, her lips fresh and red like a gory sabre. Her teeth might have been taken for pearls and her cheeks for roses. Her eyes were black and well slit, and her eyebrows of ebony resembled the rounded flourish of the *noum* traced by the hand of a skilful writer. Her forehead was like the full moon in the night.

Bahloul began to embrace her, to suck her lips and to kiss her bosom; he drew her fresh saliva and bit her thighs. So he went on till she was ready to swoon, and could scarcely stammer, and her eyes became veiled. Then he kissed her vulva, and she moved neither hand nor foot. He looked lovingly upon the secret parts of Hamdonna, beautiful enough to attract all eyes with their purple centre.

Bahloul cried, 'Oh, the temptation of man!' and still he bit her and kissed her till her desire was roused to its full pitch. Her sighs came quicker, and grasping his member with her hand she made it disappear in her vagina.

Then it was he who moved hard, and she who responded hotly, the overwhelming pleasure simultaneously calming their fervour.

Then Bahloul got off her, dried his pestle and her mortar, and prepared to retire. But Hamdonna said, 'Where is the robe? You mock me, O Bahloul.' He answered, 'O my mistress, I shall only part with it for a consideration. You have had your dues and I mine. The first time was for you, the second time for me; now the third time shall be for the robe.'

This said, he took it off, folded it, and put it in Hamdonna's hands, who, having risen, laid down again on the couch and said, 'Do what you like!'

Forthwith Bahloul threw himself upon her, and with one push completely buried his member in her vagina; then he began to work as with a pestle, and she to move her bottom, until both again did flow over at the same time. Then he rose from her side, left his robe, and went.

The negress said to Hamdonna, 'O my mistress, is it not as I have told you? Bahloul is a bad man, and you could not get the better of him. They consider him as a subject for mockery, but, before God, he is making fun of them. Why would you not believe me?'

Hamdonna turned to her and said, 'Do not tire me with your remarks. It came to pass what had to come to pass, and on the opening of each vulva is inscribed the name of the man who is to enter it, right or wrong, for love or for hatred. If Bahloul's name had not been inscribed on my vulva he would never have got into it, had he offered me the universe with all it contains.'

As they were thus talking there came a knock at the door. The negress asked who was there, and in answer the voice of Bahloul said, 'It is I.' Hamdonna, in doubt as to what the buffoon wanted to do, got frightened. The negress asked Bahloul what he wanted, and received the reply, 'Bring me a little water.' She went out of the house with a cup full of water. Bahloul drank, and then let the cup slip out of his hands, and it was broken. The negress shut the door upon Bahloul, who sat himself down on the threshold.

The buffoon being thus close to the door, the Vizir, Hamdonna's husband, arrived, who said to him, 'Why do I see you here, O Bahloul?' And he answered, 'O my lord, I was passing through the street when I was overcome by a great thirst. A negress came and brought me a cup of water. The cup slipped from my hands and got broken. Then our lady Hamdonna took my robe, which the Sultan our Master had given me as indemnification.'

Then said the Vizir, 'Let him have his robe.' Hamdonna at this moment came out, and her husband asked her whether it was true that she had taken the robe in payment for the cup. Hamdonna then cried, beating her hands together, 'What have you done, O Bahloul?' He answered, 'I have talked to your husband the language of my folly; talk to him, you, the language of thy wisdom.' And she, enraptured with the cunning he had displayed, gave him back his robe, and he departed.

Concerning Women who Deserve to be Praised

Know, O Vizir (and the mercy of God be with you!) that there are women of all sorts; that there are such as are worthy of praise, and such as deserve nothing but contempt.

In order that a woman may be relished by men, she must have a perfect waist, and must be plump and lusty. Her hair will be black, her forehead wide, she will have eyebrows of Ethiopian blackness, large black eyes, with the whites in them very limpid. With cheek of perfect oval, she will have an elegant nose and a graceful mouth; lips and tongue vermilion; her breath will be of pleasant odour, her throat long, her neck strong, her bust and her belly large; her breasts must be full and firm, her belly in good proportion, and her navel well-developed and marked; the lower part of the belly is to be large, the vulva projecting and fleshy, from the point where the hairs grow, to the buttocks; the conduit must be narrow and not moist, soft to the touch, and emitting a strong heat and no bad smell; she must have the thighs and buttocks hard, the hips large and full, a waist of fine shape, hands and feet of striking elegance, plump arms, and well-developed shoulders.

If one looks at a woman with those qualities in front, one is fascinated; if from behind, one dies with pleasure. Looked at sitting, she is a rounded dome; lying, a soft-bed; standing, the staff of a standard. When she is walking, her natural parts appear as set off under her clothing. She speaks and laughs rarely, and never without a reason. She never leaves the house, even to see neighbours of her acquaintance. She has no women friends, gives her confidence to nobody, and her husband is her sole reliance. She takes nothing from anyone, excepting from her husband and her parents. If she sees relatives, she does not meddle with their affairs. She is not treacherous, and has no faults to hide, nor bad reasons to proffer. She does not try to entice people. If her husband shows his intention of performing the conjugal rite, she is agreeable to his desires and occasionally even provokes them. She assists him always in his affairs, and is sparing in complaints and tears; she does not laugh or rejoice when she sees her husband moody or sorrowful, but shares his troubles, and wheedles him into good humour, till he is quite content again. She does not surrender herself to anybody but her husband, even if abstinence would kill her. She hides her secret parts, and does not allow them to be seen; she is always elegantly attired, of the utmost personal propriety, and takes care not to let her husband see what might be repugnant to him. She perfumes herself with scents, uses antimony for her toilets, and cleans her teeth with *souak*.

Such a woman is cherished by all men.

The Story of the Negro Dorérame

The story goes, and God knows its truth, that there was once a powerful King who had a large kindgom, armies and allies. His name was Ali ben Direme.

One night, not being able to sleep at all, he called his Vizir, the Chief of the Police, and the Commander of his Guards. They presented themselves before him without delay, and he ordered them to arm themselves with their swords. They did so at once, and asked him, 'What news is there?'

He told them: 'Sleep will not come to me; I wish to walk through the town tonight, and I must have you ready at my hand during my round.'

'To hear is to obey,' they replied.

The King then left, saying: 'In the name of God! and may the blessing of the Prophet be with us, and benediction and mercy be with him.'

His suite followed, and accompanied him everywhere from street to street.

So they went on, until they heard a noise in one of the streets, and saw a man in the most violent passion stretched on the ground, face downwards, beating his breast with a stone and crying, 'Ah there is no longer any justice here below! Is there nobody who will tell the King what is going on in his states?' And he repeated incessantly: 'There is no longer any justice! she has disappeared and the whole world is in mourning.'

The King said to his attendants, 'Bring this man to me quietly, and be careful not to frighten him.' They went to him, took him by the hand, and said to him, 'Rise and have no fear – no harm will come to you.'

To which the man made answer, 'You tell me that I shall not come to harm, and have nothing to be afraid of, and still you do not bid me welcome! And you know that the welcome of a believer is a warrant of security and forgiveness. Then, if the believer does not welcome the believer there is certainly ground for fear.' He then got up, and went with them towards the King.

The King stood still, hiding his face with his *kaïk*, as also did his attendants. The latter had their swords in their hands, and leant upon them.

When the man had come close to the King, he said, 'Greetings be with you, O man!' The King answered, 'I return your greetings, O man!' Then the man, 'Why say you "O man"?' The King, 'And why did you say "O man"?' 'It is because I do not know your name.' 'And likewise I do not know yours!'

The King then asked him, 'What mean these words I have heard: "Ah! there is no more justice here below! Nobody tells the King what is going on in his states!" Tell me what has happened to you.' 'I shall tell it only to that man who can avenge me and free me from oppression and shame, if it so please Almighty God!'

The King said to him, 'May God place me at your disposal for your revenge and deliverance from oppression and shame?'

'What I shall now tell you,' said the man, 'is marvellous and surprising. I loved a woman, who loved me also, and we were united in love. These relations lasted a long while, until an old woman enticed my mistress and took her away to a house of misfortune, shame and debauchery. Then sleep fled from my couch; I have lost all my happiness, and I have fallen into the abyss of misfortune.'

The King then said to him, 'Which is that house of ill omen, and with whom is the woman?'

The man replied, 'She is with a negro of the name of Dorérame, who has at his house women beautiful as the moon, the likes of whom the King has not in his place. He has a mistress who has a profound love for him, is entirely devoted to him, and who sends him all he wants in the way of silver, beverages and clothing.'

Then the man stopped speaking. The King was much surprised at what he had heard, but the Vizir, who had not missed a word of this conversation, had certainly made out, from what the man had said, that the negro was no other than his own.

The King requested the man to show him the house.

'If I show it you, what will you do?' asked the man.

'You will see what I shall do,' said the King. 'You will not be able to do anything,' replied the man, 'for it is a place which must be respected and feared. If you want to enter it by force you will risk death, for its master is redoubtable by means of his strength and courage.'

'Show me the place,' said the King, 'and have no fear.' The man answered, 'So be it as God will!'

He then rose, and walked before them. They followed him to a wide street, where he stopped in front of a house with lofty doors, the walls being on all sides high and inaccessible.

They examined the walls, looking for a place where they might be scaled, but with no result. To their surprise they found the house to be as close as a breastplate.

The King, turning to the man, asked him, 'What is your name?'

'Omar ben Isad,' he replied.

The King said to him, 'Omar, are you demented?'

'Yes, my brother,' answered he, 'if it so pleases God on high!' And turning to the King he added, 'May God assist you tonight!'

Then the King, addressing his attendants, said, 'Are you determined? Is there one amongst you who could scale these walls?'

'Impossible!' they all replied.

Then said the King, 'I myself will scale this wall, so please God on high! but by means of an expedient for which I require your assistance, and if you lend me the same I shall scale the wall, if it pleases God on high.'

They said, 'What is there to be done?'

'Tell me,' said the King, 'who is the strongest amongst you.' They replied, 'The Chief of the Police, who is your *Chaouch*.'

The King said, 'And who next?'

'The Commander of the Guards.'

'And after him, who?' asked the King.

'The Grand Vizir.'

Omar listened with astonishment. He knew now that it was the King, and his joy was great.

The King said, 'Who is there yet?'

Omar replied, 'I, O my master.'

The King said to him, 'O Omar, you have found out who we are; but do not betray our disguise, and you will be absolved from blame.'

'To hear is to obey,' said Omar.

The King then said to the *Chaouch*, 'Rest your hands against the wall so that your back projects.'

The *Chaouch* did so.

Then said the King to the Commander of the Guards, 'Mount upon the back of the *Chaouch*.' He did so, and stood with his feet on the other man's shoulders. Then the King ordered the Vizir to mount, and he got on the shoulders of the Commander of the Guards, and put his hands against the wall.

Then said the King, 'O Omar, mount upon the highest place!' And Omar, surprised by this expedient, cried, 'May God lend you his help, O our master, and assist you in your just enterprise!' He then got on to the shoulders of the *Chaouch*, and from there upon the back of the Commander of the Guards, and then upon that of the Vizir, and, standing upon the shoulders of the latter, he took the same position as the others. There was now only the King left.

Then the King said, 'In the name of God! and his blessing be with the prophet, upon whom be the mercy and salutation of God!' and, placing his hand upon the back of the *Chaouch*, he said, 'Have a moment's patience; if I succeed you will be compensated!' He then did the same with the others, until he got upon Omar's back, to whom he also said, 'O Omar, have a moment's patience with me, and I shall name you my private secretary. And, of all things, do not move!' Then, placing his feet upon Omar's shoulders, the King could with his hands grasp the terrace; and crying, 'In the name of God! may he pour his blessings upon the Prophet, on whom be the mercy and salutation of God!', he made a spring, and stood upon the terrace.

Then he said to his attendants, 'Descend now from each other's shoulders!'

And they got down one after another, and they could not help admiring the ingenious idea of the King, as well as the strength of the *Chaouch* who carried four men at once.

The King then began to look for a place for descending, but found no passage. He unrolled his turban, fixed one end with a single knot at the place where he was, and let himself down into the courtyard, which he explored until he found the portal in the middle of the house fastened with an enormous lock. The solidity of this lock, and the obstacle it created, gave him a disagreeable surprise. He said to himself, 'I am now in difficulty, but all comes from God; it was he who gave me the strength and the idea that brought me here; he will also provide the means for me to return to my companions.'

He then set himself to examine the place where he found himself, and counted the chambers one after another. He found seventeen chambers or rooms, furnished in different styles, with tapestries and velvet hangings of various colours, from the first to the last.

Examining all round, he saw a place raised by seven stair-steps, from which issued a great noise from voices. He went up to it, saying, 'O God! favour my project, and let me come safe and sound out of here.'

He mounted the first step, saying, 'In the name of God the compassionate and merciful!' Then he began to look at the steps, which were of variously coloured marble – black, red, white, yellow, green and other shades.

Mounting the second step, he said, 'He whom God helps is invincible!'

On the third step he said, 'With the aid of God the victory is near.'

And on the fourth, 'I have asked victory of God, who is the most puissant auxiliary.'

Finally he mounted the fifth, sixth, and seventh steps, invoking the Prophet (with whom be the mercy and salvation of God).

He then arrived at the curtain hanging at the entrance; it was of red brocade. From there he examined the room, which was bathed in light, filled with many chandeliers, and candles burning in golden sconces. In the middle of this saloon played a jet of musk-water. A table-cloth extended from end to end, covered with sundry meats and fruits.

The saloon was provided with gilt furniture, the splendour of which dazzled the eye. In fact, everywhere, there were ornaments of all kinds.

On looking closer the King ascertained that round the table-cloth there were twelve maidens and seven women, all like moons; he was astonished at their beauty and grace. There were likewise with them seven negroes, and this sight filled him with surprise. His attention was above all attracted by a woman like the full moon, of perfect beauty, with black eyes, oval cheeks, and a lithe and graceful waist; she humbled the hearts of those who became enamoured of her.

Stupefied by her beauty, the King was as one stunned. He then said to himself, 'How is there any getting out of this place? O my spirit, do not give way to love!'

And continuing his inspection of the room, he perceived in the hands of those who were present, glasses filled with wine. They were drinking and eating, and it was easy to see they were overcome with drink.

While the King was pondering how to escape his embarrassment, he heard one of the women saying to one of her companions, calling her by name, 'Oh, so and so, rise and light a torch, so that we two can go to bed, for sleep is overpowering us. Come, light the torch, and let us retire to the other chamber.'

They rose and lifted up the curtain to leave the room. The King hid himself to let them pass; then, perceiving that they had left their chamber to do a thing necessary and obligatory in human kind, he took advantage of their absence, entered their apartment, and hid himself in a cupboard.

Whilst he was thus in hiding the women returned and shut the doors. Their reason was obscured by the fumes of wine; they pulled off all their clothes and began to caress each other mutually.

The King said to himself, 'Omar has told me true about this house of misfortune as an abyss of debauchery.'

When the women had fallen asleep the King rose, extinguished the light, undressed, and laid down between the two. He had taken care during their conversation to impress their names on his memory. So he was able to say to one of them, 'You, so and so, where have you put the door-keys?' speaking very low.

The woman answered, 'Go to sleep, you whore, the keys are in their usual place.'

The King said to himself, 'There is no might and strength but in God the Almighty and Benevolent!' and was much troubled.

And again he asked the woman about the keys, saying, 'Daylight is coming. I must open the doors. There is the sun. I am going to open the house.'

And she answered, 'The keys are in the usual place. Why do you thus bother me? Sleep, I say, till it is day.'

And again the King said to himself, 'There is no might and strength but in God the Almighty and Benevolent, and surely if it were not for the fear of God I should run my sword through her.' Then he began again, 'Oh, you, so and so!'

She said, 'What do you want?'

'I am uneasy,' said the King, 'about the keys; tell me where they are?'

And she answered, 'You hussy! Does your vulva itch for coition? Cannot you do without for a single night? Look! the Vizir's wife has withstood all the entreaties of the negro, and repelled him since six months! Go, the keys are in the negro's pocket. Do not say to him, "Give me the keys;" but say, "Give me your member." You know his name is Dorérame.'

The King was now silent, for he knew what to do. He waited a short time till the woman was asleep; then he dressed himself in her clothes, and concealed his sword under them; his face he hid under a veil of red silk. Thus dressed he looked like other women. Then he opened the door, stole softly out, and placed himself behind the curtains of the saloon entrance. He saw only some people sitting there; the remainder were asleep.

The King made the following silent prayer, 'O my soul, let me follow the right way, and let all those people among whom I find myself be stunned with drunkenness, so that they cannot know the King from his subjects, and God give me strength.'

He then entered the saloon saying: 'In the name of God!' and he tottered towards the bed of the negro as if drunk. The negroes and the women took him to be the woman whose attire he had taken.

Dorérame had a great desire to have his pleasure with that woman, and when he saw her sit down by the bed he thought that she had broken her sleep to come to him, perhaps for love games. So he said, 'Oh, you, so and so, undress and get into my bed, I shall soon be back.'

The King said to himself, 'There is no might and strength but in the High God, the Benevolent!' Then he searched for the keys in the clothes and pockets of the negro, but found nothing. He said, 'God's will be done!' Then raising his eyes, he saw a high window; he reached up with his arm, and found gold embroidered garments there; he slipped his hands into the pockets, and, oh, surprise! he found the keys. He examined them and counted seven, corresponding to the number of the doors of the house, and in his joy, he exclaimed, 'God, be praised and glorified!' Then he said, 'I can only get out of here by a ruse.' Then feigning sickness, and appearing as if he wanted to vomit violently, he held his hand before his mouth, and hurried to the centre of the courtyard. The negro said to him, 'God bless you! oh, so and so! any other woman would have been sick into the bed!'

The King then went to the inner door of the house, and opened it; he closed it behind him, and so from one door to the other, till he came to the seventh, which opened upon the street. Here he found his companions again, who had been in great anxiety, and who asked him what he had seen?

Then said the King: 'This is not the time to answer. Let us go into this house with the blessing of God and with his help.'

They resolved to be upon their guard, there being in the house seven negroes, twelve maidens, and seven women, beautiful as moons.

The Vizir asked the King, 'What garments are these?' And the King answered, 'Be silent; without them I should never have got the keys.'

He then went to the chamber where were the two women, with whom he had been lying, took off the clothes in which he was dressed, and resumed his own, taking good care of his sword. Repairing to the saloon, where the negroes and the women were, he and his companions ranged themselves behind the door-curtain.

After having looked into the saloon, they said, 'Amongst all these women there is none more beautiful than the one seated on the elevated cushion!' The King said, 'I reserve her for myself, if she does not belong to someone else.'

While they were examining the interior of the saloon, Dorérame descended from the bed, and after him one of those beautiful women. Then another negro got on the bed with another woman, and so on till the seventh. They rode them in this way, one after the other, excepting the beautiful woman mentioned above, and the maidens. Each of these women appeared to mount upon the bed with marked reluctance, and descended, after the coition was finished, with her head bent down.

The negroes, however, were lusting after, and pressing one after the other, the beautiful woman. But she spurned them all, saying, 'I shall never consent to it, and as to these virgins, I take them also under my protection.'

Dorérame then rose and went up to her, holding in his hands his member in full erection, stiff as a pillar. He hit her with it on the face and head, saying, 'Six times this night I have pressed you to cede to my desires, and you always refuse; but now I must have you, even this night.'

When the woman saw the stubbornness of the negro and the state of drunkenness he was in, she tried to soften him by promises. 'Sit down here by me,' she said, 'and tonight thy desires shall be contented.'

The negro sat down near her with his member still erect as a column. The King could scarcely master his surprise.

Then the woman began to sing the following verses, intoning them from the bottom of her heart:

I prefer a young man for coition, and him only;
He is full of courage – he is my sole ambition,
His member is strong to deflower the virgin,
And richly proportioned in all its dimensions;
It has a head like to a brazier.
Enormous, and none like it in creation;
Strong it is and hard, with the head rounded off.
It is always ready for action and does not die down;
It never sleeps, owing to the violence of its love.
It sighs to enter my vulva, and sheds tears on my belly;
It asks not for help, not being in want of any;
It has no need of an ally, and stands alone the greatest fatigues,
And nobody can be sure of what will result from its efforts.
Full of vigour and life, it bores into my vagina,
And it works about there in action constant and splendid.
First from the front to the back, and then from the right to the left;
Now it is crammed hard in by vigorous pressure,

Now it rubs its head on the orifice of my vagina.
And he strokes my back, my stomach, my sides,
Kisses my cheeks, and anon begins to suck at my lips.
He embraces me close, and makes me roll on the bed,
And between his arms I am like a corpse without life.
Every part of my body receives in turn his love-bites,
And he covers me with kisses of fire;
When he sees me in heat he quickly comes to me,
Then he opens my thighs and kisses my belly,
And puts his tool in my hand to make it knock at my door.
Soon he is in the cave, and I feel pleasure approaching.
He shakes me and trills me, and hotly we both are working,
And he says, 'Receive my seed!' and I answer, 'Oh give it beloved one!
It shall be welcome to me, you light of my eyes!
Oh, you man of all men, who fillest me with pleasure.
Oh, you soul of my soul, go on with fresh vigour,
For you must not yet withdraw it from me; leave it there,
And this day will then be free of all sorrow.'
He has sworn to God to have me for seventy nights,
And what he wished for he did, in the way of kisses and embraces, during all those nights.

When she had finished, the King, in great surprise, said, 'How lascivious has God made this woman.' And turning to his companions, 'There is no doubt that this woman has no husband, and has not been debauched, for, certainly that negro is in love with her, and she has nevertheless repulsed him.'

Omar ben Isad took the word, 'This is true, O King! Her husband has been now away for nearly a year, and many men have endeavoured to debauch her, but she has resisted.'

The King asked, 'Who is her husband?' And his companions answered, 'She is the wife of the son of your father's Vizir.'

The King replied, 'You speak true; I have indeed heard it said that the son of my father's Vizir had a wife without fault, endowed with beauty and perfection and of exquisite shape; not adulterous and innocent of debauchery.'

'This is the same woman,' said they.

The King said, 'No matter how, but I must have her,' and turning to Omar, he added, 'Where amongst these women, is your mistress?' Omar answered, 'I do not see her, O King!' Upon which the King said, 'Have patience, I will show her to you.' Omar was quite surprised to find that the King knew so much. 'And this then is the negro Dorérame?'

asked the King. 'Yes, and he is a slave of mine,' answered the Vizir. 'Be silent, this is not the time to speak,' said the King.

While this discourse was going on, the negro Dorérame, still desirous of obtaining the favours of that lady, said to her, 'I am tired of your lies, O Beder el Bedour' (full moon of the full moons), for so she called herself.

The King said, 'He who called her so called by her true name, for she is the full moon of the full moons, afore God!'

However, the negro wanted to draw the woman away with him, and hit her in the face.

The King, mad with jealousy, and with his heart full of ire, said to the Vizir, 'Look what your negro is doing! By God! he shall die the death of a villain, and I shall make an example of him, and a warning to those who would imitate him!'

At that moment the King heard the lady say to the negro, 'You are betraying your master the Vizir with his wife, and now you betray her, in spite of your intimacy with her and the favours she grants to you. And surely she loves you passionately, and you are pursuing another woman!'

The King said to the Vizir, 'Listen, and do not speak a word.'

The lady then rose and returned to the place where she had been before, and began to recite:

> *Oh, men! listen to what I say on the subject of woman,*
> *Her thirst for coition is written between her eyes.*
> *Do not put trust in her vows, even were she the Sultan's daughter.*
> *Woman's malice is boundless; not even the King of kings*
> *Would suffice to subdue it, whate'er be his might.*
> *Men, take heed and shun the love of woman!*
> *Do not say, 'Such a one is my well beloved;'*
> *Do not say, 'She is my life's companion.'*
> *If I deceive you, then say my words are untruths.*
> *As long as she is with you in bed, you have her love,*
> *But a woman's love is not enduring, believe me.*
> *Lying upon her breast, you are her love-treasure;*
> *Whilst the coition goes on, you have her love, poor fool!*
> *But, anon, she looks upon you as a fiend;*
> *And this is a fact undoubted and certain.*
> *The wife receives the slave in the bed of the master,*
> *And the serving-men allay upon her their lust.*
> *Certain it is, such conduct is not to be praised and honoured.*
> *But the virtue of women is frail and changeful,*

And the man thus deceived is looked upon with contempt.
Therefore a man with a heart should not put trust in a woman.

At these words the Vizir began to cry, but the King bade him to be quiet. Then the negro recited the following verses in response to those of the lady:

We negroes have had our fill of women,
We fear not their tricks, however subtle they be.
Men confide in us with regard to what they cherish.
This is no lie, remember, but is the truth, as you know.
Oh, you women all! for sure you have no patience when the virile member you
  are wanting,
For in the same resides your life and death;
It is the end and all of your wishes, secret or open.
If your choler and ire are aroused against your husbands,
They appease you simply by introducing their members.
Your religion resides in your vulva, and the manly member is your soul.
Such you will always find is the nature of woman.

With that, the negro threw himself upon the woman, who pushed him back.

At this moment, the King felt his heart oppressed; he drew his sword, as did his companions, and they entered the room. The negroes and women saw nothing but brandished swords.

One of the negroes rose, and rushed upon the King and his companions, but the *Chaouch* severed with one blow his head from his body. The King cried, 'God's blessing upon you! Your arm is not withered and your mother has not borne a weakling. You have struck down your enemies, and paradise shall be your dwelling and place of rest!'

Another negro got up and aimed a blow at the *Chaouch*, which broke the sword of the *Chaouch* in twain. It had been a beautiful weapon, and the *Chaouch*, on seeing it ruined, broke out into the most violent passion; he seized the negro by the arm, lifted him up, and threw him against the wall, breaking his bones. Then the King cried, 'God is great. He has not dried up your hand. Oh, what a *Chaouch*! God grant you his blessing.'

The negroes, when they saw this, were cowed and silent, and the King, master now of their lives, said, 'The man that lifts his hand only, shall lose his head!' And he commanded that the remaining five negroes should have their hands tied behind their backs.

This having been done, he turned to Beder el Bedour and asked her, 'Whose wife are you, and who is this negro?'

She then told him on that subject what he had heard already from

Omar. And the King thanked her, saying, 'May God give you his blessing.' He then asked her, 'How long can a woman patiently do without coition?' She seemed amazed, but the King said, 'Speak, and do not be abashed.'

She then answered, 'A well-born lady of high origin can remain for six months without; but a lowly woman of no race nor high blood, who does not respect herself when she can lay her hand upon a man, will have him upon her; his stomach and his member will know her vagina.'

Then said the King, pointing to one of the women, 'Who is this one?' She answered, 'This is the wife of the *Kadi*.' 'And this one?' 'The wife of the second Vizir.' 'And this?' 'The wife of the chief of the *Muftis*.' 'And that one?' 'The Treasurer's.' 'And those two women that are in the other room?' She answered, 'They have received the hospitality of the house, and one of them was brought here yesterday by an old woman; the negro has so far not got possession of her.'

Then said Omar, 'This is the one I spoke to you about, O my master.'

'And the other woman? To whom does she belong?' said the King.

'She is the wife of the *Amine* of the carpenters,' answered she.

Then said the King, 'And these girls, who are they?'

She answered, 'This one is the daughter of the clerk of the treasury; this other one the daughter of the *Mohtesib*, the third is the daughter of the *Bouab*, the next one the daughter of the *Amine* of the *Moueddin*; that one the daughter of the colour-keeper. At the invitation of the King, she passed them thus all in review.

The King then asked for the reason of so many women being brought together there.

Beder el Bedour replied, 'O master of ours, the negro knows no other passions than for coition and good wine. He keeps making love night and day, and his member rests only when he himself is asleep.'

The King asked further, 'What does he live upon?'

She said, 'Upon yolks of eggs fried in fat and swimming in honey, and upon white bread; he drinks nothing but old muscatel wine.'

The King said, 'Who has brought these women here, who, all of them, belong to officials of the State?'

She replied, 'O master of ours, he has in his service an old woman who has had the run of the houses in the town; she chooses and brings to him any woman of superior beauty and perfection; but she serves him only against good consideration in silver, dresses, etc., precious stones, rubies, and other objects of value.'

'And whence does the negro get that silver?' asked the King. The lady remaining silent, he added, 'Give me some information, please.'

She signified with a sign from the corner of her eye that he had got it all from the wife of the Grand Vizir.

The King understood her, and continued, 'O Beder el Bedour! I have faith and confidence in you, and your testimony will have in my eyes the value of that of the two *Adels*. Speak to me without reserve as to what concerns yourself.'

She answered him, 'I have not been touched, and however long this might have lasted the negro would not have had his desire satisfied.'

'Is this so?' asked the King.

She replied, 'It is so!' She had understood what the King wanted to say, and the King had seized the meaning of her words.

'Has the negro respected *my* honour? Inform me about that,' said the King.

She answered, 'He has respected your honour as far as your wives are concerned. He has not pushed his criminal deeds that far; but if God had spared his days there is no certainty that he would not have tried to soil what he should have respected.'

The King having asked her then who those negroes were, she answered, 'They are his companions. After he had quite surfeited himself with the women he had caused to be brought to him, he handed them over to them, as you have seen. If it were not for the protection of a woman where would that man be?'

Then spoke the King, 'O Beder el Bedour, why did not your husband ask my help against this oppression? Why did you not complain?'

She replied, 'O King of the time, O beloved Sultan, O master of numerous armies and allies! As regards my husband I was so far unable to inform him of my lot; as to myself I have nothing to say but what you know by the verses I sang just now. I have given advice to men about women from the first verse to the last.'

The King said, 'O Beder el Bedour! I like you, I have put the question to you in the name of the chosen Prophet (the benediction and mercy of God be with him!). Inform me of everything; you have nothing to fear; I give you the *aman* complete. Has this negro not enjoyed you? For I presume that none of you were out of reach of his attempts and had her honour safe.'

She replied, 'O King of our time, in the name of your high rank and your power! Look! He, about whom you ask me, I would not have accepted him as a legitimate husband; how could I have consented to grant him the favour of an illicit love?'

The King said, 'You appear to be sincere, but the verses I heard you sing have roused doubts in my soul.'

She replied, 'I had three motives for employing that language. Firstly,

I was at that moment in heat, like a young mare; secondly, Eblis had excited my natural parts; and lastly, I wanted to quiet the negro and make him have patience, so that he should grant me some delay and leave me in peace until God would deliver me of him.'

The King said, 'Do you speak seriously?' She was silent. Then the King cried, 'O Beder el Bedour, you alone shall be pardoned!' She understood that it was she only that the King would spare from the punishment of death. He then cautioned her that she must keep the secret, and said he wanted to leave now.

Then all the women and virgins approached Beder el Bedour and implored her, saying, 'Intercede for us, for you have power over the King;' and they shed tears over her hands, and in despair threw themselves down.

Beder el Bedour then called the King back, as he was going, and said to him, 'O our master! you have not granted me any favour yet.' 'How,' said he, 'I have sent for a beautiful mule for you; you will mount her and come with us. As for these women, they must all of them die.'

She then said, 'O our master! I ask you and conjure you to authorize me to make a stipulation which you will accept.' The King made oath that he would fulfil it. Then she said, 'I ask as a gift the pardon of all these women and of all these maidens. Their deaths would moreover throw the most terrible consternation over the whole town.'

The King said, 'There is no might nor power but in God, the merciful!' He then ordered the negroes to be taken out and beheaded. The only exception he made was with the negro Dorérame, who was enormously stout and had a neck like a bull. They cut off his ears, nose, and lips; likewise his virile member, which they put into his mouth, and then hung him on a gallows.

Then the King ordered the seven doors of the house to be closed, and returned to his palace.

At sunrise he sent a mule to Beder el Bedour, in order to let her be brought to him. He made her dwell with him, and found her to be excelling all those who excel.

Then the King caused the wife of Omar ben Isad to be restored to him, and he made him his private secretary. After which he ordered the Vizir to repudiate his wife. He did not forget the *Chaouch* and the Commander of the Guards, to whom he made large presents, as he had promised, using for that purpose the negro's hoards. He sent the son of his father's Vizir to prison. He also caused the old go-between to be brought before him, and asked her, 'Give me all the particulars about the conduct of the negro, and tell me whether it was well done to bring in that way women to men.' She answered, 'This is the trade of nearly all old women.' He then had her executed, as well as all old women who followed that trade, and thus cut off in his State the tree of panderism at the root, and burnt the trunk.

He besides sent back to their families all the women and girls, and bade them repent in the name of God.

This story presents but a small part of the tricks and stratagems used by women against their husbands.

The moral of the tale is, that a man who falls in love with a woman imperils himself, and exposes himself to the greatest troubles.

BRAM STOKER

from
Dracula

Dracula *was first published in 1897 and is a Gothic masterpiece. Dramatic, even theatrical – its author Bram Stoker was at one time business manager to the great Victorian actor Sir Henry Irving. Highly erotic, it provides a disturbing insight into Victorian sexual fears and desires.*

WHEN I had written in my diary and had fortunately replaced the book and pen in my pocket, I felt sleepy. The Count's warning came into my mind, but I took a pleasure in disobeying it. The sense of sleep was upon me, and with it the obstinacy which sleep brings as outrider. The soft moonlight soothed, and the wide expanse without gave a sense of freedom which refreshed me. I determined not to return tonight to the gloom-haunted rooms, but to sleep here, where of old ladies had sat and sung and lived sweet lives whilst their gentle breasts were sad for their menfolk away in the midst of remorseless wars. I drew a great couch out of its place near the corner, so that, as I lay, I could look at the lovely view to east and south, and unthinking of and uncaring for the dust, composed myself for sleep.

I suppose I must have fallen asleep; I hope so, but I fear, for all that followed was startlingly real – so real that now, sitting here in the broad, full sunlight of the morning, I cannot in the least believe that it was all sleep.

I was not alone. The room was the same, unchanged in any way since I came into it; I could see along the floor, in the brilliant moonlight, my own footsteps marked where I had disturbed the long accumulation of dust. In the moonlight opposite me were three young women, ladies by their dress and manner. I thought at the time that I must be dreaming when I saw them, for, though the moonlight was behind them, they threw no shadow on the floor. They came close to me and looked at me for some time and then whispered together. Two were dark, and had high aquiline noses, like the Count's, and great dark, piercing eyes, that seemed to be almost red when contrasted with the pale yellow moon. The other was fair, as fair as can be, with great, wavy masses of golden hair and eyes like pale sapphires. I seemed somehow to know her face, and to know it in connection with some dreamy fear, but I could not recollect at the moment how or where. All three had brilliant white teeth, that shone like pearls against the ruby of their voluptuous lips. There was something about them that made me uneasy, some longing and at the same time some deadly fear. I felt in my heart a wicked, burning desire that they would kiss me with those red lips. It is not good to note this down, lest some day it should meet Mina's eyes and cause her pain; but it is the truth. They whispered together, and then they all three laughed – such a silvery, musical laugh, but as hard as though the sound never could have come through the softness of human lips. It was like the intolerable, tingling sweetness of water-glasses when played on by a cunning hand. The fair girl shook her head coquettishly, and the other two urged her on. One said: –

'Go on! You are first, and we shall follow; yours is the right to begin.' The other added: –

'He is young and strong; there are kisses for us all.' I lay quiet, looking out under my eyelashes in an agony of delightful anticipation. The fair girl advanced and bent over me till I could feel the movement of her breath upon me. Sweet it was in one sense, honey-sweet, and sent the same tingling through the nerves as her voice, but with a bitter underlying the sweet, a bitter offensiveness, as one smells in blood.

I was afraid to raise my eyelids, but looked out and saw perfectly under the lashes. The fair girl went on her knees and bent over me, fairly gloating. There was a deliberate voluptuousness which was both thrilling and repulsive, and as she arched her neck she actually licked her lips like an animal, till I could see in the moonlight the moisture shining on the scarlet lips and on the red tongue as it lapped the white sharp teeth. Lower and lower went her head as the lips went below the range of my mouth and chin and seemed about to fasten on my throat. Then she paused, and I could hear the churning sound of her tongue as it licked her teeth and lips, and could feel the hot breath on my neck. Then the skin of my throat began to tingle as one's flesh does when the hand that is to tickle it approaches nearer – nearer. I could feel the soft, shivering touch of the lips on the supersensitive skin of my throat, and the hard dents of two sharp teeth, just touching and pausing there. I closed my eyes in a languorous ecstasy and waited – waited with beating heart.

But at that instant another sensation swept through me as quick as lightning. I was conscious of the presence of the Count, and of his being as if lapped in a storm of fury. As my eyes opened involuntarily I saw his strong hand grasp the slender neck of the fair woman and with giant's power draw it back, the blue eyes transformed with fury, the white teeth champing with rage, and the fair cheeks blazing red with passion. But the Count! Never did I imagine such wrath and fury, even in the demons of the pit. His eyes were positively blazing. The red light in them was lurid, as if the flames of hell-fire blazed behind them. His face was deathly pale, and the lines of it were hard like drawn wires; the thick eyebrows that met over the nose now seemed like a heaving bar of white-hot metal. With a fierce sweep of his arm, he hurled the woman from him, and then motioned to the others, as though he were beating them back; it was the same imperious gesture that I had seen used to the wolves. In a voice which, though low and almost a whisper, seemed to cut through the air and then ring round the room, he exclaimed: –

'How dare you touch him, any of you? How dare you cast eyes on him when I had forbidden it? Back, I tell you all! This man belong to me! Beware how you meddle with him, or you'll have to deal with me.'

The fair girl, with laugh of ribald coquetry, turned to answer him: –

'You yourself never loved; you never love!' On this the other women joined, and such a mirthless, hard, soulless laughter rang through the room that it almost made me faint to hear; it seemed like the pleasure of fiends. Then the Count turned, after looking at my face attentively, and said in a soft whisper: –

'Yes, I too can love; you yourselves can tell it from the past. Is it not so? Well, now I promise you that when I am done with him, you shall kiss him at your will. Now go! go! I must awaken him, for there is work to be done.'

'Are we to have nothing tonight?' said one of them, with a low laugh, as she pointed to the bag which he had thrown upon the floor, and which moved as though there were some living thing within it. For answer he nodded his head. One of the women jumped forward and opened it. If my ears did not deceive me there was a gasp and a low wail, as of a half-smothered child. The women closed round, whilst I was aghast with horror; but as I looked they disappeared, and with them the dreadful bag. There was no door near them, and they could not have passed me without my noticing. They simply seemed to fade into the rays of the moonlight and pass out through the window, for I could see outside the dim, shadowy forms for a moment before they entirely faded away.

Then the horror overcame me, and I sank down unconscious.

ANONYMOUS

from
The Lustful Memoirs of a Young and Passionate Girl

The Lustful Memoirs of a Young and Passionate Girl was published in the 1890s and is a perfect example of the inventive erotica which was now flooding in from the thriving underground publishing industry.

I NEXT lived with a family named Manus. There were two girls, young women in the family. I began to get some light, on the many things that had puzzled me by listening to them when they did not suppose I was paying any attention. I got an idea of the difference in the sexes, and some confused ideas about sexual intercourse. The girls each had a beau. They used to tell each other about them, but they said many things I didn't understand. In the next place that I lived were two girls orphans, one about my own age, the other about two years older. I lived there about three years. The girls were both well informed in regard to sexual matters and they soon imparted their knowledge to me. Not far from where we lived was a neighbour who had a dairy. Among other employees were a couple of boys, two or three years older than we were. We were quite intimate with them but there had been no grievious improprieties when I again had to change my residence, this time to live with an old couple who lived adjoining the dairyman. The girls used to visit me quite often and we almost always managed to meet the boys when we were together. Julia was almost old enough now to put on long dresses while Lizzie and I began to feel a strong attraction for the male sex. Julia was really the most amorous, but Lizzie was the most reckless in words and acts. One day we girls were out in the barn where we had had an exciting conversation, so that we felt in a mood for any thing almost. Julia had taken off her drawers and pulling up her skirts to show that the hair was beginning to grow on hers. Lizzie took her's off then, and was diligently hunting for some sign of hair when the barn door opened and in came one of the boys. We had spread some blankets on the floor and had been laying on them. Julia jumped up when she heard the door open, but Lizzie and I remained on the blanket. Abner came in and seeing us on the blanket he got down with us. Julia too did the same. I know we were all glad he had come in. Lizzie soon got astraddle of him and when he rolled her off, she exposed her legs so much that I said, 'Why Lizzie! pull your clothes,' but she only rolled over two or three times with her legs bare. Then Julia began to scold her, but Lizzie only laughed and said she didn't care if he wanted to. Abner, however, seemed to care more for Julia than either Lizzie or I. For something she said or did he caught hold of her and held her fast. In her struggles she exposed her legs nearly as much as Lizzie had, but she could not get her clothes down, she was helpless. Then Lizzie began – 'Why Julia! ain't you ashamed to show your legs so. I am shocked that you would do such a thing.' Julia squirmed and asked me to pull her clothes down, but Abner said: 'Don't you do it,' and we didn't while he was trying to get her clothes up still higher. She finally got loose from him and jumped to her feet.

 He grabbed her by the ankle and over she went again and up her clothes went too. Lizzie was so pleased that she kicked up her heels as she lay on her back making no effort to hide anything. Abner got Julia's skirts up so that her thighs were naked and he got his hand up on her belly or somewhere under her skirts. Julia fairly squealed out and tried to get his hand away but didn't succeed. Instead of helping Julia, Lizzie caught hold of one of her feet and helped him get her legs separated so that he got his hand on her nest. Then Julia threw her arms across her face to hide it, and made no further objections. Lizzie and I looked on very much interested. Indeed there was a place between my own thighs that was burning and throbbing with amorous excitement and Lizzie felt much as I did. When Abner unbuttoned his pants and took out his staff, Lizzie at once took hold of it. He seemed to like it, for he rolled over partly on his back so we could get a better view of it. Julia took a look at it too, then put her hand on it. I felt of it also, – ah, how nice it felt in my hand. While we were feeling of it and commenting on it we heard a dog bark not far away. We all jumped to our feet and on going to the door saw a man coming towards the barn. Abner got away without being seen and we girls got to the house. I must now tell you of some other persons before I tell you more about the boys. Immediately after going to live with the old folks, (I call them old folks because both were past sixty. Mrs. Hall was not a bad looking woman for her age and had evidently been a fine looking woman in her younger days.) I discovered that a Mr. Brown was quite intimate with Mr. and Mrs. H. He was not more than 28 or 30 and he used to be there sometimes two or three times a week. I noticed right away that if Mrs. H. was alone when he called, I was at once sent out of doors or some where, so that Mr. Brown and Mrs. H. were left together. Of course, I was curious to know why they wanted to be alone, so I began to watch and soon managed to find a way to listen to what they said. They related to each other all the scandal they heard and did it too in plain language that showed they were accustomed to it. At that time there was a rape trial going on in town. A Mr. Hay, who lived some 8 or 10 miles from town in a lonesome place near the mountains hired a girl who lived a mile or two away to help in the house as his wife was about to be confined. The girl went with Mr. Hay to town to do some shopping one day, and on their way home the girl said he drove away from the road to a secluded place, then got her down in the bed of the wagon and raped her, after which they went on to Mr. Hay's house. Some time afterwards Mr. H. was arrested for rape and the trial excited considerable interest. Before a verdict had been rendered Mr. Brown called on Mrs. Hall. I was sent out as usual, but was soon where I could hear every word said.

After a few unimportant remarks Mrs. H. asked if the rape case was over yet. Brown said the jury were still out. 'Well,' said Mrs. H. 'I'll tell you what I think of the matter. There was no rape about it. Hay was getting all he wanted of the girl and her mother found it out and she put up the job on him.' Brown asked why she thought so. 'Why,' said she, 'If the girl had not been willing she wouldn't have gone back home with Hay and stayed a week or two before making any fuss about it.'

Another time they talked about married women taking means to avoid getting in the family way. They spoke of it in a way to show that it could be prevented, but didn't tell what the way was. I was anxious to hear that but was doomed to disappointment. This last conversation I heard just after Abner was with us in the barn. The next time I saw the girls I told them what I had heard. Julia said she was sure there was some way it could be done but she was at a loss to know how to ascertain it. Lizzie asked me why I didn't ask Mrs. Hall. 'I did rather ask Mr. Brown,' said I dubiously. 'Oh, that's it,' said Julia, 'ask Mr. Brown then,' and Lizzie joined her in urging me to ask Mr. Brown and both said they would if they had a chance. Every time I saw Mr. Brown after that I thought of the request I wanted to make and feared I'd not have courage if I had a chance. One day Mr. et Mrs. Hall went to town to be gone all day. I was all excited at once. He knocked and when I opened the door he came in and enquired for Mrs. H. It came into my mind at once that if I told him she was going to be gone all day he would go right away, so I said she is out just now. Won't you sit down and wait? So he sat down and soon picked up a paper and began to read. I was anxious to ask him, and when he laid the paper down I was afraid he was going. Without stopping to choose my words I blurted out – 'Mr. Brown won't you tell me how to keep from getting in the family way?' He looked up astonished at my question, and some how my courage came back to me at once, so when he asked what I knew about getting in the family way, I said, 'I know about screwing.' Catching me by the arm he drew me up to him and placed me on his knees. 'Now tell me,' said he, 'what you know about screwing.' He kept questioning me till I told him about Julia and Lizzie and about my hearing him and Mrs. Hall talk. While talking he felt of my bosom, then put his hand under my skirts. I didn't try to hinder him at all. When he said we must keep a look out for Mrs. Hall I told him she would be gone all day and explained why I had lied to him. At his request I took off my drawers. While doing that he unbuttoned his pants and pulled his shirt up. My goodness! his jock was as big 3 or 4 like Abner's. I was so much interested in it I forgot he had not answered my question. As I had hold of his staff of life he asked how I'd like to have that in my belly. I said I was afraid I was not big enough for it yet. 'No, you are not old enough nor large enough now, but it won't be long,' said he, 'before your pussy will be able to take in one as big as that.' He placed me astraddle his legs and then put the big red head between the lips of my pussy and rubbed it about making me feel pleasure in every nerve. He enquired about Julia and Lizzie. I told him all about them except that I didn't tell about Abner. It was yet early in the forenoon. He said if I would go over and get the girls he would tell us all about getting in the family way. Without stopping to put on my drawers I ran across the field and met Julia some distance from the house. I quickly told her that Mr. B. was waiting for her and Lizzie to tell what we were so anxious to know. Lizzie was absent so Julia went back with me. Julia was eager, but a little shamefaced when we went in where he was. He had his charmer fully exposed to view, standing stiffly and rampant.

Julia fixed her eyes on it, and as if strongly attracted by it she slowly approached Mr. Brown, he said not a word till she had come near enough for him to take her arm. He drew her right up in front of him when she at once took his stiff prick in her hand. She seemed surprised at its size and magnificent appearance. After she had handled it a few minutes he seated himself and took her on his lap. He first felt of her bosom as he had mine, then he pulled her skirts up and finding she had drawers on he asked her to take them off. When she had done so she seated herself on his lap again. He laid her over on his arm and slid his hand up to her pussy. He spread her legs and he began to titillate her clitoris and the surrounding parts till she could not keep from moving her bottom. He asked her if it felt good. 'Yes, yes,' said she, ' It feels so good.' After getting her passions all excited he said: 'You would enjoy it much better if I put this in there' and he put her hand on his cock. 'Shall we try it?' said he. Julia was too happy just then to refuse anything. Indeed he had to carry her to the bed where he quickly got her placed to suit him, then got between her legs, and carefully placing the head of his charmer between the lips of her pussy, he moved it about a little, the contact even in this manner giving her exquisite pleasure. But soon he began to push. At once I saw her countenance change. 'It is going to hurt you somewhat,' said he, 'but don't be afraid, it will soon be over.' She began to struggle but he had her so she could not avoid his thrusts, but as he shoved she exclaimed: 'Oh don't, it hurts,' her voice rising almost to a shriek as the obstruction gave way and his rod was buried in her belly. As soon as he had overcome the obstacles and effected a complete entrance he remained motionless telling her it was all over now, that she would only feel pleasure hereafter. She soon dried her tears and in answer to his question said it didn't hurt any more, only smarted a little. He kept very quiet for quite a while, but when he saw by her countenance that she was beginning to feel some pleasure he began slowly to move his sweetener out and in. 'Don't it begin to feel good?' he asked. 'Yes,' she replied, 'it does feel good!' The pleasure soon became so great that she began to heave her bottom in response to his shoves. He somehow, was not disposed to hurry matters. He would stop shoving occasionally, letting his charmer remain buried in her. While letting it soak in this way he turned to me, who was looking on a much interested spectator and asked what I thought of screwing now.

'I think it is good. I wish I was big enough,' I replied. 'Well, it won't be many months before your pussy can take it in too,' said he. 'You won't have to wait very long.' But after awhile he began to shove quite regularly. Julia quite as actively responding, then he moved faster and faster and soon he began to breath loud and to shove furiously, just as Mr. Amberg did when he was screwing my poor mama. All at once Mr. Brown ceased shoving, except an occasional, spasmatic shove, his head dropped and he seemed to become limp and lifeless, except his breathing. After he had remained quiet some time he got off of Julia, his yard still large but hanging his head, which was not of such a deep red as before, while drops of a queer looking stuff dropped from it. Julia was going to get up but he told her to lay still. I could not help noticing the change in her pussy too, as he took his handkerchief and carefully wiped it, for I could see some of that queer looking stuff running out of it. He then carefully wiped his rod but didn't button his pants and so hide it from our sight. When Julia got up she looked at his ram rod and seemed surprised to see its head dropping.

She began to handle it and the bag beneath and asking questions about them. It was not many minutes before he was preparing for another engagement. 'Would you like to try it again?' he asked. 'I'm afraid it will hurt,' said Julia. 'Suppose we try and see,' said he. Without any further urging she got on the bed and pulled up her clothing.

He got between her legs again and surprised Julia by easily shoving his charger into her without hurting her any. 'It don't hurt a bit this time,' said she, 'and it feels so nice.' After he had got his stiff one embedded in her body, he let it remain there quietly while he said 'Well girls, I promised to tell you how to avoid getting in the family way. There is one way,' said he, 'I have never known to fail.' 'What is it,' I asked. 'Keep your legs together and you will never get in the family way,' he said laughing. 'Oh!' said I, 'that ain't what we mean. Men screw their wives – what do they do to keep from getting in the family way?' He then explained that some men drew out their rod just before spending, others used a syringe, others a rubber bag over their long tom, etc. Julia asked if she wouldn't get in the family way. 'No, I guess not,' said he. 'If you do I'll take care of you.' Then he advised her not to let any man do it to her again till she got a husband. 'Then,' said he, 'you can let a dozen screw you if you are careful not to get caught. You are a woman now and will soon be getting a husband. You will give me some more, won't you, after you get married?' 'Yes,' said Julia, 'you may have all you want.' Then we arranged to meet again and he promised to tell us anything he might hear that was interesting. Julia enjoyed the delightful sensations his yard gave her while buried in her pussy so much that she could not keep still under him. He saw how fully she was enjoying it. After giving a few shoves which she promptly met he stopped and looked down in her face asked her if fucking was as good as she thought it would be. 'Oh yes,' said she, 'I wish I could stay this way forever.' They began to move again slowly at first but faster and faster after awhile, then this loud breathing and the die away. He wiped her again and after she got up and we fixed up the bed we went into the parlour again. I noticed that Julia walked a little awkwardly as if she was sore. Mr. Brown told us lots of stories of women who had been made happy by tasting stolen sweets and the time passed pleasantly till some time afternoon. Mr. Brown's charmer had long since regained its former magnificent state of erection but he didn't think it wise to put it into Julia again just then; it was some time after one o'clock when I saw Lizzie coming across the yard. I told Mr. Brown who she was and suggested that we should give her a surprise. So he let his pants down, pulled up his shirt and stood right in front of the door where she would come in, while Julia and I hid in the bed-room. Pretty soon Lizzie came bounding in but she stopped suddenly as she saw the beautiful object before her and she looked at it in open wonder. Finally she stammered, 'Where – where are the girls?' We could hold in no longer. Lizzie at once regained her wits, but kept quiet for a few minutes. She could not keep her eyes off the beauty before her however and she soon began to handle it, then she commented on it. He was amused at her remarks and finally asked her if her pussy was big enough to take it in. 'No, it ain't,' said she, 'I wish it was.' 'Well, is Julia's?' he asked. 'No,' said she, 'it would take the biggest woman in town to take that,' said she. 'Some small women have big mouths,' said he. 'I have had it in Julia twice today.' 'I don't believe it,' said Lizzie bluntly and she turned to Julia as if to get her to confirm her disbelief. 'Would you like to see me do it again?' he asked. Lizzie nodded assent.

Julia at once led the way to the bed and laying over across it pulled up her clothes and spread her legs. After getting between them he told Lizzie he wanted her to steer it, then she would know it was in sure. Without any hesitation she took hold of his beauty and placed its head at the right place and she kept hold of it till it was in so far she was forced to let go. 'Now do you believe it?' asked Mr. B. But Lizzie didn't reply, she was watching Julia, thinking it must hurt her to have such a big thing stuck into her, but when she saw no sign of pain, but evidences of pleasure she got down by Julia and in almost a whisper asked how it felt. 'It don't hurt a bit and it feels awfully good,' she replied. We watched them till it was all over. He didn't get off for some time but when he did his charmer seemed shorn of its glory, for it had shrunken in size and was soft and limp, hanging its head as if ashamed. We put the bed to rights again, then went back to the parlour. Lizzie got on his lap while he talked to us. He gave us some good advice about how to conduct ourselves so as to avoid being suspected. He cautioned us to tell no one of our meeting and managed for future meetings. He had told us too, to be careful when with young fellows for, said he, they will screw you if they can and some of them will boast of it. After he left us Lizzie and I asked Julia innumerable questions. She had at once acquired an enviable position in our estimation and she, herself, was disposed to put on airs. I met the girls quite often after that. They were as anxious as I to meet Mr. Brown again. We were out by the barn one day when we saw the boys. Abner and Van, coming. They urged us to go in the barn with them but we refused, though we stood and talked with them some time. Van put his arm around me and felt of my bosom while Abner felt of Julia's. They pleaded with us to go in the barn with them but Julia and I objected though Lizzie was willing. The boys went away evidently disappointed. Mr. Brown called one day, as usual Mr. H. – was away. I met him out by the gate. He enquired after Julia and said he wanted to see her again. 'Oh,' said I 'you want to screw her again. Well, she ain't here so you will have to screw the old woman.' 'Would you like me to screw the old woman?' he asked. 'Oh, yes, do it,' said I. 'If I do' said he, 'you must not tell the girls.' I said I would not and he went on into the house; I followed soon after and was at once sent out as I expected. Before going out I pointed to the old lady and made some very suggestive motions which of course I didn't let her see, but Mr. Brown did and he laughed as I closed the door behind me. I lost no time in getting to my place of observation. The house was originally but a two roomed board house, to which a kitchen had been added at one time, a bed-room at another, then another bed-room, but it was an 'old ram shackled' concern at the best. My hiding place was a narrow space between the bed-room and kitchen. From there I could hear what was said in any room in the house and could see into the old lady's bed-room. About the first question she asked was: 'Well, what is the latest scandal? Whose wife has been playing with her tail? He told her of some women that stories had been told about, then she told some thing she had heard about some girls that some fellow was suspected of having raised her petticoats. After some desultory talk I heard her say, 'What is the matter with you today? One would think you hadn't seen a woman for a month.' 'I haven't touched a woman's foot a long while' said he. 'You know when the last time was.' 'I'll bet,' said she, 'you have screwed half a dozen women since then.' He protested he hadn't even seen a woman's ankles. 'Why,' said he, 'I am getting so I hardly dare turn over in bed at night for fear of breaking it off.' 'If your case is so bad as that,' said the old lady, 'you ought to get some relief.' 'Well, let's go in the bed-room and see if we can't do something for it,' said he. 'Wait till I see where Laura is,' said the old woman, as she started for the door. 'Never mind,' said Mr. Brown, 'I saw her down in the field just now, there is no danger from her.' I heard Mrs. H. – lock the door, then she and Mr. Brown entered the bed-room. They proceeded to business at once. Mrs. H. – pulled up her skirts, unbuttoned her drawers and took them off. Mr. Brown took off his coat, vest and pants, then pulling up his shirt he showed her what a terrible swelling he had. 'What a terrible state the darling is in to be sure,' said she taking it in her hand. 'I think it needs a hair poultice. That will soon take the swelling down and draw the matter out of it.' Retaining her hold of it she backed up to the bed and threw herself over on her back. She was evidently experienced in such matters for she took pains to get in a comfortable position before letting him get between her legs. I could not help admiring her beautiful legs, indeed I would not have thought her past forty from what I could see of her form. But Mr. Brown soon got into place and buried his charmer in her body. She hugged him closely as if she would have been glad to take him all in. Evidently the presence of his champion in her pussy gave her great pleasure for after the hug she gave him she drew a long breath and said, 'After all there is nothing in the world that gives such exquisite pleasure as fucking.' Knowing that I could hear every word and wishing to please me Mr. Brown kept her talking. In answer to his question if she enjoyed it as much now as she did when a girl she said she could hardly see any difference, and in the conversation she told that she first tasted stolen sweets when a girl of 16. Then he asked her to tell him about it. She said there was but little to tell. She went to a dance with her beau one night and got pretty well warmed up. When she went home, about 2 in the morning she asked him in hardly expecting him to do so. They took a seat on the sofa together and he put his arm about her waist. She had on a low necked dress and almost before she knew what he was about he had his hand in her bosom. Her amorous passions had been excited by the dancing, then his hand in her bosom so excited her that she could refuse him nothing.

He soon had his hand under her skirts where his fingers quickly excited her almost to frenzy.

She took off her clothes while he disrobed and then she said, 'we took a bout on the carpet.' I enjoyed listening to their conversation and watched their actions. After they went back to the parlour I quietly left my hiding place and managed to meet Mr. Brown out by the road where Mrs. H. could not see me, after leaving the house. After talking a moment about the old woman he enquired particularly about Julia. I saw he was afraid she might be knocked up as he expressed it, but I could give him no information about it. He wanted to meet her again soon and try to ascertain. As we were standing where no one could see us he put his hand under my skirts and felt of my pussy, but he didn't stay long. A few days after that, I met the boys over by the yard where the cows were. They were in the yard, I outside. They scolded because we would not go in the barn with them when they wanted us to and asked why we wouldn't. I said we knew what they wanted to do to us was the reason. Van asked what I thought they wanted to do to us. I said 'you want to fuck us' Van laughed, 'Right you are, that is just what we want to do.' Then he got down on the ground and put his arm through the fence and his hand up between my legs. I stood still only spreading my legs and let him feel. Pretty soon he asked me to go with him around back of the stable where no one could see us. 'I won't,' said I, 'you want to fuck me and I ain't big enough.' He said I was and urged strongly but when the boys saw I would not they urged me to bring Julia over. I promised to tell her that they wanted to see her but would promise nothing more. It was some time after that, two or three months at least, when Julia told me the folks she and Lizzie were living with were going away and would leave them there alone. I at once got permission to stay with them and I managed to let Mr. Brown know the circumstances. He and I got there soon after the folks left. Mr. Brown at once took Julia on his lap and while having his hand under her skirts he questioned her about her condition and was greatly pleased to ascertain that she had escaped getting in the family way. We locked the doors and then went to the girls' bedroom where we all stripped. Lizzie and I didn't expect much attention from Mr. Brown for we knew Julia would receive most of it. He laid across the bed on his back, his charmer hard and stiff like a column of ivory with a red cap on it, attracting all our attention and admiration. We all tried to handle it at once. Finding we could not well do that Lizzie took hold of one of his hands and placed it on her nest. He got her in position so that he could better feel of her. After he had felt a minute she asked, 'Is my cunt big enough yet?' 'Hardly big enough yet,' said he, 'but I'll try it if you wish.' She didn't reply in words but quickly got on her back and spread her legs. He got on top of her then placed the head of his champion between the lips of her monkey. Before shoving any he rubbed its head about between the lips, evidently giving her much pleasure. Then he said: 'Now I am going to push, if it hurts you too much I'll stop.' Pretty soon she said: 'Oh stop, it hurts.' He at once stopped and got off. Lizzie wanted me to try it so I got in position. While he was rubbing the head of his staff in my slit I told him it felt good but when he began to push I too said it hurt. After he got off he asked Julia if she would try. She needed no urging. Instead however, of getting between her legs when she rolled over on her back, he got beside her and put his hand on her nest. Inserting a finger between its lips he began gently to rub and press her clitoris, often kissing her while doing so. I readily understood what his object was. He wished to get all her amorous passions aroused, so that the gratification of her desires would give her greater pleasure. When her actions showed that he had accomplished his purpose he got her in a position to suit him and got between her thighs. Placing the head of his instrument in the proper place he let it remain there a moment while he tightened his clasp about her. She had expected it to enter without difficulty, but her monkey had recovered from the stretching it had received so that his first shove failed to give him a complete entrance, but a second shove, which hurt her so that I thought she was going to scream. He overcame her resistance and that hard and shining shaft was again buried completely in her body. After gently kissing her he asked if it hurt her much when it went in. She said it did some. You need not fear that it will ever hurt again said he. After this time you can take in the biggest man in the state without its hurting any.

He moved gently within her, stopping occasionally to kiss her, or to toy with her breast which was getting hard, round and full. Soon her face began to flush, her eyes to sparkle and her actions more animated.

She was recovering from the unexpected hurt she felt when his charmer entered her, and was beginning to taste again the sweet pleasure only to be experienced by a woman while in the arms of a man as she was.

Still he did not hurry in his movements. He had fought too many such engagements not to know how best to cause his partner to enjoy the most of the sweetest pleasures. Mr. Brown retained control of himself but Julia's body soon became so thrilled with delight that she threw her head back, closed her eyes and moved her bottom so fast that he slid his hand down under her bottom to hold her up lest in her delirium of pleasure she might dislodge the stranger she was entertaining. After placing his hand under her bottom, he began to thrust more rapidly and only stopped to ask her if it was good. She languidly opened her eyes and held up her lips to be kissed as she threw her arms about his neck. Then began the heaves and shoving again, soon increasing in rapidity and vehemence. After a few minutes the end came preceded by his loud breathing and her exclamations. After one tremendous shove as if to send his charge of life giving sperm as far into her body as possible he let his pleasure giving rod remain buried within her as his head slowly dropped and his muscles relaxed. Soon both were still. Lizzie and I had looked on, watching every motion, both enjoying the pleasure Julia was experiencing. We both became so excited that I squeezed my thighs together while Lizzie began to try to get relief by using her finger. After awhile Mr. Brown raised his head and Julia opened her eyes. Before withdrawing he gave her a few kisses, then got from between her thighs. Neither of them seemed inclined to say or do much for awhile. But Lizzie could not restrain herself, she began to ask them both many queer but puzzling questions, which they found it difficult to answer. At length Julia said to her, 'When you have been screwed you will know all about it.' Mr. Brown entertained us for an hour or two with very interesting stories all relating to that delightfully entertaining subject sexual intercourse.

His champion had long regained its former size and stiffness but he seemed in no hurry to give Julia another taste of its quality. We were all of us stark naked as I before intimated. Neither of us girls could resist the attractions his beautiful charmer possessed. Laying on his back with his arm stiffly standing he seemed pleased to have us examine and handle it. After we had been handling it for some time Julia got down on his belly and resting sometimes on her elbow and sometimes with her head on his belly, she took possession of it. She felt of the skin that would move on the shaft though so tightly stretched, then the glowing head attracted her attention and she even opened the orifice in the end as if to ascertain where all the pleasure giving sperm came from. She felt of the bag too, and the two balls it contained. But the shaft seemed to please her most, moving her head up to it she laid it against her cheek where she let it remain a little while. Then she kissed its ruby head again and again. At last her desires became so great that she moved her face up to his and whispered: 'Don't you want to fuck me again?' 'I will if you want me to,' he replied, but he didn't make any move. Presently she said 'I wish you would.' 'How would you like to fuck me?' he asked, drawing her on top of him, he told her to get astraddle, she needed no further suggestions. Getting a leg on either side of him, she took hold of his majesty and getting his head at the entrance to her grotto she let herself down and soon had him securely imprisoned. Mr. Brown kept still and let her do just as she pleased. She kept her bottom moving quite regularly at first but her pleasure soon became so great that she was in danger of losing her prisoner by her irregular motions. Clasping his arms about her he rolled her over on her back without letting the prisoner out. He then began to move the prisoner about in his close quarters. She again gave herself up to the delights she felt. She heaved, she squirmed, she threw her arms about his neck, every act telling of the exquisite pleasure she was enjoying. He too was experiencing thrilling pleasure in every nerve. Again he spent and again they lay in each other's arms in that delicious die away languor that follows such amorous delights as they had been enjoying. Finally when they recovered their senses and he had got off, we all dressed ourselves for Mr. Brown said he dared not stay any longer. After he left I remained with the girls. I had never yet told Julia about the boys wanting her to come over to the stable but I then told her all about it. Lizzie said, 'Let's go today,' but Julia had got about all she wanted for some days so she refused. I did not see the girls for a week or ten days after that, but I met them one day out by the barn, they having come from the direction of the dairy man's. Lizzie eagerly began to tell me that they had just come from over there, that they went with the boys out back of the stable, that Abner fucked Julia and that Van fucked her. Said she, 'He didn't hurt much for his prick ain't far so big as Mr. Brown's.' After that, the girls used to meet the boys two or three times a week, usually in the evening and often in the barn, and every time they indulged in amorous delights without restraint. I was with them many times and was often urged by the boys to let them have just one screw, but remembering Mr. Brown's advice, I refused. I noticed after awhile a change in Julia. She was in the family way. About three months after Mr. Brown had been with her last she without any notice to any one was married to Abner. They went to house keeping near by for Abner still continued at the dairy. Lizzie went to another place to live where she was taken sick with inflamation of the bowels and died. Julia was delivered of a six months (?) baby just the picture of its father, Mr. Brown. I visited Julia very often, sometimes staying days with her. When the baby was about three months old Mr. Brown called to see him. I was there with Julia that day. After the baby had been duly admired Julia told him he was his. He was greatly pleased I could see, for as I said it was a handsome baby. He admired it and had it in his lap playing with its chubby hands finally he laid it down and drawing Julia in his lap said, 'Shan't we make another baby?' She made but little effort to get away, and he was soon handling her parts, then he got his hand under her skirts and unbuttoning her drawers felt of her pussy. As the drawers dropped to the floor and she stepped out of them he put his arm about her and led her to the bed. He laid her over on the bed and felt of her a few minutes, then getting between her legs he had no difficulty in inserting his instrument and quickly shoving its whole length in her. A lively engagement followed, both of them sharing in its pleasures. Of course I was allowed to look on as of old, but I realized a greater interest in what I saw and a greater desire than I had ever felt. After, she got off the bed and shook down her skirts, but didn't put on her drawers, expecting, no doubt, another bout after awhile. We went back to the parlour where he told us the latest scandal, etc. We seated ourselves on the lounge, one each side of him. He had not buttoned his pants, so when I saw his staff getting hard and stiff again, I took it in my hand. It somehow possessed a greater attraction than ever. He let me feel a few minutes, then drew me over across his lap and pulled my skirts off. My drawers being in the way, I jumped up and took them off, and resumed my place again. What sensations I felt as his hand rested a moment on my thighs. Spreading my legs his hand was at once placed on my pussy which was then surmounted by a lot of curly brown hair. His burning fingers quickly excited in me sensations I had never felt before. I can hardly tell how he did it but he very soon set my blood to a fever heat and my senses in a whirl. Presently he said, 'Let's go into the bed.' I led the way. He then nearly undressed me and removed his own garments except his shirt. I knew what he was going to do. It was what I had long wished for. I too was going to experience the supremest pleasure of existence, feel the pleasures of having that red-headed champion of him in my body, feel it pulsating and throbbing as it filled and stretched the delicate folds of my hungry receptacle. I pulled up my chemise and got on the bed. Placing myself on my back I spread my legs and awaited the attack. He didn't let me wait long. Getting between my legs he first placed the head of his champion between the lips of my nest. What pleasure just the contact of the parts gave me. Yet I knew it was but a prelude of what was to come. He seemingly was afraid of hurting me for he did not at once begin to shove. I began to be eager to feel it entering me, to feel it buried completely within me. Ah, now he shoves, gently, easily, I feel it is entering, but it meets some obstruction, still it has not hurt me. Suddenly he gives a violent shove, then another – Something gives away – I feel a sharp pain – he has overcome the obstacle and I realize that now it is where I have so long desired to have it. The pain had not been so great as I had anticipated and it was soon forgotten in the exquisite sensation that ensued. I can give no account of what followed, for my senses were so drowned in bliss that I only knew I was tasting more than heavenly pleasures. When I regained my senses he was still within me. I knew he had spent for I could feel it running down on my bottom. I expected he would get off but he didn't. He remained between my legs with his shaft still in my nest. 'Well, Laura,' said he, 'was it as good as you expected?' 'Yes, better,' said I. 'I didn't know any thing could make me feel so good.' Still he kept his position. We had not talked long before I felt his majesty swell and in a short time it was again throbbing and moving in its prison. This time Mr. Brown did not hurry any, but prolonged the pleasure a long while. Just before he spent I felt his majesty swell and then I felt the sperm coming in warm jets. When he got off we dressed ourselves and returned to the parlour. Julia was not jealous a bit at my robbing her of anticipated pleasure. She insisted on Mr. Brown remaining to dinner with us which he did leaving only when prudence said it was not wise to stay any longer. Before he left Julia asked him to come again, as often as he pleased. Soon after that, I met a nice fellow who fell in love with me at once. After a short courtship, we were married. We had but few guests at the wedding but Mr. Brown was one of them. Shall I tell you the secrets of that first night? No, I don't need to. It was all your imagination can picture.

My husband was a man, every inch of him and he has a 'long Tom' as he calls it, big enough, long enough and stiff enough to fill any women's desires. I'll only say that I got no sleep till near day light, and my chemise was starched stiff in the morning.

John had a nice home ready on our return from our wedding trip, where I was installed as its mistress. One of the first to call after I got into my home was Mr. Brown.

I at once seated myself in his lap. He kissed me and enquired how I liked married life. I said 'It's bully,' but while we were talking he was taking liberties with me that no man ought to with another man's wife. I didn't object however, so he didn't stop till he had me nearly undressed, on my back on the bed with his staff into me as far as it could go, so as he could go no further of course he had to stop. He stayed where he was, however, till he gave me another glimpse of paradise. After he had flooded my womb with great spouting jets of sperm, he got from between my legs, saying he had made twins for me. If I have any babies I wonder if I will be able to tell who their father is. You may wonder why I let Mr. Brown into my grotto and affections after my marriage, but the truth is one man is not enough for me, I can give John all he wants and then have enough left for two or three more men.

I have been admiring a good looking bachelor neighbour who lives over the way. I think with his brawn and muscle he could equal John or Mr. Brown, and every time I see him I can't help thinking of the good times we might have together if he would only try. But, dear reader, good bye.